Irish author **Abby Green** career in film and TV—v of a lot of standing in the rain outside actors trailers—to pursue her love of romance. After she'd bombarded Mills & Boon with manuscripts they kindly accepted one, and an author was born. She lives in Dublin, Ireland, and loves any excuse for distraction. Visit abby-green.com or email abbygreenauthor@gmail.com.

Joss Wood loves books and travelling—especially to the wild places of Southern Africa and, well… anywhere! She's a wife, mum to two teenagers, and slave to two cats. After a career in local economic development she now writes full-time. Joss is a member of Romance Writers of America and Romance Writers of South Africa.

CLAIMED BY THE CROWN PRINCE

ABBY GREEN

A NINE-MONTH DEAL WITH HER HUSBAND

JOSS WOOD

MILLS & BOON

First published in Great Britain 2023
by Mills & Boon, an imprint of HarperCollins*Publishers* Ltd,
1 London Bridge Street, London, SE1 9GF

www.harpercollins.co.uk

HarperCollins*Publishers*, Macken House, 39/40 Mayor Street Upper,
Dublin 1, D01 C9W8, Ireland

Claimed by the Crown Prince © 2023 Abby Green

A Nine-Month Deal with Her Husband © 2023 Joss Wood

ISBN: 978-0-263-30706-1

12/23

CLAIMED BY THE CROWN PRINCE

ABBY GREEN

MILLS & BOON

This is for the lovely country and people of Malaysia.

I was lucky enough to work and live there
for a few months a long time ago.

KL, Penang, Langkawi, Ipoh…
all hold very special places in my heart.

It's a magical place, and I hope everyone
gets a chance to visit at least once.

CHAPTER ONE

HE'D FOUND HER. A sense of intense satisfaction rolled through Dax as he took a seat in the beach bar—on the far opposite corner to where the woman sat at a table alone, with her laptop in front of her and a big floppy sun hat covering most of her hair and features.

She might have been any number of travellers in this laid-back beach bar on the beautiful Malaysian island of Langkawi. It was a mecca for backpackers and sun worshippers, with its white sand beaches and glittering green waters.

But Dax knew she wasn't just any other traveller. And she certainly wasn't a backpacker. For a start, he noted the not exactly discreet security detail keeping watch over her. Two burly men who looked as if they were desperately trying to blend in and failing miserably.

Because the woman was Crown Princess Laia Sant Roman of Isla'Rosa, a small independent kingdom in the Mediterranean. A long way away from here.

She was a queen-in-waiting. Heiress to an ancient line of kings and queens who had battled to protect their modest rock in the sea. Dax knew her history and lineage well—because he was also not just a random traveller, in spite of his khaki cargo shorts and short-sleeved shirt.

He was the Crown Prince of Santanger, the neighbouring

island kingdom and heir to his own throne, if anything happened to his brother the King and until his brother had heirs.

Which was where this woman came in. She'd been promised in marriage to his brother since she was born. A pact made by their fathers—the two late Kings—in order to ensure lasting peace and diplomacy in the region after hundreds of years of enmity and war.

But to say she was reluctant was an understatement. Dax had vague memories of her father visiting Santanger when he'd been younger, but Laia had only accompanied the King a couple of times. Dax remembered her as small and dark-haired, with wide eyes. A serious expression.

Since her father's death, she appeared to have turned avoiding his brother into an art form. And now, mere weeks before the wedding was due to take place, she'd flitted to south-east Asia.

She, unlike her security team, did fade into the crowd a little better. Especially for one so exceptionally beautiful.

Dax's insides clenched with an awareness that he desperately ignored.

Not welcome. Not appropriate.

But it was there nonetheless. And it had been there ever since they'd crossed paths one night in a club in Monaco over a year ago—his first time seeing her again since she was a young girl. Like Dax, Princess Laia had cultivated a reputation as a lover of socialising, earning her the moniker of The Party Princess.

Except, strangely enough, while Laia had been photographed at almost every 'it' social event in the past four years—most of which Dax himself had frequented—he'd never actually seen her in the flesh. Even though they'd both appeared in the papers in the days following the said events.

Dax had his suspicions as to why that was, but he'd never

had the opportunity to say it to the Princess until he'd seen her at that event for the launch of one of the biggest motor races a year ago.

She'd been on the dance floor in a green silk strapless jumpsuit, with a silver belt around her slim waist. High-heeled sandals. Hair down around her shoulders. She'd looked like the beauties who'd used to grace the iconic Studio 54 club in New York in the seventies. Except she was far more beautiful.

She'd had her eyes closed and had looked as if she was in a world of her own. Dax had felt almost a little jealous of her absorption. He'd walked over to her, and as he'd approached— as if sensing him—her eyes had opened and she'd looked directly at him.

Her eyes were huge and almond-shaped and very green. Long lashes. Exquisite bone structure. Straight nose. Lush mouth. A classic beauty, of that there was no doubt. And Dax, who was a well-known connoisseur of women, had felt—such a cliché—as if he'd never seen true beauty until that moment. Her effect on him had been like a punch to the gut.

He hadn't been able to breathe. Literally hadn't been able to find a breath for a long moment. She'd looked at him as if she'd never seen a man before. Eyes wide.

He'd seen her indicate to her security team that it was okay to let him approach. A subtle movement. The heaving crowd around them had disappeared. It had as if they were enclosed in an invisible bubble.

But then she'd blinked and, as if she'd come out of a trance, an expression of distaste had crossed her face. Dax would have sworn he'd felt a chill breeze skate over his skin. The temperature had definitely dropped a few degrees.

She'd made a small bow, but it had felt to him like a mockery. She'd looked at him.

'Crown Prince Dax of Santanger... What a pleasure to meet you in your favoured habitat.'

Dax had been surprised at the unmistakable scorn in her tone. After all, they'd never really met face to face, and she was promised in matrimony to his brother. She would become his family.

He'd felt compelled to respond with a bow of his own, saying, 'I could say the same of you, Your Highness. We seem to frequent all the same social events and yet you're as elusive as the Scarlet Pimpernel.'

She'd paled dramatically at that.

He'd frowned and put out his hand to steady her, 'Are you okay?'

Her arm had felt incredibly slim, yet strong, skin like warm silk. He'd had an impression of steeliness.

She'd pulled away from him, colour washing back into her cheeks. 'Don't touch me.'

Dax had lifted his hand in a gesture of appeasement, surprised at her vehemence. She'd looked at her security team then—another subtle movement—and Dax had found himself behind a solid wall of muscle as she'd left the dance floor.

He'd watched her leave, wondering what the hell had just happened. But he hadn't been alone for long.

'Hey, Prince Handsome, care to dance?'

Dax had torn his eyes from where Princess Laia had been fast retreating and looked down. A woman had come up beside him in a sparkling dress revealing more than it hid. Seeing her overly made-up face, and the very tell-tale glitter of synthetic substances in her unfocused eyes, he'd felt such a profound sense of ennui come over him that he'd walked straight out of the club—just in time to see a sleek chauffeur-driven SUV pull away from the kerb, followed by the recognisable security detail.

Dax had been eschewing his own security for some time by then, in spite of his brother's protests, for complicated reasons that went to the root of who he was and the burden of guilt he'd carried for years. Quite simply, he didn't deserve to be protected. He certainly wouldn't be responsible for someone putting their life ahead of his.

As he'd watched those vehicles disappear he'd felt, ridiculously, as if he'd just lost something. When he'd made it his life's purpose not to have much of an attachment to anything. Apart from his brother. It had been a long time since anyone else had made Dax *feel* anything. Not since the dark days of his mother's tragic death. A death he still held himself accountable for.

His emotions were rarely engaged now, and that was the way he liked it.

Even when he wanted a woman it was fleeting and quickly satisfied. But what had happened between him and Princess Laia had gone beyond mere *wanting*, although that had been there too.

But there had been nothing he could do about it because she was the one woman Dax couldn't touch.

She was promised to his brother.

Which was why he was here. In a rustic beach bar in Malaysia. To take her back to Santanger so she could fulfil her duty. Marry his brother and beget heirs.

A bilious knot formed in his gut at the thought of her with his brother. He chastised himself—she was beautiful and he couldn't have her. That was all it was. FOMO. He smiled mirthlessly at himself.

It was time to let his brother know he had found her and would be bringing her back.

Dax put his hand out to retrieve his phone from where he'd put it on the table but his hand found nothing. He looked down.

There was an empty space where he'd laid it just moments before. He looked up, his eye catching a small Malaysian kid on the other side of the bar, who was handing Crown Princess Laia what looked like a phone.

His phone.

She smiled at the boy indulgently and handed him some *ringgit.* The boy skipped away, delighted with himself, counting the money. She slipped the phone into a voluminous beach bag, and only then did she deign to let her gaze track over to Dax.

He could see the green of her eyes from here. It was like an electric shock straight into his bloodstream. Her smile faded. Dax stood up and walked over, through the bar, and saw her gaze tracking his progress.

He noted that her security team didn't move. Just watched carefully. He realised something then. He leaned against a wooden post beside her table and folded his arms across his chest.

'How long have you known I was here?'

She started to put away her laptop, and a notebook full of scribbles, not looking at him. 'We knew as soon as you boarded the flight in Kuala Lumpur. We've been tracking you since you landed in Langkawi two days ago.'

'Did it amuse you to wait and let me find you?'

She looked up briefly, that vivid green gaze barely skating over him. A not-so-subtle insult. He was used to women looking and lingering. But to this woman he was inconsequential. A novelty.

She said in a clipped voice, 'Not particularly.'

She stood up and Dax realised she was wearing a turquoise blue one-piece swimsuit under cut-off shorts. The floaty vibrantly coloured wrap couldn't disguise her perfect body. Not

an inch of excess flesh. She veered towards an athletic physique, but she still had curves in all the right places.

Dax had to force his gaze up from where the swells of her
breasts were barely contained by the thin material of the swimsuit. Since when were one-pieces provocative?

Her naturally olive skin was evidence of the same ancestry
as Dax. A mixture of Spanish, Italian, Moorish and Greek.

He asked, 'Can I have my phone back, please?'

She looked at him. 'That depends on what you intend to use
it for. If it's to divulge my location to your brother, or anyone
else, then, no, I'm afraid not.'

Dax was more amused than anything else. There were other
means of getting in touch with his brother. 'How do you know
I haven't already done that?'

'Because you only knew for certain I was here when you
walked into the bar.'

'So you stole my phone?'

She made a *tsk*ing sound. 'I'm not a thief.'

'No, but you employed an innocent child to do your dirty
work. What kind of a message is that sending out?'

She flushed at that, and Dax found it inordinately satisfying to see her flustered. How much more satisfying would it
be to see her flushed with arousal?

He shifted minutely and cursed his imagination.

Princess Laia said stiffly, 'I told him I knew you and wanted
to play a joke on you.'

The fact that she'd considered the integrity of what she was
doing sent a dart of something unfamiliar to Dax's gut. A mixture of humour and something soft. *Dangerous.*

He stood up straight. 'Enough chit-chatting, Princess, we
both know why I'm here. It's time to come home and fulfil
your responsibilities to the people of Santanger.'

Her eyes glittered brightly. 'Santanger is not my home and

never will be. I already have a home and responsibilities to my own people.'

Dax studied her, curious about this intransigence. The marriage pact between Santanger and Isla'Rosa made sense on many levels. Not least of which were economic and meant to foster lasting peace in the region. There hadn't been any active wars in at least a couple of generations, but there was still an underlying seam of distrust and enmity between the people in each kingdom, which was having an adverse effect on investment—even in Santanger.

Some investors that Ari and Dax had courted to do business had been put off by the merest hint of potential instability, and it didn't help that things were still stirred up occasionally by very small but effective rebel elements who seemed determined to hang on to the enmity of past generations.

Ari wanted to stamp this out once and for all through his marriage.

But the risk of stirring up unrest was one of the reasons why the marriage agreement between Ari and Laia hadn't been promoted with as much fanfare as would normally be the case. Everyone knew about it, and had known about it for years, but the details—like the wedding date—weren't due to be released until just before the event, to minimise even the small risk of rebellion in either kingdom.

'You know that marrying my brother will bring about a much hoped-for surge in goodwill from both kingdoms that will put an end to any rebel elements for good,' Dax pointed out. 'Not to mention a much-needed injection of capital for development in Isla'Rosa.'

The smaller kingdom was much poorer than Santanger. Santanger had moved with the times and grown into a modern and largely flourishing economy, with a thriving tourist scene for most of the year, thanks to its Mediterranean climate, but Isla'Rosa still lagged far behind.

It was a charming island, and attracted its own loyal tourists, who were captivated by the quaintly medieval capital city and idyllic villages and pristine beaches, but it badly needed hauling into the modern era.

'Your father did your kingdom a disservice by not allowing more growth.'

Princess Laia had gone even pinker now. Dax was momentarily distracted by that wash of blood into her cheeks.

'Don't you dare mention my father. He was a great king and beloved by the people.'

Dax shrugged minutely. 'I'm not disputing that. But our fathers were products of their time—stuck in the past. Santanger has grown and been modernised under my brother, and he can do the same for Isla'Rosa. You know this.'

'I also know that I can do it for Isla'Rosa once I become Queen, and I intend to. On my own.'

She gathered up the bag that held his phone and moved around the table. Dax's gaze tracked down over long, shapely bare legs and pretty feet in sandals.

He realised she was leaving. 'Where are you going?'

'Back to where I'm staying.'

'You have my phone.'

'If you want it you'll have to come with me.'

'I don't intend letting you out of my sight.'

Something flashed across her face at that, but it was gone before Dax could decipher what it was. A curious mixture of fear and something else. But why would she be afraid of him?

She walked out of the bar and Dax saw a slightly battered four-wheel drive appear. The driver—one of the bodyguards—jumped out and held open the back door. Princess Laia got in. Dax went around to the other side and opened the door, to hear Princess Laia say frostily, 'You can ride in the front with Pascal.'

Dax looked at her for a long moment, intrigued by this animosity, and then said, 'As you wish.'

He closed the door and got into the front passenger seat beside the bodyguard, who seemed as frosty as the Princess, not even looking his way.

Another vehicle followed them as they drove away from the beach bar—presumably the second bodyguard. She had good protection at least.

They drove for about fifteen minutes on the main road, with typical Malay houses on either side, built high off the ground to keep them cool in the intense heat. Children scampered about, along with dogs and chickens. A moped overtook them with at least four people on board and a grinning toddler on the lap of the driver. A typical sight in south-east Asia.

Then the vehicles turned down onto a dirt track and they emerged after a couple of minutes into a cleared area, where there was a jetty and two boats bobbing on the water.

They came to a stop. The driver got out and opened the door for Princess Laia. Dax got out too, bemused. A man was on one boat, readying it. Princess Laia walked down the jetty and greeted him in Malay.

Dax noted that the bodyguards carried bags of what looked like groceries and were depositing them in the first boat. Then they got into the other boat, which was larger—more like a small yacht. He followed them to the jetty. Princess Laia got into the smaller boat, helped by the driver.

She turned and looked at Dax. She arched a brow. 'Coming?'

He put his hands on his hips. 'Do I have a choice?'

'Not if you want your phone back.'

'I can get another phone. I know where you are now.'

Princess Laia shrugged. 'Suit yourself. I thought you were here to take me back, but if you're prepared to risk me disappearing again…' She trailed off.

Dax gritted his jaw. This magical mystery tour was beginning to get on his nerves. But he *was* here to bring her back, so he really couldn't risk watching her sail off into the sunset and potentially lose her, as she'd just threatened.

For all he knew she could be on a plane again within the hour and flitting off to somewhere else.

He stepped into the boat. Princess Laia was sitting primly on a seat at the back. For all the world like the Queen she would soon become. Queen of Santanger *and* Isla'Rosa. She would be a powerful woman. But he'd already sensed that power within her.

The driver indicated for Dax to take a seat too, and he did as he was told. The engines started up and the boats moved out, the bodyguards staying close.

They hugged the coast of the island for a while before heading out to sea. Just when Dax was beginning to wonder if they were headed all the way to Thailand, an island came into view. Small, and very lush. As they came closer he could see a pontoon and a beautiful beach.

A wooden structure was just about visible high on a hill, through the thick foliage. It looked like a small palace, with elaborate decorations on the roof reminiscent of royal Thai palaces.

The engine went silent as the driver guided the boat in alongside the fixed pontoon. Dax saw that the bigger boat stayed out on the almost luminously green water.

Princess Laia stood up and lifted some of the bags onto the pontoon. Then she stepped out. He followed her, feeling as bemused as ever.

When he was out, the driver handed him some bags. He

saw that they held supplies of vegetables and other food and domestic items.

He heard the engine start again and looked up to see the driver untying the boat. It was soon chugging away from the pontoon. The other boat containing the bodyguards was still some distance away.

He watched the driver wave cheerily at Princess Laia as she said something in Malay. He looked at the Princess, who was regarding him with a suspiciously triumphant glint in her green gaze.

His own narrowed. 'What the hell is this?'

'It's an island called Permata. That's "jewel" in Malay. It belonged to my mother and now it belongs to me.'

He hadn't meant that and she knew it. He'd meant what the hell was this situation. 'Why has the boat left?'

'Because he was only dropping us off.'

'How do we get off this island?'

'We don't. Unless I call for the boat or ask Pascal and Matthew to come and get us. I wouldn't recommend swimming— there are dangerous currents in the waters even though it looks safe.'

It was sinking in. With a slow certainty that was almost embarrassing. She'd caught him out.

Dax put down the bag he was holding and held out a hand. 'My phone, please.' He would arrange transport off this island with her on board within the hour.

Princess Laia held up a finger, as if just remembering. 'Ah...'

She opened her bag and scrabbled around for what seemed like long minutes. Dax's frustration and irritation were growing by the second.

'Dammit, Princess—'

She held up the phone triumphantly, with a smile. 'Got it.'

And, as he watched, she flung it out to the side and it landed in the sea with a loud *splosh*.

Her eyes went wide. 'Oops. Butterfingers.'

She picked up a couple of bags full of shopping and started to walk towards the beach and the lush hill beyond.

Dax just stood there, absorbing what had happened, looking at the place where his phone was undoubtedly sinking to the sea bed.

She stopped and looked back. 'We're the only ones here, so if you want to eat you'll need to bring those bags with you. There are a lot of steps up to the villa—you don't really want to have to make two trips.'

Dax looked at the array of bulging bags at his feet on the pontoon. Then up again. Then out to sea, where the boat that had brought them was disappearing back to the bigger island, not even visible from here.

The other boat was bobbing gently in the sea. Obviously anchored. No sign of the bodyguards. No sign of help.

Dax almost felt like throwing his head back and barking out a laugh. It had been a long time, if ever, since someone had surprised him so effectively. Taken him unawares. Blindsided him. But she'd done it with ruthless and efficient precision.

She'd basically kidnapped him, and all without hitting him over the head or disabling him. He'd followed her every step of the way into this lush and humid paradise.

CHAPTER TWO

PRINCESS LAIA DIDN'T dare look around again to see if he was behind her. Crown Prince Dax de Valle y Montero. One of the most eligible bachelors on the planet. Renowned for his good looks and sybaritic lifestyle. Renowned for lots more. Innuendo and rumours swirled around the man like a mist—not least about his sexual prowess. But she pushed that incendiary thought out of her head.

It was almost a relief to know who had come to find her and have the situation contained. Because she'd known that King Aristedes wouldn't put up with her avoidance of their arranged marriage for much longer. He'd shown his determination to force her to comply by following her to a famously remote festival in the middle of the desert just a few days ago.

Luckily, she'd managed to evade him again. But only just.

The wedding was due to take place in two weeks. Just before her twenty-fifth birthday. As agreed by her father and the previous King of Santanger. A perfectly acceptable agreement on many levels, as Prince Dax had pointed out.

But from the moment she'd been told she would have to marry a crown prince from another kingdom…a complete stranger…when she'd been just ten years old, something inside her had rebelled against it.

And that feeling had only grown stronger over the years, reinforced the few times she'd met King Aristedes—eight years her senior. He'd always seemed aloof and impossibly serious. Not remotely interested in her...in who she really was. She'd felt no connection.

And then, when her father had been dying, four years ago, he'd taken Laia's hand and said, 'My darling, don't marry for anything less than love, no matter how high the stakes. You need to be supported by someone who adores you. This job is hard and long and you deserve to be happy doing it.'

Laia's mother had died giving birth to her, and her father had lived his life in love with a ghost, devoted to her memory. He hadn't ever bowed under the pressure to marry again and have more heirs, telling people, 'I have my heir. Laia will be a great queen one day...'

And that was what the people believed, and what Laia had believed—until he'd revealed a cataclysmic secret. That he'd had a grief-fuelled affair a year after his wife had died.

Even though Laia had had time to absorb that information—and everything else that had come with it—she'd found it hard to let go of the idealised vision of love that her father had presented for so long, in spite of her knowledge of his affair.

Witnessing his devotion to his deceased wife had instilled within Laia a deep yearning for someone to love her in the same way. Yet with that came a sense of guilt—because Laia had killed her mother. Oh, she knew she hadn't *really*, but deep down, in some place where cellular memory was held, she felt guilty. Responsible.

All she had of her mother were inanimate pictures and some video footage of a beautiful, vibrant woman. She'd never been able to look at them without feeling that awful sense of guilt mixed with a hollow feeling of abandonment.

That sense of yearning for a deep and abiding connection had become even more charged as she'd grown up. As if she had a duty and responsibility not to become cynical—even after learning of her father's affair. But to honour her mother's sacrifice, and her father's grief, by aspiring to the ideals they'd set.

And now here she was, hiding out in a tropical paradise avoiding an arranged marriage, because she desperately wanted something *more* than just to be a box ticked on King Aristedes's list of things to do.

Royal wife acquired: *tick*.

Apart from that desire for a great love and supportive companionship instilled within her by her father, she also had an almost primal instinct to protect Isla'Rosa's independence. When her father had signed the marriage agreement all those years ago he'd agreed to make sure the marriage would take place before Laia's birthday, so she would have a husband and King by her side when she was crowned Queen. He'd been worried the pressure of doing it alone would be too much.

But as she'd grown up, and shown her intelligence and strength, he'd confided in her that he thought he'd make a mistake. That he should have ensured she would become Queen first, giving her more power.

Once Laia knew that her father had doubts and regrets it galvanised her to do everything she could to get out of it. She knew Isla'Rosa was badly in need of modernisation and economic assistance—she didn't need a playboy Prince to point that out. But she was determined to do it on her own and find love in the process. On her terms.

She refused to give in to the urge to look behind her to check if Prince Dax was following. Maybe he was still on the pontoon, raging at her for outwitting him.

She could still see the laser-like intensity of his blue eyes. Unusual and distinctive. She'd only seen him up close twice before, because in spite of the marriage agreement most of the meetings had taken place between the Kings, and then between Aristedes and Laia. But even those had been infrequent, due to her reluctance to meet with him.

The most recent occasion had been at a nightclub in Monaco. Unusually for her, in a social situation like that, she'd found herself lingering. For once rebelling at the constraints she'd put on herself.

In a bid to get out of her arranged marriage, she'd perfected the art of seeming to appear at every glittering social gathering she could attend, hoping she would put off the famously serious and conservative King Aristedes from marrying someone who didn't seem remotely inclined to settle down.

Ironically, she had more in common with the King than she did with his feckless playboy younger brother, even if she'd been acting the opposite. But her strategy clearly hadn't worked. Hence her current predicament—sequestering herself on an island with the last man she would choose to spend time with.

So sure about that, Princess? whispered a mischievous little voice.

She tried to block it out, but her memory transported her back to that night in Monaco with humiliating vividness.

That night she'd felt restless. Full of an uncharacteristic sense of missing out on... Fun? Her youth? The music had called to her and she'd found herself on the dance floor, closing her eyes, letting herself believe for a moment that she wasn't Crown Princess Laia Sant Roman, Queen-in-waiting, with a huge responsibility on her shoulders. A responsibility she'd borne all her life as the only heir. She'd wanted to pretend that she was just a regular young woman, with little on her mind but normal worries and concerns.

And then she'd felt an awareness. Like a faint breeze. Raising the tiny hairs on her arms. She'd opened her eyes and a man had filled her vision. Tall and broad. Unmistakably powerful. A very masculine contrast to the far more metrosexual crowd around them. As if he was from another time.

And those eyes… As blue as the clearest sea around Isla'Rosa. Laia had felt an immediate primal pull. As if on some level she'd recognised a mate. She'd wanted to take a step towards him. Absurdly. She'd even gestured to her security team that it was okay to let him approach.

And it had only been then, after her helpless reaction, that she'd realised belatedly who was standing in front of her. Crown Prince Dax. The world's most debauched and spoiled bachelor prince. The spare to the heir.

Immediately she'd felt exposed. And resentful at the brutal reminder that she wasn't just a regular young woman enjoying a carefree night out.

Along with the resentment had come a dart of envy for his freedom, and that had only made her feel even more antagonistic towards him.

To feel envy for that man was shameful.

How could she find him remotely attractive?

He epitomised everything she didn't want in a partner. The only form of love he appeared to know was self-love. He let his brother carry the full weight of responsibility for their royal obligations while he spent his days in dissolute hedonism, travelling from party to party.

As do you.

But she didn't. Not really. And that was all over now anyway. Her plan hadn't worked and now it was just a waiting game until she could return to Isla'Rosa for her birthday and the coronation.

But even if you don't marry this king now you will have to marry soon. And well. What if you never find someone who will love you the way you want? What if King Aristedes is your best chance of a happy life? Even if you don't love each other?

Laia could feel the sweat breaking out on her brow and at the small of her back as she made her way up the steps to the villa through the forest, and it wasn't just due to the high temperatures.

Lately she'd been feeling more and more claustrophobic, as if the walls were encroaching on her. What if she was painting herself into a corner and making a huge mistake, insisting on maintaining her independence and that of her country?

She forced the sensation of claustrophobia out. She reassured herself she was doing the right thing...not selling out her country to let it be subsumed by the bigger and wealthier Santanger. It wasn't the easy option, no doubt about that, but she didn't want the easy option.

She wanted to do things her way, and she wanted a life with someone she could love and respect. Not a marriage based only on duty.

Had it been totally crazy to all but kidnap Prince Dax? *Yes.* But there was no going back now.

For a louche playboy, Prince Dax had managed to find her—which had been no mean feat. So she needed her wits about her. Clearly he was able to focus when he needed to, and she had a sense that she shouldn't underestimate him.

Breathing with a bit of effort when she got to the top of the steps, she turned around—and almost fell backwards when Prince Dax appeared right behind her, taller than she'd expected. He showed no signs of exertion.

She felt churlish. Shouldn't he be a little overweight and soft around the jowls after all his partying? Instead he looked more like a prize athlete.

He stopped and looked around, taking in the open courtyard area in front of the villa with its central pond, where big golden fish swam around lazily. The villa soared dramatically above them, built on three levels. The ground floor was dramatically open to the elements, but there were screens and shutters that protected it during the rainy season.

'This is a rainforest,' Prince Dax said, looking around at the lush vegetation and tall trees.

Laia was tempted to say something snarky, but she settled for, 'Yes, it is.'

She had to admit that no other person on the planet made her feel so…so prickly and antagonistic. He had done from the moment he'd first registered on her consciousness as the younger brother of King Aristedes. She'd been just sixteen years old. That had been their first meeting.

But she couldn't go there now. Not when those blue eyes— far more alert and incisive than she'd expected—swivelled back to her.

For a moment she couldn't breathe.

Laia hated it that he had such an effect on her. She tried to assure herself she was being ridiculous. He was an undeniably gorgeous man and she was merely reacting as any red-blooded woman would. A bit galling to be as human as the next woman—or man, for that matter—but there was no accounting for hormones. It was also galling that he appeared to be the only man yet to engage her libido.

She was afraid that meeting him again face to face was only confirming something she'd feared since she'd seen him at that club. That he'd had a profound effect on her at a formative time in her life, at that very first meeting, when she'd been just sixteen—almost as if he'd imprinted on her, leaving an invisible marker on her hormones, in her blood, that had ruined her for all other men. Certainly no one she'd met since had come close to having the same effect on her.

Sending up a silent prayer that she was wrong and that

those hormones would calm down, Laia turned and walked into the villa.

She said over her shoulder, 'The kitchen is this way.'

Dax had no choice but to follow his hostess. He was still reeling a little from what had happened. The fact that he was here. And that his phone was somewhere at the bottom of the Straits of Malacca, being nibbled by fish.

All he could do now was accept his current situation, observe his surroundings, and wait for an opportunity to turn the tables on Princess Laia.

He followed her into a generous open-plan kitchen—lots of wood, from the floors to the ceilings. There was a massive island with a black marble countertop, and she'd put the bags on it. She took off the sunhat and her glossy hair hung long and wavy over her shoulders.

She was already taking the groceries out of the bags, basically behaving as if Dax wasn't even there. As inconsequential as a boat boy who'd merely helped her with her shopping.

For someone who prided himself on not having much of an ego, Dax found his irritation levels spiking again. He couldn't recall ever being so…ignored. Certainly not by someone who had gone to some lengths to bring him somewhere and incarcerate him. Albeit somewhere that seemed to be a luxury private island.

He put the shopping bags down. Princess Laia didn't even look up. She was walking over to the fridge now, the delicate material of her wrap revealing more than disguising the tantalising glimpses of her body. Her legs were long and toned. She was a runner.

Dax lifted his gaze and said, as coolly as he could, 'Well, Princess, now that you have me here, what do you intend to do with me?'

He noticed the slightest jolt in her body as she put something into the fridge. A reaction to his voice. So she wasn't as unaffected as she looked. Perhaps he'd misinterpreted that look of fear back on the main island. Maybe it hadn't been fear as much as apprehension at being alone with him.

Because she was as aware of him as he was of her?

Dax's blood pulsed at that thought. And it shouldn't. He had to control himself.

She turned around and came back to the island to pick up more groceries. She said, 'I intend to make sure you don't give away my location before I'm ready to return home.'

'To Santanger…to your fiancé.'

She'd turned to go back to the fridge, avoiding his eye the whole time. 'I am not his fiancée and I have a home of my own. Isla'Rosa.'

'I think a signed marriage agreement between our fathers would attest to my brother and you being affianced.'

He saw the tension in her body—and then she turned around and looked at him. Another electric jolt went through his body. He ignored it.

She said tightly, 'It's not a law.'

'It's not nothing, either. What about the peace agreement? You'd jeopardise the peace between our kingdoms?'

Her eyes sparked. 'Of course not—that's the last thing I want. But from what I know of King Aristedes, he's not so petty that he will undo years of peace-building just because I don't want to marry him. I am confident we can build a lasting and enduring peace without a marriage of convenience.'

'A royal dynastic marriage is a little more than a marriage of convenience.'

Princess Laia came back over to the island and put her hands on it. She really was extraordinarily beautiful.

'I am aware of that. But as your brother has refused to even listen to my side of things I've had to take matters into my own hands.'

Dax frowned. 'Ari is eminently reasonable...much more so than me.'

Princess Laia shrugged minutely. 'Not in this instance. He sees our marriage as a done deal, and when I try to talk to him about it he's not interested.'

'Why don't you just pick up the phone and talk to him about it now?'

She shook her head. 'And let him know my location? No. It's too late for that. There's no discussion to be had. We're not getting married. I will never become Queen of Santanger.'

Dax folded his arms. 'So if you're here...and so intent on not marrying him...then who is the woman purporting to be you in Santanger right now?'

The Princess went pale. Her mouth closed. Lush lips were sealed. Eyes wide. He saw the shadow of guilt in her expression. So she wasn't entirely comfortable with what she was doing. Dax would exploit that chink of vulnerability mercilessly.

He said, 'Ari knows she's not you because he's sent me after you.'

Princess Laia's jaw clenched. 'How did you find out where I was?'

'Thanks to some disreputable people I know in the security industries, I tracked you to Langkawi.'

She said, 'I guess I shouldn't be surprised that you know people on the margins.'

Dax tensed, surprised at the dart of something that felt suspiciously like hurt. He held back the urge to ask her to clarify what she meant, because he already knew and her opinion shouldn't matter.

He'd honed his own disreputable reputation for so long now

that he couldn't remember a time when it hadn't been stained with rumours and innuendo. Lots of people had said things to him over the years and it was like water off a duck's back. But not with this woman. He didn't like that revelation. He barely knew her.

He said, 'So, who is the woman pretending to be you?'

With palpable reluctance, Princess Laia said, 'She's my lady-in-waiting. Her name is Maddi.'

Dax absorbed this. 'I only saw a couple of pictures of them returning to Santanger and getting off the plane. She's uncannily like you. Hence the switch, I presume?'

Princess Laia nodded. Suddenly she did look distinctly guilty. Almost green around the gills.

He said, 'Are you sure you have the stomach for this?'

Her eyes flashed, and Dax found himself welcoming that sign of her spirit. Dark luxuriant hair slipped over one shoulder. It reached almost to the top of her breasts.

'I am absolutely fine with this,' she said. She put out a hand 'Why don't you have a look around? Make yourself at home. And please believe me when I say there is no way off this island without triggering an alarm. There is also no access to any communication devices or the internet, so don't bother looking. The bedrooms are on the third level—a guest suite has been made up for you, it's the first one on the right.'

Mercifully, the man left the kitchen and Laia sagged a little. Being in close proximity to him was like being hooked up to an electric charge. It was impossible to relax.

She continued to put the shopping away, including the bags he'd carried, hoping that doing something mundane would make her feel more centred again. But she couldn't stop her mind going back to that seismic moment when she'd first met him. When she'd been sixteen years old.

She'd been attending a charity polo match with her father in Paris, and Prince Dax had been playing for the European team against a team from South America.

Her eye had been drawn to him like a magnet. She hadn't been able to look away. He'd been so unbelievably—ridiculously—gorgeous. Dark messy hair. Stubbled jaw. A face surely carved by the same artists who had created Greek and Roman statues. A body that was lean but muscled in a way that had made her feel funny inside…as if she'd known that it was something she didn't fully understand yet.

At sixteen she'd been worldly-wise in so many ways, but not when it came to boys—or men.

She'd seen him from a distance before that, once, on a rare trip to the palace in Santanger with her father when she'd been much younger. He'd been a gangly teenager. But in Paris he'd been a man.

The VIP hospitality tent had been alive with whispers and gossip about him. His legendary sexual prowess. His string of lovers. His absolute contempt for showing an atom of responsibility. His poor brother who had to do all the work. And, worse and most salacious of all, the fiercely whispered rumour that he'd been responsible for his mother's tragic and untimely death in a car crash because he'd been driving the car.

That was a scandal in itself, because he'd only been fifteen years old—too young to drive legally. But the Queen's death had been ruled a tragic accident and no further legal proceedings had issued from it. People had commented on the entitlement of the rich and powerful, who felt they were above the law.

So, to say he'd had a reputation as an *enfant terrible* would have been an understatement. He'd appeared after the match in the tent, still wearing his mud-splattered clothes, his dark skin gleaming with perspiration. Obviously uncaring what anyone thought.

Laia would never forget his scent: earth and musky sweat and pure undiluted *male*. As potent as if he'd just climbed out of a lover's bed. She'd been struck mute by his sheer raw magnetism and total insouciance.

He'd seen her father and had come over, and she had been able to tell that her father disapproved of him. They'd greeted one another, though, civilly. And Prince Dax had looked at her then, with an appraising gaze. Laia had been mortified by the flash of heat that had washed through her entire body, making her aware of it in a way she'd never experienced before. Making her aware of the dress she was wearing, which had suddenly felt too tight and childish.

That look alone, along with her awareness of him, had unlocked something inside her. An understanding of herself becoming a woman. A sexual being.

Then he'd said, with casual devastation, 'I believe that one day I'll be your brother-in-law.'

It had taken a moment for his words to sink in. She'd been avoiding thinking about her arranged marriage very well up to that point. But with those few words it had rushed home with the speed of a freight train crashing into her.

The fact that *this man* in front of her, who was causing such a conflicting mix of emotions and sensations in her body and head, was someday going to be sitting at a table, maybe across from her, or beside her, as her *brother-in-law*, had been suddenly horrifying.

So much so that she'd felt sick.

Her father must have seen her reaction, because he'd said something and ushered her away.

He'd put her reaction down to Prince Dax presenting himself in less than pristine condition. But the truth was that for long weeks afterwards Laia had been obsessed with Prince Dax. Looking him up online. Watching his exploits unfold as he made his way from Paris to London, New York to Rome—you name it, he was there—with the world's most beautiful women on his arm and that devil-may-care grin on his face.

Gradually, mortified by her obsession, Laia had convinced herself that he disgusted her. That he revolted her with his blatant lack of consideration for anything but the good life. The incredibly louche life. Serving only himself and—by all accounts—his insatiable appetites. Whether it was for women or experiences or luxury properties or yachts...

But now that he was here, on her beloved island, sequestered with her for at least the next ten days, Laia knew she would have no choice but to face up to the fact that Prince Dax bothered her a lot.

And she was afraid that it was for far more complicated reasons than the simplistic antipathy she'd honed for years. She wasn't normally a judgemental person—never had been. She prided herself on accepting everyone as she met them. Prince Dax, however, had always uniquely got under her skin.

She was afraid that her judgement of the man was about to blow up in her face in spectacular fashion...because really, all along, it had been based on the way he made her feel and not on his lifestyle choices.

Dax stood on the generous outdoor balcony of the guest suite. He had a view out over the treetops to the sea beyond, where he could see the security team's yacht bobbing peacefully on the water. He idly wondered how long it would take to swim to the boat, climb on board, disable the bodyguards and call for help.

But, as appealing as that might be—if a little unrealistic—surely it was more prudent to win the Princess over to accepting her fate rather than coercing her into it. It was the twenty-first century after all. She was clearly a modern woman who was resistant to being treated like a chattel. Not exactly an unreasonable state of affairs.

In many respects, Dax had never really understood his brother Ari's dogged acceptance of a wedding agreement made when he'd been only eight years old. Princess Laia had been just a baby!

In every other respect his brother was a forward-thinking, modern monarch. But not in this. Even when Dax had brought it up over the years, teasing Ari about what his wife might be like, how he could possibly agree to live with a woman he didn't know, Ari had closed down the discussion. Usually by saying something like, 'You saw how it was between our parents. Do you think I want to risk that again? I'm quite happy to marry for duty and responsibility and siring heirs. I don't want anything more. Princess Laia has been bred for this. She knows the score.'

As if Dax needed any reminder of the hellscape that had been his parents' unhappy marriage... His mother had had the audacity to fall in love with her husband, and the King had repaid her love by taking numerous lovers throughout their union.

It had turned Dax's mother into a brittle and self-destructive shell of a woman. Dax had become her crutch and her confidant well before he should have even known about such things. But with Ari busy with lessons to prepare him for one day becoming sovereign, Dax had been the only one his mother had been able to turn to.

He diverted his mind from toxic memories now. He hadn't thought about such things in a long time, and he didn't welcome their resurgence.

Privately Dax had always thought to himself that while Ari was happy to accept his fate, maybe his future wife would be less so. And that was exactly what had come to pass.

Although he took no pleasure in that. Not when he was captive on a tropical island thousands of miles from his brother in Santanger. Thousands of miles from his own life.

He looked down to the ground level, where a wide lap pool looked very inviting. Sunbeds were laid out around it. The water shimmered green and blue from the mosaics underneath.

He turned around. The bedroom was palatial. Lots of wood, as was the custom in this part of the world. A massive bed dressed in cool white linen. It was a four-poster, with a simple wooden frame from which hung the very necessary mosquito net to protect him from small biting insects at night.

The bathroom was also huge, with a shower that was open to the elements. Very romantic. Dax smiled mirthlessly at the that notion. He was here with a woman who openly disdained him.

He wasn't so arrogant as to think that every woman he met fancied him, but he knew that being blessed with a pleasing physical appearance together with vast personal wealth, both inherited and created, was a powerful cocktail.

For the first time he was in the presence of someone who appeared less than impressed.

Dax spotted another door and opened it. It led into a dressing room. It was full of clothes. All brand-new. With the tags still on. More or less in his size. There was underwear. Swimwear. Leisure wear. Casual clothes. Shoes. There was even a tuxedo.

Dax left his suite to make his way back down to the kitchen, but in the corridor he spotted a door opposite. Her room? Curious, he went and tested the door. It was locked, so presumably it was hers. He had to hand it to her, she was certainly prepared.

He went downstairs to where the Princess was now chopping a range of colourful vegetables. She'd tied her hair back and up into a loose knot, and it exposed the delicate line of her jaw and neck. Her hands were deft. Short, practical nails.

Something moved through Dax at that moment—a fleeting sense of almost…protectiveness.

Rejection of that notion made his voice sharp. 'The dressing room is stocked with clothes. Did kidnapping me interrupt a lover coming to stay?'

She made a face. 'No. And don't you think you're being a little dramatic? Kidnap?'

'What would you call it, then, if not kidnapping?'

She stopped chopping, as if considering this, and then said, 'A momentary redirection.' She added, 'I took the liberty of stocking clothes because I knew you would need them.'

Dax wasn't sure whether to feel amused, bemused or insulted. Or irritated. Very few people had the wherewithal to derail his life like this. He didn't like the sensation of being powerless.

'You got the sizes mostly right, but I'm not sure a black tuxedo is entirely necessary.'

She shrugged. 'You know as well as I do that we have to be prepared at all times for any eventuality.'

Dax could appreciate that. As a royal, he did have to be prepared for literally everything, but somehow he couldn't see a black-tie event in his near future.

Then Dax thought of something—very belatedly. 'I have a hotel room. My things…my passport.'

'Taken care of,' the Princess said briskly. 'I've instructed the hotel to pack your things and put them in the safe until you return to pick them up.'

The irritation spiked. He was a busy man. 'And that would be…when, exactly?'

She looked at him. 'Ten days at the most.'

Enough was enough. 'Look, Princess Laia—'

She put up a hand. 'Please, call me Laia. I don't think we need to stand on formalities here, do we?'

Dax clenched his jaw and then said sweetly, 'Well, seeing as how we're going to be in-laws, no, I guess not. The same goes for you...just Dax will suffice.'

She flushed at that and went back to her chopping. 'I'm making a chicken and vegetable stir-fry for dinner. You're welcome to have some.'

He noted she wasn't inviting him to join her. 'Not exactly what I would have expected a princess to be doing.'

She looked at him. 'Don't judge us all by your standards.'

Dax's gaze narrowed on Laia. He didn't like the way her judgement of him pricked his skin like a sharp knife.

He put his hands on the island. 'You really don't like me, do you? Which is strange, because we don't even know each other. Maybe if you gave me a chance you'd realise that I'm not the person you clearly think I am.'

She went pinker. The fact that she couldn't hide her reactions was fascinating to Dax.

She said, 'Perhaps. But we're not really here to get acquainted.'

Dax's blood grew warm at the thought of getting 'acquainted'. He resisted her statement. It made him feel rebellious. Like forgetting he had a duty to his brother where this woman was concerned.

He wanted her.

And he'd wanted her since he'd seen her in that club. He had a feeling it was going to get harder to ignore.

'Well, maybe you should have thought about that before sequestering us on a private island with—as far as I can make out—not a whole lot to do.'

She visibly gulped at that, but it was little comfort. The magnitude of what had happened seemed to hit Dax at that moment, and suddenly he felt as caged as a captive tiger, even within this lush paradise.

With exaggerated care he said, 'Thank you for the offer of food, but I'll look after myself. I would have contributed to the shopping if I'd known what to expect.'

Laia's eyes darted to him as if she was sensing his sudden volatility. 'That's okay... We have enough supplies. There'll be leftovers if you change your mind.'

Dax turned and walked away, exerting every atom of control he could muster. He had operated outside of his comfort zone for a long time, so this situation was irritating but not disconcerting. But what he wasn't prepared for was the feeling of emotional exposure. And no way was he going to let Laia see how she affected him.

CHAPTER THREE

LAIA QUESTIONED HER sanity in thinking this was a viable option. She'd sensed Dax's volatility just now—like a crackling forcefield around him. She could only wonder how she would feel if she was in his shoes. A lot more vulnerable, for a start. Angry. *Helpless.*

Her conscience pricked hard.

Although the last thing he struck her as was helpless. In fact she wouldn't put it past him to swim out to the security boat, overcome the guards and take off. He seemed entirely capable.

But if he tried that he would set off the alarm and they'd be ready for him.

In fact, when she thought about it, he wasn't behaving as she might have expected of a playboy who was used to instant gratification and the constant stimulation of beautiful women and places. He didn't seem to be hugely perturbed. Annoyed, yes, but not petulant that he was missing whatever nightclub opening he was due to attend.

Laia scowled at herself. It wasn't like her to be bitchy. But this man appealed to her worst qualities.

Because he affects you, and you're not honest enough to acknowledge how much.

She scowled even more.

She diverted her brain away from such uncomfortable things by focusing on what she *should* be thinking about. Or *who*. Maddi, her lady-in-waiting and best friend. And, more sensationally, her half-sister, who was the product of the affair her father had had with a woman from the castle staff.

No one but them knew that they were sisters.

Her father had told her he'd always regretted how he'd handled it, because when he'd found out his lover was pregnant he'd sent her away, for fear of a scandal. He'd asked Laia to go and find her sister and tell her he was sorry.

Apparently Maddi, who lived in Ireland, had always known who she was and where she came from.

After her father's death, Laia had been too grief-struck and shocked to go looking for her half-sister. And then, as time had passed, she'd grown apprehensive. Afraid of what she might find.

Someone who was resentful? Angry? Vengeful?

But eventually Laia had been able to ignore her conscience no longer and she'd gone to Ireland. And when she had found her half-sister Maddi had been none of the things Laia had feared.

Maddi had been shy. And yet there had been a strong bond between them from the moment they'd met. Laia had begged her sister to come to Isla'Rosa with her, to see where she came from. Maddi was the one who'd suggested working as Laia's lady-in-waiting, to give her a chance to be anonymous and learn more about Laia and everything. They'd agreed that Laia's coronation would be the opportune time to reveal Maddi as a member of the royal family.

Over the past year they'd forged an even stronger bond and had become inseparable. So when King Aristedes had followed them to that festival in the desert just days ago, demonstrating his determination to make Laia his wife, Maddi had suggested taking advantage of the fact that they were so alike they could pass for twins.

Before Laia had known what was happening she'd been bundled away by her security team and Maddi had taken off in a small sleek jet with King Aristedes, pretending to be her.

But obviously, since Dax had been on her trail so soon after their switch, Maddi's impersonation of Laia couldn't have lasted more than a few hours after her arrival with the King into Santanger.

Maddi had sent her a text—obviously before she'd known the King had discovered their ruse—saying that the King believed she was Laia, that she was okay, and asking where Laia was. Laia had responded—but only mentioning that she was in south-east Asia, for fear of someone taking Maddi's phone. Since then there had been no more messages.

She knew Maddi was capable of looking after herself—she was a lot more street smart than Laia, thanks to having lived a regular life. And King Aristedes was a civilised man. He wouldn't want adverse press at this time any more than she did, which was presumably why he wasn't exposing his fake fiancée.

He would undoubtedly be expecting his brother to reappear at any moment, with Laia by his side. Was he hoping to merely switch his fake fiancée for his real one? Well, that wasn't going to happen. Once.

Laia was Queen she would be in a much stronger position to negotiate with King Aristedes—about their marriage *and* peace.

All she had to do was bide her time here until a couple of days before her birthday.

Here, on a romantic private island, with the one man in the world who makes you feel prickly and hot and full of a need you can't even name.

Laia pushed that incendiary thought out of her head and focused on cooking the food. She wasn't remotely Dax's type— not that she wanted to be, she assured herself hurriedly.

For one thing, he always seemed to favour tall, slim blondes. A dramatic contrast to his dark good looks. And she was far too boring and staid for his tastes.

The persona she'd created of being a party girl was paper-thin. She'd become an expert at appearing at the opening of an event only to be curled up in bed with a book an hour later, with no one any the wiser. She'd realised that once people *saw* you there, they just assumed you were there for the night. And she'd always made sure she appeared in the press.

Within a couple of days her guest would be climbing the trees with boredom, but there was nothing Laia could do to help that. There was no way she was jeopardising her future when she was close enough to feel the weight of the Isla'Rosa crown on her head and know that she was taking her own destiny, and that of her country, into her own hands and no one else's.

Later that evening Dax wandered into the kitchen, rubbing his wet hair with a towel. He'd just had a shower in the changing gazebo after a swim in the lap pool, and felt marginally less edgy and irritated after expending some energy.

He'd walked around the island a little beforehand. It was mostly forest and precipitous hills. There was a stunning private white sand beach on the other side of the island. And a small house that he guessed was used by staff when they were required.

It was indeed a beautiful location. But Laia was right. Unless he dived into the sea and started swimming he wasn't going anywhere.

And now, after the activity, he was hungry. He opened the fridge and spotted a Tupperware bowl filled with the leftovers of the stir-fry. There was a Post-it note attached.

Feel free to help yourself.

Strange to feel somewhat mollified at this very basic concession for having removed him from his life so spectacularly. But then hadn't he been planning on doing that to Laia? Albeit without resorting to kidnap. He could see now, though, that she wouldn't have gone anywhere with him willingly.

He took out the bowl and lifted off the airtight lid. It smelled good. His stomach rumbled. Dax had always had a healthy appetite. For everything. Life. Sex. Ambition. Winning. *Sex*.

He hadn't had sex for a few months. It had been preying on his mind...the flatlining of his libido. But lately everything had begun to feel a little dull. There was no excitement. No one causing his pulse to trip.

Until he'd laid eyes on Laia again today.

He set about putting the stir-fry in the microwave, and tried not to think about the suspicion that he'd actually felt flat since he'd seen her in that nightclub over a year ago.

Oh, he'd taken lovers since then. But for the first time it hadn't been satisfying. And so he'd subconsciously taken a hiatus from women. Focused instead on his work.

He'd even taken a call from Ari a month or so ago, his brother commenting, 'You haven't appeared in the papers in a few weeks. I'm just checking you're still alive.'

Dax had realised with a jolt that he hadn't had any appetite for going out. For the endless round of socialising that for so long had helped him not to think about things.

He'd replied, 'I'm very much alive, brother. Maybe I'm plotting to take over your throne? It's all the rage on every TV show at the moment.'

Ari had sounded weary. 'Be my guest—and while you're at it see if you can track down Princess Laia and remind her of her marital obligations, would you?'

Dax had responded lightly, belying the spike of something

sharp in his gut that had felt suspiciously like jealousy. 'Maybe she's just not that into you.'

His brother had said, 'Ha-ha,' and terminated the call.

And now he was here, with this woman who appealed to him in a way that was seriously unwelcome, and instead of being able to explore his attraction as he usually would—by seduction and indulging in slaking his desires—he had to do the right thing and encourage her go back to Europe, marry his brother and become his sister-in-law. His Queen.

Once again the resistance he felt to that idea was almost physical.

The microwave dinged at that moment and Dax welcomed the distraction. He took out the bowl of stir-fry and transferred it to a plate. He got himself a beer from the fridge, and went to sit on the decking outside the kitchen.

Dusk was cloaking everything in a lush lavender colour. The night chorus of insects was starting up. Dax noticed a citronella candle burning, to deter mosquitoes. Had Laia been sitting here eating just a short while before?

The food was delicious. Fresh and tasty, with a bit of a kick. Dax wolfed it down.

Laia was an enigma, for sure—a queen in waiting so desperate not to be married that she had run to the other side of the world to a jungle paradise where she seemed happy to cook and wait on herself.

Not the behaviour he would have expected of someone of her standing. He knew people with regular blood running through their veins who wouldn't deign to lower themselves to such mundane activities.

He was going to do his utmost to figure out how to get to her and make her see sense, and then he'd send her on her way before she could wrap his brain—*and his body*—into too many knots.

* * *

The following morning, after a fractious sleep that she blamed
Dax for, Laia felt fuzzy-headed even after a swim in the pool
and a shower. She went down to the kitchen, taking out supplies for breakfast. Pastries and fruit and granola. She made
coffee and the fragrant smell helped clear her head.

She had to admit moodily that her sleep had also been fractious because she was sharing a space with a man who made
her feel aware of herself as a woman, and very conscious of
the fact that she was that rare unicorn: a virgin. Still. At almost twenty-five.

In her defence, she wasn't exactly in a position where she
could indulge in carnal activities without risking drawing the
all-seeing eye of the press. If anything, seeing Dax's sexploits
splashed routinely across the tabloids over the years had put
the fear of God into her. And as time had gone on, and she'd
grown older, the world's fascination with her and her love-life
had assumed gargantuan proportions, making it even more
unlikely that she would indulge.

Not that she'd met anyone who'd made her feel like indulging.

Except for the man who is here right now, in your house...

She pushed that inflammatory thought aside. And then she
heard a sound and looked up and froze, even while simultaneously melting on the spot.

Dax was on the other side of the kitchen, having just walked
in from outside.

He was bare-chested and wearing a pair of short sweatpants.
He was drinking from a bottle of water. Laia was aware that
he must have been running, or maybe he'd found the gym.

Her gaze seemed to be glued to his chest. It wasn't the first
time she'd seen a bare-chested man, but it felt like it.

He was...sublime. Broad and exquisitely muscled. A light

smattering of hair across his pectorals met in a line that dissected his abdominal muscles and continued down under the top of his shorts…

Laia raised her eyes, cheeks on fire. Dammit, why couldn't she be cool? She'd never needed to be cool more than now. She felt ridiculously overdressed, in a loose linen sleeveless shirt and loose trousers. Then she noticed something else. A dark mark high over one pectoral.

He walked closer. She could see that it was a tattoo.

'You have a tattoo.'

She wasn't sure why she was surprised. It wasn't as if this man didn't have a reputation for being a rebel already.

The ink drawing was surprisingly delicate and beautiful. An intricate birdcage with a closed door and a bird inside. For some reason it made Laia feel a little sad.

'The bird is caged.'

She looked at Dax and saw he was watching her with a wary expression. It diffused something inside her…as if she'd discovered a chink in his armour.

'Yes, the bird is caged.'

'Does it mean something?'

An expression crossed his face so fleetingly that she might have imagined it, but she knew she hadn't. It had been *pain*.

He shrugged minutely. 'It was done on a drunken whim. It means whatever you want it to mean.'

'Drunken tattoos aren't usually as…considered.'

He arched a brow. 'Maybe you'd like to tell me what you think it means?'

The air around them seemed to have grown thick and charged. Laia was glad of the big solid island between them.

She changed the subject. 'Did you go for a run?' she babbled. 'We have a gym, too, fully equipped.'

'I found the gym, thank you.'

She put some fruit and yoghurt into a bowl and said, 'Please, help yourself to whatever you'd like. There's fresh coffee.'

She moved to a table on the terrace before Dax could get too close as he filled his own plate with a little of everything. He was a big man—he undoubtedly had a healthy appetite.

Not just for food, whispered a little wicked voice.

Laia tensed all over as Dax came over and joined her at the table.

He stopped before sitting down. 'Do you mind?'

Yes. She shook her head. 'Of course not.'

He sat down. Laia felt uptight. His chest filled her peripheral vision. She wanted to ask him to put a top on, but they were in the tropics. It was entirely practical to wear as little as possible. His skin gleamed. From the humidity or from exertion? She had an urge to go closer, to breathe in his scent.

This awareness of herself as a woman and him as a very masculine man made her skin prickle uncomfortably. She cursed silently. Why couldn't she be immune to him?

'So, this island…it belongs to you?' he asked.

Laia nodded, glad of a diversion from her increasingly heated thoughts. 'It was my mother's—left to her by an uncle who lived here his whole life.'

'Your mother, Queen Isabel, had links to almost every royal family in Europe.'

Laia looked at Dax. He sat in a louche sprawl on the other side of the table. Supremely at ease. Not ranting and raving about being incarcerated. She didn't trust it for a minute.

She took a sip of coffee and nodded. 'As do we all.'

'True.'

In fact he was being polite. Civil. Laia could play him at his own game and be polite too. 'Have you been to Malaysia before?'

Dax nodded his head. 'Yes, but only to Kuala Lumpur. I

am grateful for an opportunity to explore more of this beautiful country.'

Laia looked at Dax suspiciously. He had an innocent expression, as if to say, *What?* She felt a little disconcerted. She wasn't sure how to handle this sanguine man who appeared to hold no grudge for her having removed him from his life for an extended period.

Her conscience forced her to say, 'Look, I'm sorry that it had to happen like this. I'm sure you're missing lots of…engagements. I hope nothing too important?'

Dax took a sip of coffee and put the cup down. He said, 'I'd already carved time out of my schedule because my brother asked me to track you down. And that's what I've done. But I won't consider the job done until you are delivered to him in Santanger.'

Laia scowled. 'Like a parcel.'

Dax shook his head. 'Like the wife you agreed to be.'

Now Laia shook her head. 'I never agreed to it. I was never given a chance. It was a *fait accompli* from the day I was born and born a girl. How archaic is that?'

His eyes narrowed on her. 'It's the way it's done in our world. You do know that there are far more arranged marriages than so-called love matches globally?'

'You're not a fan of a love match, then?'

Now he was the one who looked slightly uncomfortable, avoiding her eye. Laia felt it like a small triumph.

He said, 'Not for people like us, no.'

'But normal people can indulge?'

He looked at her. 'The stakes are lower.'

That was one way of putting it. The stakes were definitely lower when you didn't have a duty to a nation of people and the responsibility of continuing a royal line.

Laia felt a dart of guilt before she realised that this was probably Dax's plan—to undermine her resolve.

As if reading her mind, he asked congenially, 'Why are you so against the marriage? Ari isn't a bad person. I'm told he's considered to be quite attractive.' Dax made a self-deprecating face. 'Not as much as me, of course, but he can't have everything—the kingdom *and* incredible sex appeal.'

Laia had to curb the urge to roll her eyes and smile at his confidence.

He's a charmer, reminded a little voice. *This is how he's spent his dissolute life. This is how he's trying to get to you, any way possible.*

Laia sobered. 'I'm not against marriage. I'm just against this one. Your brother has no interest in me. He expects a convenient royal wife to slot into his world and doesn't want to discuss it further.'

'So what is it that you want, if not a perfectly reasonable match with one of the world's wealthiest and most eligible men? Call me old-fashioned, but I can't see many women turning that opportunity down.'

'You're cynical.'

He looked surprised. 'And you're not?'

Laia shook her head. How had they got into this territory? 'I try not to be. I want a deeper partnership with my husband.'

A smile spread across Dax's face and Laia's breath got stuck in her throat for a second. When he smiled it was like being caught in the sun's rays...magnetic and—

He declared, 'You're a romantic.'

Laia went cold. Was she so transparent? She felt exposed under Dax's gaze.

'Don't be ridiculous.'

He shrugged. 'If you gave Ari a chance you might find that your relationship provides all that you need.'

'I did try to talk to him—after my father's funeral. He wasn't interested. He said the marriage would be happening and there was nothing further to discuss. He had his chance to convince me and now it's gone.'

Suddenly Dax looked serious. 'It's a fool's errand, looking for love in our world. It simply doesn't exist—and nor would you want it to. It only leads to self-destruction.'

Laia frowned. 'What does that mean? Who are you talking about?'

But Dax had stood up abruptly. He said, 'I'm going to clean up. Can I ask you to pass a message to one of my assistants for me? I'm sure you don't want worldwide headlines shouting about the missing Playboy Prince.'

Laia took the abrupt hint. Clearly he didn't like her question and wasn't going to answer.

She considered his request and knew she owed him this much. 'Okay.' She stood up and went to a drawer, pulling out a notepad and a pen. She handed it to Dax. 'Give me the details.'

But he said, 'I'll call them out to you, if you don't mind. I'm dyslexic, so it'll take me longer to write it all down.'

Laia stopped and looked at him. She hadn't expected him to say that. And so easily.

'I…' For once in her life she felt at a loss. Not sure what to say. Eventually she said, 'I'm sorry. I wasn't expecting to hear you say that. I didn't know you were dyslexic.'

Dax looked unperturbed. 'Both me and my brother have it—him to a lesser degree. I've learnt to navigate my way around it.'

Laia felt as if the ground was shifting under her feet. This threw a new perspective on Dax. An intriguing one.

'Okay, call out the details.'

He did, and she wrote them down. When she looked up again Dax was too close. That chest was all she could see.

And she could smell his scent. Woodsy and musky. She had the most bizarre urge to put her hand on his chest and feel his heart beating against her palm.

She backed away so fast she almost fell over.

She said, 'I'll do this now,' and fled.

Dax could still smell Laia's scent lingering in the air. Soft and flowery. But not too sweet. There was something sharp. Like her.

She'd looked at him sharply just now, when he'd told her he had dyslexia. As if reassessing him. He was used to people looking at him differently when they found out—and not necessarily kindly. Sometimes with pity. Sometimes as if his diagnosis explained something to them. As if it explained why he was nothing but a feckless royal playboy—because how could anyone with dyslexia be successful?

A total misconception, as Dax knew well. Some of the most successful people in the world had dyslexia and similar neurodivergences.

But he had been a feckless royal playboy in his younger years. So he couldn't really blame people for their lazy judgement. And if they continued to judge him based on that earlier version of himself then more fool them. And he'd proved lots of people to be fools by now.

He realised that he'd mentioned his dyslexia just now because he'd wanted to see how Laia would respond. He'd almost wanted to see that glint of *aha* in her eyes, as if she could square him away into a little box. Dismiss him.

But she hadn't looked at him like that. She'd been surprised, but not judgemental. Intrigued. She was endlessly surprising. Not least for pulling this stunt in getting him onto a private island with no escape.

And also because sometimes she looked at him the way

she had in Monte Carlo, with big eyes. As if she'd never seen a man before.

As if she wanted to devour him.

But in the next second the shutters would come down and she'd disappear back behind an expressionless mask, like she had that night.

She reminded him of a fawn. Curious, but drawing back.

She wanted him. He knew that now.

Her little glances when she thought he wasn't looking.

The way she quivered when he came near.

The almost ever-present flush in her cheeks—although admittedly sometimes that might be irritation or anger.

And you want her.

Dax turned and strode out to the terrace, to try and cool the heat in his body and brain. He might want her, but he couldn't have her. Not this woman who'd been promised to his brother from her birth.

He cursed. It *was* archaic. It was ridiculous. But it was her destiny and he had to do everything in his power to make sure it happened.

His brother had let him have his freedom and now it was Dax's turn to give Ari what he needed. A wife and a queen.

A little later, Laia was sitting cross-legged on her bed with her bedroom door carefully locked. She was on her laptop, which was hooked up to rapid broadband.

There were no headlines mentioning anything about Dax going missing. There were, however, some headlines about Princess Laia's arrival on Santanger, and speculation about the royal wedding but no real details.

King Aristedes must have realised that he'd have to postpone the wedding at the very least.

There were several grainy pictures of Maddi arriving in

Santanger, wearing what looked like a man's jacket and with long bare legs. And then there were more recent pictures of her and the King at a palace garden party.

Laia touched the screen. Maddi looked very sleekly polished and a little terrified beside the tall and stern King. Wide-eyed. Obviously the King *was* determined to maintain the fiction of his wedding proceeding, and luckily no one had seemed to notice that Maddi wasn't Laia.

They looked so alike. It was only at close quarters that someone might notice that Maddi's eyes were darker and that she was a little curvier—much to Laia's envy.

The fact that the King hadn't noticed that Maddi wasn't Laia from the very first moment told Laia she was doing the right thing. They might not have spent much time together but he knew her well enough to have noticed. If he cared.

Laia hoped that Maddi was coping okay, and vowed to get her back to Isla'Rosa just as soon as she could. Her heart swelled as she thought of what her sister had done for her so selflessly.

Laia had spoken to her most trusted and closest advisor, who supported everything she was doing. He was the only one outside of Maddi, King Aristedes and Dax who knew exactly what was going on and where she was.

She'd just had a video meeting with him, to make sure all was proceeding as planned and that nobody suspected anything was awry. The Privy Council—the group of traditionalist men who'd worked for her father and who Laia had every intention of disbanding once she became Queen, to make way for a much more gender-equal and inclusive council—were under the impression that she was, indeed, in Santanger, fulfilling her engagement duties. Thanks to Maddi.

They wouldn't know any different until she came back to Isla'Rosa, just before the coronation was due to take place.

There would be repercussions from breaking the engagement, but nothing she couldn't handle.

So now she turned to the piece of paper where she'd written down *Montero Holdings* along with Dax's assistant's email address. The name Montero Holdings rang a small bell, but she couldn't place where she'd heard it before.

Laia sent his assistant an email from a generic account, explaining that she was acting on Dax's behalf for a few days, and giving a set of instructions regarding launching a new software product online in the coming weeks. And another instruction regarding sending his apologies for not being able to make the board meeting of a charity that—

Laia stopped typing and sat back. She hadn't fully taken in what she was writing down at the time. The New Beginnings charity was very close to Laia's own heart. She'd donated generously over the years—usually anonymously.

It had been set up specifically to target babies, children and minors who had been left orphaned or alone after either a natural disaster or through migration, when they were most vulnerable and prey to being trafficked or exploited. The charity provided safe places to stay, education and resources to help them find permanent homes. It also provided scholarships for sports academies and third level education.

It was an amazing charity, and it had called to Laia as soon as she'd heard about it. Her circumstances had been vastly different, of course—she'd still had a loving father—but she'd always felt the loss of her mother so keenly, and could empathise with other children bearing that huge loss.

As far as she could make out Dax was on the board of this charity. *Interesting...* A lot of wealthy people paid lip service to charities—she'd seen photographic evidence of Dax attending enough events over the years, with a beautiful woman in tow, and she'd thought it started and ended there.

But being on a board was a responsibility—she knew because she was on a few. You wouldn't be tolerated for long if you didn't pull your weight.

Intrigued, Laia finished sending the email and resisted the urge to dive deeper into an investigation of Dax online.

She thought of the fact that he was dyslexic. The people she knew with dyslexia had had to overcome hurdles most people never had to face. They were incredibly high achievers and very successful. Ingenious.

Laia had to concede that maybe Dax had more substance to him than she'd initially given him credit for, but a man with a social life as busy as his—

A headline popped up on her web browser at that moment and she stopped and clicked on it.

Is Playboy Prince Dax finally settling down?

Below was an article speculating as to what he was up to, and with whom, because he hadn't been seen on the social circuit in a few months.

The article was from a month or so ago, so it had nothing to do with his current disappearance.

Laia breathed a sigh of relief and absorbed the fact that perhaps Dax didn't seem too put out by his current situation because he'd already been taking time out? For what? *Was* there someone special? Hardly, if he wasn't asking her to let anyone else know he was okay.

For a moment Laia wondered what it would be like to have someone like Dax care enough about you to let you know he was okay. To care enough about him to be worried about him.

She felt a swooping sensation in her lower belly and quickly shut her laptop.

Maybe she would follow Dax's lead and go to the gym...try to work off some of the restless energy she was feeling. She told herself it *wasn't* because she was more acutely aware than ever that she had one of the world's most notorious playboys on her private island and completely at her behest.

The words that he'd said to her on that first day came back in her head. *'Now you have me here, what are you going to do with me?'*

Laia let out a sound of frustration and left her room—but not until she'd made sure it was locked again.

Late that afternoon, Dax was flicking through the apps on the TV in the media room when he heard a sound and looked up to see Laia in the doorway. He went very still.

Every inch of her athletic physique was lovingly outlined by the clinging Lycra of her leggings and the tank top she wore. Her hair was pulled back and up into a ponytail. Her face was clean of make-up. A little shiny from exertion.

Dax's entire body pulsed with awareness and something much more basic—lust.

He realised she was holding something. A mobile phone. She came into the room and said, 'I have your assistant John on the phone. He wants to verify that it is you who is sending the instructions via email.'

Dax stood up. He held out his hand for the phone. But she shook her head.

She said, 'I have it on mute at the moment. I'll put him on speaker.'

Dax almost smiled. It would be nothing for him to take the phone from Laia, but he had to admit that he felt disinclined to do it. He told himself that it was because he knew gaining her trust would be far more effective.

'Okay.' He folded his arms.

Laia unmuted the phone and pressed the speaker button. She said, 'Okay, John, go ahead.'

'Dax, are you there?'

Dax didn't take his gaze off Laia's. 'I'm here. Did you get the email?'

'Yeah… I just wanted to make sure it really was you. What's going on Dax? Is everything okay?'

Laia's finger hovered over the disconnect button.

Dax said, 'Everything is fine. If I need anything else I'll contact you. I'm on a holiday and I don't want to be disturbed unless it's urgent, okay? If my brother calls looking for me, tell him I'm still working on his project.'

His assistant sounded bemused. 'Okay… Dax, do you know how long you'll be on this holiday?'

Laia took the phone off speaker and turned around, saying into it, 'Sorry, John, Dax has just stepped out. He'll be away for at least ten days, okay? Thank you.'

She terminated the call.

But Dax had barely even heard what she'd said because his gaze was glued to her behind. High and firm. More lush than he would have imagined. *Sexy.* He had a sense that she wasn't even aware of that. There was an innocence about her that made him wonder fleetingly if she might still be a virgin. There'd certainly never been any hint of a relationship or even an affair in the press, in spite of her socialising.

Or not socialising.

His suspicions about that rang even louder now.

She turned around and he lifted his gaze. Her face was pink. He unsettled her. He couldn't deny a deep sense of satisfaction that he had such an effect on her. That he could ruffle that serene surface.

And nothing will ever come of it.

A lead weight settled in his belly.

Oblivious to his inner turmoil, Laia said, 'Thank you for that. I know you could have easily disabled me and let him know everything.'

Dax felt prickly, and it was directed at himself for being weak.

'I've never laid a hand on a woman in my life unless it was to bring pleasure. I'm not going to start now. And anyway, even if I had let him know where we were and he'd sent the cavalry, how am I meant to take you back? By force? You've made it clear that's not happening. I'll just have to wait for you to come to your senses.'

CHAPTER FOUR

'I'VE NEVER LAID *a hand on a woman in my life unless it was to bring pleasure.*'

Laia's brain was fused with white-hot heat at the thought of Dax's hands on her, bringing her pleasure.

She took a step backwards and said, a little breathlessly, 'I don't need to come to my senses. It's your brother who has to come to terms with the fact that he'll need to find a new royal bride.'

Dax shrugged. 'Why don't we agree to disagree for now?'

Laia didn't trust this amenability for a second. Maybe he'd decided to play some kind of *good cop* role so that he could play on her sense of guilt and persuade her she had no option but to agree to the marriage.

No way.

Her resolve firmed, Laia went to walk out of the media room.

She was almost at the door when he said from behind her, 'If you haven't already planned something, shall I look at what we can have for dinner?'

She turned around. Dax had his hands in the pockets of his board shorts. They hung low on his narrow hips. Together with the white polo shirt that made his skin look even darker, and his messy, overlong hair, he could have passed for a sexy pro-surfer or athlete—not a royal crown prince.

'You can cook?' she asked baldly.

'I'd hardly suggest it if I couldn't, would I?'

The man was full of surprises.

'That would be nice…if you don't mind. The larder and fridge are well-stocked. I need to take a shower.' She turned to leave, and then looked back at the last second. 'I— That is… you don't have to cook for me. We don't have to eat together.'

'You've ensured I'm stuck on this island with you for the foreseeable future. I think the least you can do is provide me with some company.'

Laia felt ridiculously gauche all of a sudden. 'Yes, of course. I meant, I just don't expect you to spend time with me if you'd prefer not to.'

A look flashed across his face—something that sparked a reaction deep inside her. An intense fluttering.

He said, 'I think that horse has bolted. Go and have your shower. I'll have the food ready when you come back.'

When Laia had dried off after her shower she considered her wardrobe, which was largely made up of casual wear, considering the location. She did have formal outfits—as she'd said to Dax, she had to be prepared for every eventuality. Anything could happen. She might be taken on a plane from here straight back to Isla'Rosa to deal with any amount of situations. She even had a funeral outfit. A black shift dress and matching jacket. Simple pearl jewellery.

But she usually veered away from black and thinking about death. She'd always felt as if grief had been embedded in her consciousness from birth, along with that sense of guilt and abandonment. Because it had coincided with the death of her mother.

She spotted a navy silk wrap maxi-dress and reached for it in a bid to divert her mind away from maudlin thoughts. Driven by a compulsion she didn't want to investigate—*to look pretty?*—she pulled it on over her underwear, tying the belt around her waist.

She tied her hair back in a loose knot to let the air get to her neck. It was cooler in the evenings, but no less stifling. She was about to put on some make-up, but stopped herself.

What was she doing? Making herself up for her prisoner?

A tiny semi-hysterical giggle rose up and she put a hand over her mouth. Hands down, this was the most outlandish thing she'd ever done in her life.

There was a sound from outside the dressing room and then a deep voice. 'Laia? Dinner is almost ready.'

She stepped out to see Dax in the doorway of her room. His gaze swept her up and down, from her bare feet to her face. A wave of heat followed his gaze.

'You look…lovely.'

Laia should be cursing herself, because now he would think she'd done this for him, but she couldn't seem to drum up the necessary recrimination.

'It's nothing special…it's just light and cool.'

Why did she sound so defensive?

Dax said, 'Why don't you go down? I've prepared you an aperitif. I'll have a quick shower and freshen up too.'

Feeling slightly as if she'd stepped into some parallel dimension, Laia watched Dax turn and leave. She locked her own bedroom door and put the key in its hiding place.

She went downstairs, curious as to what she'd find. First she noticed the delicious smell, and saw something simmering on the stove. She lifted the lid. It looked like a beef stew with vegetables and spices.

Then she noticed a glass with clear liquid and ice on the counter. And a slice of cucumber. She lifted it up and smelled it, her nose wrinkling slightly. She wasn't much of a drinker, and this definitely smelled alcoholic.

She tried it. Gin or vodka—she wasn't sure which. But it tasted refreshing and light.

She wandered over to the outside deck and looked out over the view. It never failed to take her breath away.

Dusk was falling into night. She could see the lights of the fishermen in their boats. She could see her own security team's boat. The two men were operating in shifts with another team. They would be quietly coming and going, being delivered to and from the bigger island, every couple of days.

The nights here always reminded her of velvet, because the warm air felt like a caress…

And then she heard a noise behind her and her skin prickled all over. She turned around. Dax had changed into dark trousers and a white shirt, sleeves rolled up, top button open. His hair was damp. Jaw clean-shaven. Feet bare. As were hers. For some reason that made her blood pulse. It felt intimate. When really, in this climate, it was just practical.

He looked very different from the rakish, messily gorgeous man she'd met after that polo match all those years ago, but no less sexy. More sexy, if anything. He was a man now. He'd lived. His body was honed and tightly muscled. Like a prize fighter.

'Laia, if you stare at me any harder I might explode.'

She blinked, and realised she was gripping the glass tightly. She relaxed. 'I was a million miles away.'

Dax put a hand to his chest. 'You *weren't* thinking about me?'

Laia fought down the rising flush. She took a sip of her drink and tried to appear nonchalant. 'Not everything is about you.'

She sat on a stool on the opposite side of the island and watched as Dax moved easily around the kitchen. Clearly at home there.

He said, with an edge to his tone, 'Oh, don't worry, I've known for a long time that it's not all about me.'

She knew immediately what he was talking about, and said quietly, 'You mean because you're the spare?'

He stopped in the middle of chopping a slice of cucumber for his own drink. Looked at her. 'You know, you're probably one of the few people in the world who would get that straight away.'

'I don't have a spare. It's all on me.'

Dax made a face and lifted his drink in her direction as a salute. 'Having a spare doesn't necessarily mean all that much difference. I never did the same classes as Ari. In many respects I'm not remotely prepared if something happens. It's as if just having a spare is enough.'

Laia remembered what it had been like, enduring endless lessons in stuffy rooms when it had been sunny outside.

'So you were separated at lot as children?'

'From the age of eight Ari was on a different schedule. There were weeks I hardly saw him. I was six.'

'You're obviously close…'

Dax took a sip of his drink. And then he said simply, 'I'd do anything for Ari.'

Laia felt her heart squeeze when she thought of Maddi and *her* selflessness. She said, 'I always wished for a sibling when I was growing up. I used to lie awake, worrying about what would happen if anything happened to me.'

'And yet here you are. Safe and well and about to be crowned Queen. But you're choosing not to make the process easier by marrying a man who is already King and who would help you carry the burden you've been carrying alone for years.'

Laia bristled. 'Maybe I don't want "easier". Maybe I don't want to marry a king who will automatically assume that role over a country he knows little about.'

'That's hardly his fault,' Dax pointed out. 'Even with the marriage agreement, and a thawing of relations between the two kingdoms, it's not as if things improved overnight. Hence this—'

Laia put up her hand. 'Don't say it.' She stood up from the stool, feeling agitated. 'I know how it looks for me to be flying in the face of what everyone must think is the logical solution. But I know my father wouldn't want to see Isla'Rosa become a suburb of Santanger. And with the best will in the world, that's what would happen.'

'You would be Queen of Santanger—you would have your own influence.'

Laia looked at Dax. 'I don't want to be Queen of Santanger. I just want to be Queen of Isla'Rosa. That's all I need.'

Dax was stirring the stew. He turned off the heat and turned around. 'And, according to you, *love.*'

Laia felt exposed again. 'Not necessarily love. I'm not that delusional.'

She wasn't going to admit to this man in a million years that she yearned for a soul-deep connection. He'd laugh his head off.

Laia sat back on the stool and said, 'I know it's not something that comes easily for people like us. What my mother and father had was rare and special.'

Dax frowned. 'They were in love?'

Laia nodded. 'My father adored my mother. He never married again.'

But he had an affair resulting in your secret half-sister.

Laia avoided Dax's eye. She could only imagine his cynical response if she told him about that. She didn't want Dax judging her father for his moment of weakness. A moment he'd never forgiven himself for.

Something about that caught at her, but Dax cut through her thoughts.

'If he'd married again—as I'm sure he was pressured to do—he might have had more children, given you siblings and some spares, taking some of the burden from you.'

Laia shifted uncomfortably on the stool. It was as if he *knew*. She felt the urge to blurt out the truth to Dax, in spite of how he might respond, and that made her wary. Very few people made her feel inclined to open up.

She held up her glass. 'Can I have another?'

Dax raised a brow and took her glass.

Laia saw his look and said defensively, 'It's nice, fresh. It doesn't really feel like drinking. I've never been drunk.'

'It's really not all it's cracked up to be.' Dax expertly and efficiently prepared another gin and tonic with fresh ice and a cucumber slice and handed it to her. 'Take it easy. I don't want to be responsible for getting you drunk for the first time. I don't know if my reputation can handle it.'

He seasoned the stew and then turned back.

'Speaking of reputations... You've managed to carve out quite a one for yourself, considering you've never been drunk.'

Laia nearly choked on her drink. She remembered seeing Dax in the club in Monte Carlo, when he'd said to her, *'We seem to frequent all the same social events and yet you're as elusive as the Scarlet Pimpernel.'*

She looked at him accusingly. 'You knew, didn't you?'

He shrugged. 'I think I realised after that night that something was up. It was the first time I'd seen you in the flesh on the circuit, even though we'd always both appear in the papers the next morning.'

'It wasn't the first time you'd seen me in the flesh, though...' Laia wasn't even sure where those words had come from. Falling out of her mouth before she could stop them.

Dax frowned. 'What do you mean? We'd never met before that night. Not face to face, at least.'

Laia felt a dart of hurt. She lifted her chin. 'It was in Paris… after a charity polo match. I was there with my father.'

He looked at her blankly for a long moment, and then slowly she could see the dawning of recognition. It was almost insulting.

'That was…years ago. You were a child.'

Obviously she wouldn't have interested him because she'd still been a teenager.

'It was eight years ago,' Laia said, too quickly. She cursed herself. 'I was sixteen. It's no wonder you don't remember.'

Dax grimaced slightly. 'My early twenties weren't my finest moments…a lot of that time is blurry. I recall meeting your father briefly…' He looked at her and his eyes narrowed on her. 'And, yes, a young girl who looked very shy and—'

'That's okay. You don't have to say any more. That was me.' Even now Laia could remember the feeling of burning self-consciousness. The huge impact he'd had on her. That he still had on her. Mortifying. Why had she brought this up?

She wanted to drown in her drink and took a big gulp.

'You were much younger than everyone there. Then I realised who you were—Ari's fiancée.'

Laia glared at him. 'I was sixteen. I was no one's *fiancée.*'

He had the grace to wince. 'That does sound a little…weird. I used to tease Ari about being promised in marriage to a complete stranger.'

Dax was taking plates from a shelf and dishing up the stew, which smelled delicious. He was serving it with crusty bread.

He said, 'I've laid the table outside.'

Laia hadn't even noticed. She brought over the bread and Dax placed down the plates. He picked up a bottle of red wine and two glasses. There was a candle burning.

He sat down and Laia realised she was feeling a nice sensation of being cushioned against everything. Suddenly it didn't seem to matter that much that he only vaguely remembered her as an awkward teenager from that polo match in Paris.

He poured her some wine. She took a sip and asked, 'Why are you being so...calm about this? So...amenable?'

He sat down. 'Do you want to know the truth?'

She nodded and leant forward.

He leant forward too, and whispered. 'I haven't had a holiday in years.'

Laia sat back. She would have assumed he was on a permanent holiday—but then she thought of the conversation with his assistant. Montero Holdings. 'You see this as a holiday?'

'Why not? It's a tropical paradise. I have no devices to distract me. No idea what's going on in the outside world. I don't know when I'll have this chance again. I might as well make the most of it.'

Laia speared a morsel of succulent meat. 'You're making fun of me.'

'I swear to you I'm not. I've never been so cut off from everything and it's not that bad.'

Laia tasted the meat and almost closed her eyes. It was tender and tasty, with just the right amount of spiciness.

She put down her fork. 'Okay, how on earth did you learn to cook like that?'

'Aren't you being a little sexist? Where did *you* learn to cook? Neither of us grew up with expectations on us to cook or be domestic in any way.'

Laia put another forkful of food in her mouth to avoid answering.

When the silence grew taut between them Dax rolled his eyes and said, 'Okay, I'll go first. I went to a mixed sex boarding school in Switzerland for the last couple of years of high school. None of the boys took the cooking class because it was full of girls, but once I realised that I knew it was the class I wanted to be in. The guys laughed at me—but they weren't laughing when they realised I was the one with a girlfriend. And as it happens,' he went on, 'I turned out to have something of an affinity for cooking and baking.'

Laia put her fork down. She arched a brow. 'You bake too?'

'I make the most decadent chocolate cake.'

Laia couldn't quite believe what she was hearing—although she could well believe in Dax joining a class full of girls just to seduce them. That made sense.

She took another sip of wine, enjoying the velvety smoothness.

He gestured to her. 'What's your excuse?'

Laia was reluctant. This man made her feel so exposed. 'I feel like a bit of a fraud. I've got a very limited repertoire because I've only been learning in the last year...a friend has been teaching me.'

Dax raised a brow. 'A *male* friend?'

Laia blushed. 'No. A female friend.' *Her best friend. Maddi.* Impulsively she revealed, 'Apparently my mother was a good cook, so I always wanted to learn... But there never seemed to be the time and it wasn't considered appropriate.'

'Your mother died when you were born?'

She nodded, avoiding Dax's eye. She took another sip of wine. 'Just a few hours later.'

'That's tough...not to have known her.'

Laia felt ridiculously emotional. She forced it down and shrugged. 'You can't really miss what you never had.'

Except that was a lie, because she missed what she hadn't had almost every day.

She said huskily, 'My father was wonderful...at least I had him.'

Dax leaned over and topped up Laia's wine. 'My father was a serial philanderer. At least you didn't have to see something like that.'

She looked at Dax. She'd heard rumours over the years. Castle gossip. 'Did your mother know?'

He grimaced. 'You could say that. My father seemed to do it primarily to humiliate her. You see, she fell in love with him, and expected a relationship that my father had no interest in. So he punished her by showing her how weak she was for falling in love.'

Laia's mouth opened. She closed it. 'That's horrific. She must have been—'

'He destroyed her.' Dax cut her off. 'It destroyed her. Falling in love made her bitter and disappointed.'

Laia thought of Dax's tattoo. The caged bird.

'It sounds like your father's reaction to her loving him made her all those things.'

Laia remembered what people had whispered about Dax being responsible for his mother's death. Was that why he'd been sent off to boarding school? To get him away from the press and speculation?

'I'm sorry about your mother. You must have been young when she died.'

Dax took a healthy swallow of wine. 'Fifteen.'

She wondered if that had been around the time she'd first spied him in the distance at the palace in Santanger. She would have been only nine or ten. She had a vague memory of someone tall and gangly in the shadows. Had he been off the rails then? Was that what had led to his mother's death?

She didn't remember meeting the Queen—something about her not being well enough to receive them. She must have died not long afterwards.

Dax sat back and interrupted the buzz of questions in her

head. 'So, why did you cultivate a very comprehensive fake persona of a party girl?'

Laia felt embarrassed now. As if she'd been caught playing dress-up. Reluctantly she admitted, 'I thought it would put your brother off.'

Dax sat back and made a small whistling noise. He let out a sharp laugh and then shook his head. 'You know what? I can see your logic... Ari is very straight. He has no time for frivolity.'

Laia made a face as if to say, *Right?*

But Dax shook his head again. 'You underestimated his stubbornness. That man is like a mule, and if he's set on a course of action then he won't stop until he gets what he wants.'

Laia shivered slightly, thinking of Maddi.

Dax sat forward. 'Are you cold?'

Laia shook her head. He was solicitous. She hadn't expected that. He'd been solicitous that night in the club in Monte Carlo... He'd put out his hand and touched her, and his touch had burned so much she'd pulled away like a frightened maiden.

Nothing had changed in the interim. She was still an innocent.

That burden sat like a stone in her gut. Suddenly her lofty ideals about love felt very naive and unattainable. Even if she did hold out for someone more compatible, how likely was it that there'd be the kind of passion she'd always dreamed of? The kind of passion she'd read about in the romance novels she'd hidden between the covers of the classics she'd speed-read in her English classes. The kind of passion that people said was unrealistic but she knew existed, deep in her bones, because she'd seen it. Smelled it. Ached for it.

This man looking at her now had awoken something inside her. A thirst. A hunger. That first face-to-face meeting with him had sparked such a visceral reaction that when he'd told her that one day he would be her brother-in-law she'd felt sick at the thought. Because how could this man who made her feel so many things, possibly ever be her brother? The idea had been horrifying...and so wrong.

Because she wanted him. She'd always wanted him.

Sitting at the table, Laia felt dizzy all of a sudden, as that revelation sank deep into her body, making her go hot and cold and hot again.

Dax was frowning now. 'Laia...?'

She stood up and swayed slightly, suddenly very aware that she'd reached her limit and gone past it.

Dax cursed and stood too. 'You've drunk too much.'

Laia wanted to laugh, but she was afraid she might be sick, because things were spinning a little.

She put a hand to her head. 'Maybe I should lie down for a minute.'

Dax came around the table. Before Laia knew what was happening he'd lifted her effortlessly into his arms and was carrying her through the villa.

This was worse. Far worse. Because now she was pressed against all that muscle and sinew. His scent was all around her and infiltrating her blood, making it warm. Her dress was no barrier to his heat and the steely strength of his body. Her breasts were pressed against his chest. Her face was so close to his neck. If she moved her head forward even just a tiny bit she could press her lips against his skin.

They were at her bedroom door. Laia blinked. Had she really drunk that much? Dax put her down, and thankfully she didn't sway again. The spinning sensation had calmed down.

His voice was tight. 'Do you have the key to your room?'

Laia nodded. 'You'll have to turn around so you don't know where it's kept.'

Dax's jaw clenched, but he turned around. His shoulders

looked so broad, and he was so tall. The fuzziness from the alcohol was starting to wear off and she realised she was staring at Dax's back like a lovestruck groupie.

She turned quickly and took the key from its hiding spot and opened her door, slipping inside.

Dax turned around. 'Are you going to be okay?'

Laia nodded, but her head swam a bit again so she stopped. 'Fine. Thank you for dinner. It was really good.'

'You're welcome.'

'Goodnight, Dax.'

She was closing the door when he put a hand on it.

'I'd feel a lot better if you left your door open tonight.'

Laia had all her devices—phone and laptop—locked away in a safe. So there was no real reason to lock her door.

She stood back and held the door open. 'Okay, fine.'

After a long few seconds Dax backed away. 'Call me if you need anything.'

He turned and left and Laia felt very discombobulated. Who was the captor here and who was the captee?

The effects of the alcohol seemed to be fading as quickly as they'd surfaced. Maybe it hadn't been the alcohol at all, but the massive and unwelcome revelation that she really didn't want to look at.

So she didn't.

She changed into her night shorts and tank top and washed her face, and then climbed into bed. The room revolved alarmingly for a moment, but mercifully stopped after a few seconds. And then she fell asleep.

A little later, Dax stopped by Laia's open bedroom door. The muslin net around her bed was still tied up, so she wasn't being protected from biting insects.

Telling himself that he was just doing her a favour, and also delivering a big glass of water, Dax went in and put the water down on the bedside table.

Laia didn't stir. She was on her back. One arm over her chest. Dark hair spread out around her head. It tended towards the wild and wavy. He liked it. It hinted at other depths beneath the largely serene surface she projected—or had been taught to project.

He recognised it from his brother Ari. They would both have been taught at an early age not to show emotion.

And yet when he'd been telling her about his mother, just a short while before—something he avoided talking about at all costs, usually—Laia's eyes had filled with compassion.

Dax diverted his mind from how that had made him feel. He didn't ask for an emotional response from anyone.

The light sheet was pushed down to Laia's waist. One long leg was sticking out. She wore a tank top that did little to hide the firm swells of her breasts.

He could still feel them pressed against his chest as he'd carried her to the bedroom. She'd felt so light in his arms, but strong too. He'd felt her breath on his neck...warm.

By the time he'd put her on her feet his blood had been clamouring for *more*. To touch her. Explore that lithe body. Feel her under his mouth. Opening to him.

Cursing under his breath now, Dax moved silently around the bed, drawing the protective net down. This woman could not be his. No matter what she said, she was destined to be Queen of Santanger. He knew his brother, and Ari would stop at nothing to have his Queen by his side.

Dax would not betray his trust. But it might kill him in the process.

When Laia woke she was disorientated. She cracked open an eye and all she saw was fuzziness—until she realised it was the mosquito net around the bed. It was dawn outside, so mercifully it wasn't too hot yet.

She came up on one elbow and winced when her brain collided with her head. Her mouth felt as dry as sandpaper. She spied a glass of water by the bed and pulled back the net to get it.

Had she brought that up to bed? She couldn't recall. Last night wasn't a blank but it was a bit blurry. She took a big gulp of water. She recalled talking to Dax for ages. About things that she hadn't expected at all. Or had that all been a dream?

He'd told her about his parents.

He could cook like a pro.

So unexpected.

Laia got out of bed and went to the bathroom. Her hair was a big tangle around her shoulders. She couldn't look less like a crown princess right now. The stuffy Privy Council would be horrified.

As she went back towards the bed she passed her open door, leading out to the corridor. Dax's room was on the other side of the hall. Laia found her feet taking her out of her room and down the hall.

Dax's door was wide open.

So he would have heard her if she'd felt ill during the night?

She crept closer. His room was dark—it was on the west side of the villa so the sun would hit her room first.

Knowing she was intruding, but unable to stop herself, Laia went further into the room. His net was pulled around the bed, but there was a chink between two ends that was open.

It gave her a perfect view of the man on the bed. And he was naked. Laia's feet were stuck to the floor. The sheet had been thrown off completely and Dax lay in a sprawl, one leg bent. One hand was on his chest, which rose and fell rhythmically.

He was breathtaking. That was the only word to describe it.

Every muscle clearly delineated. Not a spare ounce of flesh. Corded muscles on his legs. His narrow waist. And...

Laia's breath stopped when her gaze rested on the potent centre of his masculinity.

She'd never seen a naked man in the flesh before. She knew she was transgressing a million boundaries and invading Dax's space, but she couldn't look away.

Even at rest he was impressive. Intimidating. Laia wondered what it must be like to lie next to a man like this. To wake up beside him. To have permission to touch him when you wanted because he was *yours*. To wrap your hand around—

Dax shifted on the bed and Laia froze in terror, her gaze on his face now, imagining his eyes opening. Those too-blue eyes fixing on her. Finding her ogling him. But they didn't open.

Laia backed away from the bed, the net obscuring her vision again. And then she turned around and fled, straight back to her room, closing the door silently behind her. She was wide awake now. She didn't think she'd ever get that image of Dax erased from her brain.

And she didn't want to.

He was beautiful. She couldn't deny it. She wanted Dax. She'd wanted him from the moment she'd laid eyes on him.

And now he was here.

The moment she left this place she would become Queen of Isla'Rosa and her life would not be hers again. She would have to deal with the fallout of not marrying King Aristedes and, once that had passed, everyone would be preoccupied with who she *would* be marrying.

She knew that even if she found someone she could consider a soulmate, someone who could be her companion throughout her life as Queen, she might never experience the kind of passion that she'd dreamed of. That she felt instinctively could be experienced with a man like Dax.

An audacious thought occurred to her.

He's a crown prince...eminently suitable for me to marry.

Laia's heart thumped.

But no. Crown Prince Dax of Santanger had made it very clear that his destiny was not his brother's—settling down and begetting heirs. He would be completely unsuitable. How could she even trust a man like that?

No, she didn't want him for marriage. She wanted him for something else. For something very selfish. For *her*. She wanted to know what real passion felt like before she had to settle down and live a life of duty and responsibility. Because her people would always come first. They had to.

Dax had haunted her for years. She was only realising how much now, here in this lush paradise, when she could no longer hide from herself and her desires. He didn't disgust her at all. The opposite.

Seduce him.

No. Ridiculous. Nonsensical. She didn't have the skills or the wherewithal to seduce an expert connoisseur of women. She wouldn't even know where to start... She could already feel the humiliation if she made herself vulnerable and he rejected her. He'd probably do it with kindness, which would be so much worse.

Laia started to pace. But the suggestion wouldn't fade as it should. Because surely there was no way.

If you seduce him then he will know you're serious about not wanting to marry King Aristedes.

Laia stopped pacing. Could she really be considering this? The prospect of pitting Dax against his brother...by using herself?

It wouldn't work. She wasn't so irresistible. She wasn't even sure if he wanted her. Maybe she was just imagining it when she thought she felt his eyes on her. When she thought she felt something pulse between them, alive and electric... He was a man—he was just reacting to her as a woman.

Well, then, if it won't work, what have you got to lose?

CHAPTER FIVE

A COUPLE OF hours later Laia was making breakfast. She felt on edge at the thought of trying to seduce Dax. It was almost as crazy a notion as keeping him captive on this island.

And how on earth did a virgin go about seducing one of the world's most renowned and discerning lovers? What did he feel for her? Anything? He was so hard to read.

When he appeared at that moment, with damp hair and a freshly shaven jaw, she nearly jumped out of her skin.

'Okay?' he asked.

'Fine…just…you startled me.'

He was wearing board shorts and a short-sleeved shirt, open at the top. He looked irritatingly relaxed. And gorgeous.

Her head was unhelpfully filled with images of him sprawled naked on the bed. Her cheeks grew warm.

She said quickly, 'Thank you…for last night. The glass of water. I'm sure I could have made it to bed without being carried, but…'

It was nice.

She shut her mouth quickly, and then said, 'I'm making breakfast omelettes, if you'd like one?'

'I would love one, thank you. Is there anything I can do?'

'You could make the coffee?'

Dax moved around behind her and Laia fumbled with the eggs on the pan, cursing herself silently. She managed to make two fluffy omelettes, in spite of her jitters, and carried them over to the table on two plates.

Dax had poured two coffees and brought over orange juice, bread and pastries.

Laia had only just got used to spending time with Maddi, her half-sister, in the last year. Until she'd met Maddi, she'd had quite a lonely existence, surrounded by people all the time but never in an intimate space.

That was what had made her even more determined not to marry King Aristedes. He would be as important and as busy as her. He'd been so dismissive of her all along that she could envisage a marriage where they lived parallel lives, only coming together for the necessary conjugal relations.

'Another beautiful day for a prisoner in paradise.' Dax lifted his glass of orange juice in a little mocking salute.

Laia said, 'Another week at the most and you'll have your freedom back.'

She thought of him going back out into the world and resuming his carefree existence. Being photographed with beautiful women at the opening of every glitzy event. Could she really do this and deal with *that*?

Yes, because then she'd be able to move on.

Wasn't that how it worked? That was how men said it worked—once you'd had what you wanted you were sated.

Laia sat back and cradled her coffee cup in her hand. Curiosity got the better of her. 'So what's your story? You don't have the same pressure as Aristedes to settle down and have heirs...but will you marry?'

He looked at her. 'I hope that's not a proposal, because you're already engaged.'

Laia scowled at him. 'You know that's not what I meant.'

He wiped his mouth and put down his fork. 'That's a very personal question.'

'Well, seeing as how you're so determined for me to become your sister-in-law, maybe we should get better acquainted.' He couldn't argue against that.

His eyes narrowed, but she just smiled sweetly. His gaze dropped to her mouth and lingered. Laia's smile faded. He looked up, blinked. Her pulse tripped and settled on a faster rhythm. Warmth filled her lower body.

Then the charged moment was gone. He sat back. 'I have no intention of settling down. That's my brother's domain.'

So far exactly what she'd surmised herself.

Laia took a sip of coffee. 'What do you have against it?'

'Nothing. It's just not for me. It's not something I've ever envisaged.'

'I guess I'm not surprised to hear you say that.'

'And why would that be?' he asked, civilly enough.

But she heard the thread of steel underneath. She felt as if she was skirting round the edges of something potentially fiery.

'Your…er…way of life seems to back up what you say. You don't seem inclined to sacrifice your independence any time soon. Although there are questions in the media as to why you haven't been seen for some time…'

'You've been looking me up online?'

'It doesn't take much for headlines about Prince Dax to appear at the top of any search feed.'

'Not that it's any business of—anyone's.'

He said this with a definite edge, which made Laia wonder who had said something to him—perhaps Aristedes?

He continued, 'I've been busy. With work.'

Laia tapped a nail against the side of her cup as something occurred to her. She watched his reaction as she said, 'I'm not sure if I'm the only one who likes to hide behind a certain…persona.'

Dax went very still. 'What's that supposed to mean?'

'You weren't drunk that night in Monte Carlo.'

'I haven't been drunk in years. I told you—it's overrated.'

'And yet you were there…on the scene. And I know how tedious it can be if you're not on the same energetic level as everyone else. Which is why I could never last long.'

'Maybe I was on drugs?'

Laia shook her head. 'I don't think so. You didn't have that glazed, manic look. No, I think you were doing exactly the same thing as me. You were doing your work behind the scenes while faking a façade… Why, though?'

Dax's jaw clenched. He wasn't used to this much conversation in the mornings—generally because he wasn't ever with women in the mornings. It wasn't unpleasant…but he didn't like being on the other end of scrutiny. Especially not Laia's particular brand of very perspicacious scrutiny.

He shrugged. 'Maybe, like you, I had my reasons. When people underestimate you, it gives you an edge over them.'

'But that only lasts as long as the first time. Once people know they've underestimated you it won't happen again.'

Dax arched a brow. 'You'd be surprised.'

'You run a business—Montero Holdings?'

He nodded. 'It's a software business.'

'Is that something you were into at school? How did you cope with your dyslexia?'

Before Dax could answer, she blushed.

'Sorry, I ask too many questions.'

The colour staining her cheeks made him want to touch her there, to see if her skin felt hot. He forced himself to focus.

'School was…a challenge. Until they figured out what the problem was. There was an assumption that I just wasn't that bright.'

Her green eyes were wide and filled with compassion. Dax

put it down to an automatic reflex. Ari had that ability too—
to be able to make people feel that he really cared.

She asked, 'How did you cope until they realised what it
was?'

Dax shook off the pricking of his conscience, mocking his
cynicism for judging Laia's compassion to be fake. Maybe he
couldn't handle real compassion.

*Maybe he didn't want to. Because that would be like allow-
ing a chink of light into an area he liked to keep shut away.
The place where he held his guilt and toxic memories of the
past...where he didn't feel he deserved compassion.*

He forced that out of his head and said, 'When I went to
a conventional school for those final years they caught it almost immediately. They're much better now at recognising
the signs and accommodating students who are dyslexic. I had
learnt to navigate around it. That's how I realised I was good
at computers. Not the coding so much, but an overall vision
of system designs.'

Laia said nothing for a moment, and Dax realised that she
often did that. She didn't necessarily fill a gap in the conversation with chatter. He liked it.

She put her head on one side. 'You're global, aren't you?
Your company supplies software systems for us in Isla'Rosa.'

Dax nodded. 'We most likely do. We're one of the biggest
software design companies in the world.'

'And you're on the board of that charity. There's no way
you'd be on the board if you weren't pulling your weight.'

Dax felt a little exposed. 'It's a cause close to my heart.'

'Why?'

'I have empathy for kids whose lives are torn apart, who
look around and find everything they knew is gone...every-
one they knew.'

Dax thought back to the aftermath of the car crash, when

his entire world had seemed to splinter into a thousand pieces. The crash had pulled back the curtain on the fallacy that they'd all been living a relatively functional existence.

Or it would have if he hadn't decided to do something that would protect his mother and her secrets for ever from the vultures who'd been circling. A decision that had defined his existence for a long time. *Still did.* Guilt was a canny operator.

Laia was looking at him, waiting for him to elaborate. Ordinarily he wouldn't feel inclined to, but now he did.

'The car crash that killed my mother was a pretty shattering experience. It exposed a lot of the flaws in our family. On the surface it looked perfect. But it wasn't. It was toxic. Ari was busy learning how to be King. Our father was busy parading his various mistresses in front of our mother, sending her slowly over the edge. And I... I was the only one she could turn to.'

Dax expected Laia to ask more about the crash, but she said, 'Is that why you don't want to marry?'

'It's part of it. I didn't see anything good in my parents' marriage. They certainly weren't like your parents. In love.'

Laia was quiet for a moment, and then she blurted out, 'My father had an affair.'

Dax raised a brow, glad to have the focus turned from him.

Laia continued. 'It was a year after my mother died, I was still a baby.'

'Who was she?'

'She was one of the castle staff. But then she got pregnant. My father panicked and sent her into exile. He felt so guilt-ridden. Like he'd tainted my mother's memory. I think that's why he never married again. It was some sort of penance.'

'What happened to the baby? Your half-sibling?'

Laia swallowed. 'A half-sister, actually.'

'Have you met her?'

Laia nodded. She looked guilty.

Dax narrowed his gaze on her. 'Laia, what—?'

'She's in Santanger…with Aristedes. That's Maddi—my half-sister.'

Dax's mouth closed. Opened. Closed again. He thought of the pictures he'd seen. Eventually he said, half to himself, 'That's why you look so alike. You're sisters.' Then he asked, 'Whose idea was it?'

'Maddi thought of it…but I went along with it. It was both of us.'

Dax thought of his brother, finding out that Princess Laia wasn't who he thought she was. Finding out that he had an imposter in his palace. Feeling like a fool.

Anger rose, and Dax told himself it was because of *this* and not because sitting here talking to Laia was like finding himself in a confessional, blithely spilling his guts after years of keeping them firmly tucked away from sight.

He said, with bite, 'How noble of you not to blame her entirely for duping my brother, making him look like a fool.'

Laia's hands twisted her napkin, belying what? Her guilt?

'It seems like no one is any the wiser about who Maddi really is,' she said, her tone a little defiant. 'And he's using her to make it look like all is well with the engagement, so who's duping who?'

'That's not the same. All he can do is damage limitation, thanks to you.'

Laia put down her napkin. 'If he'd listened to me back when I tried to talk to him we wouldn't even be in this situation, but his arrogance has brought us here.'

Dax stood up abruptly. He needed to get away from those big green eyes. Her gaze was too direct.

'I'm going for a walk.'

He needed to put some distance between them. Maybe then

he could get some oxygen to his brain to assess what she'd just told him.

And what you told her...practically everything.

Laia watched Dax walk out, his tall, powerful body vibrating with tension. He was angry. And she couldn't blame him after finding out the extent of how she and her sister had tricked King Aristedes.

If anything, Dax's loyalty to his brother showed yet another facet to his personality, which was evolving into something Laia had no handle on any more.

She'd thought she'd had him all sized up. In a box marked *Playboy Reprobate.*

But—as the headlines had alluded to—was he that any more? Was he changing?

She had to admit that he had far more substance than she'd given him credit for. A self-made billionaire in his own right, apart from any royal inheritance. And he'd done all that while being dyslexic—an added challenge.

Laia cleared up the breakfast detritus. Dax had disappeared somewhere into the thick foliage of the forest. No doubt cursing her with every step. So far, her plan to seduce the man was going very well. Right now, he couldn't stand her.

Brava, Laia.

She dumped the plates into the sink to wash later, and went up to her bedroom to take part in a scheduled online meeting with her advisors in Isla'Rosa. Perhaps she'd do better to focus on the very big stuff coming down the tracks—like being crowned Queen of Isla'Rosa—rather than fantasising about seducing a man way out of her league.

Dax was still angry, and now frustrated. He pushed leaves aside as he powered down yet another path. Thick foliage lined the track. Sweat was springing from every part of his skin in the humidity. He had no idea where he was heading, but he figured he couldn't get too lost because the island was small.

He eventually emerged at a small sandy beach. Its serene beauty distracted him for a moment, before he remembered to stay angry. And not to think about Laia's big green eyes. Or the expression of contrition he'd seen in them even though she'd sounded defiant.

He pulled off his sneakers and sat down on the sand under the shade of a tree.

The problem was, he was angry for his brother—of course. Ari didn't deserve this. His whole life had been dedicated to the service of his—*their*—country. And supporting Dax.

After the car accident that had killed their mother, it had been as if Ari had known that Dax needed space to get away from Santanger and what had happened. The awful tragedy, his part in it, and all the toxicity that had led to it.

Ari had persuaded their father to let Dax finish school abroad. And then a year later their father had died and it had been just the two of them. By some unspoken agreement, once Dax had graduated from high school Ari had let him carve out a life away from Santanger.

Only Ari had known the full extent of all that Dax had to carry, and Dax had known his brother felt guilty. For not noticing more. For not being there. Even though he'd had his own huge burden to carry. Taking on the weight of the crown.

But that was why Ari had let Dax have his freedom. It had been a tacit form of asking forgiveness.

So Dax had gone away. For a few years he had lived a hedonistic life as the Playboy Prince. Carousing to escape his memories and the past. But it hadn't lasted half as long as people thought it had.

He'd grown bored with it quickly—but then he'd realised that he could use it to his advantage. When people underestimated him—and that was most people, most of the time—he used it against them.

In the process he'd built up a global empire. But lately he'd had to come to terms with the fact that his reputation wasn't doing him any favours any more.

His time playing the playboy was coming to an end, and for the first time Dax wasn't sure which way to go. Ari had the kingdom and his upcoming marriage. Even if it wasn't to Laia, it would be to someone. He would be creating a new life and the next generation.

Dax knew his anger wasn't just for his brother being made a fool. It was more complicated. It was anger at himself, for wanting a woman he couldn't have.

The way Laia had looked at him just a short while before, asking questions that cut right to the heart of who he was and his *modus operandi*, had not been expected...or welcome.

'So what's your story? Will you marry?' she'd asked. As impertinently as...as a queen would.

It was rare for Dax to meet someone who was his equal in the way she was. In terms of social standing, as afforded to them by an accident of birth, but also in terms of experience.

They'd both grown up in their respective bubbles of royal courts. With great privilege. A mix of home schooling and other exclusive establishments with the children of presidents and the wealthiest people on the planet.

It was a world Dax was inextricably bound with and to, and yet he'd distanced himself from it in many ways. But, no matter what he did or where he went, he would always be Crown Prince Dax. The spare to the heir. The bad boy to Ari's good boy. A reputation he'd created and cultivated but which was beginning to feel more and more restrictive.

The burden would lift slightly once Ari had heirs and they took on the Crown Prince or Crown Princess title.

'Will you marry?'

Dax shuddered at the thought, his mind flooded with memories of his father parading his latest mistress through the palace while his mother screamed and wept in her rooms. Make-up running down her ravaged face. Breath smelling of gin. Eyes glazing over as she eventually calmed down and the medication the doctors had given her did their work in her blood system.

Dax had hated those doctors for coming in and giving her so many pills, because he'd seen the way she disappeared and became pliant. Quiet. But she'd wanted the pills. Needed them. More and more. Until she hadn't been able to get through a day without them.

Ari had come in one day after she'd had a hysterical bout and he'd looked horrified. 'What's wrong with her?'

Dax had felt guilty—as if it was his fault she was in such a state. As if he should somehow stop it. He hadn't had the appetite to tell Ari that this was how she was nearly every day. Nothing unusual. And he was the one she wanted by her side. Consoling her. Listening to her.

She'd tell him over and over again, *'Never give away your heart, Dax, they don't want it. They'll take it out and crush it to pieces in front of you...in front of everyone.'*

The silence was broken only by the call of birds, insects, and the waves gently breaking on the shore. It was hot and getting hotter.

Feeling claustrophobic after the onslaught of unwelcome memories, Dax stood up and started to strip off until he was naked. And then he walked into the sea, letting its relative cool wash over him and suck him under, where he could try and drown out the fact that he was stuck here with a woman who was simultaneously bringing back the past in a way that was most unwelcome while driving him insane with lust.

Not a good combination.

Laia emerged onto the beach from the treeline. She saw Dax's clothes on the sand. No sign of the man. She shaded her eyes and looked out to sea. She still couldn't see him.

A knot formed in her gut as she scanned the horizon, until finally she saw a speck in the distance. The knot loosened marginally as the speck got larger as he swam back to shore. Had he been trying to escape? Or just swimming…?

She went down to the shoreline, dropping her things as she did. She wore a one-piece swimsuit under a floaty kaftan that came to her thighs.

She could see Dax's powerful arms now, scissoring rhythmically in and out of the water. Eventually he was close enough to stand. The water lapped around his chest. His messy hair was slicked back and dark. He saw her, and she noticed the tension coming into his body.

'How did you find me?'

Laia's gut clenched. She felt as if she was intruding. He hadn't wanted her to find him. And why would he? She'd incarcerated him here and he'd just found out she had a half-sister who was pretending to be her.

'You set off the alarms.'

Dax splashed water onto his face, and then said, 'Well? Are you going to stand there all day or get in?'

Laia felt ridiculously awkward. And self-conscious. She told herself she was being ridiculous. This man had been to yacht parties where women cavorted with little else but a piece of string protecting their modesty.

She looked away and pulled off her kaftan. How on earth

was she going to seduce this man if she couldn't even bare herself in a one-piece swimsuit in front of him?

She threw the kaftan onto the ground, annoyed with herself now, and stepped into the water until it reached her waist. And then she dived under, hoping for a graceful surfacing near Dax, but she swallowed some water and emerged coughing and spluttering.

He was grinning. 'Okay?'

Laia nodded, regaining her composure, treading water. It was like cool silk against her skin. This was her favourite place to come for a swim.

'Look,' she said, 'I'm sorry for all this, but I truly believe I have no choice but to see this through now to the end.'

'Sorry enough to let me go?'

Laia was struck by a pang. He wanted to get away from her. Apart from anything else, she hadn't expected it to be so easy to talk to him. To tell him things.

She shook her head. 'I'm sorry, no. Not yet.'

Dax didn't look surprised. He said, 'I need to check in with my assistant John.'

Laia nodded. 'I can arrange that.'

'I'm going to get out now.'

'Okay...' Laia wondered why he was telling her this.

And then he said, 'You might want to turn around.'

'Why?'

'Because I'm naked.'

Even though she was in the cool water, heat flooded Laia all the way up to her cheeks. 'Oh, right...of course.'

She turned to face out to the horizon. She could hear Dax moving through the water back to shore. Unable to help herself, she turned her head just as he was walking out through the shallows.

His body gleamed. Strong, broad back. Narrow waist. Powerful buttocks, high and firm, those long legs.

Before she knew what was happening, he'd stopped and looked back, his body now in profile to her. It took Laia long seconds to realise that he was looking at her looking at him. Avidly.

She whirled around and ducked under the water in a bid to hide what she'd been doing. So fast that she swallowed water again and had to come up for air, gasping.

She wasn't sure, but she could have sworn she heard an evil chuckle from the beach.

Dax was sitting on the beach, dressed again, with his shirt hanging open. Laia couldn't put off coming out of the water any longer. She was acutely conscious of the way the material of her swimsuit clung to every inch of her body. It had felt conservative when she'd put it on, but now it felt as if it was indecently cut. Too high on her thighs. And low over her chest.

As she splashed out of the shallows she tried not to imagine that he was comparing her to every other woman he'd seen similarly dressed.

'You didn't have to wait,' she told him.

'I couldn't risk you getting a cramp and having that on my conscience. Some of us do have a conscience, you know.'

Laia grabbed her kaftan, but at the last second didn't pull it on. She sat down on the warm sand next to Dax.

She made a snorting sound. 'I'm sure there are legions of women all over the world who might argue that.'

'You're insinuating I treat women badly? I'm wounded.'

Laia squinted at him. The sun was high. 'With the best will in the world, some of them must have wanted…more? And been disappointed.'

'That might well have been the case…but I have never given any lover false hope. They always knew where they stood.'

Laia had to admit she believed him. But she was curious to know how it could be with a man like this.

'And where was that?' she asked.

'In something purely fun and physical for as long as we wanted each other.'

'Which was how long?'

He looked at her. And then he seemed to consider his answer before he said, 'Never longer than a few dates.'

Imagine capturing this man's attention even just for a few dates…

'What would happen if they wanted more?'

'I would end it.'

No hesitation. Stark. Absolute.

'You never found yourself transgressing your own boundaries?'

He shook his head emphatically. 'Never.'

For some reason this made Laia feel slightly giddy. And then she sobered. She didn't want to be the one to engage Dax's emotions. She only wanted him for one thing. Well, two. Passion and sex.

And then he completely took the wind out of her sails when he said, 'What about you?'

Laia's insides tightened. 'What about me, what?'

'How do you treat your lovers?'

Laia felt sure he was making fun of her. He had to know… But he was just looking at her with a curious expression.

She shrugged as nonchalantly as she could, 'Oh, you know… I make it clear that I'm not up for anything serious… how can I be?'

'Because you're engaged.'

Laia scowled at him, but was grateful for the diversion. 'No, because very soon I'll be crowned Queen and I have a life of duty ahead of me.'

'You'll have to marry and have heirs, whether it's to Ari or someone else of royal lineage.'

'Yes, I'm aware of that. But my husband will be my choice.'

'Why won't you just *do* this?'

There was an edge to Dax's voice that Laia felt deep inside. His frustration was evident. It made her prickly.

She turned to face him, trying to make him understand. 'Because if I marry Aristedes then Isla'Rosa becomes a suburb of Santanger, no matter how he might deny it. We've carved out our independence and identity after years of conflict—'

'Exactly,' interjected Dax. 'Wouldn't this bring peace once and for all?'

Laia shook her head. 'Not at the cost of our independence. It's too much. I want to lead our people out of the past and into a modern, bright future. I know that's going to be a challenge, but I can do it. My path is side by side with Santanger, not as a part of it. Peace is possible through other routes.'

Dax just looked at her, and Laia hated it that it mattered to her that he *got* it. She sensed that he sympathised with where she was coming from, but his loyalty to his brother trumped his own instincts. He was loyal to his brother, not to her, and that made total sense so why did it matter?

Because you already care what he thinks of you. You want his loyalty.

That incendiary thought drove Laia to her feet, her kaftan gripped in her hand.

'Look, Dax, you've abdicated your responsibilities—for whatever reason. You live your life from day to day, free to choose what you want when you want, with no one dictating to you how you're to live your life. You just don't get it. How can you?'

Laia went to walk away, but before she could take two steps Dax's hand was around her arm and he was whirling her back to face him. His face was like thunder.

'What the hell is that supposed to mean?'

Laia gulped. But not out of pain. Dax was barely holding her arm. It was because he was suddenly so close. And he was bristling.

'Abdicated my responsibilities?'

Laia pulled her arm free. Weakly, she said, 'I don't know what arrangement you have with your brother, but it's not as if you live a life full of royal duty.'

Dax's mouth was thin. 'No, you *don't* know anything about our arrangement, Princess. Maybe I had responsibilities that you know nothing about. Responsibilities that meant my brother got to focus on his job without being burdened by—' He stopped abruptly.

Laia wanted to ask, *Burdened by what?* But she kept her mouth shut. She wondered if he was talking about his mother.

'The way I live my life is none of your concern,' he said. 'Or anyone else's. Except maybe my brother's.'

Laia couldn't look away from Dax's eyes. They were so blue it hurt. They should have been icy, but she felt warm. And it wasn't the sun or the humidity.

She knew she should leave this alone, but words were spilling out before she could censor them. 'Did something happen? So Aristedes allowed you to walk away…?'

Dax's face tightened. His voice was a growl. 'Leave it alone, Laia, you have no idea what you're talking about.'

But it was there in his eyes, deep inside. Incredible pain. His whole body was vibrating with tension.

Without even realising what she was doing she moved closer. She'd dropped the kaftan to the sand…hadn't even noticed.

Dax said warningly, 'Laia—'

She put her hand on his bare chest. Exactly as she'd wanted to the other day. Dax's eyes flared. He put his hand over hers. But he didn't pull her hand away.

His skin was warm. Still damp from the sea. She could feel his heart. Strong and steady. Maybe a little fast. Like hers. His hand felt huge, enveloping hers.

'Laia, what are you doing?'

Her eyes fell to his mouth. It wasn't thin any more. It was lush and full. She frowned, her mind not able to let go the strand of thought it had just been picking at, in spite of Dax's warnings.

She asked, 'What happened to make your brother give you a life of freedom?'

She looked up as something occurred to her. He must have seen it in her eyes, because before she could say another word Dax had snaked his free hand under her wet hair and around to the back of her neck.

And then his mouth was on hers, and Laia didn't have any thoughts in her head any more. Because they were incinerated by the fire.

CHAPTER SIX

DAX HADN'T INTENDED to kiss Laia. Yet here he was, mouth fused to hers, and he'd never felt anything so erotically charged. She was everything he'd imagined—*fantasised*—and more.

She was soft and yet hard at the same time. Her hand was curled into his over his chest. He burned where she'd put her hand over his heart. No one had ever touched him like that. Her breasts were crushed to his chest. When had they moved so close that he could feel every inch of her lithe, supple body?

Her other arm crept around his neck. Dax desperately tried to claw back some sense of control, some coherence around why he was doing this, but it was impossible. It had something to do with needing to make her stop talking…stop looking at him as if she could see all the way down to his deepest darkest shadows.

She was lush and sweet and hesitant and bold all at once. Her mouth opened under his and Dax was lost, drowning, spinning into infinity. He'd kissed women. Many, many women. Not as many as people thought, but a lot. Enough to know that this kiss was unlike any other.

It beat through him like a drum: *his, his, his.*

He wanted this woman. He wanted to taste every inch of her and he wanted to sink so deep inside her that she would be ruined for all other men.

A klaxon went off in his brain—*she's not yours to ruin!*

Dax jerked his head backwards so fast he felt dizzy. Laia opened her eyes. They looked unfocused. Her mouth was swollen. They were still welded together—chest, thighs, hips. His body was aching and hard, pressing against her soft belly.

Dax put his hands on her arms and took a step back, pushed her away from him.

Laia blinked. 'What was that?'

'That,' Dax said grimly, 'was a mistake.'

Laia was still trying to process what had just happened. An earthquake? But the island seemed fine. The sea was calm. *No.* The earthquake had happened inside her. One minute she'd been standing there, looking at Dax, and the next...the next she'd been consumed.

She could still feel his mouth on hers, *hard*. His body against hers, *hard*. She grew warm when she registered exactly how hard...pressed against her belly.

She'd imagined that kiss her whole life. That was the kiss of her dreams and fantasies. Yet it had burnt her imaginings to dust. She'd never expected to feel so full of fire. So full of earthy lustiness. She'd never expected to feel that ache in her lower body. That pooling of heat between her legs. The way her breasts had felt heavy and tight.

Dax was holding something out to her. She looked at it. Her kaftan.

He said, 'Please, put this on.'

Laia felt uncoordinated as she took it and tried to figure out where the arm and head holes were. She heard a curse, and then seconds later Dax had stepped closer and was putting it over her head.

Laia, ridiculously, felt like giggling at Dax's stern expression. He was helping her find the armholes now and threading her arms through. The light, diaphanous material settled around her body, covering her.

Then he started striding back up the beach towards the trees.

Laia called out, 'Where are you going?'

He threw over his shoulder, 'Back to the villa.'

Laia realised at that moment that her legs were like jelly. She sank down onto the sand. She just needed a moment to assimilate different things.

Dax wanted her.

She'd felt it.

She was sure it was just a consequence of his being stuck on this island with her...he was a highly sexed man. But her plan to seduce him didn't look so ridiculous any more. At least she knew he wanted her.

She sat there in a semi stupor for long minutes. Rendered insensible by a kiss. A mere kiss. It was pathetic, really. But it was also glorious. The culmination of all her ardent longings since she'd laid eyes on him that first time in Paris. And it had surpassed anything her fevered brain could have imagined.

She visualised Dax coming back down to check on her and finding her here like this—wrecked after a kiss—and scrambled to her feet.

She tried to reduce the significance of what had just happened as she walked back. It had just been the culmination of years of longing for something—if Dax kissed her again surely it wouldn't have the same effect?

But just the thought of Dax kissing her again made Laia almost miss her footing on the path. She cursed softly. She had to get it together. She had a job to do. Seduce Dax, and in the process make it crystal-clear that she would never be marrying his brother.

And then put Dax and the past behind her and get on with her life. A life on her terms.

* * *

Dax was coming down to the kitchen level after taking a long, cold shower when Laia returned from the beach. She looked like a sexy sea nymph, with her hair in a wild sea salt tangle around her shoulders and skin burnished from the sun. Bare feet.

At least she was wearing the kaftan, which covered her body from throat to thigh. But even in spite of that he remembered what she'd felt like pressed against him, and the effects of the cold shower wore off in an instant.

Merda.

She looked at him. 'You wanted to talk to your assistant?'

He'd forgotten completely. 'Yes.'

'Is it okay if I shower first? And then I'll bring the phone down.'

Dax made some sound of assent and tried not to imagine Laia in the shower.

She padded upstairs to the bedrooms.

Dax wasn't sure what he'd expected, and it should be a *good* thing that she obviously wasn't going to make any reference to the kiss, but it also made him feel prickly.

Had she taken his words to heart and put it down to a mistake, too? Happy to forget about it? Even though he would bet that it had been as erotic an experience for her as it had been for him, if her reaction had been anything to go by.

Now he felt incensed that she seemed inclined to ignore it. Which was ridiculous. He'd betrayed his brother just by kissing her! He'd created a situation where he would have to endure watching Laia by Ari's side while the memory of that kiss burned a hole in his gut.

No. It was just a kiss. A kiss that meant nothing.

Dax cursed again and went to the kitchen, randomly pulling out ingredients. He needed to make himself busy.

After about half an hour, Laia was back.

Dax's brain went blank for a second. She was wearing cut-off shorts and a Lycra crop top that lovingly outlined her breasts. Her waist dipped in and flared out again gently. Her skin was smooth and golden. Dark hair was pulled back into a damp plait.

It took him a moment to realise she was holding out the phone. 'John is on speaker.'

Dax's brain was sluggish. He wanted to snatch the phone from her and instruct his assistant to send a plane, helicopter—*anything*—immediately. But he couldn't. He gritted his jaw and forced himself to focus, then reeled off a list of things he wanted his assistant to work on.

When he was finished, Laia terminated the call. She made a little whistling sound. 'What did your last slave die of?'

Dax forced himself not to respond. 'A lot of people depend on me for their livelihoods.' He winced inwardly. He sounded like his brother now. Uptight. Ha! Ari would laugh his head off.

Laia looked sheepish as she put the phone in a back pocket. 'I'm sorry, I know you have responsibilities.'

Dax went still. 'Not so long ago you were saying the opposite.'

A dark flush came into her cheeks. She looked at his mouth, and then back up. 'I… That wasn't fair. Like you said, I don't know the background.'

She looked at his mouth again. Suddenly all Dax could hear was the rush of blood to his head. He wanted to kiss her again. And this time not stop.

He moved back around the kitchen island. He was determined to pretend it had never happened.

And that's going really well, mocked a little voice.

'I'm making a seafood platter for dinner, okay?'

'Sounds perfect. I'm going down to the pontoon. Some fresh supplies are coming in.'

Dax looked at her. She was backing away.

'Needless to say, please don't try anything. The security guards will be watching.'

Dax was irritated that his first thought wasn't to devise some way to overcome the boatman and make his escape, but to welcome some distance between him and Laia. Right now, if she'd told him she was leaving him on the island while she went back to the mainland he would have welcomed it.

Laia carried the bags back up to the villa. Her face burned when she thought of one thing in particular that she'd ordered. A big box of condoms.

The box was light in the bag, but it felt like a ton weight. Weighed down by her hubris in thinking that she could entice Dax into more than a kiss. He'd made no reference to it just now. Clearly sending a signal that it had been, as he'd called it, a mistake.

But *he* had kissed *her*. So she knew he wanted her.

Her conscience pricked again at the thought of pitting him against his brother, but as far as she was concerned his brother had no jurisdiction here and no claim over her. This was her last few days as a free woman. And she wanted Dax to be her first lover.

What if it hadn't worked out like this? Would you still be hating Prince Dax or would you be able to move on?

As Laia huffed her way up the steps she had to concede that if she'd never come face to face with Dax again then she might have fooled herself into believing she disapproved of him and didn't find him remotely attractive.

But all it would have taken would have been a face-to-face

meeting like this one and she would have been forced to acknowledge her desire and complicated feelings for the man.

In a way, it was a blessing that it was happening now, here on this island. She could put Dax and her attraction to him behind her after this. Move on with no regrets. No unfulfilled fantasies.

First you have to sleep with him, reminded a little voice.

Laia got to the top step, out of breath, sweat running down her forehead and between her breasts.

Suddenly Dax appeared, and Laia had to take a moment to appreciate the incongruity of the image—the world's most infamous playboy with a tea towel thrown over his shoulder.

And yet it didn't diminish his sex appeal one little bit. If anything, the hint of domesticity added to it.

Once again he looked totally at ease and at home in shorts and a polo shirt open at the neck. Laia wanted to press her mouth there and then move it down, over his chest, her teeth finding a nipple, biting gently before—

'Bags?'

Dax interrupted her suddenly rampant imagination and she saw he was holding his hands out to take the bags. Laia handed them over, but at the last second remembered and kept one back, clutching it to her chest muttering, 'Feminine products.'

The thought of Dax seeing the box of condoms was too horrifying to contemplate.

He went back towards the kitchen. 'I'll put these away.'

Laia fled upstairs with her cargo and put the box deep into one of the bathroom cabinets. She looked at herself in the mirror. Eyes wide, cheeks flushed. She looked guilty. She was in full on crush mode and it was heady. She'd never really fancied anyone before.

Because it had always been Dax.

Feeling restless, Laia locked her door and dug out her phone, hoping that there might be a message from Maddi, but there was nothing. She suspected that Maddi had disabled her phone in a bid to protect Laia.

Laia went online to check what was happening, and saw pictures of King Aristedes and Maddi at a posh Santanger restaurant having lunch.

Maddi was wearing a jumpsuit, her arms bare. She looked very sleek and very beautiful. The King was wearing a suit. Laia immediately compared him to Dax. They were similarly good-looking, but where Aristedes was all clean lines and a neat, short beard hugging his jaw, Laia knew that Dax in the same scenario would be somehow…messy. Either his hair, or the stubble on his jaw that he couldn't be bothered to shave after a night of passion with his latest lover…

He'd certainly given that impression every time he'd appeared in the tabloids.

Laia emitted a sound of frustration and got off the bed to pace back and forth. Everything in her education and upbringing had schooled her to find King Aristedes attractive. Not his reprobate brother.

But his brother was the one she wanted with every pulse of her blood.

For the first time in her life she had to recognise that there was wildness in her. A wildness that had been awoken the first time she'd laid eyes on Dax. That had lain dormant until they'd met again.

It was since that night in Monte Carlo that she'd begun avoiding King Aristedes in earnest. As if she'd been reminded of what she wanted even as she'd denied it to herself.

She went back to the laptop and looked at the pictures of Maddi again. Searching for a sign that her sister was somehow in peril or unhappy. If she saw even a hint of it she would arrange for someone to go and get her out of there, but there was no hint of discomfort or unhappiness.

To the contrary. She and the King were conversing intently. Totally engrossed with each other.

A tiny seed of a suspicion formed in Laia's head as she looked at the pictures. Could it be possible that her sister and the King weren't just acting out a fake engagement?

Laia put her hand to her mouth at the notion. She knew Maddi would do anything for her, that her loyalty was true and deep. But Laia had made it very clear that she had no intention of marrying Aristedes, so even if there was something between Maddi and Aristedes, Laia wouldn't consider it a betrayal.

Laia also knew Maddi had a pragmatic approach to emotions and the notion of love. But as for desire…? As Laia was beginning to understand, once desire was involved all bets were off.

Considering her own situation… If Dax was determined to ignore the kiss, how was Laia going to remind him? And, more pertinently, encourage him to do it again?

Dax felt suspicious and he didn't know why. Well, that was a lie. He knew exactly why. Because he suspected Laia was up to something.

Since she'd brought the shopping up from the boat she'd appeared periodically during the course of the rest of the day, in those maddening cut-off shorts and the little crop top.

A tiny bikini was the only item of clothing that would have been more exposing.

First she'd helped him clear up his prep for dinner—he'd made the most of the fresh seafood the boatman had delivered and added it to the dish.

Then she'd gone off to do some gardening, reappearing with mud dotted on her knees and arms and face, carrying a big bunch of wild flowers that she'd artfully arranged in a huge vase.

Then, while he'd been watching a documentary in the media room, she'd appeared and asked very genially if he'd like anything. The sun had been going down, so he'd asked for a beer.

And now he sat here, nursing his beer and not concentrating on the documentary.

Had she really decided that their kiss was a mistake too? She was certainly behaving as if it hadn't happened.

It shouldn't be bothering him, because it had been weak and wrong to kiss her, but...

Dax's hand gripped the beer bottle. *Por Dios*, it had felt like heaven.

He gave up on the documentary and switched off the TV. He went out into the kitchen area and came to a standstill.

Laia was naked.

He blinked. She wasn't naked. But she was wearing a slinky silky slip of a dress that was approximately one shade lighter than her own skin tone.

She hadn't noticed him standing there in mute shock, taking her in.

The dress had delicate spaghetti straps that looked as if they'd slip down a shoulder at any moment. There was a slightly dipped ruched bit at the front. It belatedly occurred to Dax that she wasn't wearing a bra, because he could see no straps.

Her hair was up in an unfussy bun and her feet were bare. No jewellery, no adornment. She didn't need it.

She was the image of understated sexiness. And that was before he noticed there was a slit on one side of the dress, so when she moved a length of very toned thigh was revealed.

She saw him and stood up from where she'd been checking something in the oven. She smiled brightly. 'Shall I prepare the last bits for dinner and set the table?'

Dax had never cooked dinner with a woman before. Cooking was something he enjoyed privately. It was far too intimate to share.

'Okay.'

Laia gestured vaguely towards his clothes. 'Don't feel like you have to make an effort just because I did.'

Dax's gaze narrowed on her. His Spidey senses were tingling. 'Laia, what are you up to?'

Her eyes widened. 'What? I felt like dressing up a little. There are never usually guests here.'

'Oh, so now I'm a guest? Call your boatman friend back and have him pick me up in an hour.'

Laia's face paled a little, and for a second Dax thought she actually looked...*hurt*. Which was ridiculous. Except he had a sense at that moment—out of nowhere—of affinity. As if she knew what it was to feel alone, too.

When he and Ari had been separated so that Ari could concentrate on his important studies, Dax had spent long hours playing alone in the palace. In many ways when his mother had sought him out more and more Dax had almost welcomed it, because he'd felt lonely. He just hadn't realised how claustrophobic her attention would become. Or how all-consuming.

Dax noticed Laia was drawing back into herself, smoothing her expression. Becoming the polished Princess again. And he didn't welcome it. He had to admit that if she told him he could leave right now, he'd hesitate. More than hesitate.

And he couldn't pretend that it had anything to do with persuading her to go to his brother and fulfil her obligations.

The woman behind the Princess, who walked around in cut-off shorts and bare feet and little teasing crop tops...who kissed like a siren from a mythical tale...was tying him in knots. And he had a feeling she knew it too.

But he wasn't going to play her game. He had more control than that.

He put down his beer and said, 'I'm joking, of course. Why would I leave this beautiful place and such a generous host? I'll freshen up.'

Laia cursed herself when Dax left the kitchen. She had to stop looking so obviously hurt when he said he wanted to leave. Of course he didn't want to be here—she'd trapped him!

But still… She'd thought that in spite of everything there was…*something* between them. Apart from all the obvious things they had in common, like both being from royal dynasties.

And that kiss.

She made a face at the dress she'd chosen to wear. She'd pulled it out on a whim. She knew it was audacious. She felt naked in it. But if she was going to test Dax's control then she didn't have much time to lose.

He struck her as a man who prided himself on his control, which she realised ran contrary to what she'd assumed about him before she'd got to know him.

Like a lot of other things that ran contrary to what she'd expected…

A timer went off and Laia broke out of her reverie and turned off the grill. The array of seafood looked mouthwateringly delicious. Grilled lobster, snapper fillet, pepper prawns and calamari. She helped herself to a juicy prawn, using her fingers, and almost groaned at the taste. She could see how food like this was an aphrodisiac.

Before she made a complete fool of herself—or, worse, ate all the food, she set the table with a candle and a small posy of flowers in a vase. She turned the lighting down.

She felt anxious. She'd never tried to seduce a man before.

She heard a sound and turned around—and felt winded. Dax was wearing dark trousers and a white shirt. Open at his throat. Sleeves rolled up. His hair was damp. His jaw was still stubbled. She'd had a slight burn after their kiss earlier.

Her insides clenched tight when she thought of how it had felt when his tongue had touched hers and the kiss had spiralled into a dizzying white-hot fire.

She really, really wanted to kiss him again.

She could feel the tension in the air between them. The push and pull.

She forced her mind to focus. 'The food is ready. I can serve?'

'I'll get the wine.' He looked at her with mock severity. 'Only one glass for you.'

Laia rolled her eyes, relieved at the break in tension.

She brought the platter of seafood and some plates over to the table. At first she tried to be polite, using a knife and fork, but when she saw Dax pick up some lobster with his fingers, she gave up and joined him.

It felt thoroughly decadent, eating with her fingers, and very sensual.

The butter sauce from the lobster ran down her chin, and before she could get it Dax had leaned over and wiped it with his thumb. He looked as surprised as she felt. It had been such an automatically intimate gesture. He wiped his thumb with his napkin, and Laia's insides tightened as she couldn't help but imagine that he'd put it into his mouth instead.

She was losing it.

After that she avoided his eye for a bit. Mortified.

They ate in companionable silence, and after a few minutes Laia put her fork down and wiped her mouth. She took a sip of the crisp white wine, gestured to the half-decimated platter of seafood.

'This is seriously impressive. You could probably get work as a chef if you lost everything tomorrow.'

Dax wiped his own mouth. 'Good to know.'

'My half-sister loves food. She's a good cook too—she's the one who has been teaching me.'

Dax sat back, wine glass stem between his fingers. 'What's she like?'

'Well…' Laia hesitated.

She was wary, considering both how Dax had reacted to learning about her and what was potentially happening right now between her sister and King Aristedes. She didn't know how Dax would feel about that.

But he said, 'Genuine question.'

Laia relaxed marginally. 'She's physically very like me… as you saw. Except her eyes are more hazel. And she's curvier. And she has a gap between her front teeth.' Laia couldn't help smiling. 'She's sweet and open. There's no agenda with Maddi. She's quite shy. She's a little terrified of becoming a princess. The plan is to let people know around the time of the coronation, so that's when she'll be officially acknowledged…'

'Yet she jumped into the frying pan with Ari…? A ballsy move.'

'She's brave.'

'And she isn't resentful that she didn't grow up with great privilege?'

Laia shook her head. 'No—amazingly. But she did admit she missed not knowing our father. She's pretty special. She's much more open and affectionate than me. She's quite unorthodox… Not a hippy, exactly, but she goes with the flow…'

Dax let out a little huff of laughter. 'It sounds like Ari won't know what's hit him.'

Laia shifted uncomfortably, thinking of those pictures again.

Dax said, 'She does sound like a special person. She'd have to be to not grow up with a huge chip on her shoulder after being ostracised from a life of royalty.'

Laia said, 'The ironic thing is that I always wished for a sibling when I was growing up. I was lonely. But, as you've said, you were separated from Aristedes, so even if Maddi had been there, maybe I wouldn't have seen her all that much.' Before she could stop herself, Laia asked, 'Do you see yourself having children?'

She noticed that Dax kept his expression carefully schooled before answering.

'Like marriage, it's not something I've ever envisaged. After my experience with my parents, who didn't really parent at all, I can't say it's something I'd want to risk inflicting on my children.'

'But Aristedes has no choice.'

'Just like you have no choice.'

'I had a good experience with my father. He was loving and kind and supportive. But not having had a mother... I think I'm afraid that I won't know what to do. How to mother.'

Laia was shocked. She'd never admitted that out loud to anyone. Not even Maddi.

Dax said, 'I don't know much about these things, but for what it's worth I don't doubt that it's an entirely instinctive process and you'd be a great mother.'

Laia blinked. Startled at the sudden welling of moisture in her eyes. She'd never in a million years have imagined this conversation with this man. She'd never expected to feel such emotion.

Her voice was husky. 'I... Thank you. You didn't have to say that.'

'I don't say things I don't mean.'

No, he didn't. Just as he didn't lead women on.

He would be a good father. Laia felt it in her bones. She could almost see him with a small, sturdy toddler with dark hair, lifting him high in the air.

She stood up quickly, before any more disturbing images could pop into her head or she blurted out something else incredibly exposing. She couldn't even blame the wine this time. She'd had hardly any.

She gathered up the plates and said brightly, 'Coffee?'

'I think I'll have a digestif…a little whisky.'

Dax got up and helped clear the table, before going over to the drinks cabinet and pouring himself a measure of whisky.

Laia made coffee and went out to the deck to see if some air might help her regain some composure. There was a full moon casting a milky glow over the dark forest and the sea beyond. The lights of the fishermen shone in the distance.

She sensed Dax coming to stand near her. After that conversation Laia felt as if her skin had been peeled back to reveal a tender under-layer. She felt even more acutely aware of him, felt her blood humming under sensitive skin.

The intense heat of the day was gone, and in its place was the night-time cloak of tropical warmth. Laia turned around and rested back against the wooden railing. She looked at Dax and her heart tripped.

She said, 'You aren't at all what I expected.'

He turned towards her and hitched a hip onto the thick wood. 'What did you expect?'

'A petulant spoiled playboy with the attention span of a gnat.'

Dax made a face. 'A little unfair.'

Laia was indignant. 'You've admitted that you cultivated that reputation.'

He had the grace to look a little sheepish.

'Except now I get the impression that you're at a fork in the

road,' she went on. 'You can't keep up the playboy façade…
you've already started to retire it. People are wondering what's
going on. What's next for Prince Dax?'

Laia could see that he didn't like being questioned.

He took a sip of whisky. Looked at her. 'Maybe I'm ready
to out myself as a serious businessman?'

But not a husband and father.

Before she could quiz him any more he said, 'I've been
meaning to ask you…what was going on with you that night
in the club in Monte Carlo? You were on your own, lost to the
world…you'd obviously stayed up past your bedtime.'

Laia felt a little jolt. The fact that he'd noticed her in that
moment made her feel a little emotional.

She gave a little shrug. 'I guess I wanted to not be me for a
moment. To pretend that I was someone else. Someone without duty and obligations and every second of my life mapped
out. Right down to the man I'm supposed to marry, whether I
like it or not. I was fantasising that I was just a normal girl…
out for the night with endless possibilities in front of me. And
then I opened my eyes and there you were.'

'You didn't know who I was at first.'

Laia hated it that he'd noticed that. Noticed her little moment of exposure. 'But then I did.'

'And you realised I was the Big Bad Wolf so you ran.'

Laia looked at Dax. The man in front of her was the same
man who'd been in front of her that night, but this time everything was different.

Very carefully she said, 'I don't want to run now.'

'What did you say?'

But Dax had heard Laia perfectly well, and his body had
heard her too. Every muscle was tense with need. His pulse
was racing and his blood was hot.

She was looking at him very directly. 'I said, I don't want to run now.'

Dax knew he should be cutting this off, walking away, but a devil inside him made him say, 'Why don't you want to run?'

Her cheeks went pink, and in the midst of this heightening tension between them Dax had the urge to reach out and run his knuckles down her cheeks. He clenched his hand by his side. His other hand was tight around the glass.

He wasn't sure how he'd managed to eat and converse like a normal person over dinner, when all he'd been aware of was that slip of a dress and how it draped forward to expose the upper slopes of Laia's breasts every time she moved.

She's doing this on purpose.

Dax tried to exert some control over his body. His head.

But then she stood up straight, faced him directly, and said, 'I don't want to run because I want you.'

Dax's attempts to exert control dissolved in a flood of heat. He gritted his jaw. 'I can't deny that I want you too, Laia, but it's not happening. That kiss was a mistake.'

'It didn't feel like a mistake.'

Dax moved back into the kitchen, put his glass down on the counter.

Laia followed him and put her cup down.

No, it hadn't felt like a mistake...it had felt sweet and sinful all at once.

'You are marrying my brother.'

Laia waved a hand. 'Look around you. We're thousands of miles from Santanger. Does it look like I'm marrying your brother?'

Dax clenched his jaw again. Against the temptation she posed. He had to admit that up until the kiss he'd held out some thread of hope or futile belief that she would somehow come to her senses and return to Europe.

He shook his head, as if that would rearrange his brain cells into forgetting he wanted this woman. 'I came here to track you down for my brother. I won't betray him.'

He could see that she looked frustrated. She said tautly, 'Your brother and I have no relationship to betray.'

Laia's hair had started to come undone and was falling in tendrils around her face. Her eyes were so green they reminded him of the sea around the island. Her jaw was tight. He could feel the tension in her body, as if connected to her by an invisible thread.

So far, all his little acts of rebellion had never impacted Ari. Dax had made sure of that. He'd always stayed within the bounds of acceptability.

Laia was not the rock he would perish on. She was just a woman he wanted. She was not unique.

So why does it feel like you've never wanted another woman? How is that you can't even picture your last lover?

Like earlier, Dax knew he needed to put distance between them. *Now.*

He said, 'I'm not having this conversation. There's nothing to discuss.'

He turned and went towards the stairs leading up to his suite, where he intended on taking a very cold shower for a very long time. Maybe he could freeze this desire out of his body. In spite of the tropical temperatures.

He had his foot on the bottom step when Laia said from behind him, 'It's your fault, you know. It's your fault I can't marry your brother.'

CHAPTER SEVEN

LAIA'S HEART WAS thumping so hard she felt light-headed. Dax had gone very still. Slowly, he turned around. His expression was suspiciously blank.

He came back towards her. He stopped a couple of feet away. Laia could feel the tension like electricity crackling between them.

He gritted out one word. 'Explain.'

Laia swallowed. Dax suddenly seemed a foot taller. Broader. Darker. She hadn't fully thought through what his reaction might be. Explosive, she was guessing.

'Laia?'

How did she even articulate this? It suddenly seemed ridiculous that he could have had such a huge impact on her since—

'You do not get to make a claim like that and then say nothing.'

Dax had folded his arms, which only drew attention to his muscles, pushing against the thin material of his shirt.

'How is it my fault, exactly? And why am I the only one still talking?'

She spoke. 'The first time we met…in Paris… You…affected me. I fancied you. I developed a crush on you. A big one. You were the most beautiful man I'd ever seen. And then you told me you were going to be my brother-in-law one day and I felt sick at the thought—because how could I feel such illicit things for my brother?'

Dax's face lost some of its ferocity. 'You were only sixteen.'

Laia shrugged. 'Old enough to form a crush. And then when I saw what you were doing…how you were living your life… all the women… I think I was jealous. But I told myself you disgusted me, because you were so flagrantly disregarding the fact that you were a crown prince and had responsibilities to your King and your people. I felt ashamed that you were attractive to me when I was trying my best to prove to everyone that I could be Queen some day. But that night in Monte Carlo… I couldn't hide my immediate response to you. I envied your freedom. And then I was angry because I was weak enough to be jealous… The truth is that I convinced myself I disapproved of you to deny admitting how much you affected me. On some very deep fundamental level I knew I couldn't marry King Aristedes because I wanted you. Not him.'

Dax's voice was a little hoarse. 'You haven't even given him a chance…'

Laia shook her head. 'I saw him after my father's funeral. I felt nothing for him. *Nothing*. And he dismissed me. He's not interested in me at all. On any level. And that's not good enough. I've measured every man I've met against you, without even realising what I was doing. That's why…it's your fault.'

Dax took a step closer. His eyes were piercing her all the way down to where Laia had nothing left to hide. She'd exposed herself spectacularly. There was no going back.

Dax said, 'Ari is a good man. He would respect you and treat you well. You would want for nothing.'

'Except passion.'

Now Dax's cheeks flushed. 'You want a lot from your marriage. Passion *and* love?'

Laia felt defensive. 'I don't think that's too much to ask. After I leave here, my life will not be my own ever again. Not really. Is it so selfish to want something for myself while I can still have it? When I'm hidden from the world and no one will ever be any the wiser?'

Dax's jaw clenched. 'And then you can get on with your life and find this true love? This paragon of a mate who will fulfil all your needs? Why don't you just wait for him?'

'Because I don't think I'll be able to move on until—' She stopped.

'Until?' Dax prompted.

'Until I've *known* you.'

'You mean until we've had sex?' Dax said crudely.

Laia winced. 'Not like that.'

Except it was exactly like that.

For the first time Laia felt vulnerable. She doubted herself. Maybe she wasn't a match for Dax's control after all.

'I truly didn't know this would happen. That you would be here like this. But now the thought of meeting you at some future event or place and realising how much I want you, not having known you, it terrifies me...'

'Laia, Ari is—'

She cut him off. 'Not the man I want. Ever. I will never be with him. That's what I realised on a very deep level all those years ago. I can't be with him when I want you.'

Dax seemed to struggle with something for a long second, and then he said, with almost palpable reluctance, 'The truth is that you've haunted me since I saw you in Monaco. And until I saw you again I've had no interest in much at all.'

Laia had to lock her knees to stay standing. Her legs were turning to jelly. Was she part of the reason he'd disappeared from the scene?

Feeling emboldened, she took a step closer to Dax. She could feel his heat. And his scent, a potent mix of wood and musk and something uniquely him, tickled her nostrils.

She said, 'Let me put it this way. If I told you to send me to your brother right now, to become his Queen, would you be happy to let me go to him?'

Laia took a deep breath and made the biggest gamble of her life.

'Because if you say yes, then I'll go. Leave now. Not to go to him, but I'll go home and let the chips fall where they may. I'll never see you again.' She lifted her chin. 'I have some pride, Dax. I won't beg.'

Dax closed the distance between them. There was barely an inch now. He was all she could see.

Laia bit her lip. If he said *Yes, go now* she might very well die a little inside.

But he didn't say anything for a long moment, and then he lifted his hand and tugged her lower lip free from her teeth. Laia held her breath. Dax's gaze was on her mouth.

He said, almost to himself, 'Would I be happy to let you go to him…?'

He shook his head, and then he looked at her and she could see fires blazing in his eyes. A slow surge of euphoria made its way into her blood.

'No, Laia, I wouldn't be happy to let you go to him, or to anyone else. Because I want you and I'm done fighting it. You're mine.'

Laia trembled. She'd campaigned for this—she'd asked for it…all but begged for it. But was she really ready for it?

A kaleidoscope of pictures flashed through her head: seeing him that first time in Paris, all the tabloid images she'd pored over for years, Monte Carlo and now here. This moment. This man.

Yes.

She put her hand on his chest, over his heart, and said, 'Then make me yours, Dax.'

* * *

Dax had tipped over the edge of any control he possessed and was walking through fire. Let this woman go? Walk away? Without tasting her?

The thought made him feral.

He finally understood that Laia absolutely meant what she said. She had no intention of ever marrying his brother. In truth, he'd understood it for a while, but he'd been fighting his own desire because he'd never, ever gone against Ari in his life.

But something Laia had said had resonated with him. She selfishly wanted to take something for herself. While the eyes of the world were turned away.

In doing this, Dax would be embarking on the most selfish thing he'd ever done. And in many ways the worst thing he'd ever done. Taking his brother's promised bride.

If he'd felt tainted and damned by the past before, now he would be tainted and damned in the present. But there was no turning back. He knew Ari had no real appreciation for this woman. He'd always known it. Laia was right—Ari just saw her as the next step.

Even so, Dax knew he was crossing a line and he would never forgive himself. He would have to add this to the line he'd crossed that day of the car crash. He was good at crossing lines and accepting guilt. He'd accepted that a long time ago.

And there was no way he could hold back from what this woman was offering. She was sweet and pure and light—and, fatally, he was drawn to her as if she could offer him some kind of absolution. He did not deserve this. But he was taking it.

There was no other choice—there never had been. He could see that now—he was filled with a primal need to possess that he'd never experienced before.

He put his hand over Laia's on his chest. The way she did that…it pierced something inside him, some of the darkness.

He threaded his fingers through hers and then, taking her hand, he led her through the villa and up the stairs.

The night was warm and soft around them. Only the night chorus of insects and small animals broke the peace.

But Dax couldn't even hear that. All he could hear was the pounding of his blood. And his heart.

Laia felt as if she was in some kind of dreamlike state as she followed Dax up the stairs, her hand in his, fingers entwined, as if they'd been lovers for years.

There was no hesitation.

The lights were low, infusing everything with a low golden glow, and Dax led her into his bedroom and closed the door. He let her hand go and went over to the shutters, pulling them closed. Then he dropped the net around the bed.

Laia watched him. He turned around and came towards her. He stopped in front of her.

'Turn around.'

Laia did as he said. He pulled her hair free, so that it fell down her back. He put his hands on her shoulders and turned her again to face him. Her skin felt so sensitive.

But he didn't touch her straight away. He said, 'I've suspected something, but I need to know...'

Laia knew what he was going to say, and she knew it would be futile to pretend otherwise. So she swallowed her self-consciousness and said, 'I'm not experienced. At all.'

A muscle pulsed in Dax's jaw. 'No lovers?'

She shook her head.

'Laia...are you sure you don't want to do this with the man who will be your husband?'

She shook her head.

'I'm not naive enough to confuse sex with love.' She made a face. 'If my father's affair has taught me anything it's that.

This…this thing that's between us. You said it's rare. I might never feel this again, even with the man I choose to marry. I know that.' Just so he was in no doubt, she said, 'I choose you to be my first lover, Dax. But don't worry, I won't fall in love with you.'

His mouth twisted. 'No. Because I'm not really a suitable consort for a queen, am I?'

His words sank in and suddenly it felt as if the earth was tilting sideways. She put out her hands to find balance, but Dax was already holding her steady, his hands on her arms.

He was frowning. 'Okay?'

Laia nodded. 'Just a little rush of blood…'

But she knew something had just happened. Something profound that she couldn't—or didn't want to—analyse just yet. A desire for him to be hers in spite of all the reasons why he couldn't—because he had no intention of settling down.

Desperate to avoid thinking about that, Laia said, 'Kiss me, Dax.'

He brought one hand up, over her arm and shoulder, under her hair, and cupped her neck, tugging her closer. 'Now, that I can do.'

He seemed to take for ever to touch his mouth to hers. Laia had the slightest glimpse of his wicked smile and she was about to scowl or beg. But then everything was forgiven, because his mouth was on hers and Laia's entire body was suffused with heat and electric excitement.

She'd thought she'd made too much of their kiss earlier… that it couldn't possibly have been that transformative…but it was happening again. And it was even more profound, because now she was even hungrier for it. Desperate.

She hadn't even realised she'd twined her arms around Dax's neck, arching her body against his, wanting to feel that whipcord strength against her body, hard against soft.

She'd never considered herself a very girly girl, but she'd never felt more feminine than she did in this moment. Never been so aware of the differences between a man and a woman.

Dax's other hand was splayed across her back, and she could feel him moving it up now, over her bare skin, finding one of the straps of her dress and slipping his fingers underneath to dislodge it.

But then he tensed and stopped. Pulled back.

Laia opened her eyes. Her mouth already felt swollen. Breath fast and choppy. 'What is it?'

Dax's face was flushed, eyes glittering. 'I don't have anything with me...' He cursed softly and let her go.

Laia struggled to make her sluggish brain work. 'You don't have what with you?'

He put his hands on his hips. 'Protection. I don't have protection. We can't do this. I'm not risking getting you pregnant. That's a scandal too far even for me.'

Finally what he'd said sank in, and with it came a wave of relief.

She said, 'Wait there.' And fled back across the hall to her room, fingers clumsy with the key to the door. Eventually it opened and she almost fell inside. She went straight to where she'd stashed the box of condoms and picked it up.

She brought it back to Dax and handed it to him.

He took it and looked at it. And then her. He said, 'The delivery earlier today?'

Laia nodded, feeling self-conscious. 'I only thought of it when...after the kiss... Obviously I can't risk getting pregnant...'

Dax shook his head faintly. 'Not many women have ever surprised me... No, scratch that—actually no woman has ever surprised me as much as you have.'

Laia said, 'Is it...are there enough?'

Dax looked at the box and huffed out a laugh. He opened it and took out one foil-wrapped sheath.

'Let's start with one and see how we go, okay?'

Laia had never felt so gauche or out of her depth.

Dax seemed to take pity on her. He put down the protection and led her over to the bed.

He stood in front of her. 'Laia, I don't want you to regret this. You're about to become Queen. Life for you and my brother is different. When you meet the man you'll marry he'll probably expect you to be—'

'Pure?' Laia cut Dax off. 'I've done my best to get out of one medieval marriage arrangement. I'm not going to keep myself pure, like some sort of sacrificial offering for my husband. I'm a modern woman, Dax, and the only reason I'm still a virgin is because I've never had the opportunity to lose my virginity. Most men are too scared to come near me—they're put off by the fact that I'm promised already—and if it isn't that they're just intimidated by my status. Apart from all that, I have practically no privacy. I'm watched over day and night. Here…with you… This is the first time in a long time that I've been truly on my own. And it's not just that you happen to be here and it's an opportunity. *You're* the man I want. The man I've wanted for so long. The fact that you're here is…serendipitous. It's like a gift…*you're* a gift.'

Everything in Dax rejected her assertion that he was a gift, while at the same he was inordinately moved by her words.

Dax wasn't anyone's gift. He brought with him a legacy of guilt and tragedy. A debauched reputation. And yet here, now, in front of Laia, who was looking at him with such pure desire, he felt ridiculously that he was being reborn on some level.

He reached out and touched her jaw. So delicate, yet strong. Like her. He felt humble all of a sudden. This woman was a queen—maybe not quite yet, but she would be, very soon. And he could imagine her being a great queen. Strong and proud, but also soft and compassionate.

Ari had been a fool not to take more care to make her feel wanted. She would have been a great Queen of Santanger. But she wasn't Ari's, and in that moment Dax felt a surge of emotion as he fully acknowledged that she wanted him.

'I don't deserve you...*this*.'

Laia shook her head. 'Why would you say such a thing? Of course you deserve me. I'm really not that—'

Dax put his finger on her mouth, stopping her words. 'Don't you dare say it. You are a woman descended from great women, who have endured all manner of things to be Queen of their land. And you are about to become Queen. You're already a queen.'

He saw Laia's throat work as she swallowed. And then she took a step closer to him and put her hand on his wrist, pulling his hand away from her mouth.

'Can we just...stop talking? And make love?'

Dax couldn't help huffing out a laugh. No woman had ever accused him of talking too much. But of course with this woman everything was reversed and upside down.

'Yes, we can.'

He took a step back. He wanted nothing more than to rip that excuse of a dress from her body and sink so deep inside her that all the things she made him feel and all the contradictions would be eclipsed.

But now was not the time. He would have to go slowly, even if it killed him.

'Undress me, Laia.'

She looked up at him, her lip caught between her teeth. Dax curled his hands into fists to stop himself from touching her. She brought her hands to his shirt and started to undo his buttons. He saw how she concentrated. He also saw the almost discernible tremor in her hands. She was nervous. He'd never had to worry about that before, because his lovers had always been experienced.

He let her undo all the buttons on his shirt. She pulled it out of his trousers. Then her hands went to his belt buckle and his every nerve-ending was tingling. She opened the belt. Then the top button of his trousers. The zip.

Dax held his breath. He could hear Laia's breath coming faster. The dress dipped down between her breasts and he caught tantalising glimpses of soft, plump swells. Her nipples were hard. He imagined the silk material of the dress brushing against them. Sensitising them even more.

Unable to hold back, Dax reached out and cupped Laia's breast through her dress. She sucked in a breath and looked up. He kept his eyes on her and took his hand from her breast to pull down the other strap of her dress. She lifted her arms free. The dress gaped and Dax tugged it ever so slightly, until it dropped all the way down, exposing one breast.

'You are...beautiful,' he breathed in awe.

Her skin was luminous, dark golden. Her breast was perfectly shaped. Pert and plump. Succulent. The nipple was hard, pouting forward from the areola. Dax cupped her flesh and rubbed his thumb back and forth over the hard, straining nipple.

Laia was very still. Hardly breathing now. He looked up. Her eyes were unfocused.

He reached for the other strap and pulled it down, exposing her other breast. The dress clung to her hips.

Dax finished taking off his clothes until he was naked before her. He felt something reverent move through him, as if he was offering himself to her for her delectation.

Her eyes moved over him, shy at first, and then avid. Over

his chest and waist and then down. Colour suffused her cheeks as she took him in. Took in how much he wanted her. How hard he was for her.

He ached.

Her eyes were wide. He could see in them something that looked like trepidation. He took her hand and put it on his chest, over his heart. She looked up.

'Don't think about it. Just let it...happen.'

He led her over to the bed, pulling back the net curtain. She climbed onto the bed.

'Lie back,' Dax instructed.'

She did. Her hair swung around her head in a dark silken tangle. Dax reached forward and tugged the dress down over her hips and off. Now she just wore her underwear. Lacy and flesh-coloured. Provocative. For a moment he almost imagined she was actually experienced, silently laughing at him taking so much care of her.

When had he become so infected by cynicism?

He came down alongside her and spread his hand on her belly. He felt her muscles contracting.

She put her hand on his. 'Dax, you don't have to treat me like spun glass. I won't break.'

If she had any sense of how much he wanted her and how much it was costing him to contain it she might not be so eager. But Dax let his hand drift up to cover her breast, cupping its weight, teasing first one and then the other, before bringing his mouth to one pebbled nipple and pulling it into his mouth.

He almost lost his life there and then, at the first taste of her flesh. The first feel of that hard nub in his mouth.

Her hands were in his hair and he could feel her moving her hips impatiently. He kept his mouth on her breasts, one and then the other, teasing and tasting mercilessly, as he brought his hand back down over her belly to the top of her underwear.

Sliding his fingers under the front, he felt springy curls. She opened her legs and Dax lifted his head. He looked at her face as his hand delved deeper, between her legs, his fingers finding the hot, wet centre of her body.

His erection twitched in reaction as his brain registered how she felt. She was biting her lip again, eyes huge. On him. He explored her body, moving his fingers in and out, the slickness of her body sending Dax perilously close to spilling without even entering her.

He covered her mouth with his as his movements became faster, harder, mimicking what would come when she was ready. When he had prepared her.

She was making little moaning sounds. Her back started arching off the bed. Dax urged her on, breathing into her mouth, 'It's okay...let it go, Laia...let it out.'

She did. With a big, keening cry as her body convulsed around his fingers and the waves of her pleasure spread outwards.

Dax had to tense every muscle in his body not to come right then. He let Laia absorb what had happened. And after a minute she opened her eyes again. She was perspiring slightly, and it made her glow. The scent of her arousal was in the air and Dax had never smelled anything sexier or more potent. If he didn't sink inside this woman soon, he might just die.

'Okay?'

She looked at him. Dazed. She nodded. And then she looked embarrassed. 'I've... You know... Before...myself...'

Dax nearly groaned out loud at the thought of her exploring herself. Making herself come.

She continued, her voice slightly hoarse, 'But it never felt like that.'

Dax kissed her slowly, thoroughly. Tongues tangling. He put one of his thighs between her legs and moved his hands over her, exploring every dip and swell and inch of her silken body. She was lithe and firm and soft all at once. He felt as if he'd never really touched a woman before.

When Laia was breathless again, Dax couldn't wait any more.

He pulled back. 'Are you ready?'

Laia nodded. But he could see her trepidation. He said, 'It might sting…hurt a bit at first…but it'll pass, I promise.'

'I trust you.'

For a second Dax couldn't breathe. And then he pushed the emotion out. No room for emotion here.

He encouraged her to lift up, so that he could pull off her underwear. And then he put himself between Laia's legs. Smoothed a hand up one thigh.

He wanted to taste her. Wanted to taste where she'd fallen apart in his hands. But he was too desperate.

He reached for the protection, sending up silent thanks that she'd had the sense to think of it. She was royalty. Soon to be a Queen. The stakes were too high for her to be careless. If she got pregnant by the wrong person—

Dax shut his mind down, because that thought precipitated others, of Laia getting pregnant with the *right* person. And that was not what he wanted to think about right now, when she was spread on the bed for him like his most wicked fantasy…

Dax rolled the protection onto his erection and winced at how sensitive he was. He couldn't remember a time when he'd felt such anticipation to join with a woman.

Laia's breasts were rising and falling rapidly. He could sense her nervousness. He came down and put an arm under her, covered her mouth with his in a deep, drugging kiss. At the same moment he guided himself into the centre of her body— and died a little death at the sensation.

Laia gasped into his mouth as he entered her.

He pulled back. He could feel the sweat on his brow. 'Okay?'

He watched her taking in the sensation. He moved and she winced minutely. Dax immediately wanted to pull out, and started to, but she put a hand on his buttock.

'No, keep going,' she said. 'I'm okay.'

He could see she wasn't, but he did what she asked and thrust deeper. He let her body adjust to his. Tense muscles softening. Accepting his invasion.

Gradually her face lost its slightly pinched look. A kind of curiosity seemed to take her over and she said, a little breathlessly, 'It's okay…really.'

Dax started to move in and out slowly, with excruciating care. His passage became easier, and he could see when discomfort turned to pleasure. A look of wonder came over Laia's face. Wonder and excitement.

She moved under him experimentally, and Dax had to call on every atom of control not to lose it there and then.

She said, 'Dax…you feel…amazing.'

Knowing that she was not in pain gave Dax permission to go a little harder, deeper. He saw the way Laia's eyes were glued to him, as if she was trying to communicate something she didn't understand, and he could feel it in her body as she put her legs around his hips, instinctively chasing the same pinnacle of pleasure that he was hurtling towards.

Silently asking for forgiveness, because he was using his experience and knowledge to send her over the edge before him, Dax reached between them and touched her where their bodies joined. Laia's body tensed around his for an infinitesimal moment before the onslaught of her powerful orgasm finally sent him into oblivion and a pleasure so profound that he just *knew* it was wrong.

Because he didn't deserve anything this pure or pleasurable. Not in a million years.

CHAPTER EIGHT

WHEN LAIA WOKE she heard the call of birds outside. She was alone in her bed. And why shouldn't she be? Something was off though…the sheets were rumpled. And her body felt different, well used. Aching, but in a way that felt…

Laia sat up in bed, completely naked. Something was off because she wasn't in her own bed. Memories flooded through the temporary barrier of sleep.

Last night.

Dax. His big powerful body over hers.

In hers.

The sting of pain and then—a wave of heat washed through her body from her core—then the most incredible, unbelievable pleasure.

She'd fallen asleep with little tingles and tremors under her skin and had woken up at some point to find herself enveloped in Dax's embrace, her back against his front, her bottom snug against his groin. She'd fallen back to sleep wondering if she was dreaming.

Maybe it had been a dream, because she certainly wasn't in Dax's embrace any longer.

She reached for the sheet and pulled it up, even though she was alone. Where was Dax? What time was it? There was a faint glow of daylight from beyond the net, but not enough for it to be late, yet.

She saw a robe on the end of the bed and was touched by Dax's thoughtfulness. She hadn't expected him to be such a considerate lover.

She pulled on the robe and went to the edge of the bed and pulled back the net. It was early dawn outside, the sky a pinky grey. But she hardly noticed that, because her eye was drawn immediately to the man standing at the wooden railing that ran around the perimeter of the large deck area outside the bedroom.

His back was bare. He wore sweatpants low on his hips. His hair was messy and overlong. She was suddenly blindingly jealous of all the other women who'd seen him like this. Who'd had him in their beds.

She noticed the tension that came into his body when he heard her and a part of her didn't welcome it. He turned his head as she came to stand beside him. She belted the robe tightly around her waist.

'How are you feeling?' he asked.

Laia avoided looking at him for a moment. How did she feel? She realised that she felt powerful. In a very feminine way. As if losing her innocence had fully initiated her into womanhood. Which it had, obviously, but she'd never realised it would feel so profoundly...*significant.*

She'd always seen it as a kind of burden to be got rid of, but what had happened last night with Dax had made her feel humbled. And she realised now she was very grateful that he had been her first lover. Because it had not felt like shedding a burden, it had felt almost...spiritual.

She would have this knowledge of how it could be inside her for ever.

What if you never experience this again?

Laia went a little cold. She assured herself that she'd seduced him for this very reason—because she'd known it would be like this and this was all she wanted. It wasn't meant to be anything more.

What happens on the island stays on the island.

She couldn't shake a sudden pervasive feeling of intense melancholy.

'Laia, are you okay?'

She realised that Dax was still waiting for her answer. She took a breath and looked at him, but he impacted on her like a punch to the gut, stealing her breath again.

She nodded. 'Fine.'

Amazing.

'Are you sore?'

She shook her head, and blushed as she said, 'A little, but it's...nice.'

He turned to her fully and reached out to trace a finger along her jaw. There was something in his eyes that made her insides swoop.

'*Nice*...hmm? Was it what you expected?'

No. Because, even though she'd known the facts, Laia had had no idea the experience would be so transformative or cataclysmic. But she wasn't going to reveal that to this man who now knew her more intimately than anyone else.

'I guess...'

What she really wanted to say was *thank you*, because she had immense gratitude for what he'd given her: the knowledge of her own sensuality and desirability.

Something flashed in his eyes. 'You *guess*?'

He reached for her, putting a hand around the belt of her robe, and tugged her towards him. She came, with a little stumble, and he caught her against him. She could feel the heat of the day, sultry and humid, rising with the sun.

Dax tipped her chin up so she couldn't escape him. 'Let's see if we can improve on that verdict, hmm?'

Laia trembled with anticipation and not a little apprehension. She didn't know if she could physically survive such an onslaught on her senses—on her body—again, but then she told herself it had been her first time. Surely that was why it had been so intense? And the second time would be...*less*...

But then Dax was kissing her, and stopping her thoughts, and undoing her robe, pushing it off her shoulders and baring her naked body to the warm, tropical dawn.

And then he was leading her back to the bed, and Laia discovered far too late that the second time brought even more intensity. Not less.

When Dax woke after making love to Laia for the second time, the sun was high outside and he could feel the heat. He was in a naked sprawl on the bed, over the covers. *Alone.*

His body felt heavy, with aching muscles and a bone-deep satisfaction that had eluded him for years. The last time he could remember feeling like this had been in the heady days of his first sexual experiences. Before he'd become jaded.

He was glad he was alone, to try and wrap his head around last night and this morning. He'd known the chemistry between him and Laia was off the charts, but in his experience chemistry didn't always translate into the bedroom.

It was because she was a virgin.

Uneasily, Dax didn't think he could put it down to that. It was Laia, uniquely. With her intoxicating mix of reticence and self-consciousness and that innate confidence that came from being purely who she was.

She was a queen. She couldn't help but be regal even in the midst of learning a new experience.

The dominant thing Dax felt right now was humbled. All over again. Because she'd wanted him. Wanted him enough to be her first lover. Even though she wanted to marry for love.

She was such a contradiction. Idealistic and pragmatic at the same time.

Feeling a little exposed—literally—Dax got up and pulled aside the net. The sun was streaming in. He winced. He went into the bathroom and took a shower, and then threw on shorts and a polo shirt. Left his feet bare.

He could get used to this living outside of time feeling. Days melting into nights and back into days. And now, adding Laia in his bed to the mix…? Maybe he'd just lose himself altogether and never re-join the real world? He could understand now why people dropped out of life and went backpacking for years.

Dax heard her low voice as he passed her bedroom and stopped in his tracks, suddenly feeling a little cold. What had he expected? That she'd be downstairs making them a cosy morning-after breakfast? He'd never have encouraged that of a woman in normal circumstances.

But then this woman hadn't conformed to anything *normal* since he'd laid eyes on her in that club. And now, listening to her voice on the other side of the door, he realised that clearly Laia hadn't checked out of the real world. She hadn't lost herself.

Dax put his ear to the door but couldn't make out what she was saying. It sounded like an online meeting. With her advisors? About her coronation? About plans to get on with her life when she went back to Europe?

Quietly, Dax tested the door, but it was locked. He went colder. Last night obviously hadn't blurred the boundaries of what was happening here for her.

He had a very unwelcome feeling of something almost like *hurt*. Laia was just using him to experience what passion felt like before she moved on with her husband of choice. She'd told him as much. Dax was still a prisoner in paradise, and he'd be an idiot to forget it.

* * *

Laia terminated the online meeting. She wondered if Giorgio, her advisor, had noticed her dishevelment. She hadn't showered yet. She'd only come into her room earlier because she'd heard her phone ringing in the locked cupboard.

It had been an unwelcome reminder of the outside world after a night and morning of passion such as she never could have imagined. When she'd seen numerous missed calls on her phone she'd gone hot and cold as the pressure of her responsibilities had come back. She'd pulled on a clean top and at the last second had closed and locked her door before joining the meeting.

Giorgio had confirmed that Maddi was still in Santanger and masquerading as Laia, apparently fooling everyone. He'd shown her a picture of them at a charity event and a headline: *The look of love between King Aristedes and his future Queen!*

Laia had studied the picture and had to concede that Maddi didn't look as if she was pretending.

What was going on?

At that moment Laia had heard a sound, like the door handle being turned, but when she'd looked up she'd seen nothing.

She couldn't shake the feeling of guilt at having shut Dax out. They had gone long past the point of locking doors, so she didn't even know why she'd done it. Even if he contacted Aristedes now it was only days to her birthday and the coronation. He wouldn't be able to do anything to stop her being crowned. And sleeping with Dax had as good as put a million nails in the coffin of the marriage agreement.

The real world was encroaching relentlessly, sooner than she liked.

Giorgio had just outlined the arrangements for her return to Isla'Rosa, as soon as she gave the word. But she hadn't been able to give the word. Not yet. Even though she had no real reason to stay here any longer and a million reasons to return home—not least of which was to extricate Maddi from Santanger and figure out what was going on...

But now the meeting was finished, and in spite of Giorgio's urging for her to come home soon, Laia was filled with sense of rebelliousness. Surely another day...another night... couldn't hurt? Surely it wasn't too much to ask when soon she would be handing herself over to a life of duty?

She'd have the rest of her life to think about more serious things. Like becoming Queen. And who she would marry.

When she thought of that, though, she felt cold inside. All she could see was Dax's face above hers, intense and serious as he joined their bodies and transported her to another realm.

When she'd woken again that morning she'd been draped over Dax's naked body. She'd managed to leave without disturbing him and she'd looked back at the last moment, seeing him in that same louche, sexy sprawl that she'd seen him in before.

For a second she'd felt breathless, wondering if it had all been a particularly lurid fantasy. But no. She was naked and aching. And she'd held her scrap of a silk dress in her hand. The dress he had removed from her body.

Laia took a shower. A part of her lamented washing the scent of Dax from her body. The scent of her becoming a woman. She left her hair damp and went into the dressing room. She spotted a white bikini—something she'd never have worn ordinarily, because it was too revealing. But now she imagined wearing it under Dax's gaze, and she was filled with a newfound sense of daring. Or was it confidence?

She pulled on a loose thigh-high kaftan over the bikini and left her room. This time she didn't lock the door. And she hadn't locked away her devices.

She came down into the kitchen area but there was no sign

of Dax. She spied the leftovers of a breakfast he'd obviously cooked for himself. She felt a pang of insecurity, disappointment, but then reminded herself that men like Dax didn't *do* cosy mornings-after.

All was quiet. Too quiet.

She felt uneasy, imagining that he'd somehow managed to escape. Maybe he'd had enough and had just left. Vanished back into his life.

The thought was wrenching enough to make Laia pause for a second and consider if she really knew what she was doing. Dancing with the devil.

Except he wasn't a devil. Far from it.

Dax had exploded every misconception she'd had about him. Every judgement.

He was not the man she'd thought he was. Not remotely. She had to acknowledge that she would never have even contemplated making love with him if she'd had any reservations, or if he'd shown a smidgeon of the reputation that followed him.

She knew she wouldn't have slept with him unless she trusted him. And she did. Implicitly. She trusted him with her life.

Laia sat down heavily on a chair, her legs suddenly weak. At what point had she fallen in trust with him? She felt dizzy. She didn't want to have feelings for Dax. He wasn't the man she wanted to care about. Their lives weren't aligned. They wanted different things.

Nothing had changed. She didn't want him for anything beyond the physical. All that was between them was here and now. The present moment. For another day at the most. Twenty-four hours.

She was just feeling something for him because they'd been intimate, and she wasn't experienced enough to divorce her emotions from the sex. That was all it was. A totally natural chemical response to what had happened.

She stood up again and ignored the fact that she still felt a little shaky. As if she hadn't entirely convinced herself.

Dax had to be here somewhere.

After searching the media room and the pool, and still with no sign of Dax, Laia decided to put together a little brunch picnic and go down to the beach where she'd found him the other day.

When she emerged from the treeline she saw him straight away. He was sitting near the shoreline with his knees drawn up. His hair was wet—he'd obviously been swimming—and was wearing a pair of short swim trunks.

Laia was momentarily mesmerised by all that gleaming dark olive skin and muscle definition. She'd felt the awesome power in his body last night, and had a sense of how much it had taken for him to maintain control and be gentle with her.

As if sensing her behind him, he turned his head. She left the basket she'd brought under the trees, in the shade, and walked towards him.

She stood beside him, glad of the sunhat she wore. The hurt she'd felt that he'd not waited for her or made her breakfast still stung.

She pushed it away.

'Here you are,' she said.

'You sounded busy.'

Laia frowned. 'You heard me?'

Dax's jaw clenched. He said, 'Don't worry, it wasn't audible.'

Laia sank down beside him, guilt resurfacing. 'You tried the door, didn't you?'

'I tested it, yes.'

Laia felt something very delicate unfurling inside her as she took in his tense demeanour. He was hurt.

Because she'd shut him out.

'Dax, I did it without thinking. Not because I don't trust you. The truth is that I was talking to one of my advisors about travelling back to Isla'Rosa, making arrangements.'

Dax smiled, but it was tight, humourless. 'You've won—got your way. There will be no marriage.'

'Not between me and your brother. No.'

He looked at her. 'So there's no real reason for me to stay here now, is there? Would you stop me leaving?'

Laia's gut turned to stone. She knew what she had to say.

'No, there's no real reason for you to stay. Or me. Even if you told Aristedes where I am, there's not much he can do about it now. If you want to leave, Dax, you can. But...' She stalled.

Laia was ashamed to admit she was suddenly terrified. Terrified of what she wanted to ask and terrified of what Dax would do. This was his perfect opportunity to wreak revenge on her for having upended his life.

That cold blue gaze was so different from last night, when it had burned her alive. Laia shivered in spite of the heat.

He raised a brow. 'But...?'

Laia dared herself to be vulnerable. 'But I would like you to stay...until we have to leave.'

'To do what, exactly?'

Laia's insides dropped. He was angry, and he was wreaking his revenge, and she couldn't blame him. He would walk away from her now...leave her behind.

For the first time in her life Laia realised that she'd protected herself from this kind of pain by not forming close relationships. Deep down she'd always feared rejection or abandonment, because of her mother's untimely death.

Her half-sister Maddi was the only person she'd allowed herself to get close to, and it had taken her years to build up the courage to go and find her.

In that moment Laia felt absurdly emotional...as if she'd ruined something. She didn't get emotional. She'd learnt at an early age to hide her emotions.

Her father had used to say to her, *'You can cry in private, Laia, but no one wants to see their King or Queen be weak in public.'*

Terrified Dax would see the tears pricking her eyes, Laia got up and said, 'It's fine. Forget it, Dax. If you want to go I won't stop you.'

She turned and went back up the beach, but after a couple of seconds she heard a muffled curse behind her and Dax caught her arm, stopping her.

He came around and stood in front of her. Laia looked down. He tipped up her chin. She couldn't hide her emotion. He cursed again.

He said, 'I know it's ridiculous, but after last night...that locked door was like a slap in the face. I'm not your enemy, Laia.'

No. He was something she didn't even want to investigate.

Laia blinked back the emotion. Her chest felt very full. 'I know that. It was a reflex. To be fair, it's not as if I have all my doors open at the castle and people coming in and out as they please.'

He looked slightly horrified. 'I should hope not. That would put your safety and security at risk.'

The thought of having someone like Dax caring about her safety and security made Laia feel wobbly all over again.

'Do you want me to stay, Laia?' Dax asked.

She felt as if she was on the verge of a cliff, with nothing to stop her freefalling over the edge.

She nodded. 'Yes, but only if you want to.'

Dax cupped her jaw, a thumb moving across her cheek. 'I want to. How long have we got?'

Laia had to ignore the dart of resentment that this was finite. That she had been born to a life of duty and responsibility.

'Twenty-four hours…'

Dax smiled, and it was sexy and wicked. The tension was gone as if it had never been there.

'Now you have me here for a whole twenty-four hours, what will you do with me?'

Laia fell over the edge of the cliff. It was a dizzying, soaring, swooping feeling of letting go all the shackles that bound her to everything she knew. Dax was here of his own free will. Because he wanted to be. Because he wanted to spend time with her.

But underlying it were a thousand voices urging her to be careful. What was she doing? What was she risking by indulging so selfishly like this?

She ignored them all. Pushed them away. Embraced her finite freedom.

Twenty-four measly hours. That was all she was asking for.

She couldn't help smiling. 'First, we eat. I brought a picnic.'

'So, how many languages do you speak?' Laia asked Dax.

Dax was leaning on his bent arm, long legs stretched out and crossed at the ankle. They were under the shade of the trees, eating the picnic Laia had prepared.

Laia was trying not to ogle his body. He looked up to the sky and squinted a little as he mentally calculated, and then he looked at her and said, 'Seven.'

Laia's mouth dropped open. 'Seven? I only speak five.'

'Which five?' Dax popped a grape into his mouth.

Laia ticked off her fingers. 'French, Spanish, German, Italian and English, of course.'

'Oh, well, if we're counting English then I've got eight.'

Laia sat cross-legged on the sand. 'Okay, come on. Let's have them.'

Now Dax ticked off his fingers. 'English, Spanish, French, Italian, German, Mandarin, Russian and Arabic.'

Laia made a whistling sound. 'That's impressive.'

Dax shrugged. 'I'm able to pick up languages very easily. I learn aurally. Make me write something down, though, and it'd be a disaster.'

'Because of your dyslexia?'

Dax nodded.

'Still, diplomatically you must go down a storm if you can converse with everyone.'

'It does go well in meetings—especially when people don't think I can understand what they're saying.'

Laia could imagine people assuming Dax was all fluff and no substance.

She squinted at him. 'Are you ever going to let people see the astute global businessman?'

He made a face. 'I'm running out of people to surprise, so I might have to.'

Laia laughed.

Dax looked at her mouth.

The air crackled between them.

Laia hadn't realised how long they'd been sitting under the trees, eating and drinking sparkling wine. She'd felt deliciously relaxed, and yet now, with Dax's gaze on her mouth, she felt energised again.

She hadn't taken her kaftan off, and she suddenly felt the heat of the day. 'I might go for a quick dip to cool down.'

Dax stood up in an impressively fluid motion. He held out his hand. 'I'll come too. But we've just eaten so we should be careful.'

Another little piece of Laia's heart tightened. This man was so considerate. How had he ever managed to persuade people he was a feckless playboy?

He stepped towards her and bent to grab the edges of her kaftan, pulling it up. 'But first we leave this behind.'

It was up and off, over Laia's head and on the sand behind her, before she knew what was happening, and Dax's gaze made a slow perusal of her body in the skimpy white bikini.

This is how he got his reputation, a little voice pointed out.

Because he could look at a woman like this and turn her into a puddle of desire without even touching her. No wonder so many of his lovers had felt compelled to spill their guts about their time with him.

'Why are you scowling?'

Laia realised Dax was looking at her face. She rearranged her features. She wasn't about to tell him she was madly jealous.

'No reason. Let's go.'

He took her hand again and they walked to the water. Just before she could put a toe into the gently foaming waves Laia squealed, as the world was upended and Dax lifted her over his shoulder, striding into the sea.

She didn't even bother protesting. She was enjoying the view of his muscular buttocks too much. She pushed aside all maddening thoughts of other women aside. She was here with him now, and he was staying because he wanted to. That was all that mattered.

Dax was lying on the sarong that Laia had brought down to the beach. They were drying off in the sun, near the shore.

His stomach still hurt from laughing at Laia's indignant face after her dunking.

She'd actually said, 'You do realise I'm about to be crowned Queen?' And so he'd dunked her again.

He said now, 'I can't remember the last time I laughed that much.'

Laia huffed. 'You're easily pleased.'

Dax came up on an elbow and looked down at Laia. Her eyes were closed. Lashes long and dark on her cheeks. Her skin had taken on a deeper golden glow. That bikini needed to come with a health warning. It barely covered the firm swells of her breasts.

Her eyes opened and Dax looked away.

She squinted up at him. 'When *was* the last time you laughed like that?'

It hadn't been with a woman. No woman had ever made him laugh. He knew when, and it made him melancholic. 'With Ari...when we were kids. Before he had to start going to his lessons.'

Dax put his hand on Laia's flat belly, spreading his fingers out, revelling in the way her muscles quivered a little under his touch.

Laia came up on her elbow now, and Dax's hand moved to the dip in her waist. 'What happened with your mother?'

To his surprise, Dax didn't automatically feel like shutting down her question. It was as if something had been defused inside him.

He squeezed Laia's waist gently, and then said, 'What *didn't* happen is the question.'

Laia's eyes filled with emotion. 'If you don't want to talk about it...'

Dax had never spoken about this to anyone. The only other person who knew was Ari, and even he didn't know everything. Because Dax had kept it from him, not wanting to burden him.

'She was a broken woman. In emotional pain. She felt trapped... She probably could have left and moved on. But she didn't. She was too proud. So she hid the pain, or thought she hid it, by taking pills. By drinking. By eating and purging.'

Laia touched the tattoo of the caged bird on Dax's chest. 'This is about your mother, isn't it?'

Dax's jaw clenched. 'Love is a trap. It cages you. It caged her. It caged your father...he never moved on.'

'I never saw it like that, but you're right. He tried to move on with the affair, but the guilt of it caged him for the rest of his life.'

Laia took her hand away from Dax's chest. 'Your mother depended on you, didn't she? Too much.'

Dax didn't answer for a long moment, and then he took his hand off her waist and sat up, drawing his knees up. He looked out to sea.

'I was the only one close enough that she *could* talk to. Ari was busy. Her husband was taunting her...she had no close girlfriends or family. She was lonely.'

Laia sat up too, curling her legs under her. 'You were very young to be taken into her confidence like that. She was the adult.'

'Most of the time I felt like the adult. I was even putting her to bed at night.'

'Dax...'

'The day of the crash...she was really out of it. But she wanted to go out. Insisted. I only went with her because she refused to listen to me. I was worried.'

Laia spoke carefully. 'You weren't driving the car, were you? *She* was...'

CHAPTER NINE

A MUSCLE PULSED in Dax's jaw. He looked at Laia and she nearly gasped out loud. There was so much pain in his eyes. Pain and...*guilt*.

He said, 'I did everything I could, but she wouldn't listen. And she wouldn't let me drive, even though I knew how. I might not have been legal, but I would have been safer than her. She took a corner too fast and we went straight off the road into a ravine... I had barely a scratch on me. A broken wrist. That was it.'

Laia felt cold. 'She could have taken you all the way down with her.'

Dax said nothing for a long moment, and then, 'In a way she did.'

Laia thought of something. 'The other night you were saying that you didn't deserve me...or this... You really believe you don't deserve what...? For someone to want you?'

Dax tensed visibly. 'Because it's my fault. I didn't help her. I watched her self-destruct. I let it happen. And then I turned my back on Santanger and a life of duty. I don't believe I deserve good things. Just like I don't deserve to be protected. I won't have a security team because I won't let anyone risk their life for me.'

Laia's heart ached at Dax's pain and palpable guilt. At the thought that he wouldn't put anyone at risk because of him.

She said, 'You know, we have something in common.'

He looked at her. 'We do?'

She nodded. 'I blame myself for my mother's death too. Even though I know it's not rational. But if I wasn't here... she would still be alive.'

'And you wouldn't be here.' Dax shook his head, 'You can't possibly think like that.'

'Your guilt and sense of responsibility isn't rational either.'

'Isn't it?'

'Why did you take the blame for the crash?'

'Because I wanted to protect her reputation. It was all she had. Her pride. No one outside of the palace knew how bad she was.'

No wonder he'd abdicated so much of his other responsibilities—he'd been crushed under the weight of this one.

'It wasn't your responsibility.'

He looked at her. 'Wasn't it?'

Laia shook her head. 'No, it wasn't. But you did it because you loved her and wanted to protect her.'

And now he didn't believe in love.

For a moment it was as if the sun had gone behind a cloud, even though there wasn't a cloud in the sky. Dax reached for Laia, putting his hands on her waist and laying down, pulling her over him.

Her salty damp hair fell around them in a tangle. Her skin felt sandblasted. She was pressed against him, every inch. And she suddenly wanted him again with a hunger that rose up like a wildfire.

Her hands were splayed on his chest. Over that tattoo. She covered it with her fingers. She didn't want to think about that now. He caught her hair and moved it over one shoulder, wound it around his hand, tugging her head down to his.

Something silent moved between them.

Enough talking.

Laia needed no further encouragement to lower her head to Dax's and cover his mouth with hers. At first she was tentative, shy. Dax was under her, all that power and strength, and she felt self-conscious. Aware that she couldn't possibly be as alluring as his other lovers.

But then she felt him smile against her mouth, and she put her hands around his face and kissed him with all the pent-up emotion he was causing within her, simultaneously hating him for not just being the Playboy Prince and feeling a multitude of complicated emotions for the man he actually was.

Dax quickly took control, flipping them so that Laia was under him, one of his thighs between hers. His body was stirring against her. She moved against him. He shook his head. She pouted. He laughed.

'We are not making love here. We have no protection.'

Laia cursed her lack of foresight. Dax stood up and took her hand, pulling her up. They gathered up the picnic detritus and made their way back to the villa.

Dax took the picnic things from Laia and put them down on the kitchen table, then led her up to his suite, where he took her into the bathroom. He turned on the shower, which was open to the elements, and steam drifted upwards and all around them.

He took off Laia's kaftan again and turned her around, undoing her bikini and peeling it away. He stepped out of his own shorts. Laia marvelled that she didn't feel more self-conscious—but how could she when he was in front of her, naked?

There was something very elemental about being in this place, surrounded by heat and lush forest. Just them.

Dax stepped under the shower, bringing Laia with him. He washed her hair, working it into a lather and then massaging her skull with strong hands. Laia's head fell back at the exquisiteness of his touch. Then he rinsed her hair and worked soap into his hands again, to wash her body so thoroughly that she was shaking when his hand slipped between her legs and he found where she was so slick and ready.

It only took the barest of touches for her to come apart against his hand. She would have fallen at his feet if he hadn't held her up. She couldn't speak. She could only be manoeuvred as he turned off the shower and dried her hair, wrapped her in a towel.

He knotted a towel around his own waist. Laia looked at him, and this time she took him by the hand and led him into the bedroom. She wanted to worship at this man's feet.

She undid the towel at his waist she bent down in front of his majestic masculinity.

Roughly, he said, 'Laia, you don't have to…'

But Laia ignored him and wrapped her hand around him, in awe at the vulnerability and the strength of him. She felt powerful at Dax's feet in a way that only he had evoked within her. Powerful in her newfound sensuality and femininity.

She bent forward and experimented, flicking her tongue over the head of his erection. A shudder went through his body and she felt it all the way down to her own core, where she was still slick, aching for more. Her breasts felt tight.

Laia took more of him into her mouth, exploring the thick, hard, shaft of flesh. She heard an indrawn hiss of breath, felt the tension in Dax's body, and the way his hips started to move.

But then he reached down and pulled her up. His cheeks were slashed with colour, eyes blazing. Hot again. Not cold.

'I need to be inside you *now*.'

Laia lay back on the bed and Dax came over her, entering her body in a smooth thrust so deep and all-consuming that she arched against him. But then he cursed and withdrew, and Laia let out a little cry. It had felt so good…skin on skin.

And then she saw him roll protection onto his length. *Oh*.

Heat suffused her whole body. She hadn't even thought about protection.

He came back and smoothed a hand up her thigh to her breast. He cupped the flesh and bent his head, surrounding one nipple in hot, wet heat just as he entered her again. Laia threw her head back and gritted her jaw, as if that might help contain the building tension coiling deep inside her, stoked by Dax's body moving in and out in a rhythm that made her feverish for release.

But he kept her on the brink…a form of delicious torture… until Laia could stand it no more and cried out, begging, pleading for him to let her go.

And finally, having mercy, he did. He thrust so deep and hard that he stole every coherent thought in Laia's head. She was no longer human. She was energy and light and an immense pleasure that gripped Dax tight, deep within her body, as he found his own release and shouted out. And then they both tumbled and fell back to earth.

Dax stood on the deck outside the bedroom. It was dusk, but the sky wasn't lavender—it was grey and threatening. The air felt heavy and full of pent-up electricity. A storm was coming. He could see the fishing boats heading back for the bigger island. He noticed that even the security team's boat had moved, presumably to a more sheltered area.

But even though the atmosphere was heavy, for the first time in a long time Dax felt light. Lighter. As if a burden had been lifted.

Talking to Laia…telling her about his mother…the crash… had been cathartic. Laia's calm and compassionate acceptance of what he'd said—the ugliness he'd held inside him for so long—had been like a balm.

Maybe he was finally letting go of the crushing guilt that should never have been his to bear. Maybe he'd finally feel worthy.

Dax turned around. The net was around the bed, so he couldn't see Laia, but he could imagine her. Naked. Limbs sprawled in glorious abandon. The dips and hollows, the firm swells of her buttocks and breasts. Those eyes that opened wide when he joined their bodies and the way she had knelt at his feet like the most decadent supplicant. She'd tortured him a little. She was learning fast.

And soon she won't be yours any more. You've initiated her for someone else. Someone she can love and respect.

The thought of Laia moving on and finding this man who would be worthy of her love and respect was enough to make bile form in Dax's belly. He cursed himself and turned around again, putting his hands on the railing.

What the hell did he want? To keep seeing Laia beyond this point?

Yes. The answer was emphatic.

But it was impossible. She would be crowned Queen within days and her life would not be her own. She would be watched and commented on. If Dax went near her it would cause a sensation and a ream of headlines about his suitability.

He was not her destiny. She was not his. He had lived a life that put him firmly in the very *un*suitable bracket for a queen. He could never be a king. He'd learnt that a long time ago.

He heard a squeal from behind him and turned around to see Laia in a robe, belting it at her waist. She looked so beautiful it hurt. She was grinning.

'A storm! We have to close all the doors and shutters downstairs!'

Dax welcomed the distraction, he hadn't even noticed that it had started to rain. He told himself he must be losing it.

This tropical island paradise and the best sex he'd ever had were a potent combination for inducing crazy thoughts. Not real. Crazy.

Dax followed as Laia ran downstairs and started to pull the shutters and heavy blinds closed against the rain that was quickly turning torrential. He did the same on the other side of the room.

They met in the middle, and as soon as the room was protected against the rain he took her lapels in his hands and pulled her towards him. She went willingly, cleaving against him in a way that made his blood hum.

He smiled. 'You like storms?'

'I love them. They're so…awe-inspiring. Especially here. It feels like the world is ending, but it'll blow over in a few hours.'

It was almost as dark as night now. The storm was creating an otherworldly atmosphere. Dax had never particularly liked storms—too reminiscent of the emotional storms of his childhood. But this one was okay.

Because of Laia.

Impulsively he said, 'I'd like to take you out to dinner.'

Laia went very still. Did he actually mean take her *out* for dinner? In the real world? Where there were other people and regular restaurants and…?

It couldn't happen.

Laia imagined a scenario where she was out with Dax and the immediate frenzy of press attention.

'Dax… I don't know if that's—'

'I don't mean out there.' He jerked his head sideways to indicate beyond the villa. This island. This bubble. 'I meant here. Now. I hear there's a fabulous restaurant called La Permata? Maybe you've heard of it?'

Laia was surprised by the strength of the disappointment

she felt. But she forced a smile. This could not extend beyond the island. They both knew that. Time was slipping away from them like sand in a glass. This time tomorrow they wouldn't even—

She shut that line of thought down and put her head on one side and pretended to consider. 'I think I've heard of it... It's renowned for its eclectic menu and the novelty factor of using amateur chefs.'

'The very one. So, will you? Come to dinner with me?'

Laia's heart beat fast. 'What's the dress code?'

Dax looked affronted. 'Why, black tie, of course.'

Laia's heart thumped even faster at this side of Dax. Romantic.

She said, 'Then, yes, I would love to accept your invitation.'

Later that evening the storm had passed, as Laia had predicted. The sky was clear again, stars twinkling. There was a delicious feeling of freshness in the air and the earth smelled damp and rich from the rain. The heat wasn't as oppressive.

Laia was in her own bedroom. She'd showered and was in a robe looking for a dress. *Black tie.* It was ridiculous, really. But all Laia could think about right now was that memory of meeting Dax for the first time. When she'd been sixteen and had felt so gauche and fussy.

She realised she was living out the fantasy she'd harboured since that day. Since she'd looked at all those pictures of him with beautiful woman after beautiful woman.

She went into the dressing room and almost immediately a shimmering blue-green material caught her eye. She pulled it out. It was a maxi-dress. The simplicity of it appealed to her. It was backless. There was a silken ribbon that tied around her neck, holding the dress up, the ends trailing down her bare back. It fell in a swathe of greens and blues and teal colours down to her feet and it shimmered when she moved.

She hadn't worn jewellery since being on the island, but now she picked out some gold hoops for her ears and a gold bangle that sat on her upper arm. A gold signet ring for her little finger.

She pulled her hair back and up into a messy bun, leaving tendrils down around her face. She put on some make-up—only enough to take away the naked look. A dusting of green and gold eyeshadow. She didn't need blusher. Just thinking about the last few hours spent in bed made her blush. Some powder. A slick of flesh-coloured lipstick. Eyeliner and mascara.

She looked at herself in the mirror. After not wearing make-up for days, she felt like a clown. Did she measure up to the other women that Dax had been with? She hated this insecure, needy side of herself. But maybe this was what a passionate relationship did to you?

There was a knock on the door. 'Ready when you are.'

Laia called out, 'Okay...' but it sounded husky.

She turned away from the mirror. Slipped her feet into high-heeled sandals. She walked to the door feeling like a foal standing on its legs for the first time.

The dress moved against her body like a silken whisper, heightening her sensitivity. The only underwear she wore was knickers.

She opened her door and nearly fell backwards. Dax was standing in the corridor in a classic black tuxedo. Hair still damp. Jaw clean-shaven. It made him look no less dangerous or decadent.

His gaze moved up and down her body, and when he looked into her eyes she knew she'd never feel more beautiful than she did in this moment. He looked *awed*.

'You are stunning, Laia.'

It was hard to find her voice. 'Thank you, so are you.'

He dipped his head. 'Thank you.' He held out his arm. 'May I escort you?'

Laia slipped her arm into his, and all that heat and steely strength immediately made her feel protected.

A thought ran through her mind. *How was she going to cope without him?* She wasn't his to protect. Life as a queen's consort? He'd rejected the life of a royal a long time ago. And who could blame him?

Dax led her downstairs, oblivious to her thoughts in turmoil. But when they reached the bottom of the stairs everything in her mind blanked. The villa had surely been dressed by a set decorator?

Candles were alight everywhere. There were vases of flowers. Dax must have gone out in the dusk after the storm and picked them from the rain-laden bushes. The dinner table was on the terrace outside, with a white tablecloth and silver settings, more flowers and crystal glasses. And another candle.

Laia was breathless. She let Dax's arm go and moved into the kitchen. There was a delicious aroma of cooking...

She wrinkled her nose and looked at Dax in a bid to try and avoid thinking about all the effort he'd gone to. 'Chicken?'

'Wait and see.'

He had a bottle of champagne in an ice bucket and took it out and opened it, pouring the sparkling effervescent wine into a tall flute, handing it to her before pouring his own.

Laia waited, and when he had his she said, 'Dax, this all looks...amazing. Thank you.'

He clinked his glass against hers. 'You haven't eaten yet... reserve your judgement.'

But she already knew it would be amazing. The best meal of her life.

She took a sip of wine and said, 'I have to admit something.'
Dax said, 'Go on.'

'This is my first date. Like, my first *proper* date.'

A funny expression came over his face, but it was gone before she could decipher it. He put his hand on her waist and tugged her closer. She felt her dress moving over her bare skin.

He slipped his arm around her, his hand touching the bare skin of her back. 'Well, then,' he said, 'I'm honoured to be your first date.'

The moment and the feel of his hand on her back, now making small movements over her skin, made Laia want to melt. But not now.

Later. She pulled back a bit and said, 'Do you need help with the food?'

Dax took her hand and led her over to the table, pulling out a chair so she could sit down. He said, 'You are not to lift a finger.'

He went back to the kitchen and Laia put her chin on her hand and just watched him. He put on some music. Soft and jazzy. Perfect. And after a few minutes he brought over the plates.

He put one down in front of Laia and said, 'Chicken satay in a peanut sauce and some mezze dishes.'

It looked mouthwatering. There was houmous and pitta bread, rice balls infused with herbs, feta cheese and salad... She took a taste of the chicken and it was so tender it melted on her tongue, the peanut sauce giving it a tangy and very Malaysian twist.

They ate in companionable silence for a few minutes, and then Dax took a sip of wine and sat back. 'Tell me something about yourself.'

'Like what?' Laia felt deliciously sated. From the wine... the food...*the sex*. This place. The calls of the night insects. The soft breeze bringing tropical scents.

Dax shrugged. 'I don't know... Anything. A secret. Something other people don't know.'

Laia thought for a second and then said, a little sheepishly, 'I'm terrified of dogs.'

Dax looked at her. 'Dogs?'

Laia nodded. 'But the embarrassing thing is that it's not really my fear.'

'What do you mean?'

'My father was attacked as a child by a stray dog. He never got over the fear and passed it down to me. But I hate my fear. I'd like to have a dog. A puppy. But I can't do it. I always loved the idea of a family dog. A big shaggy thing that's goofy and silly. But if I even saw such a dog in the street I'd be rigid with fear.'

'You're brave, Laia. You'll get over that fear.'

'You think I'm brave?' Laia's insides fizzed a little.

'You stood your ground against an archaic agreement made by men and went your own way.'

'I don't know...it doesn't feel very brave to have been avoiding King Aristedes like this.'

'You're right, though, he wouldn't have listened. He would have done all he could to persuade you that you had to do the right thing. Because it would have suited *him*. We come from the same place. After what we saw, we're programmed to steer clear of emotional entanglement and drama. But, he would have been a kind and respectful husband.'

Steer clear of emotional entanglement.

That summed up Dax's attitude to relationships. She wondered if this counted as an emotional entanglement and then chastised herself. This was just sex. For him. For her...? She feared she was already way out of her depth.

But while they were here she could pretend that she wouldn't have to face the consequences of her actions.

She said softly, 'Do we have to leave here? Couldn't we just stay and pretend that the real world isn't out there, waiting?'

'We could...if you didn't have to be crowned Queen of Isla'Rosa and if I didn't have a business to run.'

Dax's easy acknowledgement that they would be leaving told her in no uncertain terms that he was already moving on.

Laia thought of all that awaited her once she left this place. She realised she didn't want to do it on her own.

She wanted Dax by her side.

That realisation lodged in her gut and in her heart like a stone.

No. She told herself. It was just sex. Messing with her head. She wasn't experienced. She was adding emotion to sex and coming up with the wrong number.

To prove to herself that it was just sex, Laia got up and held out a hand to Dax. He looked at her with those bright blue eyes. Bright enough to sear her alive.

He arched a brow. 'No dessert?'

'I'm dessert.' She smiled, but it felt hollow.

He took her hand and stood up, and Laia led him from the beautifully decorated room up the stairs to the bedroom. In the soft golden light he took off his clothes, and Laia took off all her jewellery and laid it down. She undid the ribbon at the back of her neck that held the dress up. Took off her underwear.

They were both naked.

Dax let her hair down. And then he led her to the bed. He lay down, urging her to sit astride him. Laia spread her legs either side of his hips and came down over his chest, her breasts crushed against him. He lay under her, looking stubbled and dark and thoroughly decadent.

For now, for this short time, he was hers. And she would store away these moments deep down and carry them with her through the next weeks, months and years, while she lived her life of duty with someone by her side who would love her and respect her and cherish her.

But she already knew, fatally, that they would never make her *want* like this again.

As if reading her thoughts, Dax put his hands on her waist and shifted her slightly. 'Sit up...put your hands on my chest.'

She did. Dax looked at her with such heat and desire in his eyes and his expression that Laia wanted to take a mental screenshot. He cupped her breasts, rubbing his thumbs back and forth over her nipples, making her shiver. Her hips felt restless. She wanted him. Deep inside. He put his hands back on her waist again and encouraged her to come up, before bringing her back down onto his hard body.

Laia's head fell back at the sensation. She sat for a long moment, savouring the feeling of his body in hers. And then she started to move in an instinctive dance, watching as his control started to fray and come apart at the seams. He was holding her, sweat on his brow, begging her to let him move under her, but she didn't allow it. She felt merciless as she punished him for ruining her for all other men, and it was only when he lost it under her that she allowed herself to fall behind him, collapsing onto his chest.

It might be a victory, but it felt hollow.

'Dax, wake up...'

Dax cracked open an eye. Laia was hovering over him in a robe. Hair loose. It was still dark outside. His body felt heavy.

He lifted his head. 'Is something wrong?'

She shook her head and pulled back the cover. 'No, everything is fine. I just want to show you something. Put on a robe and a pair of shoes.'

Dax got up, wondering if he was still sleeping. He pulled on the robe that Laia held out and put on some sneakers. She took his hand and led him downstairs and out of the villa, switching on a powerful torch.

They were walking down the path that led to the beach when he stopped in his tracks. This wasn't a dream. The air was warm and very still around them.

'Laia…where are we going?'

She shone the torch in his face, momentarily blinding him. 'Just follow me and wait and see.'

He did as he was told, letting her lead him all the way down to the beach. It was a clear night, with the moon sending out a milky glow. They walked down close to the shore.

At first Dax saw nothing—then he did. A bluish light coming from the waves as they crashed to shore.

Laia, beside him, said, 'It's phosphorescence…a natural phenomenon.'

It was beautiful. 'I've heard of it, but I've never seen it.'

Laia put the torch down and started taking off her robe.

'What are you doing?'

She backed away towards the water. Naked. Gorgeous. 'Skinny-dipping. Come on!'

Dax didn't need any encouragement. He threw off the robe and followed Laia into the glowing water. A blissful contrast to the humid night. The water shimmered and glowed around them as they moved. It was magical.

They didn't go far from shore, just deep enough to go under water. Dax caught Laia by the legs and she came up spluttering and laughing. He felt an acute pain near his heart, knowing he'd never experience this again with her. But she might with someone else. With her children. He imagined bringing children to see this amazing spectacle. The excited squeals. Dark heads. A girl and a boy.

To drown out the pictures, he caught Laia to him. 'Wrap your legs around my waist.'

She did. And they were joined flesh to flesh. Breasts to chest. He kissed her there in the sea, under the moonlight in the glowing water, and for the first time in his life he found himself yearning for something he couldn't even name—because he'd never allowed himself to believe it could be possible.

Laia lay awake after they'd returned from the sea and made love. Again. There was a sick sense of dread pooling in her belly. The first fingers of dawn were evident in the sky outside.

It was time.

She could drag it out for another few hours. They could have breakfast together. Maybe even make love again. But it would be the desperate actions of a desperate woman.

A few hours ago in the water...the magical glowing water... Laia had known she was in love with Dax. A man who had told her in no uncertain terms that he had no interest in settling down. Having a family. And, after what he'd been through, she could understand it.

Dax could never be hers. All she could take would be this experience. This knowledge he'd given her of herself as a sensual, desirable woman.

No man would ever make her feel the same. He'd ruined her years ago and he'd ruined her again. But this time fatally. Emotionally. And she'd let it happen. Invited it. Asked for it. *Begged.*

He moved minutely in the bed and Laia held her breath. When he didn't wake she let her eyes rove over his naked body. She'd known what it was like to lie with this man and have the freedom to touch him, to know he was hers. However briefly. But that was over now. She could never touch him again.

A sound of distress almost came out of her mouth. She had to put her hand up.

Before she could give in to the almost overwhelming temptation to touch him one last time, wake him with her body, Laia stole from the bed and went back to her own room.

She didn't look back. She couldn't. Because she knew that if she did she'd imprison them both here for ever, and that was a fantasy that could never come true.

CHAPTER TEN

WHEN DAX WOKE the next morning he wasn't sure what had woken him. He only knew that he was alone in bed. And he didn't like that.

Ironic after a lifetime of avoiding exactly that scenario.

Now he knew he wouldn't rest easy unless Laia was by his side and in his sight.

The previous night came back to him. The moonlit walk to the beach…the glowing water…

Coming back here, making love again and again. With a desperation that—

He sat up. They had to leave today.

Dax was filled with a sense of urgency. He needed to see Laia. *Now.* To talk to her. To say…

Dammit.

He didn't know what to say, but what he did know was that this couldn't be it. He had to see her again. Keep seeing her. In spite of the reasons why he shouldn't. Or couldn't.

Maybe she was making breakfast. Dax pulled on a pair of sweats and went downstairs, but even before he reached the kitchen he had the uneasy sense that he was alone.

It was another glorious day in paradise. But it didn't feel like paradise any more.

He saw a movement in his peripheral vision and a wave of relief went through him.

She hadn't left yet. She was on the main terrace.

But as he walked out and saw her fully, his sense of urgency faded and turned to wariness.

She turned to face him, and something turned to dust inside him. This was Laia, but not the Laia he'd had in bed last night, or in the phosphorescent sea. This was the Laia he'd met in Monaco, and when he'd first arrived here.

She was wearing a smart cream linen trouser suit. Silk chemise. Hair pulled back. Discreet jewellery.

Princess Laia, Queen-in-waiting. Ready to go back out into the world.

He felt exposed. Still a little fuzzy from sleep and an overload of pleasure. Dressed only in sweats.

He folded his arms across his chest. Retreated behind a wall. 'Going somewhere?'

For a second something flashed in her eyes, but then it was gone. 'You knew we only had another twenty-four hours. We can't leave together, in case we're seen. Shamil is on his way in the boat to pick you up. You'll be taken back to your hotel to get your things.'

She had it all worked out and organised.

Dax lifted his wrist and pretended to consult a non-existent watch. 'By my reckoning there are at least another three hours.'

Did he sound desperate? He felt desperate. And angry. That she was so put-together and not looking as if she was aching for him. As he was for her, even though his body was still heavy from the pleasure of their lovemaking.

He couldn't help saying, 'So that's it? You've had your secret passionate fling and now you're ready to embark on phase two of your life?'

Her cheeks flushed but it gave him no satisfaction.

'What else did you expect, Dax? Are you saying you want something more?'

He went very still. A sense of exposure prickled over his skin. Memories of his mother screeching and crying.

He said, 'Are you ready for this to be over?'

Now her eyes did flash. 'You know nothing else is possible. We can't have an affair. *I* can't have an affair.'

'Not with someone like me.'

She shook her head. She looked drawn all of a sudden. 'Even if I wanted to...we couldn't.'

Dax was tempted to say, *But you do want to?* But those toxic memories crowded his head again. The desperation he'd seen on his mother's face. He *wasn't* desperate. This was different. Infinitely different.

Laia said, 'I thought you would be happy to regain your freedom. Your life.'

It was ironic. He could now leave this island, but Dax knew that the last thing he'd feel was a sense of freedom. He saw over her shoulder that the security team's boat was approaching the pontoon. He also noticed belatedly that she had her suitcases lined up by her feet.

'You must have been up early.'

'I couldn't sleep.'

Yet Dax had slept. Like a baby. After a lifetime of insomnia.

'Dax... I...' She stalled. And then she said, 'I hope you're going to let people see the real you now.'

He looked at her. Eyes narrowed. 'What's that supposed to mean?'

'You're a good man, Dax, and you've been living a lie.'

Dios. This was even worse than he'd thought. She was trying to make him feel better. He welcomed a numbness building inside him.

'Believe me, I've enjoyed raising hell.'

'I'm sure. But isn't it time to move on from that life?'

'Settle down? Like you will?'

'I have no choice. It's my destiny. If I don't have children my line dies with me. That's hundreds of years of royal lineage.'

'I've already told you that's not what I'm interested in.'

'But…won't you be lonely? After all, Aristedes will be marrying too, having a family.'

'Like you, he has no choice. But I do. I've seen enough of family life to do me for a lifetime. The world doesn't need my genes passed down. Ari's are enough.'

As if to mock himself, Dax recalled the vision he'd had the previous night of children on the beach shrieking with excitement over the phosphorescence.

His sense of exposure went nuclear.

He could see the security men getting out of the boat in the distance. Presumably coming to get Laia and bring her luggage down.

He forced himself to look into her green eyes. 'Don't pity me in my lonely bachelor life, Laia. I'll be just fine.'

For a second she looked almost ill, but then she lifted her chin and said, 'I don't doubt you will, Dax.'

The security men arrived and wordlessly took Laia's luggage. She paused a moment before following them and said, 'Goodbye, Dax. I didn't expect for any of this to happen…but I'm glad it did. I'm glad to have got to know you.'

Was it his imagination or was her voice husky? And had her eyes been shimmering…?

Before Dax could wonder at that, and figure out what it meant, Laia was down on the beach. One of the security guards helped her up onto the pontoon by taking her hand, and for a second Dax saw red.

His hands were curled into fists at his sides. He only relaxed them when she was on the boat and sitting down. And then it was pulling away.

He could see the other boat arriving in the distance. Just as Laia had promised.

Now that she was no longer in front of him. Dax's gut swirled with emotions. He didn't want to think about how it had made him feel to hear her say, *'I hope you're going to let people see the real you now.'* The fact that he'd revealed more to her, here on this island, than to anyone else in his life was terrifying.

She'd called him a *good man*. Even though he'd all but propositioned her to have an affair. A woman who would be crowned Queen in a matter of days. A woman who deserved so much more than a tawdry affair with a playboy prince.

Every residual feeling of being unworthy and guilty swarmed up from his gut, reminding him of who he was and what he couldn't have. *Her.* And yet even now her voice came into his head. Telling him that he shouldn't feel guilty. That he deserved more.

He hadn't asked for that. He hadn't asked for any of this. And yet he knew that if someone told him right now that he could turn back time and erase the last week and a bit he would feel sick at the thought. Not to have known her? Not to have felt her moving under him? Over him? And not just the sex... The talking. Laughing. *Everything.*

'You're a gift,' she'd said to him.

Dax cursed out loud. A guttural curse. *Damn her.* He turned his back on the sight of her boat disappearing. On her. He was no gift to anyone and it was time for him to remember that. It was time to move on and get his life back on track.

Laia resolutely faced towards where she was going. Even though it killed her, she wouldn't look back at the island to try and catch a last glimpse of Dax. She'd just heard him confirm that there was no hope. He'd spelled it out clearly. Brutally.

'I've seen enough of family life to do me for a lifetime. The world doesn't need my genes passed down. Ari's are enough.'

All he was interested in was an affair. And he knew that wasn't possible. Not for her. It was time for her to be strong. She'd never needed to be stronger. Not even after her father's death. It was time to face her future and all that was ahead of her. The job of being Queen to her people.

And what about Laia the woman? asked a little voice.

She was afraid that Laia the woman had been left behind on the island and she might never find her again. From now on she was Queen first, woman second.

Two days later, Isla'Rosa

Laia was back at her desk in the castle in Sant'Rosa. Somehow holding it together even though she felt as if she was unravelling inside. Sometimes she wondered if she'd dreamt the past ten days.

She'd arrived back a few hours before and had made no comment about her upcoming nuptials, saying only that she was preparing for the coronation.

She knew she had to try and figure out how to get Maddi back—but at that moment the door to her office burst open and, as if conjured out of her head, Maddi, her half-sister, appeared.

Laia's insides dissolved into a pool of emotion. Relief and love.

'Maddi!'

They ran across the room and straight into each other's arms. Laia held on tight for a long moment, swallowing down her emotion. Then she pulled back and ran her hands all over her sister.

'Are you okay? Did Aristedes let you leave today or did

you have to escape?' She wasn't even aware of what she was babbling.

Maddi stopped her. She said, 'Laia, it wasn't like that. He found out almost straight away...but no one else knew. I agreed to slot into the engagement schedule because I thought that was the best way of letting you stay hidden...if I was distracting him... But the truth is—' Maddi broke off and walked away.

'Mads...?'

Her sister turned around. 'The truth is that I fell for him. We were...together.'

So she'd been right. 'I guess that was pretty apparent.'

Maddi frowned. 'What do you mean?'

Laia took her hand and led her over to an open laptop, where she'd been looking at the pictures of her and Aristedes.

Maddi blushed. Laia could sympathise. At least there were no pictures of her and Dax.

'I thought he was going to keep you on Santanger as some sort of a threat. That he wouldn't release you until I agreed to the marriage. But he let you go...'

Maddi's face turned to stone. 'Yes, he let me go.'

Maddi told Laia that Aristedes had come to terms with the fact that his marriage was off the table. That he'd realised he'd been complacent, expecting Laia to marry him.

'That's good. Did he say anything about the peace agreement?'

Maddi nodded. 'That you could discuss it at some point.'

'Maybe I didn't give him enough credit,' Laia said.

Just like his brother.

Her conscience stung.

Maddi took her hands. 'What matters is that you're back in time for the coronation and there's nothing and no one to stop you becoming Queen.'

Laia immediately thought of Dax.

Maddi clearly saw her face. 'What is it? What are you not telling me? Did Ari's brother find you? Did something happen?'

Laia felt like crying and laughing all at once. He'd helped her find herself.

But she just shook her head. 'It's okay. I'll tell you about it later.'

Or never—because she wasn't sure she'd ever be able to articulate what had happened.

She said now, 'I'll draft a statement and send it over for Aristedes's approval. It will say that by mutual agreement we've decided not to marry. I hope he'll countersign.'

Maddi looked emotional. 'I'm sure he will. He's a good man, Laia. I think you'll like him when you do have your talks.'

Laia focused on Maddi to stop thinking about Dax, who was also a good man. She touched her sister's cheek. 'Oh, Mads, I'm sorry... Is there any hope...?'

Maddi shook her head. 'No, he made that clear. And it wasn't as if I didn't know.'

Laia said, 'Well, you're back where you belong. And I want everyone to know who you are—if you're ready?'

Up till now Maddi had been shying away from coming out as Laia's sister. As a princess.

But now Maddi nodded. 'Yes, I'm ready.'

Laia hugged her sister tight again. Then pulled back. 'I'm so happy, Mads. I'll need you by my side.'

They smiled at each other, but their smiles were distinctly wobbly.

The same day, Santanger

Dax was bleary-eyed and dishevelled in jeans and a shirt after the long transatlantic flight. He hadn't shaved since that morning. But he'd known where he had to come first. He was in the palace in Santanger, following the way to his brother's rooms without even thinking.

The guards let him into Ari's inner suite and Dax didn't even notice their wide-eyed looks at his appearance. He went in and stood at the inner doorway. His brother was on the other side of the room, drinking. A sight as *un*-Ari as anything he'd ever seen.

Suddenly Ari turned around with a look of such hope on his face that Dax knew it wasn't because he was expecting *him*.

His expression immediately closed off. 'Where the hell have you been?'

Dax went in and gestured to the glass in Ari's hand. 'Drinking before noon, Ari? Have you decided to join my gang?'

Dax heard himself saying the words, still perpetuating the myth of his infamy even now. He hadn't drunk before noon in years.

Laia's voice sounded in his head. *'You're a good man, Dax.'*

Dax drowned it out by pouring himself a shot of whisky and downing it.

'Dax...?'

Dax looked at his brother. 'I'm sorry, Ari.'

'For what?'

'For not bringing Laia back in time. We were... She has this island...in Malaysia. That's where we've been. I couldn't leave.'

He hated even having to tell his own brother where he'd been. It was as if he was betraying the memory.

And then Dax looked at his brother as a thought occurred to him.

What if he was going to still insist—?

'You know you can't marry her, right?'

'Yes, I know.'

Dax's tension levels dropped. He said, 'You'll find another princess.'

Then his brother said, 'What happened between you and Princess Laia?'

Dax felt guilty. It must have shown, because Ari said wearily, 'It's not as if I can't put two and two together, Dax. I had no real hold over her. It was an ancient agreement. I barely knew her.'

Dax looked at him. How could he explain the unexplainable. How she'd become the centre of his world? 'I tried not to, but…'

Ari asked, 'Did you know Laia was Maddi's sister?'

Dax sat down on a chair. Legs sprawled out. He nodded. 'But I couldn't get in touch with you. She threw my phone in the sea.'

To Dax's surprise, Ari let out a sharp laugh.

Dax leaned forward. 'What's so funny? This is a disaster.'

Ari wasn't laughing any more. And neither was Dax.

Two weeks later, Isla'Rosa

'So how do you feel, *Princess Maddi*?' Laia asked teasingly.

Maddi smiled shyly. 'I don't think I'll ever get used to it. Being a princess.'

They were walking through the grounds of the castle in Sant'Rosa, enjoying the lull after the craziness of the coronation a week ago.

The world's press had descended on the small kingdom, lured by the pomp and the pageantry and the seismic announcement of a secret princess. Luckily, with the help of Laia's closest aide, Giorgio, it had all been handled with the utmost care and discretion, and after an initial flurry of headlines and shock the people of Isla'Rosa seemed to be coming around to the existence of Maddi.

She and Laia had done a small walkabout the day before, and the people hadn't been able to help but be charmed by their new Princess.

They hadn't held anything back about the King's affair. Maddi's mother had come back for the coronation, and she'd given an interview to one of Isla'Rosa's most respected newspapers. The people had sympathised with her heartbreak, and the outcome was not anger at the old King but a sense that he should have been brave enough to weather the storm to marry her.

'How are your mother and stepfather?'

Maddi smiled. 'They're good. It's been so lovely to see my mother here. Back in her home. They're already talking about moving here. Thank you for the house you've gifted them.'

Laia shook her head. 'Your mother deserves everything, Mads. She'll have whatever she wants for the rest of her life.'

She stopped when she saw tears in Maddi's eyes. 'Oh, Mads, I'm sorry—'

But Maddi shook her head. 'No, it's not that... Well, it is... and I'm so happy that she's happy. But...' she trailed off.

Laia felt her own heart contract. She *knew*. Because she felt like crying too. 'It's him, isn't it? Aristedes?'

Maddi looked as if she wanted to deny it, but she nodded. Then she looked angry. 'I never asked to fall in love with him, but he made me... If I could go back there and give him a piece of my mind—'

'Why don't you?'

Maddi stopped and looked at Laia. Eyes wide. The same eyes, just darker. 'Go back and...what?'

Laia squeezed Maddi's hand. 'Tell him that you love him. What have you got to lose?'

Laia felt like a fraud. She hadn't had the courage to tell Dax how she felt. But she'd seen those pictures of Maddi and Aristedes. She was sure that they loved each other.

'What if he rejects me?'

He won't.

Laia would bet money on it. But she said lightly, 'Then you come back here, to your home, and we'll make an effigy and stick pins in his bottom.'

Maddi giggled. And then sobered. 'You're right. I need to do this.'

'So go and do it. Giorgio will help you get to him.'

Maddi looked alternately terrified and excited. She flung her arms around Laia's neck. 'I love you.'

Laia hugged her back, feeling emotional. She couldn't stop feeling emotional these days. She said, 'I love you too. Now *go.*'

Maddi left, walking quickly through the gardens.

Laia watched her go. Selfishly, she almost felt like calling her back, because she knew that soon she'd be losing her sister again. But she said nothing. She went to the wall and looked out to sea and tried not to think about the person who dominated her every waking and sleeping moment.

Dax.

She put a hand on her belly. She'd been feeling queasy for a few days now. And she'd noticed that morning that her period was late. A trickle of fear traced down her spine, but she told herself she was being ridiculous. They'd never not been careful. It was undoubtedly due to the craziness of the last couple of weeks.

Every day she'd looked out at the people and the crowds and almost wished she would see a familiar tall, broad body amongst them. That beautiful face that could turn from serious to wicked to laughing in one instant.

But of course he wouldn't come after her. He wouldn't put her in that position. And he didn't want her enough. She'd already seen headlines saying that he was back in New York. And he'd been pictured at an event. Alone. She was thankful for that at least. She couldn't have borne seeing him with another woman so soon.

She couldn't be pregnant with Crown Prince Dax's baby. That would be the cruellest irony of all.

A month later, Santanger. Ari and Maddi's wedding

'I'd say your trip to Santanger to confront Aristedes was a success, wouldn't you?'

Maddi laughed and squeezed Laia's hand. She looked shy all of a sudden. 'I think we can say that, yes.'

The guests were mingling after the wedding reception in the beautiful ballroom at the Santanger palace. Guests spilled out through open French doors onto balconies and the sky was turning dusky. It was magical.

Laia felt emotional. *Again.*

'I'm so happy for you, Mads. Truly. You deserve everything the world has to offer—*Queen Maddi.*'

Maddi paled a little. 'I've only just been getting used to the idea of being a princess. This is ridiculous...'

Laia shook her head. 'You can do this. You're a natural.'

She spotted Aristedes coming over from the other side of the room and stood back. He winked at her and smiled as he took Maddi's hand to lead her away.

This marriage had already done so much for the two kingdoms. There had been some mutterings of dissent, but everyone was so happy to celebrate something joyful that they had been drowned out.

This really was a new era for Isla'Rosa and Santanger. Side

by side. Just as Laia had wanted. It was a just pity that she was single-handedly going to ruin it all for everyone with a scandal. Any day now.

The ever-present queasiness was worse now. Much worse.

At that moment she spotted Dax across the room. As if she hadn't been aware of him, mouthwateringly sexy in his morning suit, for every second they'd shared the same air, during the wedding and the reception.

Somehow, miraculously, she'd managed to avoid coming into close proximity with him—no mean feat considering she was maid of honour and he was the best man.

Those blue eyes moved over the crowd and stopped on her. As if he'd been looking for her. She felt it like a jolt of electricity. Panic galvanised Laia. She simply could not come face to face with him. Not now. Not yet. She'd fall to pieces.

Her phone rang in her bag and she welcomed the distraction, taking it out. But when she heard what her advisor Giorgio was saying her legs nearly gave way.

The scandal was upon her.

She had to go. Leave now.

She found Maddi and told her she had to go, assuaging her concern by telling her it wasn't anything too serious, but serious enough that she had to return to Isla'Rosa.

She wouldn't ruin Maddi's happy day.

The news would come out soon enough.

Dax was staring at Laia so hard he was surprised she didn't have two holes in her forehead. Never in the history of weddings had the best man and maid of honour had less to do with one another.

For the life of him he couldn't seem to get across the room to her, where she was talking to Maddi. It was like a recurring dream, where he was following her but she kept disappearing. She'd turned avoiding him into a sport.

She was maddening. She was beautiful.

She wore a long, simple teal-coloured gown in the same style as the bride's very simple wedding dress. High-necked and long-sleeved, it was the epitome of classic elegance, but all Dax could see was that lithe body underneath. And was it his imagination or did she look even curvier?

Her hair was up and swept back in a smooth classic chignon. Her jewellery was discreet. The newly crowned Queen of Isla'Rosa was not putting a foor wrong.

Dax had watched her coronation on repeat for days. Obsessing over the fact that she looked pale. And serious. Who was supporting her? Caring for her? Protecting her?

She was obviously close to her sister, who'd been at her side throughout. He could be thankful for that. But he was also incredulous that Ari had been taken in by Maddi's subterfuge. To his mind they didn't look remotely alike.

He'd even lifted up his laptop one day and brought it into Ari. He'd pointed at the screen and said incredulously, 'Really, Ari? You really thought that *she*—' he'd stabbed at the screen over Maddi's face '—was *her*?' He stabbed at the screen over Laia's face.

Ari had just scowled at him, and soon afterwards Dax had left to go back to New York—where he'd alienated everyone around him with his bad mood. He'd even started to frequent Irish bars, seeking solace in their whiskey and their maudlin ten-verse songs about heartache and pain.

And now he was back in the eye of the storm. And Laia was ignoring him so determinedly it was a wonder her head didn't fall off.

He had to admit that his brother had never looked happier. And since when had he been a fan of public displays of affection? He couldn't keep his hands off his new wife. The new Queen of Santanger.

Ari had got his strategic marriage after all...and a woman he loved.

Dax had to admit to envy. Because what he wanted now was the same, but with the only woman who—

When Dax next looked for Laia she was gone.

Again.

Dammit.

He pushed through the crowd, determined to find her this time.

And say what? prompted a voice.

All Dax knew was that the thought of not seeing her, speaking to her...*touching her*...ever again was unconscionable. No matter what the consequences.

He finally made it to the other side of the ballroom and stepped out into the blessedly empty corridor. But there was no one. Nothing. Acrid disappointment filled his gut.

Then he saw a flash of dark green out of the corner of his eye. *Laia.*

Dax followed her. She wasn't going to escape again. He saw her then, walking fast towards an exit.

No way.

She'd stopped for a second, as if wondering which way to go, and Dax seized the opportunity. He'd caught up with her and said her name before she could move again.

He saw how she tensed and everything in him rejected it. Slowly she turned around. *Por Dios.* He'd missed her.

He shook his head. 'Laia, you've been avoiding me for the whole day...what the hell is going on? Can't we even be civil with each other?'

Her face went red. A sign of life. Dax welcomed it.

She said. 'Of course. I didn't mean for it to be like this. But, look, I have to go back to Isla'Rosa. Something has come up. An emergency. A crisis.'

She turned around again and Dax caught her arm. She pulled away jerkily. Dax gritted his jaw against the hurt. She couldn't even bear to be touched by him.

He realised she looked very alone at that moment, and in spite of her obvious reluctance to be with him he felt protective. 'What's going on? Do you want me to come with you?'

She paled and backed away. 'No way. You are literally the last person I want to come with me right now.'

Dax felt winded. All he could do was watch as Laia started walking again. She went to the exit, where a car was waiting, and got into the back. He watched it pull away.

When Dax's brain started functioning again he wondered if he'd been deluded on the island. Had he really meant so little to her that she couldn't bear to be around him now? Did she regret everything in spite of what she'd said?

He wanted to turn away, leave and nurse his hurt. But something stopped him. Some instinct.

In spite of Laia's rejection she'd looked terrified. Something was going on.

Cursing himself for being such a sap, Dax got his things and arranged transport to Isla'Rosa.

When he arrived a couple of hours later he checked into a mid-range hotel, to draw less attention. Wearing a baseball cap, he left the hotel and walked around the capital city, Sant'Rosa. He was charmed by its quaint medieval streets, but he could see that it needed drastic modernisation and development.

He'd never been here before—it hadn't been considered necessary for him to visit when Ari had—and then Dax had wanted to put Santanger behind him. So Isla'Rosa had never really been on his radar.

The imposing castle stood on a hill overlooking the town.

Not unlike the palace in Santanger, albeit on a much smaller scale. Laia was up there now. Dealing with whatever was going on.

Dax cursed himself for being an idiot and went back to the hotel, vowing to leave again first thing in the morning. Clearly she wanted nothing to do with him. She'd moved on.

But when he went out for coffee the following morning all he could see were huddles of people talking in whispers. Looking worried. He saw a newspaper stand and the picture of Laia on the front page caught his eyes.

He didn't even have to buy a copy to see the blazing headline, and when it sank in he realised what the crisis was.

And also that he wasn't leaving Isla'Rosa any time soon.

CHAPTER ELEVEN

One day later

LAIA SAT AT the head of a long boardroom table in the castle in Sant'Rosa. The capital city. But that was a bit of a stretch. It was more of a big town, with a lot of its medieval infrastructure still intact, which was lovely for the tourists but not so much for a modern economy.

Her head throbbed.

About twenty men looked at her with varying expressions of shock, dismay and disgust. There was only one of compassion. From her advisor Giorgio.

He'd called her with the news at the wedding reception. The news that was going to break all over Isla'Rosa's media. And it had. Yesterday. Luckily it didn't seem to have filtered through to Ari and Maddi on their honeymoon. *Yet.*

One of the men stood up at the end of the table. Laia vaguely recognised him as one of her father's less favoured advisors. She really had to do something about this motley crew.

He was shaking with agitation. 'Queen Laia, since no one else here seems prepared to say the unsayable, I must. How on earth is it possible that our virgin Queen is pregnant?'

Laia had the absurd urge to giggle, but Giorgio caught her eye and shook his head. She stood up. She needed to get more women into this room.

'Gentlemen. I know this comes as a huge shock, and believe me, I truly didn't plan—'

But she was quickly drowned out by a cacophony of voices. All the men were asking questions now, and predicting disaster and destruction.

One man's voice was more strident than everyone else's as he shouted out, 'Who on earth is the father? Is he even a royal?'

Before Laia could answer, the door at the end of the room swung open and a man appeared. Laia's legs wobbled so much she almost fell back into her chair. She locked her knees.

Dax stood there. In a three-piece suit. Shaved jaw. He'd even had a haircut. He hadn't looked this suave for his own brother's wedding.

He said, firmly and clearly, '*I* am the father of Queen Laia's baby. And, yes, I am royal. For anyone who doesn't recognise me, I'm Crown Prince Dax de Valle y Montero of Santanger.'

There were a few gasps around the table.

One of the men blustered, 'You can't just barge in here like this.'

Dax looked at Laia. This time there was no hiding. His blue gaze was mesmeric. She didn't want to look away. She felt tired. As if she'd been running for a long time.

He said, 'If you would all excuse us, please? I would like to talk to Queen Laia in private.'

One of the men gasped in outrage. 'You can't dismiss us.'

Laia didn't take her eyes off Dax. She was afraid if she did he'd disappear. She said, 'Please leave us.' And then, more softly, 'You too, Giorgio. I'll be fine.'

The men sidled out of the room with lots of mutterings and deep sighs. At last the door closed and they were alone. It was silent.

Dax walked towards her.

She said, 'What are you doing here? How did you know?'

He stopped a few feet away. 'I followed you back from Santanger, even though you'd made it clear I was the last person
you wanted to see.'

Laia winced. 'Why?'

'Because I was worried about you.'

Laia's heart clenched. 'You've seen the newspapers?'

He nodded. 'I presume that is the crisis?'

She nodded. 'I hadn't been feeling well for the past month…
a persistent queasiness.' She blushed. 'My period was late.
Very late. I suspected what it was, but I was too terrified to
get it confirmed. But eventually I had to go to the castle doc-
tor, and he did a routine pregnancy test a couple of days ago.
I think he was as shocked as me. One of his staff must have
leaked it. Giorgio told me the media had the story the day before yesterday.'

Dax frowned. 'At the wedding—that's why you left?'

She nodded.

'But you already knew you were pregnant.'

Laia nodded. 'Only just. That's why I was avoiding you. I
couldn't bear to look at you in case you saw… I was in shock.
Trying to get my head around it. I felt so raw. If you'd come
near me, touched me, I was afraid I'd combust or fall to pieces,
and it was Maddi and Ari's celebration. I was terrified it would
come out…somehow.'

'I thought you were avoiding me because you couldn't bear
to look at me. Because you were ashamed of what had happened between us.'

Laia shook her head. She stepped out from the table and
faced Dax. He came towards her and then stopped. Her hands
itched to touch him. Feel him.

'Dax, I—'

But he closed the gap between them and put a finger to her

mouth. Laia instinctively pressed a kiss against it. His eyes flared.

He took his finger away. 'I just have one thing I want to say.'

Laia swallowed. 'Okay...'

He cupped her face with his hands. 'I love you, Laia. I adore you. You changed my life on that island and I never want to return to being the person I was. Cynical and closed off and afraid to ask for *more*. Afraid to forgive myself. I'm sorry I didn't tell you this before I let you leave, but I was too scared to admit it.' He made a face. 'Okay, that was more than one thing. But I—'

This time Laia put a finger to his mouth. She smiled. She was coming apart inside, walls crumbling, hope rising, joy seeping into her blood and veins.

'I have a few things to say.'

She took her finger away. Dax said, 'Okay.'

'I love you too. I adore you. But I truly believed that you weren't interested in anything more. And I have to have more...because that's what is expected of me.'

Dax winced. 'I felt threatened when you asked me if I was going to let people see the real me. I hadn't realised until that moment how much I'd shared with you. You knew more than Ari. I'd never trusted anyone with so much. I knew deep down that I wanted you—and not just for an affair. But in that moment the thought of revealing that to you was...terrifying. Because I really believed you wouldn't choose me for a partner. Why would you? I have my reputation and all my baggage. You deserve someone far more worthy.'

Laia looked at his mouth. 'You are more than worthy, Dax. I don't want to ever leave you again. Please, kiss—'

She was in his arms and his mouth was on hers before she'd even finished speaking. It was bliss. She'd never thought she'd experience it again.

She pulled back, breathing hard. Dax's hair was messier now. Better.

She said, 'I've hated you for ruining me for all men.'

He smiled and it was wicked. 'Good. Because I've been hating you too—for being the only woman I want to have a life with that I never even wanted before. Now it's all I can think about.'

Laia shook her head. 'I don't really hate you. I love you, Dax.'

'I don't hate you either. I adore you.'

Dax led her over to the window seat and sat down, pulling her into his lap. Laia couldn't stop looking at him. Touching his face.

She said, 'You look so elegant.'

Dax blushed.

Laia laughed, joy bubbling up. 'What is it?'

'I knew I had to come here today and I wanted to make a good impression. I didn't want to give anyone an excuse to say I wasn't good enough.'

Laia put her hand on his cheek. He turned his head and pressed a kiss into her palm. She said, 'Oh, Dax, you're more than good enough.'

Then she bit her lip and brought his hand to her belly and its very delicate curve. 'We haven't even talked about this... How do you feel?'

'How do I feel?' Dax shook his head. 'I feel like bursting with pride. And happiness and joy. And I'm also terrified. Because my father was not a good role model, nor my mother... But with you, I want to be a father. That night when we went down to the sea...?'

Laia nodded. Her eyes were already pricking with tears.

'I imagined a family,' Dax continued. 'I imagined you with

children, hearing their excitement. And I wanted to be part of that.'

Laia was crying in earnest now. 'I would love that.'

Dax put his hand over hers on her belly and said, 'Let's do it. Let's do it all together. For ever.'

Laia nodded and wrapped her arms around his neck. Dax's hands roved over her body, feeling every inch, relearning her shape. Making her blood grow hot. Making her want him. Right now.

She caught his tie, started to undo it. His hands were cupping her breasts, already fuller.

Then he said, 'Wait. I have to show you something.' He pushed his tie aside and undid his shirt, pulling it open.

Laia looked—and sucked in a breath. There, high on his chest, near the tattoo of the caged bird, was another tattoo. Identical in style, except for the fact that in this tattoo the cage was open and the bird was flying free.

It was very new. Still raised and dark with ink. She touched it softly, reverently. Tears blurred her vision again. 'It's beautiful.'

There was a knock on the door. They looked at each other.

Laia called out, 'Two minutes.'

Dax gently put Laia off his lap and stood up. They rearranged themselves and Laia giggled. Then she sobered up for a second and said, 'Are you sure you're ready for this? You'll be the Queen's Consort. You might even have to walk a few feet behind me... I've always wanted to change that.'

Dax said, 'Slight issue, my love. You haven't agreed to marry me yet. But in theory I will walk ten feet behind you if I have to. That way I can look at your ass and make sure you're safe.'

Laia giggled again. Then she said, 'You'd better hurry up and ask me, then.'

Dax got down on one knee, and to her surprise took a box out of his pocket.

He said, 'This visit was only ending one way or I was never going to leave.' He looked up at her and said, 'My darling Laia Sant Roman, Queen of Isla'Rosa, will you please do me the honour of becoming my wife, mother of my firstborn child, and hopefully more?'

He opened the box and Laia gasped. It was a stunning emerald ring, glittering in a diamond and platinum setting. He took the ring out and held her hand, looked at her.

She looked back at him. 'What?'

'You haven't answered me yet.'

She moved down and bowled him backwards onto the floor, her arms wrapped around him. 'I thought that was obvious. Yes, yes, *yes!* I will marry you, Prince Dax. Now, can we please go somewhere and make love?'

Dax grinned and put the ring on Laia's finger, where it shone like the seas around Permata island.

A few minutes later they opened the door to Giorgio, who took a step back at the sight of their slightly dishevelled appearances.

Laia held up her hand with the ring and said, 'Can you organise a press conference? Say for tomorrow morning? And let's see how fast we can organise a royal wedding. And cancel all my meetings for the rest of the day and don't let anyone disturb us, okay?'

Giorgio nodded frantically, and then grinned, and he watched as the Queen of Isla'Rosa led her husband-to-be by the hand up to her private rooms.

EPILOGUE

Four years later, Permata

'PAPA, WHAT IS THAT? Is it magic?'

Dax looked at Laia in the moonlight and smiled. He turned his attention back to his daughter, Liselle, held high in his arms. They stood at the shoreline on the beach on Permata.

'No, it's not magic, but it looks like it, hmm? It's called bio-luminescence, or phosphorescence.'

Their three-year-old daughter tried to repeat the word. 'Fozzi-essence?'

Dax chuckled. 'That's it.'

Liselle clapped her hands. 'Can I touch it?'

'Of course. Let's go into the water.'

Laia smiled as she watched her husband wade into the shallows holding Liselle by the hand. She was squealing with delight, exactly as Dax had envisaged.

And soon, when their son Demetriou started walking—which looked like any day now—he would join Liselle in the magic water. He was asleep on Laia's shoulder now, his sturdy body a welcome heavy weight.

Laia looked up to the moonlit sky in a bid to keep back emotional tears. She had everything she'd ever dared to dream of and so much more. A man she loved who loved her. Endless passion. A family.

A growing family!

Maddi and Ari had just had twins, so now they had three children. Max, who was almost the same age as Liselle, and Tomas and Sara.

They hadn't been able to come on this trip, due to the twins' imminent birth, but Permata had become a private special haven for both families.

And Isla'Rosa was developing at a rate of knots—thanks to her clever husband. Much to Ari's chagrin, it was fast becoming one of Europe's biggest hubs for software development, keeping young people from emigrating and drawing people who wanted to live and work in a Mediterranean climate from all over the world.

The people of Isla'Rosa adored Dax, their King Consort. And the peace pact between Santanger and Isla'Rosa was a solid and enduring thing. Healing generations of hurt and pain.

Dax came back, holding Liselle. He put her down and reached for Demi, and Laia handed him over. Their little boy made a sound, but promptly fell back to sleep on his father's shoulder.

Dax took Laia's hand, and in her other hand she held her daughter's.

'Home?'

Laia nodded.

He saw her emotion and he kissed her. It was an acknowledgement and a promise of so much more to come.

She smiled. 'Yes, let's go home.'

* * * * *

A
NINE-MONTH DEAL
WITH HER HUSBAND

JOSS WOOD

MILLS & BOON

PROLOGUE

Twelve years ago

'I'M SORRY TO disturb you, but Millie Magnúsdottir is here.'

Benedikt Jónsson looked up to see his late business partner's daughter charging into his office, every muscle in her body taut with tension.

Millie's dyed coal-black hair hung over her shoulders in two fat braids and her light green eyes were heavily rimmed with kohl. 'He's going to charge me with theft and if I get convicted I might end up with a permanent criminal record.'

He'd heard the news this morning from his irate in-house lawyer, who'd spent more time on Millie's escapades than any corporate lawyer should. According to Lars, the night before last, Millie had appropriated her father's Ferrari for a midnight joy ride with her friends.

He wished the teenager would stop looking for trouble. This month alone, she'd been photographed leaving three clubs three nights in a row in the early hours of the morning, carrying her two-inch heels. She'd 'forgotten' to pay for a gold lamé top at an exclusive boutique and was, supposedly, having an affair with a famous Danish drummer twenty years her senior.

Every press article mentioned she was the wayward, uncontrollable daughter of Magnús Gunnarsson, widower of Jacqui Piper, the founder of PR Reliance, the company half owned by Ben. Every time she hit the headlines, for all the wrong reasons, Millie generated bad press for the company and their competitors laughed, delighted. She was an unmanageable PR nightmare.

Ben told Millie to sit, but she ignored him, choosing to pace the area in front of his desk.

'Taking his Ferrari for a joyride was stupid, Millie.'

Why had she taken Magnús's brand-new car? Was she trying to push his buttons simply because that's what eighteen-year-old rebels did? And why was she here, talking to him about it? They'd little to do with each other. He was just her mum's business partner, a guy whom she'd met only a handful of times over the years. Before her death, Jacqui had kept her business and personal life separate.

'Sit down,' Benedikt told her, linking his hands across his stomach and leaning back in his chair. She heard the command in his voice, released an audible sigh and perched on the edge of a chair, a scared bird ready to take flight. Or peck.

'What do you want from *me*?' he asked. He could try to persuade Magnús from pressing charges, but didn't think it would help. Magnús loved to thwart him: he'd always resented his and Jacqui's close relationship. If Benedikt said something was white, Magnús would insist it was black. Dealing with him since Jacqui's death had been three years of hell. Worse than that, PR Reliance was simply ticking along.

And he was stuck with Millie's father for another seven years because Millie would only take control of her trust fund, and the half-share of PR Reliance she'd inherited, when she turned twenty-five. The thought of dealing with Magnús for another seven weeks, never mind seven years, made him feel ill.

Millie's eyes slammed into his and he saw the determination in hers, and desperation. He'd mourned Jacqui, but his grief was nothing compared to Millie losing her mum at fifteen. Her numerous scandals, each one worse than the last, were surely desperate cries for attention. He didn't know much about teenagers, but he suspected Millie was trying, first by acting out and then by rebelling, to get a reaction, good or bad, from her father.

Benedikt wished she wouldn't. It made his job ten times harder than it needed to be…

'I have a proposition for you,' Millie quietly stated.

This should be good. But whatever it was, he'd have to say no. He didn't make deals with teenagers who were barely adults. No matter how much maturity, determination and sense of purpose he saw in their eyes.

'I want to get married.'

Benedikt blinked, then frowned. She was eighteen, far too young for marriage.

Millie pushed her heavy fringe from her face with a black-tipped finger. 'You're wondering why I'm telling you this. Can I explain?'

Benedikt nodded, disconcerted by the direction of their conversation.

'Magnús is not my real dad,' Millie stated, looking down. Benedikt's attention sharpened even further. What was she talking about?

'Why do you think that?' he asked, keeping his tone even.

'Magnús let it slip during an explosive argument recently. He told me he's glad I don't carry his DNA because I'm a complete embarrassment.'

Beneath her pale foundation, he saw stripes under her eyes and a tension in her mouth no one her age should have.

'He wasn't supposed to tell me, he'd promised my mum he wouldn't, but I think he's relieved I know.'

Ben rubbed his jaw, not sure what to say or do, or how this related to her wish to get married.

'It explains why Magnús and I never got along,' Millie added.

He glanced at his monitor and wished he could get back to work. He didn't understand why she was talking to him about this. He ran the company, he wasn't her confessor.

'I wish I knew why she lied to me and why she never told me who my real dad was.'

The pain in Millie's eyes was tangible, a living, breathing thing, and Benedikt wanted to pull her into his arms, to give her the support she so badly needed. But he didn't know her well enough. She was his dead partner's kid—to her he was the guy who now ran her mum's business. They weren't friends—hell, they were barely more than acquaintances.

But Benedikt did wonder why some people—he and Millie, for instance—won the 'one bad parent' lottery.

'It's obvious Magnús wants me out of his life and I most certainly would like him out of mine,' Millie told him, sounding much older than her eighteen years.

Ben would like Magnús out of his life as well, but he didn't see any way of that happening any time soon. Sadly. Benedikt noticed the gleam in Millie's eyes and recognised it as the same one her mother had when she was hatching a plan…

Danger ahead.

'Magnús has a lover, she's been around for a few years,' Millie stated. 'I'm not sure if their affair started before or after Mum got sick, but he's besotted with her. Or besotted with her money.'

He was aware of Magnús's wealthy lover.

'He wants to move to Italy with her but, per Mum's will, he can't leave Iceland. He has to stick around and look after my interests until I turn twenty-five,' Millie continued. 'The only way he can leave Iceland, and be rid of me, is if he resigns as my trustee.'

'But that will only happen in seven years,' Benedikt pointed out.

Millie's gaze was steady on his face. 'Or it could happen sooner if I marry,' she stated. 'I looked at her will. If I marry, my husband can take over as my trustee.'

This was another of her crazy schemes and Benedikt felt ice invade his veins. Millie, Reykjavik's wild child marrying?

'That's a crazy idea, Millie!'

She shook her head. 'No, it would work! If I choose the right man and if I made a deal with him.'

He couldn't believe he was having this mad conversation, but Benedikt was intrigued enough by her mature tone and her direct gaze to roll his finger, suggesting she continue.

She leaned back, crossed her legs and folded her arms. 'I think a marriage of convenience would be the way to go and the marriage would be nothing more than a legal document. I want to go to the UK to study, get out of Magnús's life and start a new chapter. I know Magnús will be thrilled to be rid of me. He might even forget about charging me with theft of his Ferrari.'

'Those charges won't stick.' He hoped.

'Maybe not, but it'll be another scandal.'

'You've told me why marrying would work for you and for Magnús,' Benedikt stated, 'but what's in it for the guy who you plan on marrying? He's got a stake in this, too.'

He recognised her sly smile and narrowed his eyes at her. She'd borrowed the smile from her mum and it meant trouble. 'I know you have someone in mind, Millie,' he told her, feeling sorry for her victim.

She nodded. 'I do. He'd get rid of Magnús and be able to run this place without interference, from either Magnús or me. He'd be able to live his life exactly as he did before—we'd both pretend we weren't married and wouldn't impose any conditions on each other.'

Right. *He* was her intended victim. *Gut-punch.*

Millie continued her explanation. 'I want to do an art degree and become a jewellery designer. When I take control of the trust and the shares, in seven years, I'll sell you my half of the business. All you'd have to do was to stay married to me until then.'

By marrying Millie, he would gain complete control of PR Reliance and could implement everything Magnús had vetoed. He could expand, venture into new markets and take some risks he knew would pay off. He'd have freedom in his business life. And, if he was hearing Millie right, in his personal life as well. Since breaking his engagement to Margrét, Ben had had only puddle-shallow encounters with women. He had no intention of marrying, or making *any* type of commitment, to a woman again. Marrying Millie wouldn't cause a ripple in his personal life, but it would reinvigorate his business life.

Once he moved past the shock factor, Benedikt couldn't for the life of him see a flaw in her plan.

Apart from their age difference, it was a no-brainer. But if this was going to be a hands-off, business-only, don't-have-anything-to-do-with-each-other marriage, would the eight-year difference between them matter? She knew what she was walking into, what she wanted from this arrangement.

After allowing him to think for a few minutes, Millie arched her black eyebrows. 'Well? What do you think?'

Benedikt rubbed his jaw before speaking again. 'I have two conditions,' he replied.

Her eyes closed and she shook her head. 'Of course you do,' she muttered. 'I thought I covered all the bases. Why can't anything be simple?' She sighed. 'What is it?'

He allowed a small smile to touch his lips. 'One, you stop hitting the headlines. And, two, you allow me to run PR Reliance without any interference from you.'

'I have no interest in my mum's business, so I'll agree to that. But you've got to promise never to lie to me.'

He far preferred the truth, however hard it was, to dishonesty. The promise was easy to make.

Benedikt pulled a notepad towards him and picked up his fountain pen. It seemed they had a deal to make, a marriage to undertake.

He looked at Millie and nodded. 'Right, let's hammer out the details.'

CHAPTER ONE

Present day...

IN REYKJAVIK, outside the hotel she'd booked last week in the historical heart of the city, Millie left the taxi and icy air burned a path down her throat. Man, it was cold. And, at nearly three in the afternoon, daylight was fast disappearing. She smiled at the driver who'd parked directly outside the entrance and thanked him for collecting her from the airport before turning to thank the harried-looking porter pulling her case from the boot of the sedan.

It was about a hundred degrees below and she buried her nose in her cream scarf as she walked up the steps to the front door of the hotel, wishing she was wearing another four layers of clothing.

Despite only being outside for no more than a minute, she was mind-numbingly, toe-curlingly cold. She managed to stutter a greeting to the doormen and immediately headed for the freestanding fireplace in the centre of the impressive room. She held her hands to the warmth and her fingers started to tingle.

Man, she'd forgotten how far north Iceland was and how cold it could get. Life in London had made her soft.

After defrosting, she peeled her scarf from her neck and undid the buttons on her thigh-length coat. She wore tight jeans tucked into knee-high, stiletto-heeled leather boots and a cranberry-coloured jersey that skimmed her hips and ended at the top of her thighs. She brushed a hand over her long hair, which she'd pulled back into a low tail.

She could murder a cup of coffee…

Draping her coat and scarf over her arm, she looked around the small lobby and her eyebrows lifted. The hotel had more of a feel of a modern country house, with long, comfortable sofas and exceptional art on the walls. There was no reception desk and she wondered where to check in…

'Ms Piper?'

Millie greeted the tall, thin and extremely stressed man who'd addressed her. 'Hello.' She smiled at him and thought he could do with a half-bottle of homoeopathic stress drops.

'I'm surprised to see you here, Ms Piper.'

Piper looked at the name tag attached to his lapel—Stefán, General Manager. Why should he be surprised? She'd made a reservation and she'd arrived. That was the way hotels worked, wasn't it?

A young woman approached them at a fast clip and touched Stefán's arm. 'Sir? Will you come? *Now?*'

Stefán picked up the urgency in his colleague's voice. 'Ms Piper, will you excuse me?' He pointed to a couch behind her, facing the snowy street. 'I'll be right back, if you'll wait?'

Well, it wasn't as though she had a choice. Millie nodded and watched as he fast-walked across the lobby and disappeared behind a door. She noticed her suitcase standing next to a pot plant and grimaced. She hoped there wasn't a problem with her booking.

Now a lot warmer, Millie took off her coat and sat on the edge of the backless couch and looked at the huge Christmas tree in the corner, white fairy lights its only decoration. Christmas was just three weeks away, but she wasn't overly excited about the holiday.

Without a family, the holiday season was more of a trial than a celebration. Millie placed her chin on her fist and sighed. The last Christmas she truly enjoyed was when she was fourteen, the year before her mum died. She and her mum had decorated their Reykjavik house with greenery and fairy lights and made a wreath for the front door. They'd polished off many hot chocolates and belted out Christmas carols on the piano as snow covered the city. It had been a happy time, mostly because Magnús had been away for most of that December...

At fourteen, she'd believed her mum when Jacqui told her her dad was working, that he was in a different time zone and that's why he couldn't call her. That, despite being unemotional and distant, Magnús definitely loved her.

But she'd still wondered why Magnús never hugged her, why he'd never shown her a hint of the affection her friends' fathers gave them. Magnús didn't show any interest in her, or her life, and, despite her mum's reassurances, she genuinely believed, for the longest time, she was defective and unlovable.

That there was something wrong with her...

Losing her mum had rocked her world and, despite her thinking he couldn't be more distant or emotionally unavailable, Magnús retreated from her life in every way he could. She felt as though she was sharing the house with a stranger, someone who occasionally used the bedroom he shared with her mum.

She'd so desperately wanted his attention, good or bad, so she resolved to make him notice her. She started bunking school, acting out, dressing in weird and alternative clothing styles.

She picked fights and taunted him, wanting to see if she could penetrate his mask of cold disdain. It took him a few years, but his mask finally cracked when she'd taken his car that time. He'd lashed out, calling her a barnacle and a leech, someone he couldn't stand. He'd had to share Jacqui with her and he resented all the attention her mum gave her.

'But I'm your child, too!' she'd protested, feeling as though he'd gutted her with a sharp scalpel.

'You're not mine, thank God! I would hate to think such a useless, snivelling, pathetic creature carried any of my DNA!'

It was one sentence, twenty-one words, but after hearing and digesting them, Millie finally understood his nearly two decades of emotional uninterest. She'd been furious and so hurt but, because she was her mother's daughter, she'd had enough pride to come up with a solution to banish Magnús from her life. And, damn, it had worked well.

Her stepfather was now a distant memory, someone she tried not to think about. But Millie still didn't understand why her mum had lied to her for so long and why she died without telling her the truth. She and her mum had been so close and they'd shared everything. But she would never have known the truth if it weren't for Magnús losing his temper.

Millie couldn't help wondering who her real father was and why her mum had thought it so important to keep his identity a secret. Did he know about her? Did she look like him? Did she have any siblings?

She loved her mum, always would, but damn, sometimes she hated her for leaving her with so many unanswered questions. For leaving her to live with lies, for leaving *her*. Death, the ultimate form of abandonment.

Her mum's death, her secrets and lies and Magnús's uninterest in her, had coloured the rest of her life. Millie found it exceptionally difficult to trust anyone and, while she had friends, she wasn't close to anyone. Nobody knew that behind the semi-famous jewellery designer was a messed-up woman with massive trust and family issues.

There was only one person she trusted fully, only one man who'd never lied to her or let her down—her husband of twelve years. The one she'd travelled to Reykjavik, unannounced, to see.

Today would be their second meeting. He'd find this one as unexpected as the first and she hoped this meeting would go as well.

When she'd suggested she and Benedikt marry it was a shot-in-the-dark solution, but within a few days Benedikt had a lawyer draw up a prenup and that was it.

They'd hammered out another agreement on his notepad and, despite it not being a legal document, it carried the most weight. Millie easily recalled their terms…their union would be a marriage in name only and Benedikt would not exert any control over her, provided she stayed out of legal trouble and out of the headlines. As her husband and trustee, he had agreed she could use her trust fund to study what she wanted, where she wanted, provided she got a degree, *any* degree. And that he would entertain any other reasonable requests she made for money.

They would correspond via email and would live their own, very separate lives.

After she turned twenty-five, they would discuss divorce and Millie agreed to give Ben the first option to buy her shares in PR Reliance International, when he was ready to do so.

Seven years had come and gone, then ten. Magnús had passed on. She didn't go to his funeral and wasn't surprised when he left everything to a lover. And, after studying jewellery design, she'd become a sought-after jewellery designer. Another two years passed and, in name only, she'd been married to Benedikt for twelve years.

Now it was time for them to divorce...

Because, while she never wanted to be married in the usual sense of the word—she had too many trust issues to risk her heart—she *did* want a child. She wanted the close relationship she'd had with her mum with her own child, she wanted to regain the feeling of being part of a team, her and her mum's *it's us against us the world* feeling.

But she was also very tired of being alone. She wanted someone to share her life and a child was a much safer bet than a lover. She could pour her pent-up love into a child. To give it to a lover was far too dangerous.

She'd had relationships and some lasted longer than others. But when her partners started pushing for more, when they started using words like 'love' and 'commitment' and 'taking this to the next level', she always found a reason to call it quits.

Her and Benedikt's marriage was a marriage of convenience and she knew he'd had many, many affairs over the years. Their marriage was need-to-know information and nobody, to date, needed to know. And since the death of Magnús, only she and Benedikt knew they were hitched.

But everything would change, everything *needed* to change, if she brought a new life into the world.

Millie swiped her finger across the screen of her phone and the sperm bank website she'd been looking at earlier populated her screen.

She intended to make full use of technology and have a baby the modern way. Just in case something went wrong down the line, she'd had her eggs harvested and now all she needed was a sperm donor to create her own little family.

Millie was surprised at how many men featured on the sperm bank's database, and the range of diversity, and couldn't decide whom she wanted to be her baby's biological dad. Brains and athleticism were important to her, but, while she'd like him to be handsome, his looks weren't crucially important. She had to make a choice and the baby doctors would do their magic in a laboratory before placing the viable embryos back inside her.

The image of Benedikt flashed on the big screen of her brain and Millie frowned. What made her think of her handsome, but uncommunicative, husband in name only? On paper, he would make a great donor, he was super-smart, very athletic, and, because he'd grown PR Reliance into an international empire and made them both ridiculously rich, she knew he was ambitious and driven. But she didn't know any more about him than she did about the donors on the sperm bank website.

She glared at the screen. She wanted more, she needed the personality quirks of the donors. How would she know if she was choosing a man who was reticent and uncommunicative, narcissistic and selfish? How did she know if her baby's father was outgoing? Or sensitive? Or temperamental?

And that was why she was struggling, the reason she couldn't make a choice. She didn't much care about eye colour or height, but she did care whether her child was going to inherit its father's fatal flaws. Look, she wasn't perfect, she was emotionally closed down and she struggled to trust and make friends, but she tried to be kind, tried to be a good person.

Millie sighed. Even if she had a donor in mind, she wouldn't allow herself to become pregnant while she was still married to Benedikt, because it didn't seem, or feel, right. She wanted to leave the past, all of her past, full of lies, behind her. Her mum, the person she had loved the most and who had loved her, had lied to her and died without telling her the truth about her biological father. Magnús colluded in the lies because, Millie presumed, he'd loved her mum.

To her, love was twisted, tainted for ever by untruths and deceptions. Honesty was her highest value and she couldn't trust anyone to be completely honest with her. Love, a partnership and raising a child together required transparency and a level of trust impossible for her to reach, or believe in. No, it was better for her to raise a child alone. If she did this alone, she'd never be disappointed, hurt or lied to again.

It was a trifecta of self-protection.

That was why she was here, in Iceland after twelve years. Sending Benedikt an email with a blithe request for a divorce seemed like a cop-out. She felt she needed, at the very least, to have a face-to-face meeting with the man.

Millie looked up at the hotel manager's approach and stood. 'I'm sorry we were interrupted,' he said.

'Not a problem. Is there something wrong with my reservation?'

Stefán rubbed the tips of his fingers across his forehead. 'I take it you didn't get the email we sent yesterday?'

Millie wasn't about to explain she wasn't good at checking her personal emails. She'd skimmed through her mail yesterday, seen a message from the hotel and presumed it was a standard, looking-forward-to-seeing-you letter.

'Our correspondence strongly suggested that, unless it was an emergency, you postpone your trip. We have a blizzard on its way and your plane would've been one of the last to arrive. We have guests who can't leave and a dire shortage of rooms.'

'I was raised in this country, Stefán, blizzards are not that big a deal,' Millie said, as her heart sank to her toes.

'As someone raised here, you should know how the weather influences travel, especially in winter, and you should know how important it is to stay well informed.'

Millie felt like an errant schoolgirl being reprimanded by the headmaster, but Stefán wasn't wrong. She *did* know better and she should've checked on what was happening with the weather. But when she got to the airport, her flight was on time and she'd assumed all was well.

'This one is going to be one of the worst in two decades.' Stefán twisted his hands together. 'As per our email, we cancelled your reservation because you didn't confirm your arrival and we needed the room. We do not have a room for you.'

Dammit! Millie cursed.

'You said that you grew up here,' Stefán said, looking hopeful. 'I don't suppose you have anyone you can stay with?'

Yes, Benedikt. But also, no. She wasn't going to ask her husband/stranger whether she could ride out the storm with him. What if he had a lover living with him? Having his wife in the spare room would be, at best, problematic.

Aargh!

'I will try to find you accommodation, Ms Piper, but it might require you to share a room with another single female guest.'

Millie couldn't think of anything worse than having to be cooped up in a hotel room with a stranger. That sounded truly awful. 'I'll phone someone,' Millie told Stefán.

'Thank you,' Stefán replied. 'I will not start with my calls until I know whether or not you have been successful. I *do* hope you come right, Ms Piper.'

She did, too. She'd come to Iceland to ask her husband for a divorce, but now she'd have to ask Benedikt for help, too.

Blast!

She wouldn't get a place to stay, or a divorce, if she didn't call the man. Ignoring the nauseous feeling in her stomach, Millie did what she'd never had cause to before and placed a video call to Benedikt. He'd given Millie a mobile phone number the day they married and this was the first time she'd used it.

'Millie, are you all right?'

She blinked at the sound of his chocolate-over-gravel voice, which was deeper than most. His face in her tiny screen came in focus and she took in those still familiar features, that ruggedly angular face, his high cheekbones and sensual mouth. His eyes were a deep blue, tinged with violet, and she noticed flecks of grey hair within his blond hair. The creases at the edges of his eyes were deeper than before. Millie wondered where he'd picked up his tan and could easily imagine him on a windsurfer or a surfboard, sunlight and seawater on his broad shoulders and muscular arms.

Millie met his eyes. He looked older, hotter and even more inscrutable than he did twelve years ago. 'Hello, Benedikt. I'm glad this number still works.'

He lifted one shoulder, covered in what she could see was a very expensive designer shirt. The discreet logo on the pocket was a dead giveaway. He wore a perfectly knotted mint-green tie.

'Millie, again, are you all right?'

'I'm fine, why wouldn't I be?' she asked.

He released a sigh and sat back, his shoulders dropping. 'Forgive me for thinking that, the first time I get a phone call from my wife, something might be wrong.'

Fair point. Millie pushed her long fringe off her forehead and tucked it behind her ear. 'Sorry, I didn't think about that.'

She should tell him why she was calling, but she felt like an idiot. Benedikt would surely never ignore his emails and be caught out by an approaching blizzard. She decided to make small talk to build up her courage to ask him a favour. The first in twelve years...

'So, I'm going to be attending Star Shine's Gala Concert on the twenty-second. It'll take place at the Harpa Concert Hall.'

Every five years, the foundation her mum had established held a benefit concert to raise funds for the foundation and, as Jacqui's daughter, she was always invited to attend. She'd missed the last one due to flu and the one before that because she hadn't felt ready to return to Iceland. Bettina, her mum's best friend and the CEO of the foundation, would tolerate no excuses this year.

It was also the twenty-fifth anniversary of the establishment of the foundation and Bettina wanted Millie to do a tribute speech to her mum. The Gala Concert was one of the major social events of the decade and the idea of talking to the great and good of Europe made her quake in her boots.

'I thought I'd let you know,' Millie added, feeling like an idiot.

'The foundations' trustees will be glad to hear that,' Benedikt calmly replied. As one of the country's most celebrated business people, he would've been at the top of the list to receive an invitation to purchase a ticket to the much-anticipated Gala Concert. She knew he'd attended previous concerts and Millie wondered if he'd bring a partner to the event this time, although he hadn't before. Should she bring someone? But who? And why did she feel it was weird to take a date knowing her husband would be attending the same event?

He's not *your husband, Millie, he's the man you made a deal with. Stop being naive...*

The silence between them turned awkward and Millie cast about for something else to speak about. 'I was also wondering if you knew about a safety deposit box. I've had a letter to say it's come up for renewal, but I don't know anything about it,' Millie gabbled, trying to fill the silence between them.

Millie named the bank and Benedikt shook his head. 'I wasn't aware you had one.'

'Me neither, but it was opened around the time we married,' Millie explained.

His expression didn't change—he was so hard to read—but his eyes narrowed, just a fraction, and his left eyebrow raised a millimetre, maybe two. 'Not by me,' he stated.

Millie wrinkled her nose. 'I suppose Magnús must've opened it on my behalf. But I wonder what's in it?'

'It could be anything,' Benedikt said 'The only way to find out what's in it is to open it yourself. They won't allow anyone else to. So, you came back to Iceland to check a safety deposit box?' he asked, sounding sceptical.

Millie wished she'd made the trip for something so simple, but…*no.*

I need to start a new chapter of my life. I need to move on. I need to ask you for a divorce.

'Partly.'

'Isn't this a busy time for you with people buying jewellery for Christmas gifts?'

He wasn't wrong—a Millie Piper ring or pendant or bracelet made a perfect, but very pricey, Christmas gift. But her clients understood quality and artistry couldn't be rushed and they'd put in their orders months in advance to avoid disappointment.

'No, I'm done until the new year. Then I'll have to start working on an emerald and diamond choker for the wife of an American internet billionaire. He bought some emeralds when he was in Colombia—' She was rambling, dammit. Benedikt still made her feel off balance and gauche. Millie gave herself a mental slap. She wasn't eighteen any more, she was a grown woman with a successful business!

It didn't help that he was treating her as though they'd

spoken yesterday, as though her out-of-the-ether call wasn't in any way a surprise. Millie wanted to punch through his impenetrable façade and shake him.

I'm your wife, she wanted to scream, but that urge quickly faded.

She wasn't, not really. Not in any way it counted. She was just a woman he'd married so that they could both get Magnús out of their lives. She'd been lucky Benedikt agreed to marry her because she'd been on a fast track to self-destruction. While she'd thought up the scheme for them to marry, Benedikt had helped her step off the tracks and out of the way of an incoming train.

But he wouldn't have helped her if there hadn't been anything in it for him and she understood that. But why hadn't he asked for a divorce before now? When she had turned twenty-five, he handed her the control of her trust but agreed, when she asked him, to act as her financial adviser.

For a year she'd tried to follow his directions—buy this stock, sell that one, liquidate this account, open that one—but she'd made mistakes, costly mistakes. When Ben offered to take back the management of her investment portfolio, north of fifty million pounds, and her trust, she'd handed it back to him with a huge sigh of relief. He wasn't scared of all those zeros, but they petrified her.

But why did he do that for her? Why did he never ask to buy her out of the company, the international empire he'd grown and built? Why did he never ask for a divorce? Why didn't he cut ties with her years ago?

It wasn't as though they were friends—before their marriage they'd been barely more than acquaintances. That didn't change after she became his wife.

'Now that we've danced around a bush or two, are you going to tell me why you really called?' Benedikt asked.

Right. *That.*

'I'm in a bit of a pickle.' His gaze sharpened, but he didn't pepper her with questions, he simply lifted one thick eyebrow and waited. 'I'm actually in the city, I landed a little while ago.' She saw curiosity flick over his face and spoke before he could ask any questions. 'But I didn't read my email from the hotel and it turns out that there's an incoming blizzard and they are overbooked.'

'And you need a place to stay,' he blandly stated.

She pulled her bottom lip between her teeth. 'The manager said he would try to find me a room, but he looks as though he's about to have a panic attack. And I get the sense that, because I didn't read his don't-come-to-Iceland-because-a-blizzard-is-coming-and-you-didn't-confirm email, I'm way down on his list of priorities.'

'Why did you fly in now? The concert isn't for another two weeks. Why didn't you wait?' he asked.

That was a very good question. Maybe it was because, once she made up her mind, she needed to put her plan into action. Because if she didn't speak to him now, she might lose her nerve and not face him at all. Having a baby was her primary goal, but there were things she needed to do first. Getting a divorce was the first bullet point on her 'Steps to Falling Pregnant' list.

She couldn't explain any of that now, not in an increasingly crowded lobby and not over the phone. 'Can we talk about that when I see you? But, for now, can you suggest a place for me to stay?'

'I should be able to manage that.'

'At a hotel?' she asked, sounding hopeful.

'Mmm.'

Excellent. Staying wherever Benedikt stashed her would be a lot better than sharing a room with a stranger. Being one of the most influential business people in the country, Millie was pretty sure he would be able to find her a hotel room somewhere in the city. Hotel managers were always eager to do favours for someone who wielded as much power and financial clout as Benedikt did.

And, yes, a fancy room in an excellent hotel would cost her a lot of money, but she could afford it and she'd ride out the storm in comfort.

Millie released an audible sigh of relief and looked around the lobby to see Stefán looking at her. She gave him the thumbs up and he looked, momentarily, relieved. Then he turned back to talk to another guest and Millie knew he'd mentally crossed her off his to-do list and had moved on.

'Where are you?' Benedikt asked her.

Millie gave him the address of the hotel. 'Okay, stay put. I'll send my driver to pick you up. He'll know where to take you.'

Millie shook her head. 'That's not necessary, Benedikt, I can order a taxi.'

Benedikt just stared at her and Millie sighed. She should dig her heels and be a little more vociferous in her arguments but a) that stare was pretty damn intimidating and b) she knew he had numerous personal assistants to do his bidding. It wasn't as though he was going to personally run to her rescue—he'd send a minion to yank her out of her jam.

Millie nodded. 'Okay, thank you, I'll wait here for your driver. I appreciate your help. I'd also appreciate it if you could spare some time for us to meet. Obviously only when the blizzard is over and regular activities resume.'

'I'll be around,' Benedikt assured her. She saw a ghost of a smile touch his lips and his eyes lightened to the colour of a deep, dark sapphire. 'It'll be...*interesting* to see you again, Millie.'

She managed a small smile and disconnected the call. She was looking forward to seeing him. Madness, since she rarely thought of the man. He was still, as he'd always been, on the periphery of her life.

Her husband. Sort of.

CHAPTER TWO

DÉJÀ VU.

It felt like yesterday, but it had been twelve years since she last took this lift to Benedikt's office. She'd been eighteen years old and she'd been quaking in her boots. At nearly thirty, she wasn't quaking, but her stomach was definitely doing a number on her.

She looked at the tall man who'd followed her into the lift. When he walked into the hotel lobby earlier, he'd introduced himself as Einar Petersson, Benedikt's assistant. He had, he explained, instructions to take her to PR Reliance International Headquarters.

'Why did Benedikt ask you to bring me here?' Millie asked. Einar said he spoke little English, but Millie suspected he understood a lot more than he'd let on. She'd asked him the same question earlier and then, like now, he'd spread his hands out, looked blank and lifted his shoulders.

Oh, well, it wasn't as though she had somewhere else to go. She'd checked her weather app and the blizzard was supposed to start in a few hours. They were predicting very high winds—up to one hundred miles per hour in the north—and a massive snow dump, but the storm would only sweep in in a few hours. She had time to get to wherever Benedikt had arranged for her to go.

The lift doors opened and Einar guided her past an empty desk towards a long, wide office with floor-to-ceiling glass walls. She frowned and looked around. Extensive renovations had been done to the building. If she wasn't mistaken, the walls between Benedikt's office and the office Magnús had used had been knocked down to make a light and airy space with a huge desk and a seating area.

Einar opened the glass door and ushered her inside. He gestured for her to take a seat on one of the couches, but she crossed the room to the floor-to-ceiling windows. A wooden terrace ran the length of the room and lights flickered from a glass and steel building to the left. She recognised it as being the famous Harpa Concert Hall. It was a spectacular view at night, lights danced across the sea, but Millie knew Benedikt's office views would be equally spectacular in daylight.

Millie ran her fingers along the back of a sleek, Scandinavian-inspired couch. A massive flat-screen TV dominated another wall and there was a telescope in the corner, its nose pointing at the sky.

She wondered if Ben could see the Northern Lights from here. As a child, she remembered taking a trip with her mum north and they'd stayed in a cabin in the woods somewhere. They'd spent four nights sitting around a fire, bundled up in their all-weather gear, watching the sky flicker with ribbons of green and yellow light. She'd been entranced by the depth of colour and never forgot the experience.

Her mum had promised another trip, but time passed and, before they knew it, their time together was over. Millie was determined to see them again—spent a lot of time watching videos on YouTube—and she wanted to see the full light show instead of the trailer she'd witnessed as a kid.

Einar walked over to a trolley in the corner of the room and Millie saw it held coffee cups and a modern, silver, coffee jug. The smell of excellent coffee drifted over to her and she wondered where Benedikt was. Judging by all the empty offices she'd passed, all his staff had been sent home already.

As Einar walked over to her, carrying a cup of coffee, she placed a hand on her stomach, hoping to still the butterflies flapping their wings renting space in there. She was nervous about meeting Benedikt and she shouldn't be. He was nothing more than a man with whom she'd struck a deal a lifetime ago.

A marriage deal, but still a deal.

It was time to end it, to move on to the next chapter in her life. She'd have a family, even if it was one she had to make herself. She was so sick of living alone and rattling around her empty, quiet flat. She wanted a baby to love, someone who couldn't be taken from her. She wanted hugs and laughter, someone to cuddle, to fill up her empty apartment and break the long silences.

She wasn't a child any more, she was nearly thirty, for goodness sake! She'd done what she thought she should: she'd been to university, partied at Glastonbury and Burning Man, got her degree and established a career where she could make good money and set her own hours. She was financially secure and it was time to do something she'd been thinking about for years…

But as much as she wanted a child, as lonely as she was, she couldn't trust a man to share her life and family with. When you realised your mum, the person you thought loved you more than life itself, had lied to you and kept you in the dark, it made trusting anyone else impossible.

That, and she'd witnessed Magnús's possessive streak. He'd wanted her mum all to himself, all the time. He hated Jacq's independent streak and resented Millie being in her mum's life. Magnús's love was tainted by a slick, destructive layer of control, sprinkled with obsession.

She'd never let that happen to her and wasn't prepared to take the chance on loving someone who might end up trying to change or cage her. She didn't want her baby to have to live with, or witness, anything similar.

Millie heard the sound of a throat clearing, blinked and looked at the coffee cup Einar held out to her. She took it with a shaking hand and immediately lifted the cup to her lips, desperate for a jolt of the hot liquid, for a hit of caffeine. Being back in Iceland, the first time in for ever, had her feeling more emotional and off balance than she'd expected.

She had to pull herself together before she met Benedikt.

'Hello, Millie.'

Millie spun around, saw his tall frame standing at the door and tried to replace the cup on its saucer. She missed by a mile and coffee spilt on to the pale, hardwood floors and splattered over her boots.

Damn. She'd really been looking forward to that cup of coffee.

As his assistant wiped up coffee, Ben looked at Millie, taking in her similarities, cataloguing the differences. The black, Goth-inspired hair was gone and so was the thick makeup she wore back then. She'd pulled her hair, as sleek as an otter's coat and roughly the same colour, into a sleek tail and her makeup, if she wore any, was understated. Dark eyelashes and gently arched eyebrows framed her clear, light green eyes. Once too skinny, she'd filled out and his mouth watered as he took in her gentle curves. Put simply, she was gorgeous.

'Hi, Benedikt,' she murmured, her hand on her throat.

The last person he'd expected to see today, or see any time soon, was Millie. He'd been preparing to leave his office when her call came in—he'd already sent everyone but Einar home. That she was in his city shocked him and he was insanely curious as to why she wanted to meet.

She'd never expressed any interest in the company and he made all the decisions concerning their now jointly owned business. They communicated via infrequent emails.

They'd been legally married for more than a decade, but he knew little about her and her life.

So why was she here?

Ben forced his feet to move and hoped his normal implacable mask was in place as he walked over to her. He took her elegant hand in his, felt the tingle of attraction skitter over his hand and up his arm, and bent his head to kiss her cheek. She smelled of wildflowers and something deeper, darker, sexier.

'Hello, M...'

Hell! Her name wouldn't move over his tongue. Shock held him rigid and his grip on her hand tightened. Was he about to stutter? *Now?* And after so long? It had been years since he'd struggled with his speech, but this woman—his *wife*—had his words catching in his throat.

He tried to stop the slide into the past, to push away the unrelenting memories of being a child, cursed with shyness and a terrible stutter, raised to believe he was a disappointment, frequently told his profound stutter was something he could overcome if he worked hard enough and wasn't ineffective and weak. His uninterested, nuclear engineer mother also thought mocking and denigrating him for his affliction would cure him of it sooner.

It hadn't.

He'd eventually, with no help from her, learned how to converse normally. He thought he had his stutter under complete control until a year before Jacq's death. While trying to make a toast to his then bride-to-be at his engagement party, it had roared back into his life. His fiancé hadn't been impressed when he walked away from the podium after two sentences and ripped into him for not telling her he had a 'disability'.

That he'd met her at a business conference where he was the keynote speaker and hadn't stuttered once during his ninety-minute presentation, or since that day, went straight over her head. Accepting that his stutter only appeared when he felt emotional, he quickly found the solution: if he avoided emotion, his stutter would never raise its ugly head again. So far, his theory had proven true.

He and Millie weren't emotionally connected, so why did he stumble?

Recalling his training, and those hard, endless lessons, he took a deep breath and kissed Millie's other cheek to buy himself some time. He cleared his throat to gain another few moments of calm before he spoke. 'Hello, Millie. You're looking—'

Her eyebrows lifted. 'Older?'

He wanted to tell her she looked fantastic, that he hadn't expected her to pack such a punch. He settled for telling her she looked lovely. The girl he remembered had amused him and he'd admired her courage, but this woman had his knees melting and his heart thumping. He'd always mocked the idea of having butterflies in his stomach—it was such a asinine notion!—but his were about to take flight. Ben felt sweat pooling at the base of his spine and he swallowed as his eyes drifted over her body, taking in her full breasts, long legs and round hips.

His wife packed a hell of a sexual punch.

Ben stepped back and looked at Einar, who'd crossed to the other side of his office to give them some privacy. 'Would you please pour Ms Piper another coffee, Einar? Then you can go home.'

Einar nodded. 'Certainly.'

Einar did as he asked and, after reminding him that the weather was closing in and he shouldn't dawdle, left him and Millie alone.

Ben checked his watch. He had to leave the office within the hour, no longer. That would give him enough time to get home before conditions drastically deteriorated. Ben walked to the drinks trolley in the far corner of the room to pour himself a whisky, which he threw back. He lifted the bottle and nodded his approval. The whisky was part of a limited run from a distillery in Speyside. Fantastically expensive, but exceptional. It was technically too early to drink, but it wasn't every day his wife in name only made an unexpected appearance.

'May I have one of those?'

He nodded, poured a decent measure into her glass and carried the glass over to her. He pushed the heavy tumbler into her hand and his fingers brushed hers, a touch as light as a feather and as hot and fast as an electrical shock. Power ran up his hand, through his arm, and smacked into his heart. His gaze connected with hers and found cool green lightning in her eyes. Her chin lifted, just a little, and he noticed the flush on her cheeks, the tick in her jaw.

He was old enough, experienced enough, to recognise their mutual attraction and the urge to drop his head was overwhelming.

Her scent swirled around him and he lowered his head just a fraction, the distance between their lips lessening. The air between them tasted of coffee and whisky. He was about to kiss Millie…

He was…

About to…

Kiss Millie.

The thought landed, his eyes flew open and he jerked up, stepped back and rubbed the back of his neck, utterly disconcerted at their instant, intense attraction.

This was Millie. His *wife*.

He pulled away, took a step back and pushed an agitated hand through his hair. Needing time, he picked up his phone, pretended to check for messages and tried to regulate his over-excited heart. Stupid thing. Its job was to pump blood, nothing else.

'I like the changes you made to your office,' Millie stated, after sitting on his couch and crossing one long leg over the other.

Thank God for the change of subject.

'When I bought the building, I refurbished the entire place,' Ben replied, keeping his eyes on his phone, needing a little time to take her in. She was everything, and more than, he'd thought she'd be. The wild child was gone, and she'd come a long way in twelve years.

He knew a little about her…she'd attained a degree in art history, was a jewellery designer and owned and lived in an apartment in Notting Hill. He sent her company statements, which she never queried, and he paid her share of the profits into a bank account she provided. They weren't emotionally connected and there was never anything more between them than a piece of paper and a legal agreement.

She'd married him to avoid a jail sentence and take control of her life, he'd married her to take control of the business he loved, and they both got Magnús out of their lives permanently.

Ben sipped his whisky and felt the welcome burn in his throat. Millie drank hers and looked out the window, seemingly entranced by the view. He eyed her profile—which was lovely—and looked for something to say. *How was your flight?* seemed trite, *Welcome to Reykjavik* even more so.

He sighed. In a work environment, talking was never an issue and he was suave enough, unemotional enough, to talk a woman into bed. But when someone meant something to him—and as his wife and business partner and as Jacqui's daughter, Millie did, just a little—he found making small talk difficult. Keeping tabs on his stutter harder.

That she'd morphed from a girl who'd worn nothing but black as a teenager into one of the most beautiful, self-possessed, and stylish women he'd encountered in a long time didn't help at all. If she was just another woman he wanted, his words wouldn't stick in his throat. But she wasn't. And wanting Millie in all the ways he shouldn't rocked him to his core.

For the first ten years of his life, he could barely hold a conversation, and when he found someone with the patience to listen to what he had to say, they were both exhausted at the end of their discourse. Picking out words between the stutters was hard work for everyone. It was easier not to talk at all; if he kept silent then he didn't receive as many pitying glances and rolled eyes.

Memories, unbidden and unwelcome, rolled over him. At thirteen and already struggling to fit in at his local school, his mother, who wholly believed in the 'if you put your mind to it, you can achieve it' school of thought, decided that boarding school would *sort him out*.

If he thought he'd been bullied and teased before, it was nothing to what he endured at one of the best boys' schools in the country. If he tried to speak, he was bullied. If he didn't, he was bullied even more. He was the ultimate easy target and his frantic text messages and emails to his mum—he was far too upset to try to get the words out on a call—begging her to pull him out of school went unheeded. Four months into what, for him, was hell on earth, he knew nobody was riding in to save him and he was on his own.

He'd been on the point of running away when his English teacher stepped in and roped in the school's counsellor. She referred him to a speech therapist, who helped him get the worst of his stuttering under control. Then he signed up for a university trial, working with a language professor. Using his innovative techniques, Ben's stutter all but disappeared. The bullying died down when his stuttering did and his sudden growth spurt at fifteen also helped. Running and skiing made him fast and strong and he was able to fight back, which made him less of a target. He finally made friends and then girls also started paying him attention.

He learned, quite quickly, that females really did go for the strong and silent type.

As he got older, grew stronger, and more confident,

his mother's once-powerful intellect started to diminish. As he gained knowledge, at school and university, his mum lost hers and the once sharp, cutting and undeniably charismatic woman grew confused, a victim of early-onset Alzheimer's. Her condition deteriorated rapidly and, in his last year of university, Ben made the hard decision to put his mother into a residential home. She'd screamed, insulted him and called him a million names. As her brain withered, she lost all her filters and informed him she should've had the abortion, she'd never wanted him, and that embarrassing stutter of his was a constant source of humiliation.

Six months later she passed away, the day after he graduated from university.

Wanting to get out of London, he'd applied for a job at PR Reliance in Reykjavik and was pulled under Jacqui's wing. He not only found her knowledgeable, and easy to talk to, but in her he found the older sister and best friend he'd so desperately needed.

She'd been the only person he talked to about his struggles to communicate and, with her encouragement, he started dating, had a few relationships and then fell in love. When Margrét tore into him at their engagement party, yelling at him for embarrassing her in front of her family and friends, it was Jacqui who'd steered him out of the room.

Jacqui didn't agree with his decision to avoid love and relationships, she believed being emotional required mental strength and bravery. Ben didn't often disagree with Jacqui, but he did about that. Emotion was a weakness and one he wouldn't tolerate.

It was highly problematic that Jacqui's daughter made his words—temporarily, he hoped—stick in his throat.

And that wasn't, in any way, acceptable. Theirs was a legal arrangement, nothing more or less. Business.

Get it together, Jónsson.

He sat on the chair opposite the couch, leaned back, hitched his suit pants up and placed his ankle on his opposite knee. Ben wanted to see her in a business light, but the impulse to push the coffee table out of the way, pull her band from her hair and lower his mouth and body to hers was unbelievably strong.

He wanted to know how she tasted, whether the skin where her neck and jaw met was as soft as it looked. He wanted her hands sliding down his stomach, over his hip, her lips on his jaw, his neck, his hipbone…*lower.* He wanted to pull her jersey up her body and cover her full breast with his hands, trace her curves, kiss her hip, her lower back, between her legs…

He *wanted* her. With a ferocity that rocked him. Women were great, he liked them—they were smart and creative and intuitive—and he enjoyed them in bed and out. But he had never felt the overwhelming need to discover, to explore, as he did with Millie.

Annoyed with himself, Ben took a deep breath and forced himself to think about business. Why was she affecting him like this? What was it about her that made him question his control over his tongue? Women didn't do this to him, he didn't *allow* it.

'So, why are you in Reykjavik, Millie? On the phone you said you needed to talk…what about?'

Ben noticed the tension in her neck and how her spine straightened. A knot formed in his stomach and he knew, without her needing to say anything, what she was about to say.

He'd been expecting this conversation for years. 'You want a divorce, don't you?' he stated.

Her eyes slammed into his. 'How did you know?'

'It wasn't hard to work out, Millie. You've never asked for a face-to-face meeting before, we always correspond via email. There is only one thing you could want from me that would require a face-to-face meeting and that's a request to end our marriage.'

She nodded before slowly placing her glass on the coffee table. He noticed her trembling fingers. 'It's been a long time, Ben, and I think it's time.'

'I'm perfectly happy with the way things are,' he told her.

'Don't you want...' she hesitated '...more?'

'More what?'

'More than a convenient marriage! What about being in a loving relationship, having kids, establishing a family?'

He had no intention of doing any of the above. He linked his hands across his stomach and wished they were on her. 'I've never wanted to get married—'

Okay, that was a lie, he had wanted to once, but he'd learned the hard way that the people you loved could hurt you the most. He wouldn't love again. It was very simple.

'I have affairs, but I don't get involved. I have never had the desire to put a ring on anybody else's finger.'

Not quite a lie, but not quite the truth either.

A marriage of convenience to Millie suited him perfectly. They hadn't put any restrictions on what they could do or who they could be with. They were both free to take lovers and had done so. They didn't report to each other or even kept each other updated. So the only reason Millie could want a divorce after so long was that

she wanted more than what she had right now. A proper, committed relationship, perhaps even a proper marriage.

Could he blame her for that? Of course not, she deserved to be loved, deserved to have a man adore her. He couldn't be that man for her, not now and not ever. He could never be that man for anyone. And he would never risk getting so close to a person again—being emotionally sliced and diced by his mum, then his fiancé, was more than enough.

He tried to smile, but found it incredibly hard. When he spoke, he didn't achieve the lightness he was aiming for. 'So who's the lucky guy?' he asked.

Millie looked at him, her eyebrows pulling down. 'What?'

At the thought of another man kissing her, wrapping his arms around her slight body, doing all the things he wanted to do, Ben's gut twisted. The whisky he'd swallowed sloshed in his stomach and he felt seasick.

Nobody affected him like this.

It had to be the shock of seeing Millie all grown up, her now being a woman and not a girl. That's *all* it could be. All he'd allow it to be. Anything else was impossible. Yes, maybe he was attracted to her, she was lovely—who wouldn't be?—but he was old enough to know he didn't need to act on it. In fact, it would be far more sensible not to. Less complicated. Smarter.

'I'm not seeing anyone, Ben,' Millie told him.

He frowned and her words sank into his jittery brain. 'Then what's the problem? Why do you want things to change?'

Millie stood and walked over to the glass doors that led on to the balcony and watched fat snowflakes fall out of

the sky. They were running out of time, the blizzard was roaring in, but he stayed where he was and watched her.

Millie placed her forehead against the cool glass, her shoulders rose and fell and she released a long sigh. Her breath put condensation on the window and she dragged a finger through the wet patch. When she turned, he saw the frustration in her eyes and the tilt of her chin implied she could be stubborn. Like mother, like daughter.

You don't get apples from orange trees, Jónsson.

She managed a self-deprecating smile. 'Aren't you sick of me? Aren't I a millstone around your neck? I'm happy to sell you my stake in the company. I'm a grown woman and I could find someone else to act as the trust's financial adviser.'

'I don't have the money to buy out your stake right now, not without finding investors and taking out loans with crippling interest rates, and it's not top of my list of priorities. And you've been able to look after everything for many years now, Millie, and I've never doubted your ability to do so. You could manage your own money—'

'But then I'd have to learn about the stock market, amortisation, capital gains and the difference between a hedge fund and a mutual fund.' She shuddered. 'I don't understand any of it.'

'You don't want to understand because it bores you.'

'It really does. You're so much better at investments and things. And you said you didn't mind,' she muttered.

'I don't mind,' he pointed out. 'It takes me minimal time and it's something I'm still happy to do.'

Her trust was incredibly healthy, partly because he made the same sound decisions for her as he did for himself, but mostly because she seldom pulled money from its overflowing coffers. She'd only taken money to buy her Notting Hill apartment and her car, purchases he'd approved of. She didn't need his approval, but he admired her willingness to support herself and establish a career without using her inheritance as a cushion.

Being a workaholic himself, he appreciated hard work.

Ben climbed to his feet and went to stand beside her. He pushed his shoulder into the glass and looked down at her bent head. 'If you want a divorce, Millie, that's fine. It's not as though our arrangement was supposed to last for ever. And I would be happy to stay on as your financial adviser if that's what you wanted me to do.'

Her gorgeous green eyes, the colour of green grapes, met his. 'You would?'

'Sure.'

He wanted to touch her, to stroke his thumb over her lower lip, across her cheekbone, down the cords of her lovely, long neck. He jammed his hands into his suit pants to stop himself from doing something so idiotic.

'I just want to know *why*, Millie,' he said. He wasn't good with unanswered questions.

She managed a smile, just a small one. 'My mum always said that you were tenacious and that you never gave up. I guess that's how you expanded the business so quickly and came to be one of Europe's best business people.'

'So what's the real reason you want a divorce, Millie?'

She sighed before looking him in the eye. 'I want a baby. And I didn't think it's fair to have one while still being married to you.'

CHAPTER THREE

MILLIE HELD HER breath while Benedikt processed her words. While he did have an inscrutable face, his eyes were a different story. A lighter blue meant he was amused, darker meant he was either angry or turned on and lightning-tinged purple indicated he was shocked. And, yes, a lightning storm was happening in his eyes right now.

'You want a baby?' he asked, his voice holding the slightest hint of a croak.

'I'm not getting any younger, Benedikt,' she told him. But more than that, she was very tired of being on her own, of having no one to love. And loving a baby was the safest option she could think of.

'You are a few months off your thirtieth birthday, you're not about to qualify for an old person's pension,' he snapped. 'I'm thirty-eight! What's your age got to do with any of this?'

'Apparently, eighteen is the best time, physiologically, for a woman to have a child. And, from her mid-thirties, a woman is thought to be a geriatric mother.'

'That's ridiculous,' he snapped.

'That's science,' she retorted. She lifted her hand, her palm facing him. 'We're getting off track… I've always wanted a baby and I think it's the right time to have one.

My business is established, I work from home and I make my own hours. I can afford to hire help and, most importantly, I think I'm mentally ready to invite a little human into my life.'

Sometimes her dreams about holding her baby felt so real, she could smell his sweet smell, hear his cry and feel his warm little body snuggled into her arm. Millie felt the familiar tug in her womb and nodded. Yes, she wanted her little boy...

Benedikt rubbed the back of his neck before pulling down the knot of his tie. He opened the top button to his shirt and pulled the tie over his head, still knotted, and jammed it into the inside pocket of his suit jacket, which he then yanked off and tossed over the back of the couch.

Millie watched as he rolled up the sleeves of his shirt, marvelling at strong forearms covered in blond hair. When he was done, he rolled his shoulders and tipped his head up to look at the ceiling.

'So you want a child.'

'I do,' Millie told him. 'But I don't think I should be married when I have one.'

Benedikt sat on the back of the low couch and stretched out his long legs. 'You told me that you don't have a partner, so how are you going to "have" one, Millie?'

She sent an anxious glance towards his window and grimaced. 'Shouldn't we be going? There's a storm coming,' she reminded him.

He glanced at his limited edition Patek Philippe watch. 'We still have some time before we need to leave. I don't live that far away and it will only take me twenty minutes, even in this weather, to get home.'

'Yes, but you have to drop me off first,' Millie told

him. When he didn't say anything, she narrowed her eyes. Oh, no. *No, no, no.*

'I'm not staying with you, Jónsson,' she told him.

Uh-uh, no way.

'Einar made some calls and he couldn't get you a hotel room at such late notice. And it made no sense to keep calling when I have a perfectly good guest suite.'

A guest suite was fine for one night, but not if they were housebound because of the weather!

'It's a big house, Millie,' Ben told her. 'It has a gym and sauna and a library. We won't be tripping over each other.'

'We don't know each other!' Millie wailed. She didn't want to spend a couple of days cooped up with a man to whom she was intensely attracted.

'We're married,' Ben calmly pointed out.

Back then he was an adult and she'd been a young woman, looking to spread her wings and leave the city. They had been miles apart, mentally and socially. Twelve years later, the gap between them had narrowed substantially. He was hot and sexy and she hadn't been this attracted to a man in years. If ever.

She'd wanted him to kiss her earlier. Had been about to lift on to her toes to meet his mouth when he'd pulled back. Disappointment and frustration rolled over her, hot and sour. Honestly, had she left her brain and self-control back in London? And how was she supposed to share a house with a man she desperately wanted to see naked? Nope, not happening. She needed a hotel room, a room in an Airbnb, a stable or a caravan. Anything.

'I can't—'

'You'll have to because there's nowhere else for you to go,' Ben crisply told her and she knew she'd lost the argument. She had to be sensible and take whatever accommodation was on offer. She was out of choices.

'Let's get back to *how* you plan on getting pregnant.'

Why was he hung up on that? Why was that an issue and why did it concern him? But she wasn't ashamed of wanting a family, nor was she ashamed of her plan of how to fall pregnant. She wanted a family, she was so sick of being alone. 'I'm going to choose a sperm donor and be artificially inseminated, Benedikt.'

He pulled a face and Millie threw up her hands. 'Well, what other choice do I have? To go pub or club trawling at the right time of the month, find a guy I like the look of and have a one-night stand, crossing my fingers that he isn't a psycho?'

'That wouldn't be wise,' Benedikt stated.

'Of course not,' Millie retorted, unsure of why she was discussing this with him. They might be married, but they *weren't* friends. 'That's why I'm going to choose what I hope will be a nice man from a website that gives me statistics about his medical history and IQ and looks and genes. And pray he's a decent human being!'

Benedikt's eyes clashed with hers and Millie wondered what he was thinking, trying to ignore what *she* was thinking: he would make the most delicious father himself. He was tall, athletic, smart as a whip and not a psycho. He was just a hardworking, driven billionaire currently married to her. There was no way he'd consider...

You're being ridiculous, Millie! You're asking for a divorce so that you can cut the strings with this man, and asking him to give you his biological matter would be like using a ship's rope to bind you together.

She was just being fanciful, feeling a little disconcerted and off balance about being back in Reykjavik—the place held so many good and bad memories. Memories of her lovely mum and her awful dad…*stepdad*.

Meeting Benedikt again…

Flip, how she wished he'd grown plump and started to go bald, was in a relationship himself or was too busy to see her. If she'd managed to avoid him, then she wouldn't be feeling all hot and bothered, tingly and weird. Yes, Benedikt made her feel shaky and off her game.

'So, what's the next step?' she asked, placing her open palms on the glass behind her back.

'I drive you back to my place and settle you into my guest suite.'

'I meant with us getting a divorce, Benedikt. Shall we see a lawyer together, get our own? I'm not going to claim anything from you…' She couldn't—they'd signed a prenup and their individual assets were protected. Their divorce should be a quick and easy process.

Benedikt looked, surprisingly, a little disconcerted. He always seemed so together, so unshockable—he'd barely blinked at her offer of marriage—and she hadn't thought he could be caught off guard. 'Uh… I… I'm not sure. I need to look into it.'

He paused, hauled in some air and paused again. He was a confident and super-capable businessman, maybe he had a thing about picking and choosing the right words. 'I can set up a meeting with my lawyer and he can advise us on how to go forward,' he stated. 'He's also my cousin and closest friend. Olivier is one of the best lawyers in the country.'

Of course he was—a man in Benedikt's position wouldn't have anyone but the best. 'Could we meet tomorrow?' Millie asked. 'I fly tomorrow afternoon.' Then she remembered the storm. 'I *was* flying tomorrow afternoon.'

'I'll contact Olivier now,' he said. Benedikt picked up his phone and typed in a super-fast message.

'Olivier is working from home and he's suggested a video call. We can talk about legalities when we get back to my place. He's annoyed because he wanted to meet you in person.'

'Why?' Millie asked, confused.

'Because he's been your trust's lawyer for over eight years, Millie.'

Oh, right. *Olafson.* She'd seen correspondence from his law offices many times over the years. He'd answered many of her legal questions and she wanted to meet him, too. 'Maybe we could all have lunch when I come back on the twenty-second.'

'I'm not going to be in the country, I'm flying to St Barth's that day for an old friend's stag weekend,' Benedikt told her. Oh. Well, that answered the question about whether he'd be attending the gala concert or not.

'We'll video call him when we get home,' Benedikt said, standing up. 'We do need to get going, I do not want to be driving when the storm hits.'

She was going home with him and they would be alone.

Millie picked up her bag, feeling tired, out of her depth and emotionally drained. She looked around. 'I don't know where my luggage is, Benedikt,' she told him.

'For goodness sake, call me Ben,' he told her, gesturing for her to leave his office in front of him. He flipped off some light switches. 'And Einar transferred your luggage to my car.'

Millie followed Ben to the lifts and stepped into one

that was empty. In the confined space, she inhaled Ben's cologne, a fresh scent that made her want to bury her nose in his throat, and lick her way across his collarbone.

Once more she was bombarded with thoughts of how Ben would look naked, whether that sensual mouth delivered wicked kisses and what it would feel like to have his broad, masculine hands moving over her skin. She hadn't felt this attracted to a man in...ages. Truthfully, she'd never felt this much this quickly. Nobody ever had her mentally undressing him, thinking about his mouth and his hands...

She wanted him and she *so* didn't want to want her husband. And she could never, ever let him suspect she was attracted to him.

This marriage of convenience was now very inconvenient indeed!

Ben's car was a four-wheel drive Range Rover with all the bells, whistles and, best of all, heated seats. The wind had picked up and it was snowing quite hard but, because she knew Ben had been driving in extreme conditions for twenty-plus years, Millie settled back in her seat.

As they drove through Reykjavik she noticed the exquisite shops, decorated for Christmas, and an abundance of white fairy lights. She had hoped to take a tour of Reykjavik to see the city decorated with its Christmas lights, but she didn't know if she'd manage it this trip. Twelve years ago, she'd felt like a local, now she was a little better than a tourist.

Millie looked at Ben behind the wheel and took in his strong profile. He'd draped his wrist over the steering wheel and she'd felt a buzz of lust between her legs. She'd been in Iceland for just a few hours and spent a lot of that time thinking about his hands and how they would feel on her bare skin.

She'd spent almost as much time imagining his mouth, how he would taste…how amazing he would look naked. He had an athlete's build, tall, rangy and muscled, and she suspected that a few of his muscles had muscles of their own.

They stopped at a traffic light and Ben reached across her legs to open the glove compartment, his hand brushing her knee and her thigh. He murmured a quick apology as he pulled out a phone charger, the side of his hand skimming over the top of her hand.

He plugged his charger in and Millie noticed a muscle ticking in the side of his jaw. The atmosphere in the car turned heavy and sultry, wickedly intense. He looked at her and they exchanged another of those I-can't-believe-how-much-I-want-you glances.

Then the traffic light changed to green, Ben hit the button to let in a gust of fresh, snow-tinged air and the moment passed. It was, she supposed, a viable alternative to a cold shower.

Her unexpected attraction to him was both tiresome and problematic. Millie wiggled in her seat and slipped out of her coat. She'd never before thought of Ben in terms of sex or being stripped of his clothes. Up until yesterday, he'd been the name at the end of infrequent email messages.

Most days, and for most of their marriage, she rarely thought of him and she never, not once, found her marriage to him any sort of handbrake. The terms of their engagement were clear: it was a business deal and their lives were never, in any way, to be impacted by it. They both had the freedom to see other people, sleep with other people, and do what they wanted when they wanted.

She had no idea how many lovers Ben had had—she'd seen the occasional picture of him with some socialite or celebrity at fancy functions over the years—but she knew he'd been anything but a monk. Neither had she been a nun. She'd had two relationships at university, neither of which panned out—she wouldn't let them—and another two lovers since then.

The thing was, while she could never see herself getting married and settling down—if she couldn't trust her mum, the person she loved the most and whom she always believed loved her, to tell her the truth about her biological father, how could she trust anyone? Ever? And love and trust went hand in hand. Neither was she cut out for casual sex and random affairs. They were fine for a lot of women, but sharing her body was an intimate act and sex with a stranger made her feel a little ick.

So she was stuck in no man's land. Because she didn't like hurting guys and didn't like to lead them on, she always laid her cards on the table. If she liked a guy enough after a couple of months of dating, she made it clear she wasn't interested in a long-term relationship. Some stuck around, mostly because they thought they could change her mind, but most didn't. She kept a close eye on the ones who stayed. If she thought their feelings for her were deepening, she called it quits.

But she'd never had such an intense reaction to a man, ever. Something about Benedikt called to her and she was both mentally and physically curious. She wanted to know why he'd stayed married to her for so long, why he was so anti settling down, why he was such a lone wolf. She wanted to know his likes and dislikes, what made him laugh, and the things that caused him to feel mad, sad and frustrated. But most of all, she wanted to know how good he was in bed.

She thought he'd be excellent, even brilliant. Possibly, *probably*, mind-blowing.

Millie looked out the window and told herself to get a grip. She was in the country for, at most, the next thirty-six to forty-eight hours and nothing could, or would, happen. They'd get divorced, pretty quickly because they'd been separated for ever and because it was something they both wanted. They weren't going to fight over assets or money or kids and, in a couple of months, she'd be free of her husband on paper, the man she married but didn't know.

In January, she'd make a concerted effort to wrap her head around a sperm donor. She'd find somebody nice, smart and, hopefully, sexy. And in a year or two, she'd go back to the same donor to try for a sibling for her toddler. She'd been an only child and hated it, and desperately wished she had someone who knew her and her backstory, someone to whom she could talk about her parents and the past.

Millie crossed her legs as they passed through a pretty neighbourhood with old houses. 'Where do you live?' she asked Ben.

He looked at her quickly before returning his eyes to the road. 'Ah, I inherited my father's house close to Ingólfur Square.'

Her mum and his dad had been friends and Millie vaguely remembered Jon's house. It was, if her memory was right, built of grey stone and Jon always boasted that it was one of the older houses in the city. 'I remember the hallway had lots of wood,' she told him.

'That's the one. I did quite a bit of remodelling. The wooden panelling is gone, but I kept the original parquet flooring and renovated the kitchen and bathrooms,' he explained.

She really hoped he left the garden alone. She'd built fairy houses in the small backyard and imagined that butterflies perched on the rims of the moss-covered urns.

'At some point, I have to do something about the garden, but it's been way down on my list of priorities,' Benedikt explained.

'Do not touch the garden,' she told him, sounding fierce. For some reason, she could see her little boy climbing the thick branches of the tree near the wooden gate, looking for Huldufólk, the country's version of elves. She imagined a little girl building and decorating a house from sticks and stones on the stone flags so one of the hidden folk families could make it their home.

She saw his eyebrows shoot up and waved her hand away. She was projecting her desire for children on to him and felt heat in her cheeks. 'Sorry, it's your garden and you can do what you want with it. I loved it, though. I thought it was magical.'

'Are you sure you are remembering the right place?' he joked. 'The one with the cracked flagstones and the slippery moss paths?'

'That's the one. I don't ever remember seeing you there.'

'I only visited my dad a few times when I was a kid.'

Millie half turned to face him. 'Did you ever come to our house?'

He tapped his finger on the steering wheel. 'Once, twice maybe. Magnús didn't like your mum bringing work home. And he and I didn't get along.'

'Join the club,' Millie muttered.

'I do remember a barn and Jacqui telling me about her animals.'

'Mum and I were both crazy about animals,' Millie replied, smiling. 'If anything was sick, pretty much anywhere within fifty kilometres, it ended up in our barn. It drove Magnús mad.'

The animals took up Jacqui's attention, just like Millie and her business did, something Magnús hated. He'd wanted her mum all to himself, all the time. No wonder she was terrified of being controlled.

'Magnús frequently threatened to have the animals put down. I spent so many nights wide awake, worried that the rabbit or horse or pig we'd just rescued wouldn't be there in the morning.'

Benedikt's expression darkened. 'Really? Man, he was an unfeeling sod.'

That wasn't the worst of it. 'The week after Mum died, that's exactly what happened. I came home from school and all the animals in the barn had been removed. He told me they'd been relocated, but he wouldn't tell me where they were. I'm convinced he had them put down.'

Those animals had been a distraction from her grief, a connection to her mum, and Magnús had ripped them away from her, she explained to Ben. She wasn't sure why she was telling him this, maybe it was because he knew, and didn't like, Magnús. Because he understood the reasons behind her hatred for her stepfather.

Ben's jaw tightened and she knew he was angry for her. So was she. She was so angry for the vulnerable girl she'd been.

'What else did he do?' he asked. 'I know there was more.'

He was right. Magnús hadn't had a sliver of sympathy for her in the weeks and months after her mum's death. It had been such a desolate, lonely, awful time. 'Oh, he wouldn't let me have any input into her funeral and he insisted on white lilies at the funeral when he knew her favourite flowers were gerbera daisies.

'Soon after the animals left, I came home to find strangers packing up my mum's clothes,' she said. 'I called him and screamed at him, told him that there were things of hers I wanted, that he had no right to ask strangers to pack up her belongings.'

'He told me not to be hysterical, she was gone and the sooner I got used to the idea, the easier it would be for him. I was becoming tiresome, he told me, and he was sick of seeing my long face day in and day out.'

'And this was how many weeks after she died?' Ben asked, horrified.

'Two? Maybe three?'

'What a complete moron,' Ben stated. 'I never suspected any of this, Millie.'

'Why would you? You were a part of Mum's working life,' she replied. She played with the hem of her jersey, knowing she could be more candid with Ben than she could be with anyone else. He had known her mum well.

'To the world, my mum was this independent, incredibly strong woman, but nobody knew how much Magnús tried to control her. He hated anything that took her time away from him and resented the attention Mum gave me. If you weren't fully focused on Magnús, he thought you were ignoring him.'

'I only knew him in a business environment, but he could be a difficult bastard.'

Whenever Millie thought she might be missing out on

something by not having a man in her life, she remembered what her mum went through with Magnús. She'd never allow that to happen to her. She'd rather be single and uncontrolled than married and miserable.

'So after your mum died, you thought that rebelling was a good idea,' Ben murmured. Millie stiffened and then realised there was no judgement in his voice.

'I was hurt, angry and confused. I wanted his attention so I acted up. After I found out he wasn't my dad, I wanted to punish him for not loving me and for not telling me sooner he wasn't my real dad, for *not* being my real dad,' she explained, her shoulders up around her ears. 'I tried to make his life as difficult as possible.'

Ben mused, 'I was, reluctantly, impressed by how well you handled his Ferrari. You were clocked at some ridiculous speed on the highway. How did you manage not to kill yourself in that thing?'

She grinned, remembering the exhilaration of having all that power under her control. 'I was, am, a very good driver,' she told him. 'I did clip a pavement going too fast turning into a one-way street. I put a deep gouge in his midnight-blue paintwork.'

'Good for you,' Ben told her. He flipped the windscreen wipers on to a higher setting and Millie noticed that snow was falling in a steady stream. While she'd been nattering away, the weather had turned worse.

'Are we close to your house?' she asked.

'Very,' Ben assured her. 'We'll get home safely, I promise.'

He pushed a button on his steering wheel and tuned into a local radio station. The female presenter was talking in fast Icelandic and Millie quickly lost track of her words. Her Icelandic was very rusty indeed.

She caught Ben's grimace. 'It's getting worse,' he said. 'The northern parts of the country are being hammered. The city will be shut down tomorrow. It'll remain shut for a day, maybe two.'

It took Millie a moment to process the information. 'So, my flight tomorrow afternoon will be cancelled?'

He nodded. 'Definitely.'

She grimaced. 'I have an appointment with the bank tomorrow, to get into my safety deposit box.'

'They will postpone it,' Ben told her, swinging into a snow-covered drive. He pushed a button on his visor and a double garage door rolled up. He entered the tidy garage, filled with big boy toys, and parked his SUV next to a Ducati superbike. A snowmobile and a jet ski sat on trailers. 'If you need to get back to London urgently, then you should try to rebook your flight as soon as possible, maybe go on standby to get the first flight out.'

Millie shook her head. 'I'm not in that much of a hurry. There's nothing I *need* to get back for, I'm free until the New Year. But I don't want to take advantage of your hospitality,' she added when he didn't reply. She rooted around in her bag and pulled out her phone. 'Can you give me five minutes while I contact the airline?'

'You could do it when you get inside.' Ben's smile made him look younger than his thirty-eight years. 'Or you could ask me to organise it for you. One of the perks of working a thousand hours a week and enjoying some success is that I have people to do that for me.'

'But I don't,' Millie pointed out.

'While you're with me, you do,' he told her and told his onboard computer to call Einar and, in English this time, asked him to find her a London-bound flight as soon as the airport opened. Einar agreed.

Ben left the car, stood between his open door and her seat and bent his head to meet her eyes. 'When you come back in two weeks, Millie, you will be able to do everything you didn't do this time.'

But Ben would be in St Barth's, so her list of things to do when she returned to Reykjavik wouldn't include sleeping with her husband.

CHAPTER FOUR

'I'M SORRY, I don't understand,' Millie said, looking from an onscreen Olivier to Ben and back to Olivier again.

She sat next to Ben on the couch in his home office. In his home across the city Olivier sat on a couch, his forearms resting on his knees. He was a little older than Ben, dark-haired and dark-eyed.

Ben didn't waste any time explaining to Olivier that they were married, or why they'd married twelve years ago. He simply told Olivier it was time to end their association. Olivier didn't react to Ben's statement and Millie wondered if implacability was a trait that ran through Icelandic veins. What shocked them? She'd loved to know.

'Are you saying that we can't get divorced until we've been legally separated for six months? But we haven't lived together for twelve years! We've *never* lived together!' Millie protested.

'But the state doesn't know that,' Olivier gently told her. 'You need to file a permit notifying that state that you want to get divorced, then proceedings can start. Divorce doesn't happen quickly in Iceland.'

'How long?' Ben asked.

'It usually takes around a year after the period of legal separation has passed. I don't expect it will take that long with you, you have nothing to argue about, but it's best to be prepared.'

Millie groaned. That long? Was she supposed to wait a year before she tried to fall pregnant? No way!

Nobody, least of all Ben, was stopping her from going ahead and making her arrangements to have a baby, but it didn't feel...*right*. Yes, she knew it was silly, theirs was a business arrangement, but she couldn't help the way she felt.

She could, she supposed, carry on with the baby-making process after they were legally separated, but the thought of falling pregnant by someone else—even if he was an anonymous someone!—while she was married to Ben didn't sit well with her. It was silly, she didn't have a relationship with the man, barely knew him, but she still felt as though she couldn't take this next massive step until she'd cut ties with him.

She looked at Olivier. 'And there's no way around that?' she asked, sounding a little desperate.

Olivier looked regretful. 'I'm sorry, but it's the law. I can submit the forms to get the ball rolling in the meantime. Would that be okay?'

What choice did she have? If she wanted to dissolve her marriage, then these were the hoops they needed to jump through. It was annoying, but none of it was Olivier's fault. Or Ben's. She was the one moving the goalposts so she couldn't whine.

She pulled a smile on to her face. 'Yes, please, I'd be grateful for your help.'

Olivier nodded, his dark eyes holding hers. 'If you are dissolving your marriage, does that also mean that you intend to replace Ben as the person managing your trust?

If that's the case, then documents need to be filed with the authorities to remove him as a trustee.'

They'd done it before, but Millie had reinstated him a year later.

Ben stiffened. He looked as impenetrable as ever, but she sensed his tension. Locking her fingers together, she shrugged. 'I don't want to,' she admitted. 'Ben has done a marvellous job looking after my investments, but I feel bad asking him to spend time on my—'

'It's a few hours here and there,' Ben interjected. 'I told you, it's not a big deal.'

But Millie couldn't help thinking that if they were going to get divorced, then they should completely split and have nothing to do with each other any more. Divorcing him but still allowing him to run her trust's investments didn't make sense. It would be better if they were either in or out.

Millie told Olivier she'd let him know and, after a few more minutes, Ben disconnected the call. She stood and picked up the glass of red wine he had poured for her earlier and sipped. Holding the glass against her chest, she walked over to the large window and looked out, watching the wild wind bend the trees. A thick layer of snow covered the cars parked on the street and a young man staggered from his car to a house opposite. Millie was relieved when he managed to get his front door open and stumbled into his house.

She remembered days like this from her childhood, but they seemed softer, smudged somehow. There was nothing gentle about what was happening outside. The blizzard raged on, ferocious, elemental…primal. Snow hurtled to the ground, thick and fast, and the curtain of snow allowed only the occasional sighting of cars and trees, lampposts and street signs. The snowflakes were bigger than she'd ever seen before, twirling in the air and smashing into each other.

The wind howled as it whipped the snow and sent it swirling through the air in chaotic, random patterns, and seemed to grow louder and more ferocious by the minute. Ben's street, now impassable—the snow was waist-high in some places—was completely deserted, as anyone with sense was inside, enjoying the warmth and safety of their homes.

Millie couldn't remember when last she had felt so alive. There was something about the wild, uncontrollable aspect of nature, something about being here in Iceland, being with Ben, that made her feel more like the girl she used to be, more like young Millie than the staid Londoner she'd become.

Ben joined her at the window, his big hand wrapped around the bowl of his glass. After showing her where the guest suite was and telling her they were due to talk to Olivier in fifteen minutes, he'd left her to freshen up.

When she found him in his home office, she noticed he'd changed out of his designer suit into dark blue jeans and a bottle-green crew-neck jersey. The soft wool hugged his broad shoulders and showed the definition in his big arms. He looked relaxed and the thought of spending the night in his house, spending alone time with him, made her heart bang against her ribs and her stomach do back flips.

The thought of living with him, even for such a short time, terrified her. Mostly because she didn't know how she was going to keep her clothes on. And her hands off him.

She wanted him, she really, *really* wanted him. And

wanting him, in this basic, biblical way, complicated her life in ways she'd never expected. She wasn't supposed to feel desire for her husband, who was nothing much more than a stranger.

Then again, every aspect of her Icelandic trip had gone haywire, so why not this, too?

Their eyes connected. Ben lifted his big hand to hold her cheek and Millie kept her face tipped up, frozen in place. His hand was warm and his big body was now close to hers, radiating heat. She wanted to push her breasts into his chest, her stomach into his hips, she wanted proof he wanted her as much as she wanted him.

She watched as smouldering desire morphed into a blazing wildfire. Any minute now, their clothes would start to fly. She hoped.

'I'm sorry, but I need to kiss you. I can't go another minute without having my mouth on yours, without knowing how you taste.'

There was zero chance of her saying no. Kissing Ben was what she most wanted to do.

He lowered his head and Millie watched his lips descend to hers, and her eyes closed when they touched hers. She lifted her hand to touch his jaw, her fingertips running through his three-day scruff. Her body sank against his as he lightly explored her mouth, his lips moving gently along hers, learning the shape of her lips.

It was a *'hey'* kiss, and a *'so this is how you feel'* kiss. Millie placed her hands flat against his chest and his hand landed on her lower back and he pulled her into him. He kissed her as if he'd finally found what he'd been looking for most of his life, as though she was the biggest, shiniest, loveliest present under the Christmas tree. It was heady stuff to be wanted so much, to feel as though he'd been waiting for months, years, to kiss her like this.

Smart Millie knew he was just a spectacular kisser—she was reading too much into the first meeting of their lips, but she didn't care. It was magical, lovely, fairy footsteps dancing across her soul. Reality would slam into her soon enough. She was happy to take this moment and experience all the feels. Reality could wait.

He smelled of snow and wind, but his cologne reminded her of sunshine and the sea. His body was harder than she expected, more muscled than she'd imagined. He was strong and masculine and felt like a barrier between her and the world. For the first time since her mum died, she didn't feel so utterly alone.

Millie's tongue darted out to touch his lips and Ben stiffened. For a moment Millie thought she'd pushed the kiss too far and asked for too much, too quickly. But then his hand gripped the back of her head and he tugged on her hair, so very gently, silently asking her to tip her head back.

Then he took her mouth in a firestorm of want and need. His tongue slipped between her teeth to slide against hers and Millie, ridiculously, felt her knees melting and her muscles loosening. His hand on her back pulled her into his body and that connection was all that kept her from sinking to the floor.

But her temporary paralysis didn't matter, all that mattered was that Ben was kissing her as though she held all the secrets to the universe and the answers to her most burning questions. And she never, ever, wanted to stop.

Their kiss was as hot as the wind outside was cold. Fireworks flared under her skin and the world faded away, the snowstorm and the howling wind forgotten.

Ben placed his hand on her lower back and pulled her to him, her stomach pushing into his oh-so-hard erection, heady proof he wanted her.

Needing her hands on his skin, she pulled his shirt from his pants with rapid tugs and sighed when she encountered the heat of his back, his muscles and the bumps of his spine. She pushed her hand between his back and the band of his pants, frustrated when she couldn't go any further. Their tongues tangled and Ben dialled up the heat by covering her lace-covered breast with his big hand, his thumb swiping across her already hard nipple.

This felt so good, he felt *amazing*. She loved the way he made her feel… Millie wanted more. She wanted everything. Immediately.

Millie reached for his shirt, but she'd barely tugged it an inch upwards when he dropped his hands and yanked his mouth off hers. *What?* Why did he stop? She wanted more…so much more. Their heavy breathing filled the room, interspersed by the screeching wind outside.

Ben ran his hands over his face and tugged his shirt down, and Millie noticed he was a shade paler than he was before. Millie hauled in a deep breath and slowly, oh so slowly, lifted her gaze to meet his. He didn't, thank goodness, look as remote as he normally did. There was a faint flush in his cheeks and his eyes glittered with frustration and need.

He wanted her and their attraction was now an out-of-control wildfire blazing through drought-ravaged forests. For the first time in years, she wanted to fling herself into that firestorm, to taste fire on her tongue. She really wanted a tour of his bedroom. And his bed.

Millie knew how to ask for what she wanted, she was

Icelandic enough to be direct. 'Shall we continue things upstairs?'

Ben released a half-laugh, half-snort sound. Was he upset she asked first, because she put what they were both thinking into words? She hoped not, those attitudes were so last century. She was a liberated woman and while she wasn't in the habit of asking guys to sleep with her, she couldn't remember when last she did, she *could*.

She tipped her head to the side. 'I thought that men liked it when a woman takes the lead? You know, less pressure, making it easy?' Right, she was beginning to feel a bit idiotic, as though she'd misread the situation. She might be liberated, but she was very out of practice. Had she done something wrong? Gone too fast? Come on too strong? What?

'Right, since you're not tugging me up the stairs, I presume that's not something you want to do.' She threw up her hands and pulled a face. 'So what do we do now?'

His gaze, as it so often was, was steady and sincerity replaced lust.

'Now, we take a breather and I see what I can find to feed you. When last did you eat?'

Really? How was she supposed to think about food when he was all she wanted to feast on? Millie rubbed her hands over her face. She'd had a cup of coffee on the plane and hadn't eaten breakfast.

'How did we go from a hot kiss to talking about food?' she asked, puzzled.

He sighed. 'Millie, you're in my house, through necessity, not by choice. I don't want you to feel pressurised or coerced into doing anything you don't want to. I kissed you, that's as far as I'll go.'

'But I told you I wanted—'

She tipped her head to the side, silently waiting for him to explain. After lifting his hands and dropping them in an I-don't-know-what-I'm-doing gesture, he spoke again. 'Look, I never expected to be this attracted to you. Wanting my wife was the last thing I expected and I'm feeling a bit off balance. I expect you are, too.'

Unbalanced? No, she felt as though she'd been sideswiped by an avalanche.

His thick eyebrows pulled together. 'It's been a long, strange day, a puzzling one. We haven't seen each other for more than a decade and we've been thrown into sharing my house for a day, maybe more. We're getting divorced, you want a baby. We both want to see each other naked. What was once a simple deal is now complicated.'

His sensible words obliterated her impulsiveness. Millie folded her arms and rocked on her heels, feeling a little embarrassed and, dammit, grateful. While she'd been happy to skip into the inferno, he'd looked beyond their hot-as-the-inside-of-the-sun attraction to consider the consequences. She'd been impetuous, he thoughtful.

Millie wished she could argue with him, but she couldn't. It *had* been an exceptionally weird day. And now, below the lust, the longing, a streak of hesitation pulsed, a layer of should she, shouldn't she? She'd felt off balance all day and was old enough to know it wasn't a good time to step on to a sexual merry-go-round. Nothing good came out of impulsively throwing yourself into a man's arms...

'Right, point taken,' Millie admitted.

'I'm backing off because it's the right thing to do right now, Millie. But if you decide I'm what you want later, you just have to ask, and I'll have your clothes off so fast your head will spin.'

Millie blinked, letting his words sink in. Getting the firestorm that they created inside her under control.

'I'm going to head to the kitchen and distract myself by looking for something to eat for supper.'

'Ben—' Millie sighed. She didn't want him to go, he couldn't stay. She wanted him to kiss her again. She needed to find her room and take a sanity break.

She was supposed to be breaking their ties, not forging new ones. She'd come to Iceland to close the book, to put her past on the shelf, to move on.

She had to be a sensible adult.

Divorce, pregnancy, baby, a new life, her own little family. She'd made her plan—there was no space for a brief affair with her never there, stranger-husband. Ben wouldn't be a part of her future, no man would.

She needed to keep it together, to consider the future. Sleeping with him would be instant gratification, a wonderful step out of time, but it could have…unintended consequences. Ben was a potent man and she'd kissed him and propositioned him, something that normally took her weeks to do with other men. She was acting out of character and needed time and space to clear her head and start thinking clearly.

There was a blizzard outside and a bigger one happening inside her head.

She had to back off, with as much dignity as she could manage. 'You're right, with me wanting a divorce, and a baby, it's too complicated, too messy,' Millie told him. She bit the inside of her lip. 'Sorry, I lost my head.'

'Don't apologise, Millie, it's not necessary,' Ben said and she heard regret in his voice. 'Our marriage was once a very simple arrangement. Now it's…n-not.'

She looked out of the window, hoping against hope that

the storm had cleared and she could leave, find somewhere else to stay. But, no—if anything, the blizzard was just getting started. She was stuck here, feeling awkward and sexually frustrated. Not a great combination.

'I'm sorry if all of this has inconvenienced you, Benedikt. I would go if I could.'

'I'll be in the kitchen…give me a half-hour or so. When *you* are ready, join me.'

Millie nodded, understanding his need for some space. She needed that time, possibly more, for Sensible Millie to slap Turned On Millie back into shape.

Sleeping with Ben would be a ghastly mistake. But there was still nothing she wanted to do more.

In his kitchen, Ben heard her on the stairs as she made her way up to the guest suite. Running his hand through his hair, he walked over to a kitchen cupboard and yanked out a bottle and a shot glass. It might be a little early for alcohol—it was only two in the afternoon—but he desperately needed a drink.

After swallowing a shot of Brennivín, his Icelandic father's favourite drink, he placed the empty glass against his forehead and closed his eyes.

Millie was upstairs, in one of the three spare bedrooms, and she was going to be sleeping in that bed tonight, tomorrow night. And he'd told her that nothing would happen between them…

Unless she asked.

Ben walked over to the window and placed his shoulder against the window frame and watched the wind toss big, feathery snowflakes on to the glass. The wind screamed its fury outside, and Ben could barely make out the huge branches of the trees in his garden and couldn't see the gate or the street. The blizzard was causing chaos and disorientation outside. Millie did the same inside his mind. Ben was fairly certain both storms were going to intensify.

It had been obvious Millie wanted to leave after the dust settled on their kiss and, had there been a way, he would've helped her go. But the snow was thigh deep, the visibility impenetrable, the roads were undrivable and the wind strong enough to blow trucks off the road. This wasn't weather you took chances in, it was supremely dangerous out there.

It was marginally less dangerous inside his house, for vastly different reasons. He and Millie were snow-bound, forced to share the same house. If she were another woman he was attracted to, he'd consider it a perfect situation. With the storm raging, he wouldn't be able to go into the office and he could spend long, lazy hours in bed, having sex, giving and receiving pleasure. He couldn't remember when last, if ever, he had three days of uninterrupted time with a lover...

But the woman upstairs wasn't just someone he was head-over-ass attracted to, but his wife of twelve years. His attraction to her was stunning, and inconvenient, mostly because he didn't like how out of control Millie made him feel. He looked at her and he wanted, he touched her and he burned. He never dated women who made him feel more than a passing attraction, interest, who made him tip his head, intrigued. He ran, as far and as fast as he could. Millie made him feel all that and more and there was no damn place to run to, no way of putting some distance between them.

For the past two decades, sex had been a tool for plea-sure, fun and a way to burn away stress. It had never been preceded by such need and constant thoughts of having her and how he would take her. Millie had been back in his life for a few hours, but the storm in his head matched the ferocity of the blizzard outside. She was a hurricane rushing through his soul, a tornado spinning through his mind. He wasn't quite sure which way was up...

Absurd!

He wasn't a man who allowed himself to get carried away, he prided himself on being rational and calm. He didn't believe in love or excess emotion, he knew it always led to hurt and disappointment.

The woman he'd allowed himself to love had let him down and there was no way he'd allow that to happen again. He'd worked exceptionally hard to become the emotionally independent, sometimes ruthless, impassive man he now was and he'd never put himself at the mercy of needing a woman's love again. Emotional distance and not allowing himself to have feelings of attachment to anything—not to money or people or things—gave him a sense of freedom and security.

Staying away from emotional situations also kept his stutter at bay.

Yes, he'd hesitated once or twice, and felt the prickles in his throat when his words took longer than usual to appear. But that could be due to stress, to the surprise of Millie dropping back into his life. There was nothing to worry about; he hadn't spent enough time with Millie to know whether she could sneak under his defences, whether she was able to burrow her way inside his steel-hard carapace and look past his carefully constructed veneer of implacability.

But he had to be careful of her, he couldn't start feeling more, feeling *anything* for his on-paper wife. And he knew he shouldn't sleep with her...

He needed a good excuse to spend time away from her. Work would work and he could spend more time in his basement gym.

Ben tapped his empty glass against his thigh, his attention moving to what Olivier had said about their divorce. He had no problem with waiting to get divorced, it wasn't a problem for him.

But he'd seen Millie's look of horror and knew the waiting period would derail her plans to have a baby. She didn't want to start this new chapter of her life until the ties were cut between them. He could understand that. He believed, like Millie did, that a clean break should be made before one moved on...

She wanted a child and he could see her with a baby. She had so much love to give and, like her mother, was warm and affectionate. Millie would be an exceptional mother, and he wanted that for her. He wanted her to be happy. But despite trying, he was finding it difficult to wrap his head around her using a sperm donor to fall pregnant.

Yes, yes, it was the modern way of doing things, a choice she had the absolute right to make—her body and her choice—but it just felt...*wrong*.

He couldn't explain it, he just didn't *like* it.

But he was also bemused by her deep desire to have a child.

Unlike her, he'd never given a lot of thought, if any, to procreation and the urge to do so wasn't innate. It was easy to find excuses—there were enough kids in the world as it was, he had no time, his career was his primary focus.

Nothing, as far as he was concerned, was missing in his life, he didn't see how kids would fit in with his schedule, the little free time he had or the life he'd worked his tail off to attain.

Millie wanted children, but he didn't. He was attracted to her, she was a gorgeous woman, and he was a man with normal sexual desires. He liked women and liked to sleep with them. It was a fun, completely normal urge.

And if she was anyone other than his wife, and his business partner, if he wasn't involved with making the financial decisions about her vast investments, he wouldn't think twice about spending the next two days in bed with her, naked.

But she was his wife, the wife who wanted a divorce so she could have a baby. They co-owned a company and he'd offered to continue to handle her trust's huge investment portfolio. They were already dealing with a lot and sleeping together would be a flame inserted into a gas line.

He'd worked exceptionally hard to get where he was, to have the career and business he enjoyed, to find the ninety/ten balance between work and play. He liked his life, sometimes he even loved it. He couldn't allow his no-longer-convenient wife to upset it. He had to be sensible, he should avoid complications…

But he really hoped she would ask.

CHAPTER FIVE

AFTER SPENDING TWO nights in Ben's wonderful house, Millie was starting to climb the walls. Despite using the state-of-the-art gym in his basement she wanted to breathe fresh air, go for a walk and to put some space between them.

Living with someone she was so desperately attracted to wasn't, in any way, fun and staying in a hotel's broom closet might've been a better idea. Being housebound was a lot easier for Ben, he had work to do, and he spent hours in his downstairs study doing whatever the CEO of PR Reliance International did. He didn't have time to sit around wondering how it would feel to have his hands on her body, the scrape of her leg against his, his big hands lifting her up as he slid into her…

Aargh! Honestly?

Millie picked the magazine she'd been reading and frisbee'd it across the room in a fit of pique. Ben chose that moment to walk into the smaller of his two reception rooms and the magazine slammed into his thigh. His only reaction was to lift his eyebrows. He picked up the magazine and placed it on the nearest side table. 'Problem?' he asked.

Millie blushed, swung her sock-covered feet off the couch, leaned forward and placed her forearms on her knees. She hoped her hair dropping on either side of her face would hide her flaming cheeks. She was acting like a stroppy child.

After tossing another log in the fireplace, Ben sat next to her and pulled back a hank of hair and tucked it behind her ear. A soft, sky-blue cashmere blanket fell to the floor. 'Have you got cabin fever?' he asked.

She shrugged, not willing to admit she was suffering from I-want-to-sleep-with-him fever more than any other ailment. 'Yes,' she admitted.

'This is the worst storm we've had this decade,' Ben told her, leaning back. He smothered a yawn and rested his head on the back of the couch and closed his eyes. His thick eyelashes rested against the faint blue stripes beneath his eyes—he was more tired than she'd realised. Wasn't he sleeping?

Why?

'Tough day?' she asked, shuffling back and lifting her feet on to the couch, then wrapping her arms around her bent knees.

'No more than usual,' he told her, rolling his head in her direction before opening his eyes. 'Why?'

'You look tired. And stressed,' she stated, allowing herself the pleasure of tracing the darkness under his eyes with the tip of her index finger. Touching him was a compulsion and she was tired of holding herself back.

His eyes didn't drop from hers, holding her gaze.

'I'm not sleeping because I spend most of the night talking myself out of walking down the hallway and slipping into your bed.'

Icelandic people were generally blunt—it was a trait she had taken to London with her when she left. She liked knowing where she stood. After her mum's lies about her father and Magnús's cold deceit—if she hadn't pushed his buttons so hard and so often, she probably would still think *he* was her father—honesty was a refreshing and welcome change. And Millie recalled his promise to her. He would never lie to her. As far as she knew, he hadn't.

If he did, she'd find his deceit devastating. In a world full of shifting opinions and fake news, she'd relied on him to tell her the truth about the business, her investments and the trust's business.

'I've been doing the same,' she admitted and managed a small smile. 'It would've been kind of funny if we met in the hallway rushing to each other's rooms, wouldn't it?'

Ben's intensity didn't waver and wasn't distracted by her weak joke. 'Since you arrived, I've been trying to talk myself out of taking you to bed, praying you'd cave and ask me again. We're both single and we want each other. Why are we denying ourselves something we both know we're going to enjoy?'

She swallowed. 'Because we're married? Because if we sleep together, it will change things. It will affect our arrangement,' she said, the heat in his eyes raising the temperature of the already warm room.

'I've been thinking about that,' he mused. 'How would it affect anything? We've never allowed other lovers to affect our marriage deal—what difference would it make if we are each other's lovers?'

'I don't know!' Millie rubbed her hands over her face. 'Ben, this isn't helping!'

'We're trying to dissolve our…arrangement,' he pointed out. 'But our attraction to each other has nothing to do with the deal we struck, the dissolution of that deal. It's a separate issue.'

Was it? To her, everything was jumbled up. She felt as

though she was in an industrial washing machine, being tumbled this way and that. Sex, baby, their marriage, being business partners...they all bled into each other.

Ben didn't move from his indolent position, but every muscle in his body was on high alert. He was waiting for her to say the word and he would take control. She was so close to saying yes and words like *please love me... take me to bed* and *I want you* hovered on her tongue, desperate to be verbalised.

'We can get the divorce you want and I'll stay on as your trustee if that's what you want. Your wanting a child doesn't, so you've said, c-c-concern me—'

She'd caught his sporadic, barely-there stutter and found the small imperfection charming. And reassuring because Ben sometimes seemed too together, too polished. His infrequent stammer made him seem a little fallible.

'But, more than anything else, I want to take you to bed,' he continued.

Millie hesitated and Ben caught it. He sat up, his expression serious. 'This will only become complicated if we let it, Millie. This has nothing to do with our arrangement or our divorce.'

'It's about the way we feel when we look at each other,' Millie murmured. She'd never had a man look at her with such intensity, as though she was all he needed for him to keep breathing, and existing.

To be desired by someone so much was a heady experience and it was something Millie doubted she'd feel again. Ben was such a *man*, masculine and hot, and to know that someone so sexy wanted her flooded her with a confidence she couldn't remember feeling.

She was done with thinking, finished with denying

herself what she really wanted. Ben was right—this didn't need to be complicated.

'This is about sex, a fling, a step out of time,' Millie quietly stated. 'It can't mean anything.'

Ben nodded. 'So…can I kiss you now?'

Millie looked temptation in the eye, nodded her agreement and followed it over to the dark side. She wanted him, he wanted her, this was going to happen…

Millie dropped her knees and moved to straddle Ben's lap. His hands came up to hold her hips and surprise, then delight, flashed in his eyes. Millie pulled up his black cashmere sweater and placed her hands on the bare skin of his stomach, felt his muscles tighten beneath her fingertips.

She lowered her mouth to kiss him, but Ben's whisper stopped her before she could make contact. 'Are you sure you want this, Millie? Because once we start, I'm not sure I'll be able to stop.'

Of course he would, of that she had no doubt. Ben was a man who exuded control, over his actions and words. She absolutely knew he would stop if she asked him to. But she had no intention of stopping before he gave her an earth-moving orgasm. Or two or three. She wanted to know what making love to this amazing man felt like. 'I'm sure, Ben.'

She remembered him saying that she needed to ask him to kiss her, to make love to her, so she decided to say the words, to leave him in no doubt. 'Will you take me to bed, Ben? Will you love me?'

He lifted his hand and, with one finger, traced the curve of her cheek, the line of her jaw. 'Does it have to be in my bed?' he asked. 'This couch and the carpet in front of the fireplace are incredibly comfortable and I can't wait that long.'

She smiled, her lips curving as her hands skimmed over his pectorals. 'We can start here and make our way upstairs as the night progresses.'

'That,' Ben said, between kissing her lips, 'sounds like a very good plan.'

They were doing this. He closed his eyes as Millie's hands danced over his ribs and he shivered. All he could do was echo her actions, so he pushed his hands under the hem of her long-sleeved silk T-shirt. His fingers moved slowly up her ribcage and flirted with the sides of her full breasts. He ran his thumb over her nipple, rasping over the lace cup of her bra. She felt so incredibly good... Amazing, feminine and completely delightful.

He banded an arm around her waist, lifted her up and off him and slowly, so slowly, lowered her to the cushions of the couch. He smiled at the combination of excitement and desire on her face and her grape-green eyes seemed lighter and brighter than they normally were. She wanted him...she'd *asked* him.

He lowered his mouth to hers, sucking on her bottom lip, then sliding his tongue into her mouth. Her hands skimmed his sides and she dug her fingers into his butt, her hands sliding as far down the back of his thighs as she could reach. Lifting her hands, she placed them on either side of his face and the combination of that sexy, tender gesture nearly undid him. Millie pulled her mouth off his and ran her tongue over his jaw, down his neck and, after pulling the neck of his T-shirt away, dragged her teeth over his collarbone.

'You feel amazing...you're so sexy,' she murmured.

Ben couldn't remember when last he was complimented, in bed or out. He tugged on the hem of her T-shirt, a silent plea to remove the barriers of clothing between them. Millie did as he asked and tossed the shirt over the back of the couch. Ben took a minute to take in creamy breasts nestled in a deep purple bra.

Millie arched her back and he knew she was quietly begging him to touch her, to pay attention to her nipples. Ben was happy to oblige. He dropped his head and sucked one into his mouth, lace and all, and she released a deep, appreciative groan. Her fingers tunnelled into his hair, gripping his head to keep him in place.

She was what he'd craved since the moment he saw her yesterday, the reason why he couldn't sleep. When he did drift off, making love to her was what he dreamed of—he'd wanted these moments—he craved the ebb and tide of hot, delicious sex. Ben needed to touch her everywhere and he wanted her to know him, to explore him in the same way he intended to explore her.

She would be returning to the UK soon and when she next returned to Iceland, he'd be in St Barth's. He didn't know when, or if, he'd see her next. If this was the only time they had, if this night was all they got, he wanted to know her inside out, what made her sigh and what made her scream. And he wanted her to know him, to remember him...

He wanted to be her only memory when sex slid into her mind...

But as he touched her, as his mouth moved down her body to explore her belly button, to drag his warm, open mouth over her mound, he knew he could, if he wasn't careful, become addicted to her, to this. She could become something he couldn't get enough of.

She was skimming in and out of his life, and soon, the fragile ties that bound them would be broken. She wasn't for ever, he didn't do that long. He wasn't into commitment, of any length or any type. This was about pleasure, nothing more. And if he kept telling himself that, maybe he would, at some point, start to believe it.

Ben divested Millie of her underwear and, sitting on his heels, he looked at her, gorgeously naked. He was entranced by her delightful body, her long, shapely legs and her creamy, scented skin. 'You are exquisite, Millie.'

Millie's eyes darkened, her lips curled up and she sighed, but her eyes didn't leave his. Although he wanted to kiss her more than he wanted to breathe, Ben kept his eyes on her face and watched emotions slide in and out of her startling eyes and across her face. Lust, desire, crazy attraction—they were all there, but he thought that under the want was affection, a little fear and a lot of anticipation.

He wanted to remind her, remind himself, that romance had no part in this. This was about sex and escapism. They were doing what women and men did best...

Ben pulled away from her and lifted his hand to grip the back of his shirt. He pulled it over his head in one easy, fluid movement. Millie growled and ran her hand over his chest, lightly touched with hair. He flipped open the buttons to his jeans, hooked his thumbs into the waistband and pushed his jeans down his thighs, taking his underwear with them.

The sigh that followed was one of pure female appreciation.

Naked, Ben gripped her waist and moved her down the couch. When she was where he wanted her, he lay down on top of her, chest to chest, his erection finding its natural place between her thighs. Wanting more, he pulled back to kiss his way down her neck, across her collarbone. She was so lovely, and he couldn't get enough of her. He pulled her nipple into his mouth and her fingers twisted in his hair. She liked that, seemed to like everything he did. She was so damn hot…

He was so close to making her his…one little push and he'd be in heaven. But…*aargh*! He needed a condom or Millie would be getting that baby sooner than she thought.

He looked up and pushed a strand of hair from her face. She gripped his hips and dropped her legs open. Ben groaned and shook his head.

'What's the matter?' she whispered, immediately tensing. He saw the vulnerability in her eyes—she thought he was slamming on the brakes. There wasn't a remote chance of that happening.

'I need to get a condom, sweetheart. I'll be back in a sec.'

Ben reluctantly pulled away from her. He knew he had a condom in his wallet, which lay on the hallway table, just outside the door to this lounge. He moved quickly and came back into the room, scattering cards and cash over the intricate parquet floor as he searched for the condom he'd shoved into one of the compartments a few months back. Finally digging it out, he ripped it open, sheathed himself and lowered himself back down to the couch, settling himself back between her thighs.

Ben kissed her gently before skimming his thumb over the spot between her eyes. 'Second thoughts?' he asked. He wanted her, wanted this more than anything he'd ever wanted before, but he needed to know whether she felt the same. If she didn't, his withered heart might just crack…

Her ankles were already curved around his calves, and she was lifting her hips, trying to push him deeper into her. 'No, but I'm tired of waiting. I *need* you.'

Oh, he liked her like this, a little breathless, hunger in her eyes, her body pushing up into his, wanting what he could give her. He deliberately brushed his chest against hers, teasing her nipples with his chest hair. Unfortunately, his teasing backfired and he knew he couldn't wait much longer to make her his. He was running out of patience.

'Quick question?' she asked.

His eyes bored into her. 'Make it very damn quick.'

'I was just wondering how long you are going to tease me?'

'This long.' Ben entered her with one fluid stroke, burying himself to the hilt. Yeah, this was what he loved, what he craved, being encased by a woman, enveloped in her heat and scent, feeling her lift her hips in a silent but powerful demand for him to go deeper, to take her harder. Then Millie lifted her mouth to find his and Ben forgot how to think.

All he could concentrate on was the warm, sparkly sensation building in a place deep inside him, each spark igniting another until a million tiny fires danced under his skin. Ben placed his hand under her back, yanked her up and he pushed deeper into her, and those fires joined and created an explosion that consumed him from the inside out. All he wanted was this heat and light and warmth. Her. He wanted *her*. This. Again and again and again.

Millie's internal muscles clenched around him, he felt her wet gush against him and heard her sob his name. He'd had good sex before, great sex often. But this was better, hotter, brighter. And that, Ben thought as followed Millie into that white-hot, blinding rush of sensation, was a huge problem.

Much, much later, after Ben had loved her thoroughly and exquisitely again, Millie heard the sound of his deep breathing and watched him in the low light coming from his spectacular en-suite bathroom. Millie lifted his big hand off her bare stomach and held her breath, waiting for him to wake up. He didn't, so she slipped out of his enormous bed and picked up one of his long-sleeved T-shirts lying on the back of the chair in the corner of his spacious room. She pulled it over her head, rolled up the sleeves and, after finding her panties and pulling them on, padded downstairs, needing to be alone.

She approved of Ben's renovated, now contemporary, split-level house, with all the levels arranged around the original, central courtyard. All the rooms had parquet floors, high ceilings and big windows, letting in as much natural light as possible. She loved its layout, and its decor, not overly minimalistic, and she felt at home.

Moving down the steps, Millie walked into the kitchen area with its mahogany cupboards, granite counters and stainless-steel appliances. A big island dominated the room and to the left was a spacious, casual eating area under a massive window. The built-in, L-shaped couch half framed the dining table and it was wide enough to sleep on.

Millie took a bottle of water from the fridge and cracked the top, took a long swallow and looked out, sighing at the still-falling snow. She needed a few min-utes to make sense of what had happened upstairs and to get her brain to restart. If that took a while, she wouldn't be surprised—she felt as though she'd been hit by a massive power surge.

She'd had a few lovers over the years, but sex with those men couldn't compare to what she'd experienced with Ben. He was a tender and thorough lover and he'd shown her how fantastic sex could be. It was an eye-opener to realise she'd only ever had boring sex, mediocre sex and okay sex. Making love to Ben was a transformative experience and she'd never be satisfied with anything less than brilliant sex again.

That shouldn't be a problem because, after she left Reykjavik, her focus would move from having a lover to acquiring a baby. She doubted she'd be interested in sex while she was pregnant and, after the baby was born, all her focus would be on her child. Hopefully, by the time she finally turned her attention back to her own sexual needs, the memory of this incredible night spent in Ben's arms, and how brilliant he was in bed, would've dissipated.

Millie sat on one of the bar stools at the island and crossed her bare legs. She pulled her laptop towards her—she'd left it here earlier—and switched it on. They'd had sex, it had been stunning and amazing, but she had to put it into perspective: it was a fling, not destined to last. It didn't matter that she wanted more than one delicious night, wasn't important that she needed more of his growled compliments, to hear his murmurs of appreciation at how fantastic she made him feel.

He'd made her feel more like a woman, fierce and fantastic, than she ever had before, but where did that get her? The harsh reality was that there was nothing more between them than a once-convenient marriage and pheromones.

Unfortunately, she hadn't expected to like him so much. They'd both had good reasons to marry back then—she to get her stepfather out of her life, he to get her stepfather out of the company. Things ticked along happily until her biological clock started setting off alarm bells...

Millie wondered if Ben had ever wanted kids, if having a family was something he'd ever considered. She knew little about his family and wondered why he'd never married or had a long-term partner. If he had, she would know about it, it was part of their pact to be honest with each other.

Ben, she suspected, was married to the company and his career. He'd taken the business to unimaginable heights, making them both—well, him and her mum's foundation, because that's where her share of the company profits ended up—exceptionally rich. Success like that required pinpoint focus and dedication.

But, for some mad reason, she could see him married, see him as a dad. She could easily imagine him standing at that stove, dressed in a T-shirt and plaid pyjama pants, his feet bare as he flipped pancakes for his toddler son and dropped kisses on the head of his flaxen-haired daughter. His lower face would be rough with stubble, his usually neat hair would be messy, and happiness and contentment would make him look younger than his years. He'd smile when she walked through the door...

Whoa, brakes on, Millie!

Too much and too fast. Ben wasn't going to be her happy-ever-after, because she didn't believe her happiness rested in a man's hands. And she had too many trust issues to let a man that far into her world and heart. Ben would never be the man she created a family with, the man she'd spend the rest of her life with. There wasn't going to *be* a man. No, it was better to be a single mum and not risk her heart.

She was going to have her family, and it would be just her and her kids. And the donor of the biological matter she needed would be anonymous. If her kids wanted to know who he was, and if he was open to that, they could track him down when they were adults, but she never wanted a relationship with the man.

Stop thinking about Ben and start thinking about your Ben-free future, Millie!

Now, or some time very soon, she had to work out when to get pregnant. But before she did that, she had to get past her reluctance to fall pregnant while she was still married to Ben. It was stupid to wait up to eighteen months to get pregnant because she felt 'uncomfortable' about being married to Ben while carrying another man's child.

She wasn't properly married to Ben and the baby would be hers. Neither man would play a part in her or her baby's life going forward so she was being incredibly stupid. She had to get over herself. Immediately.

She needed to get serious about finding a sperm donor, so she opened her laptop and pulled up the website of the sperm bank she favoured using. Millie idly scrolled through the website. If she and Ben got divorced shortly after their government-imposed, six-month waiting period, then she could have the baby any time after July next year. It made sense to start trying to fall pregnant in the New Year, as her first attempt might not be successful.

Derek is a super-smart, persistent and very kind man with a fun, open personality. He also has gorgeous blue eyes and light brown hair, with impressive cheekbones and a straight nose. He's on an impressive career path, has two degrees, in genetics and pharmacology, and wants to establish his own bio lab to tailor-make drugs to individuals. Derek has a large family he is close to...

Admittedly, Derek looked sexy and athletic, but Millie wanted to know more. Did he sulk? Was he the type to lose his temper? Did he make promises he didn't keep? Millie sighed. She could never fill in all the blanks—nobody could, not even in a proper relationship—but she wanted to know more, dig deeper. This was someone who would pass on a hefty chunk of his genes to her baby, she wanted to know the good, the bad and the ugly.

How was she supposed to make a choice when she didn't know *everything*?

Millie looked out of the large windows that were a feature of Ben's open plan living area and sighed at the endlessly falling snow, wondering when the wind would ever stop howling. She felt tired but energised, sleepy but her mind was on a spin cycle.

'He sounds too good to be true.'

Millie slapped her hand on her chest and spun around to see Ben standing by the island, his eyes on her computer screen. Yawning, he scratched the side of his neck and walked towards the enormous fridge. He removed a bottle of orange juice, slammed the door closed with his foot and took a glass from the cupboard next to the fridge. He downed a tall glass of orange juice before re-filling the glass and coming to stand next to her.

'Should I be offended that you are looking for sperm donors after we nearly set the house on fire?' he asked, his tone mild. He stroked his hand over her hair and she responded by lifting her face, silently and subconsciously, asking for a kiss. His lips met hers with gentle heat.

'They are separate issues,' Millie quietly reminded him. 'I still want a baby and I'm not going to get one until I decide who I want the sperm donor to be.'

'So what's the problem?' Ben asked, sitting next to her and placing his forearm on the counter. He'd pulled on a pair of sweatpants and a T-shirt and, yes, his big feet were bare. He looked like the man she'd imagined earlier, the one flipping pancakes...

Stop it, Millie!

'I can choose everything: hair colour, eye colour, height and build. His ethnicity,' Millie explained, pushing her hands into her hair. And, yes, it felt weird discussing this with him. 'But I can't tell what sort of personality he has. How does he react to stress? To hardship? Is he a bully or is he sensitive?' Magnús's face popped up on the big screen of her mind. 'Does he have a temper? Does he say one thing and do another?'

'Are you thinking about how Magnús treated you? If you are, then you are giving him too much power,' Ben told her.

Millie silently cursed, wishing he wouldn't read her mind. Maybe she'd told him too much earlier. Why had she told him about Magnús's hatred towards her because she'd never shared that with anyone?

Not even her mum understood how much Magnús detested her. Millie had always sensed his dislike, but didn't understand how deep his hatred ran until their big blowout. He resented having to raise her, resented the attention her mum paid her, resented her mum's insistence that he claim her as his.

Why had they both promoted the lie? Iceland was an accepting society and having a child by someone else wasn't that big a deal, even thirty years ago. Millie didn't understand their motives and she definitely didn't understand why they'd kept her real father's identity a secret.

There would be no lies in her family, no secrets. Her children would, when they were old enough to understand, know everything about her and her family.

'To be fair, most couples take years to know each other that well,' he stated. 'It's not something you can discover in a few conversations.'

It took her a minute to work out that Ben was referring to her statement about not knowing the ins and outs of her potential sperm donor.

Funny that Ben was the person she'd known the longest, the man who'd been on the outside of her life for most of her life. A spark of an idea flared in the deepest part of her.

Ben had been amazing these past twelve years. He was always polite, always calm and he'd made great decisions for the company and her. She trusted him. He was smart, good looking and healthy, and making a baby with him would be so much more fun than the soulless clinic visit she was anticipating.

The spark flared into a flame. Had she found a neat solution to her dilemma? He'd married her, they were business partners and now they were lovers, possibly even on their way to being friends. She hadn't come across anyone on the website of sperm donors who could match him.

'You're plotting something,' Ben said, resting his forearms on the counter. Her eyes darted back to the website and then to him and back to the website again. When fear jumped into his eyes, she knew he'd worked out what she was thinking...

'You can't possibly be thinking that I...' He stopped talking, still shaking his head.

'That I would like you to be my father's baby?' Millie looked him in the eye and nodded. He'd be perfect. Well, not perfect, but miles better than anyone on any website.

Ben linked his hands behind his head, still calm. Would she ever be able to surprise him? She doubted it. 'That's a chemical reaction to us having great sex, Millie.'

Was it? She didn't think so. She knew Ben, she trusted him. She liked him. They'd already slept together. 'Nobody comes close to you on the sperm donor website, Ben.'

He shot a look at her laptop and Millie closed the lid.

'I cannot believe that you are asking this,' Ben muttered. Millie frowned. Right. Her request might not be a surprise, but it wasn't a welcome one. 'I don't want to be a father, I never planned on having kids.'

Millie frowned at him. Oh, damn! He'd grabbed the wrong end of the stick and was impaled on the sharp point.

She lifted her hand and shook her head. 'Whoa, hold on! I'm not asking you to be involved in his, or her, life.'

'Th-then what are you asking, Millie?'

She fully intended to raise her baby alone, without anyone's input. This baby, and its sibling, if she was lucky enough to be able to do this again, would be her family, she would be a single parent and responsible for raising her child. She didn't want any outside input, thank you very much. Her body, her baby…

'I don't want a *father* for my baby, Benedikt, that's not what I'm asking. I intend to raise this baby on my own. All I'd require is for you to help me become pregnant. I still want a divorce. I wouldn't expect you to pay me maintenance or to be involved in my child's life. I'd happily sign any legal documents stating that.'

'So you just want my sperm?' he clarified, with a strange look on his face.

She lifted one shoulder to her ear. 'Yes.'

'I'm not sure whether to feel relieved or insulted,' Ben stated. Millie couldn't read the emotion in his eyes and she didn't like it when he closed down mentally and emotionally. Looking closely, she saw that there was heat within those blue depths, as well as irritation. She bit down on her bottom lip.

Had she completely spoiled what had been a lovely night by tossing this idea into the equation? Possibly. Probably. But she wasn't good at waiting for what she wanted. Once she decided to embark on a course of action she jumped in with both feet and her whole body.

Millie twisted her lips. 'I'm sorry, I've thrown this at you late at night and after...after we just had an amazing time together in bed.'

Ben sent her one of his enigmatic looks, the one where she had no idea what he was thinking and feeling. Millie felt like an absolute fool...and wasn't sure what to do. She'd erected this huge barrier between them—she'd couldn't flip back into being his lover...

Why hadn't she thought more and spoken less? 'Uh... so I'm going to go to bed.'

What else could she say? Do? She hesitated a minute and hoped Ben would say something to reduce the tension between them, to take them back to where they were a few hours ago. She'd messed up and she was hoping *he'd* get her out of her jam. She wasn't being fair...

'I am sorry, Ben. Having a baby is important to me and...' she said, feeling the need to explain.

When his eyes remained steady on her face, she knew she was digging her hole deeper and making the situation a lot worse. Thank God he'd worn a condom tonight; her falling pregnant accidentally was the last thing she wanted. She would never take the decision out of his hands and she hoped he knew that. She thought about reminding him of that and decided not to, it would only make the situation worse.

Ben released a long, drawn-out sigh and rubbed the back of his neck. 'Go to bed, Millie.'

There was nothing else she could do, nothing else she could say, so she did as he suggested. She climbed the stairs to the guest bedroom, knowing she'd spend the rest of the night, not that there was much of it left, cursing herself for asking him to be her baby daddy.

And praying for a miracle he would agree.

CHAPTER SIX

THERE WAS FLIPPING things upside down and then there were emotional nuclear strikes.

When Ben followed Millie downstairs he'd expected maybe a whisky-flavoured hot chocolate in the kitchen, running his hands up her bare legs as they watched the still-falling snow through his huge windows.

He had not been expecting her to ask him to give her a baby.

Ben opened a cupboard door, pulled out a bottle of whisky sans hot chocolate and reached for a glass. Dumping a healthy amount into the glass, he threw it back, welcoming the heat as it slipped down his throat. He started to pour himself another shot and stopped, thinking that alcohol would not add any clarity to the situation.

He walked over to the L-shaped couch in the corner of the kitchen, underneath the wide, tall windows, lay down and rested his head on a cushion, with his forearm over his eyes.

The sex they shared had been brilliant and he'd enjoyed feeling completely in sync with another person. Millie had been as into him as he was her and they seemed to be reading from the same book, singing the same tune. He instinctively knew how to touch her, what she'd like and didn't. She hadn't been shy about exploring his body and she'd paid attention to his responses. In some ways, it felt as though they'd made love a hundred times before, yet coming together was still new and exhilarating.

She'd rocked his world and he knew he'd returned that favour. They'd had simple, uncomplicated, unbelievably amazing sex…*twice*. And he'd thought they'd spend the rest of the night having more brilliant sex. But her question changed their dynamic in a heartbeat.

Could he give her a child?

Wow. And what the hell? He had no idea how he'd managed to keep so calm, to not react. Maybe he'd been too shocked to react.

He wasn't sure whether to be irritated by her question, hurt or annoyed.

Ben dropped his arm, sat up and glanced out of the window. Still snowing…*dammit*. The usual sounds of his busy street were drowned out by the snow-filled wind. The dim street lights cast long, distorted shadows on the snowbanks, creating an eerie atmosphere.

Ben tipped his head back to look up at the ceiling. On the next floor, somewhere directly above him, Millie slept. He rubbed his hands over his face. On his *What-will-Millie-do-next?* bingo card, getting her pregnant didn't feature. He'd married her to protect his business interests and he'd looked after her interests, and the personal trust she'd inherited from Jacqui, as he would his own money. Giving her a baby wasn't part of that agreement.

He didn't want to be a father and had never had any interest in raising a child. He had no idea how to juggle a kid and a career and was scared to try because his mum had been so shockingly bad at being a mother and having a career. And, thanks to his mum being difficult about visitation rights—she didn't want him to stay with her, but she didn't want him to spend time with his dad either—he and his Icelandic father had had a cordial, but not particularly close, relationship.

He hadn't had a decent role model, nobody to teach him how to be a good parent. His mother had veered from thinking he was mildly intellectually challenged—for a super-smart woman, she could be amazingly dense—to being uninterested in him. His dad was welcoming when he made the rare trip to Iceland, but hadn't gone out of his way to make sure Ben spent time with him.

Neither of them had paid any attention to his progress at school and never expressed any interest when he stopped stuttering or guided him in any way, shape or form. He was expected to get on with it, so that's what he had done.

He'd become the person he was, confident and successful, all by himself. He had his mother's ruthless streak, he could also be uninterested and quickly grow bored of things that didn't hold his attention. He wasn't father material and he didn't have time to learn how to be one...

But Millie didn't want him to be a father, she didn't want him involved in his child's life at all. She wanted to raise the baby alone, with no input from anybody else. How would he be any different from a sperm donor?

And if he did get her pregnant, could he stay uninvolved? He liked control, having it and wielding it, so would he be able to stick to his promise to stay out of her, and his child's, life? His mother had never liked him, but she liked having power over him. His father had been fine with, or without, Ben's presence in his life. If he had a child, in whose footsteps would he follow?

Questions tumbled through his mind, just like those

fluffy snowflakes tumbled through the night, and he couldn't find any answers. Could he keep his distance from Millie during the pregnancy and after the baby was born? Would he be able to carry on a relationship, even if it was business, and ignore her child...*his* child?

And what about his stuttering? He pushed his hands into his hair, irritated with his grasshopper thoughts.

His stuttering was, to an extent, hereditary—one of his uncles on his dad's side had a stutter, as did his grandfather. What if he passed his chronic stuttering on to his kid? How would Millie feel if he told her there was a chance her kid would inherit his speech impediment? Would she say *'thanks, but no thanks'*?

If she did that, and she most likely would, it would hurt like hell. His stuttering had caused him so much pain, but he'd overcome it. He'd made a few mistakes lately when speaking to Millie and those small lapses scared him to his soul. What was it about her that made him lose a smidgeon of his hard-fought-for control? He only stuttered when he got upset or was overly emotional.

He knew that having people in his life he cared about would lead to a resumption of his speech impediment. He'd proved that with Margrét and he'd promised himself he'd never go back to that deep, dark place where words stuck in his throat and his world closed in. To feel less than, stupid and unaccepted. No, he couldn't risk that, he'd worked too hard to go back to the place he was before.

He needed to run, to put as much distance between them as he could.

But then a tantalising thought dropped into his brain. What if he didn't?

What...what if he ran *to* her, had a fling with her and

then let her go when their time was up? Millie was an outlier, an absolute temptation, and she pulled unwelcome feelings to the surface. He accepted that.

Normally, when he met a woman who interested him, who made him feel more, he never, after taking her to bed, followed up. He was terrified he'd feel something, *anything*, and was constantly on edge, waiting for his stutter to be triggered by even the smallest hint of emotion. He so was tired of being ruled by fear…

Oh, he had no intention of falling in love with Millie, being overcome by emotion—it wasn't an option. But Millie got to him quicker than most and he sensed lust and like, affection and joy flittering on the outer edges of his mind. They were softer, brighter, lovelier emotions and ones he refused to entertain. He knew his stutter walked in their shadow…

But what if he *managed to* control his feelings towards Millie? What if, instead of running away, instead of having brief encounters, he had a fling with Millie and spent concentrated time with her? What if he danced with his devils instead of running away from them?

If he could keep emotions under control with her, then he knew—*knew*—he'd have absolute control of *every* emotion going forward.

Absolute control over his feelings meant he'd never have to worry about his stutter again. He'd be free of it, free from its invisible but still strong chains. Free from the fear of its reappearance and he'd finally wash the stain on his soul away. He'd never be the boy who couldn't speak again.

It was an opportunity, one that wouldn't roll around again. And when he had his emotions under control, then he could decide whether or not to give her a child.

* * *

Millie walked down the stairs to the kitchen, dressed in a pair of jeans, a long jersey the colour of butter and knee-high, flat-soled boots. Because she'd spent most of the night looking out of the window, she knew it had stopped snowing around four and, by eight, the heavy clouds had lifted, allowing what little light there was to filter through the gaps in the clouds. With every hour that passed the day lightened. As much as a winter's day in Iceland could.

She wished she could say the same thing about her state of mind.

At the bottom of the stairs, Millie paused and placed her fist into the area between her ribs. She had to face Ben at some point and all she could do was apologise for the timing of her question. She couldn't, *wouldn't*, apologise for asking him to give her the baby she so desperately wanted.

But she hadn't approached the subject in the right way and for that she was sorry. She needed him to know she hadn't used sex as a means to butter him up, another thought that had occurred to her in the early hours. She hadn't, not even once, equated making love with having a baby…she only linked Ben and babies after they'd made love.

She'd wanted him. She'd wanted to know him in the most primal, biblical way a man and woman could know each other. She'd only considered the possibility of Ben as a donor after looking at the website and long after they'd had blindingly good sex. She wasn't, couldn't be, that manipulative. Did he understand that? If he didn't, she needed to convince him.

She wasn't good at heart-to-heart conversations, at exposing herself emotionally or mentally. Since her mum's death and that blowout conversation with Magnús, she far preferred to keep people at a distance, that way they couldn't hurt or disappoint her.

But talk to Ben she would. She had to… But maybe she could do it later.

Ben's deep voice drifted over to her and stopped her flight up the stairs. 'Are you going to hover or are you going to come into the kitchen and have a cup of coffee?'

Right, *busted*. Millie wiped her damp hands on her jeans and pulled up a smile. Or tried to. She forced her feet to move, but when she saw him standing next to the island, looking down at his phone, all the air rushed from her lungs. Heat rocketed from her stomach to her womb and between her legs.

She wanted him again, desperately. She wanted to pull his navy sweater and white shirt up and over his head, tug that leather belt apart and drop his grey pants to the floor. Her hands itched to explore his chest, those lovely abs and his muscled back.

She wanted to fall into his kisses, and into the magic they'd found last night.

Ben looked up and their eyes connected. Heat flared in his eyes and his Adam's apple bobbed. Their physical attraction was undeniable, and she wished she could wipe the slate clean, go back to last night and start all over again.

Ben managed a small smile. 'Coffee?' he asked, putting his phone down on the counter.

'Morning. And, yes, please,' Millie slid on to a bar stool and linked her hands together. Ben turned to the expensive coffee machine and Millie looked past his broad shoulders to the drifts of snow outside the window.

In the weak light, not dawn or daylight, his neighbour-hood was now a pristine white landscape, as if Mother Nature had painted everything with a soft, fluffy brush. The trees lining the street were weighed down, their branches drooping under the weight of the snow. Ici-cles dropped from the eaves of the house over the road. 'Wow, that's a lot of snow,' she said, wincing at her inane statement.

'The main roads will be cleared in a few hours,' Ben explained, his back still to her. 'And they should open the airport soon.'

Right, he was hinting she should go back to London. She could do that. She *should* do that as soon as possible. But first, she had to apologise to Ben for making such a hash of things last night.

She pulled in some much-needed air and started to speak. 'I'm really sorry about last night, sorry I threw that at you and for the timing of my question. The thought popped into my brain and then left my mouth. I should've thought it through a bit more.'

Damn, she wished he'd turn around, she hated talk-ing to his back. 'It's a huge ask. Also, I don't want you to think I only had sex with you because I was buttering you up to ask you to give me a baby. I don't operate like that, the one thing had nothing to do with the other and I only thought about you being a donor after I—'

Ben walked over to her and slid a cup of coffee in front of her. He gripped her shoulder. 'Breathe, Millie.'

'I will, in a minute, I just need you to understand—'

'Millie, take a breath and stop talking,' Ben com-manded her.

Millie's mouth snapped shut. She looked at Ben and

when she was reasonably sure he wasn't going to speak, she started talking again. 'I just need to say that I'm—'

'Millicent.'

Millie heard the exasperation in his voice and stopped talking. Her shoulders slumped and she dropped her head, letting her hair hide her hot face. She'd made such a hash of everything, and she felt like such a fool. She desperately wanted the floor to open up and swallow her whole. Millie felt Ben's hand skate over her hair and then burrowed under her hair to hold her neck in a gentle grip. 'Look at me.'

It took Millie twenty seconds, maybe more, before she mustered the courage to look at him. And when she did, she saw he was smiling and that his expression held no mockery and a hefty dose of compassion. 'Can you possibly keep quiet for a minute while I speak?' he asked and she heard the gentle teasing in the question.

She nodded. Well, she'd *try*.

'I didn't, for one minute, think that you were manipulating me last night. And I'm smart enough to recognise when I'm being used.' His grip on her neck tightened, just a fraction. 'I don't know you well, but you don't dissemble and you aren't manipulative.'

A whole lot of tension left her body and she sighed, relieved. Weight dropped off her shoulders, but she couldn't relax because he was going to shoot down her proposal. 'Thank you,' she murmured. 'I appreciate you saying that.'

Ben picked up her cup of black coffee and took a sip. 'I can see the question in your eyes, Millie. You still want an answer.'

She nodded. 'I do.' It was the truth after all.

Ben pushed an agitated hand through his hair, his

mouth taut with tension. 'I can't give you one, I'm afraid. I know I should say no, but I can't. I can't say yes, either.'

'You need more time to think about it,' Millie said. She understood that and was perfectly happy to give him all the time he needed. Within reason. She wasn't going to hang around for ever waiting for an answer. She had a baby to make, a new life to start.

'I do,' Ben agreed.

Fair enough. 'That makes complete sense and I know I can't expect an immediate answer.' She'd like one, though. She thought about pushing him for a date, an end point and knew she was pushing her luck.

Rein it in, Piper. It's not as though you are asking to borrow some sugar or asking him to give you a lift to the airport.

'How long do you need?' she asked him.

He lifted his hands, puzzled. 'I don't know, Millie.'

She stared at her coffee cup, thinking hard. She'd been mentally prepared to delay getting pregnant until she and Ben were, at the minimum, legally separated. It would take them, at least, eighteen months to get their divorce through the system. Could she delay the baby-making process for half that time, say nine months, the same amount of time she required to grow a baby?

She wasn't crazy about the delay, but she was willing to wait if it meant there was a chance of having Ben's baby. She knew him, she trusted him and she wanted her child to carry his genes as well as hers.

'Do you think you could give me an answer in nine months?' Millie asked him.

She'd finally, finally, managed to crack his mask of imperturbability and shock, hot and blunt, flew through his eyes. 'You are prepared to wait *that* long?'

She lifted one shoulder. 'Yes. You are the only person I would consider entering into a nine-month baby deal.' She tried to smile, but knew she didn't succeed. 'My only request is what I've always asked of you, Ben, and that's for you to be honest. The moment you know whether you will, or won't, please tell me.'

He nodded, looking more serious than usual. 'I promise to tell you as soon as I can, Mils. And I promise to continue being honest with you.'

That's all she could ask. Right, time to move on from this awkward conversation. She was feeling like the one-night stand who'd overstayed her welcome and Ben had work to do. 'Can you check with Einar whether he managed to get me on a flight back to London?' she asked him. 'And do you think the bank will be open today?'

Ben nodded. 'I don't see why not. Why?'

'Well, I'd like to see what's in the bank deposit box Magnús rented in my name before I leave,' she told him, looking at the hands that had glided over her body last night. She wanted more of the wonderfulness they'd shared last night, but she couldn't ask him to take her back to bed. She torpedoed that option when she blurted out her baby-making idea.

Ben pushed his hip into the island and crossed his arms. He was so close she could count each of his individual, dark and stubby eyelashes and could see the faint, white scar on the right side of his jaw underneath his stubble. His big brain was working overtime and she wondered what he was thinking. She sighed. He was probably counting the minutes until he got the crazy woman out of his house.

'Why don't you stay?'

Millie blinked, unsure if her hearing was playing tricks on her. 'Sorry?' she asked.

'Stay,' he said. 'Here. With me.' Ben tapped his index finger against his bicep, the only hint he wasn't as insouciant as he sounded. 'I'm flying to St Barth's in two weeks, the afternoon before the gala concert—'

'I'm not happy about you missing the concert, Jónsson.' She narrowed her eyes at him, trying to channel Bettina. She also just wanted a minute to take in his words. Ben was asking her to stay. What did that, what *could* that, mean?

'I was hoping to talk you into the speech I've been asked to do,' she added.

'I'd rather die,' Ben growled and she wondered if he'd really turned white, or whether it was a trick of the light.

'You give speeches to hundreds, thousands of people all the time,' Millie countered. She'd caught a couple of his speeches on social media and she'd been impressed. Benedikt Jónsson, it was said, knew his stuff.

Ben's expression hardened. 'That's business, not personal. I don't *do* personal.'

His words were bullet hard and the hard light in his eyes suggested she not pursue this now.

'Spend the next two weeks with me,' he said, repeating his earlier suggestion. 'I'll take some downtime and I'll hand off some of my responsibilities to my second-in-command, and we can explore Iceland. It's been years since I've been snowshoeing or on a snowmobile.'

It had been even longer for her and she'd always loved Iceland best in winter. It had a stark beauty that took her breath away. Millie desperately wanted to reacquaint herself with this ancient, mystical land, and her first instinct was to shout yes, loudly and with force, but she managed to swallow her response.

'Why?' she asked instead. He couldn't do the speech for her, he didn't do personal, but he was asking her to stick around. She narrowed her eyes, suspicious. 'Why are you ditching work to spend time with me?'

Ben shrugged. 'Part of the reason is that I need to decide on whether to give you a baby and I think I need to know you better, and get to know you as an adult, to make that decision.'

His answer made sense, but it sounded… Millie bit the inside of her cheek. What was the word she was looking for? Rehearsed, maybe? Not a lie, but not the full truth either.

'And the other part?' Millie pressed him.

He scratched his neck, and his eyes slid off hers. 'You are like a human lie detector test. Look, I promised never to lie to you and I don't want to. Can I say that I am trying to work something out and leave it at that?'

She wanted to push, but sensed it wouldn't help. 'And you want me to stay in Reykjavik?' she clarified.

'Iceland is pretty special this time of the year and I thought it might be a good time for you to rediscover the country, as you've been away a long time.'

She had and she'd missed being here—she'd lost touch with her Icelandic roots. After their hasty marriage, she'd been desperate for a new life and a new place. It had taken her twelve years to return and she'd yet to lay all her ghosts to rest. Maybe if she spent some time here, she could work through the last of the resentment she held towards Magnús, she could remember her mum better and she could close the circle.

But there was another elephant in the room and this

one was wearing very sexy lingerie. What about sex? Would Ben expect her to share his bed? Could they go back to where they were last night? She wanted to spend long, lovely hours in his arms, but was having a fling with him the clever thing to do?

But how was she supposed to *not* want to sleep with him? He was smart, interesting, gorgeous and had superior bedroom skills. And she *liked* him. She'd never liked any man as much as she did Ben.

Maybe she should forget everything—using him as a baby maker, exploring this land she once called her home, their explosive attraction—and go back to London and resume her life there, eventually forcing herself to make an uncomplicated choice from a sperm bank website. But she'd asked Ben to give her a baby. It wasn't a request she could take back.

Millie rubbed her hands over her face and, when she lowered them, she saw that Ben was looking at her, his eyes steady and warm. 'Stay here, spend some time with me and when it's time for you to go home I'll, hopefully, be able to give you an answer about giving you a baby.' His eyebrows pulled together in a frown. 'But I feel I should warn you that the chances of me saying yes are not high.'

'I told you, you don't have to do anything, be anything—'

Ben jammed his hands into the pockets of his pants and frustration flickered in his eyes. 'Millie, we went over it. I know what you said and I'll think it through, okay?' He looked at his watch and then picked his coffee off the counter. 'So, are you staying or are you going back to the UK?'

It was a choice between spending time with him or

spending time in London, mostly alone. It was a choice between having his body wrapped around her when she slept, waking up to the smell of good coffee and a rumpled man in the morning and a series of great orgasms to…well, boredom. Loneliness.

Nobody, she decided, should be lonely at this time of the year. But before she agreed to stay here, she needed to know whether they were going to pick up where they left off. 'And are we going to keep sleeping together?'

Ben didn't drop his eyes from hers. 'Last night was amazing, but—'

Oh, dear, here came his *but*…

'Obviously I'd love to keep making love to you. But I don't want you to feel pressurised, that it's a condition of you staying. If we both want to, we can. If not, we remain friends.' He sent her one of those warm smiles that could melt her insides at fifty paces.

There was no point in trying to play it cool. 'I want to, Ben.'

A rare, full smile bloomed. 'Yeah, I do, too.'

'And are we friends, Ben?' Millie asked, tipping her head to the side.

'We're on our way,' Ben told her. It was a fair statement, but Ben knew her better than she knew him. 'Two weeks, Mils, let's go play. Let's forget about babies, work, divorce, the trust and what happens in the future and live in the moment. A two-week step out of time.'

Oh, that sounded like heaven. But the thought that life didn't work like that niggled at the back of her brain. They still had to be smart. 'Same terms as before?' she asked. 'No strings sex, complete honesty?'

He placed an open-mouthed kiss on her lips. 'That works. Can I get Einar to cancel your flights?'

Millie nodded quickly. 'Yes, please. Could you also ask him to see if he can get me an appointment at the bank so that I can deal with those safety deposit boxes?'

He nodded, scooped up his phone and in an instant he was talking to Einar, issuing a set of instructions in his machine-gun-fast Icelandic. Man, she had a long way to go before she became even mildly proficient in the language again. Thank goodness most Icelandic people spoke excellent English.

Millie slipped off the stool, but her progress to the coffee machine was halted by Ben's strong arm around her waist. While still talking to Einar, he deposited her back on the stool, but only on the edge and lifted her thigh to hold it over his hip. He smiled down at her as her core connected with his erection and she was pretty certain her eyes rolled back in her head. Because she wanted him to moan her name, she placed her hands on his hips and stretched out her fingers and allowed her thumbnail to scrape his long, hard length.

Ben was in the middle of a sentence about delaying some meeting—or she thought he was—but then his eyes darkened and he shuddered. He disconnected the phone mid-sentence and it clattered on to the surface of the island, coming to rest quite close to the far side. It buzzed with an incoming call, most likely Einar, but Ben ignored it and lowered his mouth to hers and slid his tongue past her teeth, to tangle with hers.

He jerked his head off her and stared down at her, his eyes blazing with need and passion. 'I'm taking you back to bed,' he told her in a deep growl. He lifted her and Millie wrapped her legs around his hips, loving his strength. Ben walked her up the stairs to the landing where he stopped to kiss her.

'I want you so damn much, Millie,' he told her, yanking her jersey up and over her head.

His need for her was obvious. It was in his touch, in the way he attacked her clothes, in his need to get her naked as soon as possible. She wanted him as much, as mindlessly, as completely.

CHAPTER SEVEN

LYING IN THE enormous bed in their exquisite room at a private, exclusive spa north of Reykjavik, Millie yawned and rested her head on Ben's shoulder after an extremely satisfying bout of lovemaking. She felt soft and floaty, a sorbet that had been left to melt under a hot summer sun. She pulled her knee up to rest it on Ben's thigh and felt the pull in her thigh muscles. *Ow.* Thank goodness she'd had a massage that afternoon—if she hadn't, she doubted she would still be able to walk.

She and Ben were a week into their Icelandic adventure and muscles she didn't know she possessed were saying 'hi'. Loudly and resentfully. Millie thought she was reasonably fit, but a week full of outdoor adventures—skiing, snowshoeing and ice skating—had her thinking that a few hours spent in the gym each week didn't amount to much.

They'd taken snowmobiles and explored Langjökull, the second-largest glacier in Iceland, but driving a snowmobile was so much harder than she remembered. But the experience had been amazing and sore muscles were a small price to pay to explore the amazing winter wonderland.

She'd forgotten how compelling and magical Iceland was, how endlessly beautiful. How effortlessly romantic.

'Have you ever been in love?' Millie asked, her voice breaking the comfortable silence.

He pulled back to frown at her. 'That's an out-of-the-blue question,' he stated. She shrugged. Did his body tense? Just a little?

'We're in a romantic room in a romantic place. I haven't, not really. I haven't experienced I-can't-live-without-you love,' Millie told him.

Ben stroked her head, then her shoulder. 'Have you enjoyed rediscovering Iceland?'

'So much,' she told him, kissing his chest, aware that he didn't answer her question. 'It's been brilliant.'

She'd always be grateful to Ben for joining her on her tour of rediscovering the land of her birth. Together, they'd marvelled at the Gullfoss waterfall, watched geysers shoot from the ground and walked through ice caves. And she'd never forget seeing a massive chunk of ice calving into the water and floating towards the sea at Jökulsárlón. Her Icelandic was, very slowly, improving and Ben, apart from taking and making a few phone calls, had left work behind.

Ben's phone lit up. He picked it up and squinted at the screen to read the message. Who was rude enough to send messages so late at night? Putting it back down on the bedside table, Ben turned his head to kiss her forehead and she expected a sleepy goodnight.

'Let's get up.'

She dragged her eyelids open and tipped her head back. It was shortly after midnight, what could he possibly want to do? 'Let me think about that...' she told him, yawning. '*No.* Go to sleep, you maniac.'

Instead of following what she thought was a very sensible suggestion, Ben left their bed and flipped the covers back. He slid one hand under her bum, the other under her back, and walked her to the en-suite bathroom. The huge shower was tucked into the corner and Ben placed her on her feet and flipped on the taps to the multi-headed shower.

'Can we not do this in the morning?' Millie asked as he handed her a band to keep her hair out of the pulsing spray.

Ben dropped a kiss on her nose. 'We could,' he agreed.

Millie's eyes widened as Ben stepped under the spray and quickly and efficiently washed. Shrugging at his hurried movements, she stepped under the lovely, hot spray and allowed the power shower to pummel her stiff shoulders. Mr Efficient could power his way through the shower, but she was in holiday mode and intended to enjoy every experience at this luxury geothermal spa. And that included spending many, many luxurious minutes enjoying this power shower.

She'd booked another spa appointment tomorrow and later they were taking a private tour to hunt for the Northern Lights. They could drive for hours, Ben warned her, and not see anything. Nature's most amazing light show only appeared when conditions were perfect—their appearance had something to do with solar activity, cloud cover and the darkness of the night sky. They might get lucky, or they might not.

Unlike Millie, who had been getting very lucky a *lot*.

Ben used a soapy flannel to wash her down and Millie's eyes flew open. 'I can wash myself, thanks,' she told him, irritated by his brisk strokes.

'Then can you hurry it up?' Ben asked, sounding uncharacteristically impatient.

What was his problem? If he wanted to get back to bed, he could leave her here to enjoy her shower in peace.

'You're killing me here, Mils,' Ben said, with a low

groan. He dropped the flannel and used his hands to smooth soap across her body and Millie's protests died away. Her body, as it always did, melted under his skilled hands and she placed a hand on the wall to keep her balance when his hands moved between her thighs. She rocked against him, closing her eyes…he'd pulled more than a few orgasms from her earlier, yet here she was, on the edge again.

'Nope, not happening,' Ben muttered, shaking his head. 'Not right now.'

Millie looked down, saw he was interested and if they sat on the built-in ledge, they could add shower sex to their ever-increasing repertoire of sexual positions. Instead of stroking her, Ben yanked his hand from between her legs and pushed her under the shower so she could rinse the expensive shower gel from her body.

When she was free of soap, Ben turned off the shower and handed her one of the extraordinarily fluffy bathrobes hanging on a hook in easy reach of the shower door. He yanked his on and pulled her out of the bathroom.

Instead of leading her back to bed, he led her through the sliding doors on to the wooden deck outside and Millie yelped when her feet hit the icy planks. The cold air was a shock and she tried to turn around to rush back to the warmth of their bedroom, but Ben planted his feet and held her in place. 'Trust me, Millie.'

Millie hopped from foot to foot. 'Where are we going?' she demanded. 'And will you pay for my medical treatment when my toes drop off from frostbite?'

In the darkness, Ben's white teeth flashed as he smiled. 'The planks are nowhere near cold enough to give you frostbite, they are heated. Stop being dramatic and start walking. I promise it will be worth it.'

Millie glared at the back of his head as he led her down the wood deck path. Just a few yards away was a geothermal pool. Right, she remembered reading something about each room having its own pool. Yes, her toes were about to fall off, but having a midnight swim in a thermal pool was a perfect idea.

Then she remembered that it would be a skinny dip and her swimming costume was back in her room. She tugged on Ben's hand. 'Ben, we can't swim naked,' she protested.

Ben stopped at the edge of their pool. Millie couldn't see any of the other pools now, only the wild north Atlantic as it crashed on to the rocks below them. 'Nobody can see us, and we can't see them,' Ben told her. 'Everyone else is asleep.'

He shrugged out of his dressing gown and Millie thought he'd never seen anything better than Ben standing on the side of the pool, tall and strong and utterly masculine. The night sky was clear, but so dark, and Millie thought it would be amazing to sit in the pool while fat snowflakes fell from the sky.

She heard the hiss of the geothermal spring and watched Ben slide into the water, his eyes closing in sensual delight. She saw a sign attached to the wall and moved to read it, barely able to make out the words in the dim light. It was a request that all the bathers shower before entering the pool. Right, that explained Ben bundling her into the shower.

'Come on in, Millie,' Ben told her.

Millie undid the sash, hung her robe alongside Ben's and tried not to feel embarrassed about being naked. It was no different from when they were in bed, she told herself. She darted a look at Ben and his look of appreciation imbued her with confidence. Using the steps, she slipped into the water...

And in five seconds, she died and went to heaven. The hot water was silky against her skin and her body heated instantly. She bent her knees and the water covered her shoulders. It was official: she might never leave this place.

Ben wrapped his arms around her waist and dropped a kiss on her temple. Millie looked up and took in the black velvet sky and the ice drop stars and felt completely happy, unbelievably content. Right now, right here, with this man, was where she most wanted to be.

'It's the most stunning night, cold but so clear,' Millie whispered, feeling the need to keep her voice down. It felt wrong to talk at normal volume when the air around them was so still.

'It is,' Ben agreed. He guided her to a ledge and sat, positioning her back to his front so they could look out to sea. He cupped one breast with one hand and laid the other on her thigh and Millie leaned her head back to rest her head on his collarbone. Hot water, an amazing sky and Ben. What else could she need?

'Bettina sent me the slideshow they are going to play at the concert, Ben, and a rough draft of the speech detailing her work with the foundation,' Millie lazily told him after they'd been silent for a few minutes. She could be quiet with Ben and she didn't feel the need to fill every minute talking.

'And?'

'It's good,' Millie said. 'Humorous and lovely without being maudlin. It'll be so hard to speak without crying, especially knowing you won't be there. I wish you'd change your plans and do the speech for me—'

'You need to do it, Millie,' Ben told her and Millie

heard the *don't go there* note in his voice. A few days ago she'd asked him, again, whether he'd read the speech for her and got a curt, harsh 'no' as a reply.

'But I could delay my trip to St Barth's and fly out after the concert, if you *really* wanted me there.'

She tipped her head back and up so she could, sort of, look at his face. 'I *really* do want you there, Ben. And Jacqui loved you and I think your absence would be noticed.'

'I know,' he admitted, his voice sounding rough. 'It's j-just…' He hesitated for a few beats, before taking in a deep breath. 'I still miss her and I thought it would be easier to be somewhere else.'

Millie understood that. Being around people who loved her mum, and who wanted to talk about her, brought a lot of the pain of losing her back and it was a sharper stab than before.

'I'll change my plans, Mils, and I'll attend the gala concert with you. I'll fly out when it's done.'

'Thank you.' And maybe, somehow, she'd persuade him to do the speech for her. She sighed and tipped her eyes to inspect the bold, brash sky, filled with stars. 'This land… I'd forgotten how enchanting it is.'

She felt Ben drop a kiss into her hair—it was still in the messy bun she'd pulled it into before she went into the shower. 'It's nice to see you enjoying Iceland, Millie,' he murmured. 'The last time you were here, you couldn't wait to leave.'

True enough. She'd desperately wanted to get away from Magnús and start a new life somewhere else. 'Iceland was too small for both of us,' she replied.

'You and me or you and Magnús?'

'My stepfather and I,' she clarified. 'Our relationship was nightmarish.'

Ben took a while to answer her. 'I now know that you had your problems after your mum died, but I thought that you two got along well before Jacqui died. Icelandic people don't get hung up about step kids and parentage. They're pretty welcoming. Why wasn't Magnús?'

'He resented me, resented the attention my mum gave me.'

'Why didn't Jacqui tell you about your biological father?'

It was a question she'd asked herself a thousand times. 'I don't know. She was unbelievably honest, yet she lied to me about Magnús until the day she died.'

Ben's chest lifted with his sigh. 'I've wondered about that, too, because Jacqui wasn't secretive.'

'Well, she kept one hell of a one from me,' Millie said, sounding bitter. 'And, yes, I'm still angry with her for leaving me with all these questions and what ifs.'

'What ifs?'

'I don't have a family, Ben…so what if my dad is out there and what if he needs a family as much as I do? What if I have an underlying medical condition that I have inherited from him? What if I pass on something from him to any kids I might have?' Behind her, Ben tensed. She was spoiling this night by talking about her past and she should stop.

She sighed. She knew she was being overly dramatic. 'Not knowing who he is, whether he is still alive or whether he even knew about me, keeps me awake at night, Benedikt.'

He stroked her arm, from her shoulder to the tips of her fingers. 'I know, sweetheart.'

'And it would help if I understood why my mum kept

it from me.' Millie half turned to face him. 'You don't know anything about him, right?'

He looked her in the eye and pushed a strand of damp hair off her forehead. 'No, sweetheart. I didn't know anything about this until you told me.' Ben cuddled her close. 'I'm so sorry, Millie. If it helps, I wish I could go back in time—I'd change that for you.'

Millie traced patterns on his wrist and up his arm. 'I just wished she'd trusted me,' Millie said. 'Between them, they did a good job of teaching me not to trust anyone.'

'Explain that, Mils.'

'If my mum, the person who I loved, who loved me, could lie to me, I think anybody can. And will. But Magnús messed me up as well,' she added. 'I hate the thought of being controlled and, because he could never love me, I doubt anyone can, except, maybe, any children I have. I wasn't a bad kid, Ben, I tried so hard to be a good daughter, someone he could love, but I never got there.'

'You do know it was his issue, Mils, and not yours?'

'Intellectually I do, emotionally, I still have my doubts. I've had guys who told me they loved me, but I could never quite believe it and, because I couldn't trust what they said, or them, they eventually gave up on me. Or I gave up on them.'

'Oh, Millie,' Ben murmured.

'I've spent so much emotional energy on trying to figure my mum and stepfather out, trying to work out their motives for doing what they did,' Millie told him, wiggling her toes. 'The only thing that gives me a little comfort is that I made Magnús's life hell for a few years. He took some hits for his daughter, the walking, talking PR disaster.'

'Yeah, you landed a few blows, Mils. Unfortunately,

Magnús didn't take the heat, I did. You wouldn't believe how many times I had to sweet-talk a client, how many times I heard the "why should they give me their PR account when we couldn't manage to keep the founder's daughter out of the news cycle" question. I became an expert in tap dancing.'

Millie turned to face him and scrunched her face. 'Oh, Ben, I'm so sorry. I never imagined you'd take the flak for what I did.'

'I think I overcame the hurdle you presented, Mils,' he drily informed her.

Since he—they—now owned a multi-international firm with clients based all around the world, it was obvious he had.

Millie leaned her back against the bath's wall and pulled her knees up to her chest. 'Thank you for marrying me, Ben. Thank you for giving me an out and for looking after my interests so well.'

'Why did you trust me enough to put yourself in my hands?' he asked, after a short, emotional silence.

She thought for a minute, wondering how to explain. 'I think it's because my mum did. And when I suggested that we get married, you didn't throw me out of your office, you listened to what I had to say. And you were so straightforward, so…blunt. I appreciated that. And I appreciated you writing down the terms of our marriage, what we could and couldn't do, what was expected.'

Ben picked up a curl that had fallen loose from her bun and rubbed the damp hair between his fingers. 'You do know our agreement couldn't be used in a court of law, right?'

Millie rolled her eyes at his question. 'Of course I do, Benedikt, I knew it back then, too. But that you wrote it down, with our signatures, meant something to me. I've always disliked shadows, but I felt back then, as I do now, that you are a man who stands in the sunshine. With you, I get what I see.'

She felt him tense and frowned when he pulled his shoulder and leg away from hers. What did she say? Why was he pulling back? Had she, in some way, got that statement, or him, wrong?

No, she was being ridiculous. Ben had been the same man for the past twelve years, nothing had changed. He was still as forthright and blunt as he ever was, as most Icelandic people, except for Magnús, were. She was letting her imagination off its leash. But she had to ask. 'Is there something I should know, Ben? Something you aren't telling me?'

Ben dropped his head and brushed his lips across hers in a kiss that was both racy and reassuring. 'Sweetheart, you're getting worked up and that's not what I thought would happen at half-midnight in a hot pool.'

Right…he was *right*. But Millie noticed he didn't answer her question. She thought about asking him again, pushing for more, but suspected Ben would retreat behind his armour of implacability and reserve. No, she was being silly and was spoiling the moment.

Then Ben smiled, placed a hand on her shoulder and released an audible sigh. 'Finally,' he murmured. 'I was about to give up on you.'

Millie wondered who he was talking to, but, before she could ask him, he slipped off her seat and walked to the other side of the tub. Ben placed his forearms on the side of the tub and she copied his movements.

'What are we looking at, Ben?' she asked, noticing that his eyes were fixed on the horizon.

He lifted his hand and Millie looked to where he was pointing. She saw a hint of green and thought her eyes were playing tricks on her. Then the sky started to pulsate with the strangest, most beautiful luminous green light. Millie's mouth fell open and she clutched Ben's arm, digging her nails into his skin.

'Are those...could those be...am I looking at the Northern Lights?'

Ben gently removed her hand from his arm and pulled her to stand in front of him and bent his knees so that their bodies were immersed in the water.

'I received a text alert when we were in bed saying that the conditions were optimal and that there was a good chance of them making an appearance. I didn't tell you because I didn't want you to be disappointed if they didn't appear.' He rested his chin on the top of her head as yellow joined green in a slinky, sensuous tango across the sky. 'I was about to call it a night and take you back to bed when I saw a hint of green on the horizon.'

Millie nodded, unable to speak as more of the celestial dancers took to the sky. Pink waltzed with blue, orange with purple in an indescribable light show. It felt as though some mystical force in the universe was finger painting, drawing an omnipotent finger through a palette of brightly coloured oil paints.

Millie stood in Ben's arms, utterly transfixed. It seemed to her that the world was holding its breath and the sea had stopped throwing waves against the rocks in deference to the majesty of the lights. She didn't want to talk or examine how she was feeling—her thoughts and emotions and her entire existence were all inconsequential right now. She was glad that Ben seemed to understand that words would spoil the moment.

He just held her, occasionally drifting a finger across her skin under the water to remind her he was there, here with her. Millie forgot her face was cold, that the night seemed darker than it had been before. All she could do was to try, in the best way she could, to take it all in.

She wanted to make memories and wanted every hue, every wave, every drumbeat of colour to be burned on her internal memory bank. She knew she was privileged to witness this, to stand under a majestic sky and be both overwhelmed and entertained. She couldn't tell how long they watched the lights, it could've been minutes or days, but she didn't care. Although he'd witnessed the ultimate light show many times before, Ben didn't rush her, he just waited until the last flicker of colour faded away before leading her out of the pool. Bemused, and bewitched, Millie kept looking at the sky as he shoved her into her gown, before pulling on his own. It was only when he guided her on to the icy wooden path that led back to their suite that she was shocked back into reality.

'I can't believe that happened,' she whispered. His hand tightened around hers and she felt rather than saw his contented smile.

'It was one of the more intense ones I've seen,' Ben admitted, his deep voice sliding over her skin like melted molasses.

She tugged on his hand and braked. Ben stopped and turned around. When he lifted his eyebrows, she cleared her throat and tried to speak past the emotion. 'Thank you. That was…um…unbelievable. I will never forget…' She dashed her tears away with impatient fingers.

Seeming to understand she couldn't express what she wanted to say, how emotional she felt, Ben dropped his head to kiss her temple. 'Let's go to bed, sweetheart.'

CHAPTER EIGHT

MILLIE THOUGHT THAT after a good sleep her revving-in-the-red-zone emotions would die down. But the next morning, watching Ben—dressed only in jeans and a cashmere sweater over a long-sleeved shirt—talk on his mobile outside, she knew everything had changed.

She wanted Ben in her life. Permanently. She wanted him as a lover, a husband and the father of her children. But loving someone meant trusting them, something she found intensely hard to do. She couldn't handle Ben lying to her, couldn't cope if he disappointed her. He could hurt her and cut her into a million emotional pieces.

But, despite their amazing Icelandic fling, him showing her the country of her birth, the laughter and the loving, she knew he hadn't caught as many feelings as her. Or any at all.

She was his wife, but in name only. He was her lover, but he'd given her no hint he wanted to continue seeing her after the gala concert, and they hadn't spoken again about her sperm donor request.

Despite them spending every moment of the last ten days together, she didn't know him much better than she had when she first arrived in Reykjavik. It was obvious there was so much below his urbane façade and she couldn't access any of his hidden depths. Millie didn't know if she ever would. Ben was an island, a place you got to visit, but never to know.

It was so typical of her that the one man she loved, the only person she'd ever fully trusted, was the one man who only wanted a specific amount from her and no more. He knew so much about her, far more than anyone else, yet what she knew about his inner world would fit on a postage stamp.

Something was bugging him, he was wrestling with an issue. What was he trying to work out? Why couldn't he share it with her? Why did he need to hide it? Why wouldn't he let her help? She wanted to be the person he confided in, the woman who knew him better than anyone else. The one he turned to, valued, whose opinion was important.

Millie placed her hand on the cold glass and sighed. Ben's back was to her, and she took in his height, his strength, his solidity. Was she imagining herself to be in love with him because he was exactly what she wanted in a man? As a father for her children? Oh, he wasn't perfect, far from it. He could be impatient and unbelievably, tactlessly blunt, but he was, at the core of him, solid and calm. But so emotionally elusive...

Ben turned, saw her looking at him through the window and his slow smile heated her from the inside out. He dropped his phone to his side and walked over to the door, sliding it open. Millie stepped back and squealed when he put his cold hand on her cheek.

'How can you be out there without a jacket?' she asked.

'Viking blood,' he quickly replied. 'It's a couple of degrees warmer than it was yesterday.'

Millie shook her head. 'That doesn't help when the temps dip below zero, Jónsson.' She saw that the light was fading and shook her head. It wasn't even three in the afternoon yet!

Ben tossed his phone on the coffee table that stood between the two couches and perched on the arm of the nearest couch. 'I was just talking to Einar about rearranging my St Barth trip. I'll be missing the first night of my friend's stag do, but that's not an issue.'

Millie winced. 'Look, if you need to be there—'

'All I'll miss is the hangover the next morning,' Ben assured her. 'Einar also spoke to Bettina who is, supposedly, delighted I will be escorting you. It's good PR,' he said, humour dancing in his deep blue eyes.

'Jacq's daughter and ex-partner arriving together will make a good story and will generate headlines and good press for the foundation.'

Was that why he had agreed to accompany her to the gala concert? Because it would be excellent PR for the Star Shine Foundation? Did his change of heart have anything at all to do with her? She thought he'd agreed to be there to support her, but now she wasn't so sure.

'Imagine the headlines if they knew we were married,' Millie said. 'There would be a firestorm of press attention.'

Ben pulled a face. 'I manage people who find themselves the target of a camera lens, not the other way around. Extricating celebrities from their self-created dramas is, *was*, the least favourite part of my job.'

Millie laughed. For a guy who ran an international PR firm, he should show more enthusiasm for celebrities and their need for good PR than he did, she told him. 'How on earth did you handle the PR for Daft Peanut and Gladys?' she asked.

She'd caused a few headlines in her day, but the antics of the young, over-the-top DJ who'd burst on to the music scene ten years ago and the bad girl of Scandinavian music were enough to turn any PR person grey.

'I tore my hair out with both of them,' Ben told her. 'The greatest day of my life was when I handed the clients over to my subordinates. I was finally able to run the business without having to stop to deal with their drama. Then, as soon as I could, I diversified and appointed an excellent manager to handle the high-value, high-drama clients. As you, as part-owner of the business, should know.' The comment was pointed and showed Millie that her lack of interest in their jointly owned business frustrated him.

'I have just enough interest in business practices to run my small operation, Ben. PR Reliance was my mum's baby, not mine,' she told him. She pointed a finger at him. 'And, be honest, you would hate having an involved, interested partner. It suits you just fine for me to be a silent partner.'

Ben placed his empty cup on the coffee table and folded his arms. 'Maybe,' he conceded.

'Maybe my foot,' Millie retorted.

Ben tapped his index finger against his bicep. 'We were talking about the gala concert,' he said, changing the subject because he knew she was right. 'Because of you, I have to smile at the cameras and people, and shake many, many hands and kiss many, many cheeks.' Ben pulled a face. 'And I'll have to wear a tuxedo, which I hate.'

'Poor baby,' Millie gently mocked him. 'At least you don't have to do a speech honouring your dead mum.'

'*Touché*. You've definitely got the tougher gig,' he softly said. He ran his hand down her hair. 'You'll be fine, Mils.'

'You'd be finer,' she whipped back.

'Give it up, Mils, I'm not doing your speech for you,' Ben wearily stated, gripping the bridge of his nose.

She didn't want an argument with him, so she rested her temple against his bicep and wound her arms around his waist. He gathered her close and placed his chin on the top of her head. 'Didn't you say that you had booked a spa treatment some time soon?' he asked.

She had. 'Mmm. At three-thirty.'

'It's half two, now,' Ben told her, stepping back from her. She caught his mischievous smile as he gripped her hand in his and led her to the bedroom. 'That means I have forty-five minutes. Between sex and your spa treatment, you're going to need a nap later.'

Millie tried, but couldn't find any problems with his statement.

Ben took her empty takeaway cup and asked her if she wanted another hot chocolate. Millie debated for a minute—of course she did, they were delicious!—and it took all of her willpower to shake her head. 'I'd better not,' she told him, 'or else there is no way I'm going to fit into my dress for the gala concert.'

She thought of the gold, tight-fitting jersey top and the lighter gold flowing skirt she'd bought yesterday, after seeing it in the window of a small boutique on Laugavegur Street. While she didn't think that one hot chocolate would cause her to put on weight, the pastries she was addicted to, and the other delicious Christmas foods Ben kept insisting she try, would add to her waistline.

At this rate, she might not fit into her plane seat when she flew back after New Year. Ben threw their cups into a rubbish bin as Millie took in the square. The market at Jólaþorpið was fifteen minutes from Reykjavik. It echoed the beauty of the town of Hafnarfjörður and was a typical Christmas market.

Twinkling fairy lights criss-crossed the space between the booths and jaunty instrumental music floated through the air. Millie had picked up a few Christmas gifts from stalls selling homemade jams and jewellery, Christmas decorations and woollen products. And there was food... so much food.

The long hours of dusk, that magical light, made the market extra festive, but it was cold and Millie stamped her feet, trying to get her blood flowing.

'Cold?' Ben asked, running his bare fingers down her cheek.

Since her nose was probably red, she couldn't lie. 'I am. But I'll be fine once we start moving.'

Ben curved his hand around the back of her neck and his warm lips met hers. 'Then let's walk. Do you want to try to find the Huldufólk?'

The Huldufólk, or hidden people, were elves in Icelandic folklore and were said to be supernatural creatures living in the wild. They looked and acted like humans and could make themselves visible at will. So it was said.

Millie squinted at him. 'C'mon, Ben, you don't really believe in them, do you?'

He shrugged. 'I don't *not* believe in them. It's part of the Icelandic tradition and culture and every culture needs a little magic.'

Millie remembered talk about the hidden folk from when she was little. 'I always thought your house had Huldufólk living in your garden,' she admitted. 'I loved visiting your dad, I would spend hours in the garden hoping I'd see one.'

Ben took her gloved hand in his. 'Well, Hellisgerdi Park is not far from here and they say it's the home of many Huldufólk. It's also a pretty walk and decorated for Christmas. Want to see it?'

Millie nodded, feeling the heat of his bare hand through the wool. He radiated warmth and she immediately felt warmer as they headed for the park. As they approached the park, whispers of déjà vu fluttered inside her and she was certain she'd visited here with her mum when she was very small. Candy canes and twinkling Christmas lights provided light to the cleared path, but snow covered the ground, small hills and the branches of trees.

'I think I only ever came here in summer,' Millie told Ben. 'It looks like an enchanted garden, doesn't it?'

He nodded. 'There are lots of lava formations that are blanketed in moss, so it's easy to convince kids, and adults, that elves live here. My dad insisted the hidden folk were real.'

Millie looked up at him, surprised. 'I think that's the first time you've ever mentioned your dad,' she said. 'You don't talk much about your family.'

He looked away. 'You know the basics, English mother, Icelandic father. I went to boarding school in the UK. I spent a couple of school holidays with him.'

'No siblings?'

'No.' So they were both only children of only children. And Millie knew it was a lonely way to grow up.

She'd like to know much more than the basics of his past. And because he opened the door, she strolled on through. 'What was he like?'

'Stoic and direct, a big believer in the Icelandic philosophy of *þetta reddast*.'

'Everything will work out,' Millie murmured.

Ben rocked his hand from side to side. 'Sort of, but not quite,' he replied. 'It's less starry-eyed optimism and more the idea that you sometimes have to make the best of things, just work through it.' He gestured to the banks of snow.

'Take the recent blizzard for example. It's not the first, it won't be the last and it wasn't nearly the worst the country has seen. We've got volcanoes and glaciers and we have to live in this hostile environment and make it work for us. We accept that sometimes life does work out and sometimes it doesn't, but you have to try.'

'And that's how you built up PR Reliance,' Millie said. 'But you took it from a small national concern to an international empire.'

'That's my English mother's bull-headed determination. If you tell me I can't do something, then I will.'

'Are you more English than Icelandic?' Millie asked him, intrigued.

Ben looked down at her. 'What do you think?'

She took some time to sort through her thoughts, before answering him. 'You are very blunt, so you are Icelandic in that. You're punctual, that's English because Icelandic people are not. I know that you are a huge believer in equality and that's very Icelandic. But I think you are very English in your outlook on relationships.'

He stopped walking to look down at her. 'What do you mean by that?'

'Well, I want a baby, as you know.'

'You might've mentioned it once or twice,' Ben replied, a little drily.

She narrowed her eyes to fake-scowl at him. 'Anyway… Iceland has one of the highest birth rates in Europe and there are young women everywhere with babies and who are pregnant. Some are in relationships, some aren't. But Icelanders have this idea that babies are always welcome and there isn't angst around blended families. Yet you are—' She hesitated, unsure of how to put this into words.

'I'm what?' he prompted her.

'I think the English part of you is hesitating—if you were fully Icelandic, I'd probably be pregnant by now.'

'I appreciate your confidence in my baby-making skills,' Ben murmured.

But he didn't contradict her and that was interesting. 'So you don't subscribe to the-more-the-merrier idea of kids? Or *þetta reddast* when it comes to having kids?'

He took her hand, tucked it into his elbow and they started walking again. 'No, I don't.'

Right, don't overwhelm me with information, Jónsson.

Millie started to tell him he didn't need to be involved in the raising of the baby, but held her words back. Two weeks ago, she thought she wanted to be a single mum, but now she wasn't sure. She now wanted more from Ben, as a lover and as a father.

'It's unlike you not to take the opportunity to try to convince me to give you a child, Mils,' Ben commented.

She scrunched up her nose and hoped he didn't notice. She wasn't sure what to say—her heart wanted to beg him to love her, to create a family with her, and to plan a life together—but she knew he would run a mile if she suggested any of the above. Ben didn't do commitment, he'd told her that. More than once. And at some point, she had to let that sink in, take it onboard.

'What was your mum like, Ben?' she asked instead. Maybe if he understood more about his past, she would understand him a bit better.

He sighed. 'Driven, cold, emotionally stunted.'

Wow, okay then.

'She was a nuclear engineer, right?'

'Yes, she worked for a company I'm pretty sure is a cover for the British government,' Ben told her. 'She was obsessed with her work and I got my work ethic from her.'

'And, possibly, your dad. People in Iceland aren't slouches when it comes to working.'

'Point taken, but my mother was a next-level workaholic. Nothing ever came between her and her work,' he said and Millie heard a note of…something in his voice. Longing or resentment—a combination of both? She wasn't sure.

'Tell me something good about her,' Millie said, wanting him to move on to a happier memory. It was what she did, or what she was trying to do, when she got caught up in the *Why didn't my mum believe me or be honest with me?* spiral. 'Did she binge eat chocolate or have a funny laugh?'

She'd never met his mum and she wondered about the woman who'd birthed him. She felt Ben pull away from her, just a little, and she followed, tucking herself back into his side. She wasn't going to allow him to scoot away, emotionally or physically.

'She was super-intelligent, her IQ was off the charts,' Ben eventually told her. 'She would never mix her food— if she had potatoes, vegetables and meat on her plate, she'd eat each one separately. Ah, what else? She was utterly unemotional, brutally honest and had no concept of tact. If she thought you were an idiot, then that's what you were. She believed you could do anything you wanted to, achieve anything at all, as long as you put your mind to it and worked hard. She didn't accept failure, ever.'

Millie rubbed her cold and itchy nose with the side of her hand. She knew, from those few sentences, that she hadn't been fun to live with and her expectations of Ben had been off the charts. Being raised by somebody like that had to have been difficult. No wonder he wasn't a warm and fuzzy type of guy.

'Is she the reason you don't want to have kids?' Millie asked. 'Because you suspect you might be like her?'

Ben stopped and looked down at her. In the half-daylight, half-night light, his eyes were a hard blue. 'I'm exactly like her, Millie, don't think I'm not.'

She laughed and Ben jerked back. 'Don't be ridiculous, you're nothing like that! Sure, you don't wear your heart on your sleeve, but you know how to laugh and you know how to make a woman feel special. You've listened to me talk about my mum and my issues with Magnús. You helped me re-balance those scales. You took me all over the country on a holiday trip I'll never forget and were thoughtful enough to hang around in a hot pool, hoping for the lights to appear because you knew how much I wanted to see them. You *see* me, Ben.'

'You don't know me, Millie, not really,' Ben told her.

He looked so serious and Millie felt a frisson of fear run up her spine. 'Of course I do,' she protested. 'Okay, maybe I don't know all your history, but I know what makes you *you*. You embody what I value most…'

'And that is?' he challenged.

'Honesty,' she told him. 'You've always been honest with me and that means more to me than anything else.'

Ben released a tiny snort, part-laughter, part-derision. 'You're seeing me through rose-coloured glasses, Millie.'

'Are you telling me that you haven't been honest with me?' Millie demanded.

'I'm telling you that you've chosen to see what you want to see. You still think that I'm going to cave and give you a baby, don't you?'

How had a massive chasm opened up between them, why were they suddenly arguing? Millie saw the annoyance in Ben's eyes and, when he repeated his question, she threw her hands up in the air. 'I'm hoping that you are,' she admitted. She was also hoping he'd come to love her and that they'd have a life together.

'Please don't bank on it, Millie.'

CHAPTER NINE

BACK IN REYKJAVIK, Millie left the taxi and walked up the path to Ben's front door. She slipped inside his house, kicked off her boots in the hall and hung her coat up on a rack. She rested the package on the hall table, still unable to believe the contents held within the plain cardboard box.

Finally alone, she slid down the wall to sit on the cold floor of the hallway and tears, hot and acidic, slid down her cheeks. The house had underfloor heating, but the hall, separated from the rest of the house by frosted glass doors, was chillier.

She just needed a moment to get herself under control, a few minutes to make sense of what was in the box. She'd wanted answers, but they weren't what she'd expected. Not even close.

Millie heard the glass doors opening, but she didn't look up, silently begging Ben to go away. She didn't want to explain the reason for her tears, wasn't sure if she could. There were no words...

Not for what she'd just discovered.

Millie felt Ben's hand on her head and then he crouched down in front of her, easily balancing on the balls of his feet. He placed his finger under her chin and lifted her face, but Millie slammed her eyes shut, not wanting him to see her cry.

'Ah, sweetheart, what's got you in such a state?' Ben asked, placing both his hands on her bent knees.

She darted a look at the brown box. 'I went to the bank,' she told him.

'Okay,' Ben said. 'You can tell me all about it, but we need to get you up off this cold floor first.'

He stood, gripped her hands and pulled her up. Cupping her face, he used his thumbs to brush away the tears before holding her head against his chest. Millie buried her nose into that space where his shoulder met his neck, inhaling his sea-and-sunshine scented cologne, her arms around his waist. Ben held her close and Millie knew he'd hold her until she was ready to talk, to make the next move, or leave his arms.

She could stay here for ever, he gave the best hugs, but she knew she had to face down the contents of that box. She couldn't avoid it or ignore it, she couldn't choose only the best parts of her past.

'I didn't expect you to be here,' she told Ben.

'Nothing needed my attention at the office. I was missing you, so I came home,' Ben told her.

Millie stepped back and bent her knees to pick up the box, but Ben got there first, lifted it and tucked it under his arm. He opened the glass door leading into the open-plan lounge, dining and kitchen area and placed the box on the wooden table in the kitchen area. He suggested that Millie sit and asked her if she wanted some wine.

She glanced at the oversized clock on the cherry-red wall above the stove. It was only three in the afternoon and a bit early.

'I'm done with work for the day and you're on holiday, so why not?' Ben asked.

Why not indeed? Millie watched as he chose a bottle of wine from the rack next to the fridge, remembering he had a state-of-the-art cellar in the basement. It was next to the state-of-the-art gym and the sauna, which was also top of the range.

Millie took the huge glass Ben held out to her and sipped. Ben slid on to the bench across the table from her, waiting for her to tell him the reason for her tears.

If she didn't tell him, if she changed the subject and moved on, he would let her. Ben didn't push. Millie took another sip of her wine and stood, moving to stand at the head of the table. She lifted the lid on the box and looked at Ben.

'As you know, I went to the bank to find out what Magnús put in the safety deposit box. And it was Magnús, he paid to rent it and I'm the only person who can access it. I have no idea why he didn't send the contents to me, directly.'

'I suppose there are no gold bars, loose diamonds or wads of cash?' Ben asked.

She shook her head. 'No, nothing like that.' She picked up the top file, saw that it was labelled with her mum's name and rested it on the table between the box and Ben. 'These are some of my mum's papers, her birth and death certificate, her schooling records, letters between her and her parents. I never thought to ask where they were, I assumed you had them.' She picked up a picture, smiled at the two stick-like figures and handed it to Ben.

He studied her childish drawing and the side of his mouth lifted in a sexy smile. 'I see your sketching skills hadn't yet kicked in,' he commented.

'I was four,' Millie protested. She pointed to the purple bobs around her mother's neck and at her ears. 'I did draw her necklace and earrings, though.'

Ben chuckled and handed the drawing back. She looked at it again, saw her wonky handwriting, Millie and Mum, and thought she might frame it and put it in her baby's nursery. Dipping her hand into the box, she pulled out a thick file. It was unlabelled and she handed it to Ben.

He frowned, placed it on the table in front of him and flipped open the cover. His expression became more puzzled as he flipped through the papers. 'These are prison records, Mils.'

She sat on the bench next to him and Ben shuffled over to give her more room, but kept his strong thigh against hers, giving her the anchor she so badly needed. 'Yeah, he was in and out of jail for most of his life. Icelandic jails, Danish jails—he even did a stretch in the UK.'

Ben picked up a photograph of a narrow-faced man with dark hair and winged eyebrows. He looked from her to the photo and back again. 'This is your dad,' he quietly stated. 'You have his nose, his eyes, his eyebrows, the line of your jaw.'

Millie nodded. 'Yep.'

She tapped her index finger on the photograph between them. 'His name is Hans Grunsmar, his mother was Icelandic and his father Finnish, according to his birth certificate. He was thirty-eight when he died and thirty when I was born. He was in jail at the time.'

'Wow.'

Millie thought she might as well tell Ben the rest. Or as much as she'd gathered from skimming the police records and letters her mum and parents exchanged. 'He and my mum were never married and they met when she was young, eighteen or nineteen. He was ten years older than her and he was married. Her parents freaked at their relationship and banned my mum from seeing him. So they ran away together, to Manchester.'

Millie blinked back her tears, thinking of the letters her mum wrote to her parents and never sent.

'He was abusive, emotionally and physically. He made my mum believe her parents didn't love her any more and wouldn't take her back, that they were ashamed of her. As a result, she spent far longer with him than she should've.'

Ben's big hand came to rest on her back and his rhythmic strokes calmed her down.

'Tell me what you found out, Mils,' he softly commanded.

'She fell pregnant with me and when she was six months pregnant, he put her in hospital with a broken jaw.'

Ben released an angry growl and Millie rested her temple on his shoulder. 'That's not the worst of it, Ben.'

'There's more?'

Unfortunately. 'While she was in the hospital, she found the courage to call her parents. They dropped everything to go to her. They'd tried to contact her, but he monitored her mobile and deleted their calls, emails and messages. Anyway, with them in her corner, she laid charges against him. Mum told them she had hidden photos showing the other beatings he gave her. When the police searched his stuff, and their flat, they got more than they bargained for.'

Ben tensed.

'They found evidence linking him to sexual assaults

and burglaries. He'd attacked many women over many years. The man was awful.'

Ben released a soft curse. 'Did your mum go back to live with her parents?'

Millie nodded. 'Yes, she lived with them until I was born, and afterwards. But when I was six months old, they were killed in a car crash. That's when she moved to Iceland.'

Ben's hand curled around her waist as he flipped the folder closed. 'That's awful, Millie. I'm so sorry.'

'You know, I've been so worried about what bad genes my baby will inherit from an anonymous donor, but now I'm worried about what genes he might inherit from my father!' she said, sounding a little unhinged.

'I believe nurture will trump nature, Mils. None of your bio father's genes came out in you and they won't come out in your kid.'

He sounded so certain and she wanted, desperately, to believe him. 'Are you sure, Ben?'

'Jacqui was an amazing mum, Mils, and you will be, too,' Ben told her, without a hint of worry in his voice. He closed the files and stacked them. His complete certainty calmed her fears. 'I'm so sorry that happened to her.'

'Me, too. She had such a hard time,' Millie stated. 'But now I understand why she kept my real father a secret and why she pretended Magnús was my dad.'

'She was trying to protect you from the knowledge that your father was a serial rapist.'

Millie turned to face him and put her elbow on the table. 'I think it would've been a lot better and healthier for me if she just told me that my dad was a bad man and left it at that. Thinking Magnús was my dad, but knowing he didn't love me, did some damage, Ben.'

He ran his hand over her hair. 'I know, Mils.' He pulled her in for a long side-to-side hug before pushing her heavy, long fringe off her face. 'I'm going to try to say this as gently as I can...your childhood is over, Millie. You've got to let it go. You can't keep carrying that baggage around with you.'

She nodded, tears streaming down her face. 'I *know*. I do know that, Ben, I just don't know how to put it down, to walk away from it. Tell me how to do it and I will,' she gasped the words out, her chest heaving with the concentrated emotion of a lifetime. 'Tell me how not to be angry and hurt and devastated and I will change, I will be better, I promise you!'

Ben pulled her into the shelter of his big body and wrapped his arms around her, holding her tight. 'Ah, Mils. Just be you. You are more than enough. You always were and always will be.'

She sobbed and held on to his words.

As the limousine made its way through the still snowy streets of Reykjavik, Millie smoothed down her golden skirt and touched her hair, pinned up into a romantic wavy bun on the back of her head. The loose style was supposed to look, as her stylist said, as if she'd just rolled out of bed, but it had taken hours for her to do.

Ben took her hand in his and squeezed it. 'You look wonderful, Millie.'

'For the daughter of a criminal, you mean,' Millie snapped back. She closed her eyes, immediately remorseful. She'd had a long, tough day and was still coming to terms with the contents of the safety deposit box. 'Sorry, I didn't mean that. I'm just on edge and tense and so nervous about making this speech.'

Ben gave her a reassuring smile. 'If I'd had any idea what you were going to find in the safety deposit box, I would never have asked the bank manager to see you on the same day as the concert.'

He'd pulled some strings to get her the appointment and she was grateful.

'It's not your fault, Benedikt,' Millie told him. Man, he looked amazing. He wore a classic tuxedo, but instead of a bowtie, he wore a plain black silk tie. He looked stunningly handsome and very debonair. She wondered what the press would think about them arriving together in the same limousine, then remembered the world knew them to be business partners.

In the eyes of the world, they were the two people closest to Jacqui and there was nothing to be read into them attending the gala concert together.

'It's not your fault either, Millie,' Ben told her, his tone suggesting she not argue with him.

She nodded. She took his hand and slid her fingers between his, grateful he'd lifted the privacy screen in the limo and that the windows were so darkly tinted that no one could see inside. She looked at Ben and managed a smile.

'I know, Ben. And I do understand why Jacqs didn't want me to know about him, he wasn't a very nice man. No, he was an awful man, but I'm choosing to believe I inherited all my genes from my mum, she made me the person I'm today.'

'She did,' Ben agreed.

'And I can see why she thought Magnús would be a good dad for me, he was handsome and educated, cool and controlled. He was everything my biological father wasn't. When she married him, she couldn't see into the future, she didn't know he couldn't love me. In fact, I don't think she ever admitted to herself that Magnús didn't love me. She always had an excuse for why he wasn't affectionate or loving or interested.' Millie folded the fabric of her dress into creases. 'It was as though she was trying to convince herself as much as me.'

'Stop fiddling with your gown,' Ben gently told her.

She sighed and smoothed the fabric back into place. 'I understand why she chose not to tell me—if I was faced with the same choice of protecting my little girl, maybe I would make the same decision. She kept the secret because she believed not knowing was best for me.'

'I agree. You were her whole world, and she would've fought dragons for you.'

It was true, her mum loved her more than life itself and Millie could understand, possibly even forgive her actions. And since it was the only misstep Jacqs ever made as a mother—for all of her life she'd been the awesome mum most girls dreamed of—she could stand up on that stage in front of two thousand people, Europe's princes and princesses, CEOs and celebrities, and talk about her mum. Well, theoretically.

In reality, she was terrified of messing up and making a hash of her mum's tribute speech. Her stomach lurched up into her throat. She hadn't done any public speaking, ever, and now she was going to talk in front of two thousand people the day she'd discovered who her real father was.

In the reflection on the window opposite, she saw her bone-white face. Yep, terrified. 'I don't know if I can do this, Ben.'

Ben's smile was warm and reassuring. 'Of course you can, Millie.'

'Can't you do it for me?' she demanded. 'I might freeze or stumble or mess it up.'

'You'll regret not doing this later, Millicent,' Ben told her, moving towards her to drop a kiss on her temple. 'You *must* do this, for her.'

She really didn't think she could and told Ben so.

'You'll have a teleprompter in front of you and two on each side of you. You just have to read the words on the screen, words you helped write, Millie. The speech is great and you've practised it many times.'

After her fifth rehearsal, Ben, who had something of a photographic memory, could correct her without referring to the printed page. It was most annoying.

'You can imagine the audience naked if it helps, Mils,' Ben told her, sitting back. He reached for the glass of champagne he'd poured earlier, an exceptional Taittinger, and forced it into her hand. 'And drink this.'

She pushed the glass away. 'I should keep my head clear.'

He pushed the glass into her hand. 'One is fine, two or three would be a disaster.'

'Is that what you do, Ben, when you do your presentations?' she asked after the lovely liquid streamed down her throat. 'Drink champagne and imagine your audience naked?'

Ben snorted. 'The image of my colleagues naked is one I'd prefer not to have in my head.'

Millie laughed. 'So how do you do your big speeches?' she asked. 'You've spoken to far bigger audiences than I will tonight.'

'Mine are business speeches, Millie, very dry and boring. And longer,' Ben said, throwing his champagne back.

'Yours will be shorter and lovelier and you'll be talking about someone you love.'

Millie nodded and blinked back her tears. She rested her head against the window and closed her eyes. Ben was flying out after the concert to St Barth's for a friend's stag weekend and she was booked on tomorrow's afternoon flight back to London.

Theoretically, they were done, whatever they had was over. Neither of them mentioned their affair continuing after tonight and Millie didn't know when, if, she'd ever see him again. How could anyone expect her to walk away from him? How could this just *end*? And why hadn't they spoken about this? Had she hoped that by ignoring it, it wouldn't happen?

'I don't want you to go,' she told him. She kept her eyes closed. 'I don't want this to end.'

'We said two weeks, Mils,' he murmured.

She recalled every word they had exchanged, so she didn't need him reminding her of their deal. 'No strings, keep it simple, don't complicate the issue,' she muttered.

'Millie, this isn't the time to discuss this.'

She forced herself to look at him. 'Will there ever be *a* time?' she asked him, needing to know.

An emotion she didn't recognise flickered in his eyes. 'I think there should be. We have things to say to each other.' Oh…*oh*. Thank goodness.

'What if I fly into Heathrow on Christmas Eve?'

'I'll meet you at the airport,' Millie told him, immediately feeling lighter and brighter. He was coming back, it wasn't the end. All would be well.

'No, that's not necessary. I'll let you know when I'm on my way.' Ben stroked her cheek. 'You've had a hell of a day, darling. Try to relax.'

Yeah, *right*.

'I'm still really nervous, Ben.'

Ben plucked her glass of champagne from her hand and looked at his watch. 'We have ten minutes until we arrive. Let's see if I can change that.'

Millie immediately recognised his expression. She was now easily able to recognise passion when it flared in his eyes. She checked that the privacy screen between them and the driver was in place and held up a hand. 'You can't mess up my hair or make-up, Ben.'

'I'm not going to kiss you, Millie. Well, not on your mouth, anyway.'

He sent her a wicked, wicked grin and ran his hand up and under her skirt, creating streaks of lightning on her skin. His fingers slipped under the brief thong she wore and skimmed over her feminine lips, instantly finding her core. He spread her moisture over her bead and Millie was astounded, as always, at how quickly he could rocket her from zero to gasping.

She dropped her head back against the cool leather seat and widened her legs, not able to believe that Ben was stroking her in the back seat on the way to a very upmarket event.

Ben slipped one finger into her and she gasped at the lovely, lovely intrusion, her channel gripping his fingers. He pulled his hand away and she protested. He impatiently moved her panties to the side and Millie closed her eyes in relief when his middle finger joined his index finger inside her again.

'Look at me,' he commanded her.

Millie opened her eyes and stared into those deep blue-purple depths, mesmerised by the lust she saw in his eyes. She couldn't believe that this amazing man wanted her so much. She could see everything he wanted to do to her in his eyes.

In all that blue, she could see clips of all the times they'd made love, rolling around his bed, in the shower, up against the wall of his hallway when they were too hot for each other to wait until they got inside the house properly.

He took her hand and put it on his steel-hard erection. 'I wish I could lay you down and take you here, right now, but that's further than we can go…right now, at least,' he muttered, his thumb brushing her clitoris in a barely-there stroke. Millie still released a deep moan.

'But I can make you feel good, I can make you feel *amazing*,' Ben told her, placing his lips on the space where her jaw met her neck and gently, gently sucking. 'God, you smell delicious.'

Millie felt herself building and she rocked her hips as Ben increased the stroke of his fingers, the pressure on her bead. She wanted to kiss him, but knew she couldn't, so she concentrated on his fingers, feeling her pleasure building. Her legs felt shaky and her breasts full, and lust shimmered in the air.

'You've got to come now, Mils,' he growled against her skin. 'We're going to be stopping soon.'

Millie heard the warning in his voice and as Ben stroked her harder, she flew apart, encased in a light, bright band of pleasure that spun her away. When she came back to earth, softly panting, Ben was gently wiping her with a cotton handkerchief he'd taken from the inside pocket of his jacket.

She sent him a weak smile and his mouth twitched with amusement. 'Still nervous?' he asked, sounding more than a little smug.

The car was crawling now and Millie lifted her hand to pat her hair. 'Just a little worried about my hair,' she airily told him, inwardly cursing her husky voice.

'You look fine, sweetheart, hair and make-up intact. I am,' Ben loftily and arrogantly informed her, 'damn good at what I do.'

Millie sat in a highchair in a small dressing room somewhere behind the stage, watching her reflection in the mirror as the make-up artist fluttered around her, dusting her nose with powder, and refreshing her lipstick. Bettina had whisked her off, telling her she needed a touch-up before she went on stage. Millie agreed. Her lipstick had faded and one of the curls on the back of her head felt loose.

The make-up artist gave her a shy smile and Millie, needing a couple of minutes to get her thoughts in order, was grateful for her silence. In the few hours, she'd discovered who her father was—a monstrous predator—cried all over Ben, got herself ready for this function, travelled from Ben's house in the limo, had a stunning orgasm, posed for a million photographs, shaken even more hands and smiled.

And smiled. And smiled some more. She'd met a lot of people whose names she had no hope of remembering, she felt emotionally depleted and she longed for a glass of champagne or a stiff whisky.

Millie couldn't wait to get the speech over so she could, metaphorically, let down her hair…

She shouldn't look at the photos projected on to the big screen behind her and on screens all over the theatre, Ben informed her, as they would show heart-tugging photographs of her mum. She wouldn't. They'd been chosen to elicit emotion and the last thing she wanted to do was cry in front of strangers. So, no, she had no intention of looking behind her at the big screen. She'd read her speech and get off the stage.

And then she'd have an enormous glass of champagne.

Millie heard the door behind her open and in the mirror in front of her saw Bettina slip into the room, carrying a crystal flute, filled with pale gold liquid.

'That had better be for me,' Millie muttered, holding her hand out.

Bettina passed the glass over and Millie took a huge sip. 'Where's Ben?' she asked.

'Pacing the corridor outside. Given his history, he's probably even more nervous than you are now,' Bettina said, resting her hip against the counter running against the wall and below the mirror.

Millie's head jerked and the make-up artist, Anna, groaned when her hand slipped. Millie looked straight ahead again, her eyes connecting with Bettina's in the mirror. 'What do you mean by that?' she asked.

Bettina shifted from foot to foot, looking uncomfortable. 'Um, you know, because of what happened with Margrét?'

What happened? And who was Margrét? 'What are you talking about, Bets?' Millie demanded.

Bettina winced and sent a longing look at the door. It was obvious she was desperate to escape. 'I thought that, given how close you and Ben seem to be, he would've told you...'

Millie glared at her mother's best friend. 'Bets, what do I need to know?'

Bets looked down and ran an elegant finger, red nail

polish glistening, around the edge of the glass. 'Didn't he tell you why his engagement ended abruptly?'

Millie's mouth dropped open in surprise. As far as she knew, he'd only ever had surface-skimming relationships. '*Ben* was engaged?'

'Did you not know?'

No, she bloody well didn't! How could she not know? And why, when Ben knew all her deepest secrets, hadn't he told her? 'When was this?'

Bettina waved her hand in the air. 'Oh, a few years before your mum died. He was pretty young, but so in love. She came from a very wealthy, very connected family.'

Anna stepped back, declared she was done, but Millie couldn't be bothered with her appearance.

Mille wanted to scream with frustration when someone called Bettina's name and she hurried away, looking relieved to be let off the conversational hook.

Damn, because she wanted to know more about Ben and his broken engagement. Over the past two weeks, she'd told him so much about her childhood—and her future hopes and dreams—but Ben had shared very little about his past. Millie could think of at least ten occasions when he could've mentioned he'd been engaged and that he'd once thought about marriage. She'd even asked him whether he'd ever been in love, but he never answered her.

He never answered her...

She was a gushing geyser; he was a hidden away ice cave. He was aware of how much her mum's secrets had hurt her and knew how insecure she felt as a child, knowing she wasn't loved by Magnús and not knowing why. She'd cried all over him, told him about her father, exposed herself and shown him her soft underbelly but he didn't feel enough for her, or didn't trust her enough, to show her his. He loved her body and enjoyed her mind, but he kept his heart safely tucked away.

He hadn't been dishonest, but neither had he been truly honest, and that realisation was hard to swallow. They said that girls fell in love with men who were either like, or the exact opposite, of their fathers. Ben, in his inability to communicate, was very like the man she grew up with. Like Magnús, he kept himself emotionally isolated.

She was having an affair with her husband and was in love with him, but he couldn't emotionally engage with her. She needed more than surface, she always had. She'd never been able to break through Magnús's reserves to find the man behind the armour and it seemed as though she was repeating that mistake with Ben.

It was possible she was banging on a door that would never open.

Her choices were to keep banging, hoping it opened a crack and she could slip in through, or to give up on trying to get him to confide in her. Which way to jump? Right? Left? Not at all?

They'd agreed to talk later...could she talk about this?

She knew what she wanted and that was to carry on seeing him. Would he want to continue their relationship if she asked? But was what they had, right now, *enough*? He was her best friend, her confidant, but she didn't want to keep taking, she wanted to give as well. She wanted him to confide in her, to be his best friend, to support him when he needed propping up.

But would he open up if she asked him to? Could he? If he couldn't, and if she wanted Ben in her life, then she'd have to accept his emotional distance. Could she live with him being like that? Could she have someone in her life who knew everything about her, but she knew nothing of him? She didn't know...

Millie knew she didn't want to spend the rest of her life begging him to let her in. She knew how it felt to be continuously rebuffed, how frustrating and soul-destroying it could be. If Ben couldn't give her what she needed, then it might be better for her, better for *them*, if they called it over...

It would hurt—she loved him, how could she not?—but she could walk away. She *would*. She had to because she'd fought this battle before and it had dented and damaged her.

But before she did anything too drastic, said words she couldn't take back, she and Ben needed to talk. She wanted a relationship with him, but he'd have to emotionally unbend.

She couldn't be the only one with emotional skin in the game.

CHAPTER TEN

BEN STOOD IN the wings on the impressive stage, shoved his hands into his suit pockets and watched as Millie walked to the podium on what he knew were shaky legs. Millie had asked him to come backstage with her and he'd agreed, knowing she needed his support.

Public speaking, especially at such an important event, was always hard, but talking about your dead mum was doubly so. If he could do it for her, he would, but he couldn't take the chance.

He didn't know if, as soon as he spoke Jacqui's name, emotion would flood his system and his words would disappear. He didn't know if he'd stammer the first few sentences and then dry up. He couldn't risk freezing, embarrassing himself and spoiling the evening for everyone else. He wouldn't do that to Millie, or to Jacqui's memory. No, he was in the right place.

Ben noticed the hesitation in her usually fluid steps. Nerves had taken hold of her again and he couldn't blame her, he felt as though his were also on fire. Honestly, he felt as though he was perching on the rim of the volcanic crater this stunning auditorium, Eldborg, was named after. The auditorium, built in concrete and covered with red-varnished birch veneer, reflected his red-hot inner core.

He had to calm down. If he didn't, he would transfer his nerves to Millie, and she was jumpy enough as it was. Ben took a deep breath and looked across the orchestra to where rows of elegantly and expensively dressed patrons sat. The woman wore Dior and Givenchy, Armani and Chanel and the men wore custom-made tuxedos from Brioni, Tom Ford and Cesare Attollini.

Behind the podium, and on strategic places throughout the hall, were screens so that the guests in the cheap seats didn't have to watch a tiny Millie speak. The screen would show images of Jacqui as Millie gave her moving tribute to her mum. There were words on the teleprompter and all she had to do was get through the next fifteen minutes.

Ben looked at his wife, his lover, thinking how stunning she looked. She looked like the heiress she was, elegant and sophisticated and lovely. But she was also kind and accepting and non-judgemental.

He'd thought he'd been so smart thinking he could control his emotions when it came to her. Another woman maybe, but not Millie. Had he grabbed on to the idea of linking his emotions to his stuttering as a way to rationalise keeping her around? Had his subconscious looked for a way to keep her by his side? Did it know, instinctively, that she was the one person, the only woman, he could imagine having a deep relationship with, even a measure of permanence, and he was searching for a way to keep her in his life?

Yeah…

His stammer now seemed relatively unimportant, keeping his feelings under control less so. He could even imagine giving her the baby she so desperately wanted. He might even be able to be a dad. He knew he wanted to try…

With Millie to guide him, he could do this. And if his kid stuttered—no he couldn't go there, not yet. Not now…

But in the future, yes. Ben was starting to believe that, with Millie at his side, he could do anything. There was no way they were done…not yet. Not for the next sixty or so years.

He watched as Millie cleared her throat and touched the slender microphone. He mentally urged her to start talking—the longer she stood there, the more her nerves would take hold. He silently urged her to start the speech, his fists bunched at his sides.

Just don't look at the screens, Mils, and don't watch the photos.

But Millie, being Millie, did exactly that. He silently cursed when the first picture hit the screens. It was a favourite of his. It was a candid shot of Jacq and Millie, who was probably around ten, sitting on the beach, laughing uproariously. It was clear that they not only loved each other, but took enormous pleasure in each other's company. It was a highly emotive and beautiful shot.

The picture on the screen flipped over to one of Jacq holding Millie, shortly after she was born, a red-faced baby with lots of hair. Jacqui, sweaty and make-up free, was laughing, triumph and love blazing from her eyes. It was another intensely emotional picture and one he knew would hit Millie hard. This picture had been taken just a few months after she was beaten up by her ex. If Millie started thinking about the past, her biological father, she'd collapse in a heap.

He watched, horrified, as she looked at the picture and despair jumped into her eyes. She lifted her fist to her mouth and Ben heard the collective intake of the audience. Everyone was on the edge of their seats, waiting to see what happened next. Millie dragged her eyes off the screen and her head whipped around, and Ben knew she was looking for him. Their eyes connected and held, and Ben saw the unspoken words on her face...

I can't do this. Please help me.

If he had to, he would do that damn speech for her, he would stutter and stammer his way through it, but Jacqui would be honoured. Without giving himself time to think, Ben strode on to the stage, keeping his eyes locked on Millie's face. He reached her, placed his hand on her back and bent to speak in her ear. 'Can you do this? Or must I?'

Please let her say she could.

He held his breath as he waited for her answer. Then he felt her spine straighten. She tipped her head back to speak in his ear, so softly that the microphone couldn't pick up her words. 'I want to try, for her. Can you stand next to me and, if I fumble, can you pick it up from me?'

'Always,' Ben assured her and she had no way of knowing he'd do it in every way he could, for as long as she would let him.

Millie heard the thundering applause in her ears as she walked off the stage, Ben's hand on her back. Her head buzzed with a million thoughts. She'd got through her speech without crying, she'd done her mum proud and the audience liked what she had to say. The hardest part of her evening was over. Well, until Ben left.

Dammit.

'I'm so damn proud of you, Mils,' he told her, ducking his head to kiss her mouth.

When he stood again, he had lipstick on his top lip and Millie lifted her thumb to wipe it away. The tears she'd been holding back threatened to spill and she blinked rapidly. 'Thank you.'

'I wish I didn't have to leave tonight. All I want to do is take you home, strip all that gold material off you and spend the rest of the night making love to you,' Ben softly stated, looking frustrated.

She held her breath and saw her feelings in his eyes. Maybe she wouldn't have to say anything, maybe… 'Ben, we really need to talk.'

He cupped the side of her face with his big hand and rested his forehead against hers. 'I know, sweetheart. There's much to say and we'd be having that conversation tonight if I didn't have to rush off. I'd stay if I could.'

'You made a commitment and you've already missed tonight's celebrations,' Millie told him. 'I'm grateful to you for being here. I couldn't have done that without you.'

'Of course you could, you are amazing.' Millie heard someone calling her name and she sighed as Ben dropped his hand and stepped away from her. He looked past her shoulder and grimaced.

'There are hordes of people, including Bettina and some of the trustees, waiting to congratulate you.'

She'd rather lie down in a bed of fire ants. And they only had a half-hour before the concert was about to start. 'I don't want to spend the little time I have left with you watching a concert. Will our absence be noticed?' she asked as he steered her away from Bettina's group. Ben was leaving directly after the concert and she…

Did not.

Want him.

To go.

'Since we are seated in the front row, in the middle,

with trustees on either side of us, I'd say yes,' Ben told her, his smile warm but frustrated.

'Damn.' She slipped her hand into his and rested her head against his shoulder as he steered her down a few steps into a quieter area empty of guests. 'I could do with a drink.'

He walked over to a waiter in the distance and returned with two glasses of champagne, then led Millie through a series of doors before finding a small, empty room and pulling her inside.

Ben lowered his head to kiss her and Millie sighed when his lips hit hers. She waited to be swept away, to fall into the magic of their kiss, but an annoying imp shouted questions from her shoulder.

Did he kiss her—Margrét—like this? How much did he love her? Did he still think about her?

She pulled back and Ben squinted down at her. 'What's the matter?' he asked.

She needed the answer to one question now—curiosity was burning a hole through her stomach. 'Why didn't you tell me you were engaged?' Millie asked him.

He quietly cursed and she knew he didn't want to answer her question. Doubts, hot and sour, rolled over her. It was all very well saying that they should talk, to find a way forward, but was she setting herself up for disappointment? If Ben couldn't talk to her about his ex, someone she presumed he was over, then what hope was there for him opening up about everything else?

Fear invaded her body. What was she doing? She was risking her heart, risking getting hurt...

Ben frowned. 'I didn't think it was relevant and it was a long time ago.' He touched the frown lines between her eyebrows. 'Why are we talking about this now?'

Because she needed some reassurance to get her through the next few days apart? 'I hate that you don't talk to me, Ben. And I don't feel as though you were honest with me.'

'I never lied to you,' he countered.

'I asked you if you'd ever been in love,' she shot back. 'It was a perfect time to tell me you'd been engaged, to explain what happened. You loving someone else isn't a big deal, you not telling me you were engaged *is*.'

'I'm not good at expressing myself, Mils,' he replied, sounding frustrated. She didn't blame him—he'd come in here to spend some time loving her, wanting to give her a send-off that'd carry them through the next few days, but she was throwing up barriers between them.

'I know, but I wish you would try,' Millie said, sounding a little desperate. 'I've lived with half-truths and I hate feeling as though I'm standing on shifting sand. I need to know everything, the good, bad and ugly.'

Oh, stop, Millie. Just let it go.

But she couldn't. The floodgates were open and she couldn't hold back the tide.

Ben lifted his arm and rested it against the wall above her head. Millie looked up into his masculine face.

Her breath caught at the emotion in his eyes—there was something there she'd never seen before. Something softer, kinder, but also bolder and braver. 'Are you sure you want the truth, Mils?'

'Always,' she assured him, her heart speeding up at the tenderness in his eyes. Was he about to…? Could she hope that he…?

Ben rested his forehead against hers. It took him a few minutes to speak. 'There are so many things I want to s-say, Millie, b-but we have so…so little time,' he said, his voice deeper than usual. 'I... I...th-think... Ca-ca-ca-*crap*!'

He hauled in a deep breath, closed his eyes and Millie's eyebrows raised. He looked as though he was in physical pain. What was going on with him?

'La-la-*look*,' Ben spat the last word out with the speed of a bullet. His F-bomb came out far more fluently than any of his words before.

'Are you okay?'

'Of ca-ca-course I... I'm bl-bl-bloody okay!'

She'd never seen him like this, abruptly distressed and flustered and upset. She was so used to Ben being controlled and urbane and she didn't recognise the wild look in his eyes and didn't know the reason for the heat in his cheeks. 'Seriously, Ben, what's wrong?' she asked, gripping his arm. 'Should I call someone?'

He whipped his head back and forth in what she presumed was a sharp no. 'Okay, I won't call anyone. Yet. But only if you relax and take a couple of deep breaths.'

Another very fluent, very loud curse bounced off the wall and Millie took a step back, not understanding his anger. She lifted her hands and stepped back further, feeling as though she was walking through a field planted with landmines.

Ben jammed his hands into the pockets of his pants, misery and horror on his face. Then he dropped his hands and shoved his hands into his hair, whirling away from her. Frowning, she stared at his big back and lifted and bit down hard on her bottom lip. What was going on here?

She stepped towards him and placed her hand on his back, utterly confused. 'Ben?'

He shrugged her hand off and walked away from her. She watched as he put both hands on a wall and dropped his head. Every muscle in his body tensed—he was a pulled-too-tight cable about to snap. She wanted to go to him, to wrap her arms around his waist and tell him that everything would be okay, but knew he needed her to keep her distance.

She just wished she understood. Just a few minutes ago he was kissing her, now he was emotional and upset. All she could give him was time...

But they didn't have much of it.

After what felt like an age, but was only a few minutes, Ben straightened. He turned around, did up the button to his dinner jacket and when he finally lifted his head, she saw that Cool and Collected Ben was back. He looked as though the past few minutes hadn't happened and when their eyes met, all his many barriers were back in place.

He lifted his arm and made a production of looking at his watch. 'I think we should go, the concert will be starting shortly.'

Millie stared at him, flabbergasted. Would he walk away from her without an explanation? Oh, no, they were not going to brush his odd behaviour under the mat.

'Shall we?' Ben asked in his smooth, nothing-to-see-here voice and gestured to the door.

'No.'

When his eyebrows raised, giving her a look that suggested she was being unreasonable, she lifted her chin. 'Ben, darling, I don't understand. I'm worried about you—your reaction is completely out of character. I need to know what just happened.'

His eyes dropped from hers, for just a second. 'Nothing happened, Millie.'

'And you say that you are honest with me! Are you kidding me?' She released her own milder curse and slapped her arms against her chest. 'No, you don't just get to act the way you did and then walk away without an explanation, Jónsson!'

'What the hell do you want from me, Millie?' Ben shouted, that cool mask falling away.

'I want you to tell me what just happened, I want you to open up! I want you to talk to me!' Millie shouted back.

Ben looked furious, but still so, so cool. Cold anger was so much scarier than an overheated temper. 'Okay, so do you want me to tell you that I stutter, that I've always stuttered? There have been times when I haven't been able to form a sentence or make any sense. I've heard more "just relax" and "take a breath" comments than you've had cups of coffee!'

Sure, she'd caught the odd stammer, nothing serious, and he didn't stutter as a rule. 'I have never heard you stutter until a few minutes ago,' she told him. 'I never suspected it.'

'That's because I've worked damn hard to overcome it because it's not part of who I am any more,' Ben whipped back. 'Here's the honesty you want… I stutter when I'm emotional, when I feel too much. It's always worse when I'm upset or when I'm feeling overwhelmed or out of control.'

She was trying to make sense of what he was saying, trying to sort his words into concepts she could understand. She shrugged her shoulders and lifted her hands. 'Stuttering is *not* a big deal, Ben.'

Her words were barely out when she'd realised, once again, she'd said the wrong thing. His eyes turned a violent shade of purple and two strips of pink coloured his cheekbones. He took a couple of deep breaths—closed his eyes—and pulled out his phone. He scrolled through it and eventually held up the phone so she could see the screen.

Ben was a child in the video, maybe eleven or twelve, tall and gangly and as pale as a ghost. She saw the tracks left by tears on his cheeks, but his eyes were full of defiance as he tried to read from the book he held in his hand. Every word was torture and she only understood every couple of words. His sentences made no sense at all.

'It's all a matter of mind over matter, Benedikt! If you decide not to stutter, you won't,' a strident voice coming from his phone's speakers made her jump. His mother, she presumed. 'My teachers assure me that you're not stupid, but, right now, I have my doubts.'

Millie closed her eyes, feeling lava-hot anger run through her. How could his mum speak to him in that way? How could she be so cruel and heartless?

Ben jabbed a finger at his screen. 'That's who I was, that's how I spoke when I was a child. Sometimes it was much worse. That's how I get when I allow emotions to get in the way! I will *not*—I refuse to go back to being that person again!'

Millie felt as though she was still walking through that field of landmines, uncertain of what path to take. 'You worked so hard to overcome it, Ben.'

'You'd think, right? I thought so, too, until I stood at my engagement party, trying to make a toast to my bride, who I was crazy about, and my first sentence was a train wreck. She dumped me a few days later, telling me she didn't think we were suited. I knew it was because I embarrassed her that night.'

'Why do you think I refused to do that speech for you?' Ben demanded, his tone still as harsh as the wind flying off the Langjökull glacier. 'It's because I loved your mum and I knew I'd become emotional. And when I become emotional, I stutter. When I stutter, I feel...'

His words trailed away, and Millie didn't need him to fill in the blanks, to connect the dots. When he stuttered he felt out of control, as though he was a kid again, as though he was in that space where he thought nothing would ever be okay again.

'Your stutter does not make you *unlovable*,' she insisted.

Ben didn't take in her words. 'After Margrét, it was easy to work out that emotion and my stutter are inexplicably intertwined and I vowed I would never allow my relationships to go more than surface deep,' he stated.

But he'd stuttered with her earlier. What did that mean? 'But you have feelings for me,' Millie said, taking a stab in the dark.

He nodded, not bothering to deny her claim. Instead, he simply shrugged. 'And that's why I'm walking out of here, jumping on my plane and going to St Barth's. And why I won't be spending Christmas with you or having any contact with you in the future. Nor will I give you a child. It's not going to happen, Millie. I can't do this, I can't do *any* of it.'

Just like that? Did he really think she was going to stand for such a bloody awful explanation? 'Oh, that's such a cop-out, Jónsson, you are such a coward!'

Anger suffused his features and the blood drained from his face. 'What did you say to me? How dare you?' he asked her through clenched teeth. 'Do you know how long it took me to get my stuttering under control? Do you know how many tears I shed, how many walls I punched, and how often I screamed and shouted in my head when my words got stuck in my throat?

'I had no support from my parents—my mum thought I wasn't trying hard enough—my dad simply believed it would come right on its own and I had to find my own counsellors and my therapists! I'm *not* a coward!'

'You are if you are keeping it from letting you love me,' Millie told him. It wasn't a good time to tell him that, despite never having seen him so angry or out of control, she'd yet to hear him stutter. Yeah, he might have a couple of words go amiss here and there, but if he could yell at her without stuttering, then he could love her without it being a problem, too.

'And I think you might love me, Ben. I love you,' she stated. 'And I'm so furious that you've put this barrier between us when there was no need to do that. I'm so angry that you couldn't tell me that you stuttered and that you kept this from me.'

'I won't discuss my speech impediment, Millie.'

Ben looked away, but his stubborn expression remained. She knew how obstinate and determined he could be—he hadn't built an international empire without deciding on a course of action and pursuing it with zeal. He looked at his watch again. 'You should get back to the concert,' he told her.

It was obvious he was emotionally retreating and even more obvious he wasn't going to join her in the front row to watch the gala concert. *Marvellous.* Nor would he come to see her in London. Millie felt her throat tighten and remembered long-ago conversations with Magnús, wondering why she could never break through, wondering why he couldn't love her, wondering what was wrong with her. And here she was again, standing in front of a man, begging him to love her, and, once again, she was being batted away.

She was done. She couldn't give her love to someone who didn't want it. But before she walked away, she had more to say.

'I want to say a few things and I'll hope you'll give me the courtesy of hearing me out,' she said, hearing the wobble in her voice and hating herself. 'I cannot tell you how little I care that you stutter. I'm sorry you went through such a torrid time as a child, but you've been shouting at me, emotion blazing, without stuttering once, so I'm wondering if it's as bad as you think it is.

'So you got choked up and your words didn't come quickly enough. So *what*? Again, your stutter does not make you less you, less lovable, less anything. If you couldn't speak at all, I would still love you. I think I always have,' she said, sounding sad. 'You've never let me down...until today.'

She blinked and couldn't help the single tear that slid down her face. 'I trusted you to tell me the truth, but you held back and you didn't trust me with this. And that hurts, so much. Secondly, you are the best person in my life and over these past two weeks, I've come to love you. But I will not beg you to trust me or to love me. I did that with Magnús and I nearly destroyed myself in the process.

'It's your choice to love me or not, Benedikt, your choice to stay on your emotional island or to join the rest of us who are prepared to flounder our way through love. Be alone or be with me but...' she swallowed and looked him dead in the eye '...if you are with me, then you are *with* me. And that includes talking to me, letting me in. I'm not prepared to keep banging on the door, demanding entrance into your inner world.'

He rubbed his hand over his mouth, up his jaw, and

Millie saw the misery in his eyes. 'I can't, Millie. You're asking too much.'

No, she wasn't. But she couldn't make him see that.

She wasn't going to cry, not yet. She still had to walk out of this room with her dignity intact and sit through a concert. She could cry later, on the plane back to London tomorrow. She couldn't cry here.

'Okay, then,' she told him and heard her voice crack. She needed to leave now, before she begged him not to throw her away. Faced with the immensity of her need for him, with the reality of what she was walking away from, she wanted to grovel to him to keep her. She fought the urge to tell him she'd accept anything he could give her.

But, if she did, in time she'd come to resent him, just as she had Magnús. No, it was better to walk away. Millie forced herself to kiss his cheek, to touch his cheek with her fingertips. 'Take care, Benedikt.'

Gathering every bit of courage she possessed, she walked out of the empty room they'd taken refuge in.

CHAPTER ELEVEN

EDEN ROCK HAD been voted one of the best hotels in the world and every time he came here, Ben was reminded why. The setting, being right on the beach, was perfect, the service was exceptional and the amenities were varied and wonderful. With golf, tennis and a range of water sports on offer, it was also a perfect spot to host a stag weekend for a group of guys who liked to be active, but who weren't into pub crawling and getting wasted.

He'd arrived in St Barth's mid-morning two days ago, just in time to be included in a round of golf and from there he and his friends hit the beach, finding that Anders had arranged jet skis for them. They'd spent the next two hours on the water, had a quick shower and met up again for drinks on the terrace and then an exceptional supper. Then, to toast the groom-to-be, they got stuck into the hotel's exceptional wine and whisky list.

He hadn't thought about Millie or the train wreck he left behind in Reykjavik. Or, more accurately, he tried not to. And every time he felt his heart splitting in two, he had another glass of wine or threw back another whisky.

As a result, he felt like death warmed up. So sick and so sad. Ben walked out of the warm, clear sea and pushed back his hair, wishing Millie was by his side, or that she was waiting for him in their room, or on a lounger or at the breakfast table. He wished he could make his life with her, take a chance on her, wished he could believe that their love would last for ever, through thick and thin, through stammers and stutters.

She'd told him she didn't give a damn about his speech impediment, that it meant no more to her than the birthmark on his thigh, or the scar on his chin, did. But how could he believe that when it meant so much to him? How could she brush away something that defined the way he lived his life? It was the barrier he'd erected between him and the world, the impenetrable bulletproof glass shield excuse that didn't allow him to emotionally engage.

Ben picked a towel off the lounger and roughly swiped his chest, before sitting on the lounger, inspecting the fine-grained sand between his feet. He didn't want to be here, the sun hot on his shoulders and the gentle wind ruffling his hair. He wanted to be in London, wet and drizzly, or in snowy Iceland. He wanted to be with Millie.

But being with Millie meant being vulnerable, opening himself up and taking a chance she wouldn't hurt him.

Olivier and Anders, walked towards him, dressed, like he was, only in board shorts. They both wore dark sunglasses and Ben wished he'd thought to pick up his own before leaving his luxury room. His eyes felt as though they were being slowly roasted on an open fire.

'Ben, we are flying out just after lunch. What time are you leaving?' Anders asked when they stopped to speak to him. Ben looked up at him and shrugged. It was Christmas Eve tonight and he was supposed to fly to the UK, but he hadn't thought of an alternative arrangement.

'I'm not sure,' he told Anders. 'I might hang around for another day or two and solo celebrate your last few days of being an unmarried man.'

Anders, always so serious, tapped his temple with his index finger. 'I've been a married man, in my heart, since I met Jules. These few days with my friends are just a nice break and not a goodbye to my old way of thinking.'

Ben looked up at him, as his words settled on his skin. He understood what Anders was trying to say—he'd married Jules, emotionally, five years ago and all they were doing with their wedding was making it legal and celebrating their love. He and Mille had made things legal a long time ago, but they'd only discovered each other on an emotional level recently. She'd said she was in love with him, he knew he loved her.

He just didn't know if love was *enough*.

Anders told them he had to find some aspirin for his pounding head and left him and Olivier alone. His cousin dropped to sit on the sand in front of him and extended his long legs. He leaned back on his hands, beach sand covering his fingers.

'On a scale of one to ten, how rough are you feeling?' Olivier asked him.

'Fifteen,' Ben replied.

'Is that from the booze or because you walked out of the gala concert and left Millie to watch it alone?' Olivier asked, keeping his tone low.

Ben jerked his head and immediately wished he hadn't. He groaned. 'How do you know that?'

'I've seen the articles. You stormed out of the concert hall into your waiting limo, Millie returned to her seat. And every paper, printed and on-line, published a photograph of a devastated-looking Millie sitting next to your empty seat.'

Ben cursed and rubbed his face with both his hands. When he'd left the Harpa Concert Hall, desperate to get away from her and his feelings, he hadn't considered that the gala concert was one of the most covered events of the year, that social diarists and journalists from all over Europe attended the event.

Millie's speech was a big deal. His coming on to the stage to support her, and the intimacy of the gesture, would've raised their *Is love in the air?* suspicions. His bolting, just a half-hour later, would've added fuel to their journalistic fire. *Dammit.* This situation had gone from bad to worse to terrible.

'Millie had to fight her way through a group of journalists outside your house when she left for the airport,' Olivier told him. 'There were more photographs of her in the papers.'

'How did she look?'

'Hard to tell because she was wearing enormous sunglasses and a floppy hat.' Olivier shrugged. 'But pale. She looked pale.'

Ben cursed again, keeping his tone low because kids were running past him and he didn't want them to learn words they shouldn't.

'So, what happened, Benedikt?'

Ben told him about their fight, that he'd started to stutter, his terror when emotion swamped him. He couldn't allow emotion back into his life because if he did, he would start to stutter again and he refused to allow that to happen.

Olivier tipped his head to the side, looking confused. 'So, you started to stutter at the beginning of your argument with Millie?'

'Mmm,' Ben replied, feeling twelve again. He dragged his foot through the sand.

'So you stuttered, told her you couldn't be with her and left, right?'

'No, we argued. She told me she loved me, that we could be together, that she didn't care about my stutter,' Ben explained. 'Can we stop talking about this now?'

'No,' Olivier retorted. 'And you argued for how long?'

Been shrugged. 'Ten minutes, fifteen? Twenty? I can't remember, we both had a lot to say.'

'And did you stutter while you were arguing with her?' Olivier asked.

The question punched Ben between his eyeballs. He stared at his cousin as the importance of his words sank in. 'No. I was fine.'

Olivier rolled his eyes at him. 'So you had a quick relapse, but kept fighting with her because a couple of sentences came out wrong? You broke her heart over a *couple* of sentences?'

Words, not sentences. But he wasn't going to help Olivier make his case. Ben sighed and gripped the bridge of his nose with his finger and thumb. When Olivier put it like that, it sounded stupid. *He* sounded stupid. He thought he should try to explain why he was running from Millie. Maybe if it made sense to Olivier, it would make sense to him. 'Emotion scares me. I was feeling emotional and I started to stutter. If I don't nip this in the bud now, I might regress.'

Olivier's look suggested he'd been out in the sun for too long. 'Get real, Ben, we both know that's not going to happen. You've worked far too hard and too long to let that happen. And if you stutter with the people who care about you, who the hell cares? The people who love you—me, Millie—love you whether you stutter or not. Heads up, perfect speech is not a requirement to be loved.'

Millie said the same thing, love wasn't conditional. But could he believe it? His mum was supposed to love him, but she couldn't. Neither could Margrét. Ben bit his lip and shook his head. 'Lo-lo-love hurts, Olivier. It's hurt m-me.'

'No, *love* didn't hurt you. Your mother, because she had the emotional range of a crowbar, hurt you. Margrét, because she was more concerned about how your relationship looked to the outside world, hurt you. But do you know what hurts more, Ben?' Olivier demanded, sitting up and resting his arms on his now bent knees. 'Loneliness hurts. Rejection hurts. Walking away because you're an idiot hurts. Trying to protect yourself hurts. We blame love for hurting us, but it doesn't. Love doesn't hurt. Love heals those wounds and fixes the bumps. It gets you through the day.'

Ben met his cousin, and best friend's, eyes. He couldn't speak, partly because emotion was bubbling in his throat and if he tried to push words past that mess, he'd make a mess of what he was trying to say.

'You've been married to that girl for twelve years, Ben, and I've never seen you happier than I have these past few weeks. You might not have known it at the time, but she was always the girl you were supposed to be with.'

He shook his head. 'I d-don't know, Ol.'

'Of course you do,' Olivier told him, ignoring his stammer. 'You're just being stubborn. You want to love her, you want to be with her, you want to spend your life with her, but you're scared of taking that leap, of being emotionally vulnerable.' Olivier reached across the sand and punched his thigh. Hard. *Dammit, ow!*

'Pull your head out of your—' He saw a little girl building a sandcastle quite close to them and adjusted his words. 'Out of the sand and go and be with her. Throw your lot in with hers and see what happens.'

'What h-happens if it f-falls apart?' Ben asked, terrified at the idea.

Olivier shrugged. 'Then your heart gets shattered and you can go back to being the introverted, unemotional robot you were before.'

'I feel like that now,' Ben reluctantly admitted, rubbing his aching thigh.

'Then you might as well take a punt and be happy before you feel like that again,' Olivier cheerfully told him. 'But I don't think that's going to happen. I suspect that when Millie jumps in, she does it with both feet and all of her body.'

Ben took the hand Olivier held out and allowed his cousin to pull him to his feet. 'I'll think about what you said,' he told Olivier.

Olivier shook his blond head. 'No, you and thinking are a dangerous combination. Just tell your pilot to get your jet ready, get to the airport and fly to London. When you get there, go to Millie. She'll do the rest…'

'Your faith in me is touching,' Ben told him, his tone dry as they walked back to the hotel.

Olivier grinned at him. 'And tell Millie to let me know whether I should withdraw your divorce petition. And for God's sake, buy the woman a ring, Jónsson. Actually, *don't*, she's a jewellery designer, you'll probably get it wrong. Let her choose her own.'

Ben stopped and rolled his eyes. When Olivier finally stopped talking, he shook his head. 'Are you done telling me what to do?' he asked, a little bemused by this volley of instructions.

Olivier slapped his hand on his back and the movement propelled Ben forward. 'I intend to be your shadow until I get you on your plane and see you taking off. I'm not letting you bail, Cousin.'

Ben didn't think he would. Living with his fear might be hard, but living without Millie was impossible. 'Why don't you organise your own love life and stay out of mine?' Ben grumbled.

'Where's the fun in that?' Olivier demanded, laughing.

Millie aimlessly wandered around her top-floor Notting Hill apartment, feeling unsettled and off balance. Nothing, it turned out, stopped the ache of a broken heart. Her entire body was slowly crumbling and she was a hostage to sadness. Since she watched Ben walk out of her life, her nerves started vibrating at a higher intensity and every bump, scrape or bruise was so much more painful than anything she'd experienced before. Her heart was shattered and so was her spirit.

She'd been hurt when Magnús rejected her and by her mum's inability to tell her who her father was. Discovering the identity of her real father upset her, but Ben choosing not to love her was pain on an industrial scale.

What made their situation worse was that she knew he felt something for her—it might not be love, but it was close—and she couldn't believe he'd chosen to walk away from her, dismissing all they could be. He was choosing loneliness and solitude over her and that added a layer to hurt she'd never experienced before.

How could he think that being miserable and lonely was better than being together?

Millie looked out of her window on to the street below, taking in the flickering light of a Christmas tree in the window of the flat opposite. It was Christmas Eve and she was spending it alone. For once she didn't mind—if she couldn't be with Ben, then she preferred to be by herself.

She could cry in peace, she wouldn't have to put on a happy face and pretend to be jolly.

Millie placed the balls of her hands into her eye sockets and pushed back her tears. She'd cried more over the last two days than she had since her mum died and knew her red nose could rival Rudolph's. Her hair was a tangled mess and she wore her most comfortable pair of yoga pants, thick fluffy socks and a sweatshirt of Ben's she'd nicked from his closet.

She should eat, but whatever she swallowed immediately wanted out. She wasn't sure if a broken heart or starvation would kill her first.

Stupid, *stupid* man for not giving them a chance.

Later, she'd try to eat tea and toast. Tomorrow she'd eat something more substantial. The day after tomorrow her heart would feel a tiny bit better and it would start to heal in minuscule increments. Because, even though it didn't feel like that right now, Millie was mature enough to know her heart would, in some way, heal. She would smile again. Not today or tomorrow, possibly not next week or next year, but at some point, she'd learn to live again. She hoped.

And in the New Year, she would force herself to choose a sperm donor from the website, she would go to the clinic and be artificially inseminated. Hopefully, she'd fall pregnant straight away, but if she didn't she would try again. She would continue with her pre-Ben plans—they were good plans and made sense. Married or divorced or separated, Ben or no Ben, she wasn't putting her dreams on hold any longer. Not for any man.

She needed a family, someone to love. She wanted a

child, she wanted children. It was a pity that Ben couldn't get past his fear to share her life, and her his, and share children with her. But she wouldn't let him derail her plans.

She would be okay. Not today, but at some point.

Millie rested her head against the window, noticing the low dark clouds. They were predicting snow in London, just a few flakes, but after experiencing an Icelandic blizzard, she wasn't even marginally concerned or impressed. A black London taxi turned down her street, moving slowly along the road, before pulling up next to her flat. Some lucky person in her building, or maybe in the one next door, was home for Christmas...

Millie watched as the door opened and she placed a trembling hand on the cold pane when she saw a big foot, covered in a trendy trainer, hit the pavement. Ben had a pair of trainers just like those. She closed her eyes and rested her forehead on the glass. She had to stop thinking about him...she was driving herself mad.

When she opened her eyes again, she saw flat, fluffy snowflakes cascading past her window and a tall man stood next to the taxi, a small overnight bag in his hand. Her eyes travelled up his body—jeans, a navy pullover, a black scarf and a camel-coloured coat and, taking in his messy hair and tired, oh-so-familiar face, her heart started to gallop.

Ben stood below her window and he was looking up at her, his face pale in the fading afternoon light. She stared down at him, wondering if she was hallucinating, possibly caused by her lack of food, sleep and extreme sadness.

But then he lifted his hand and pointed to her door, silently asking if he could come up. Millie nodded and a few seconds later her intercom buzzed. Was this really happening? Ben's deep voice sounded a little strained. 'Can I come up? We need to talk.'

'The last time you said that ended in you walking out of my life,' Millie told him, cursing her shaky voice.

'Mils, I'm cold and tired. Let me in, dammit.'

Millie hit the button to unlock the downstairs door and went to her front door and opened it. She heard the sound of Ben's feet as he jogged up the wooden stairs and she swallowed, wondering why he was here and what he would say.

Leaning against the door frame of her front door, she waited until he reached her landing, her heart pounding at a million beats per second.

Ben stopped in front of her and used his free hand to rake back his hair, dislodging a melting snowflake. He looked as though he hadn't slept any more than she had.

She gestured for him to follow her into her flat and re-minded herself she wasn't looking her best either.

Ben closed the door behind him and she turned to look at him. He dropped his overnight bag to the floor and jammed his hands into his coat pockets.

'Coffee? Tea? A drink?' she asked.

He took a long time to answer her and when he finally spoke, he only uttered one word. 'You.'

Ben kept his eyes on Millie's face, taking in the various emotions skittering across her face. With Millie, even if it was on a second-to-second basis, you could always tell how she was feeling if you looked quickly enough. Hope flared first, then delight, then worry and resignation.

Shaking her head, she walked out of her bright and happy sitting room—cream couches with bright cush-ions, lots of plants and colourful Persian carpets on the old wooden floors—and he followed her slim figure to her small, equally light kitchen. He stood in the doorway while she fiddled with her kettle and reached for two mugs. It looked as though he was getting coffee whether he wanted it or not.

He took in the tension in her slim back and noticed her shoulders were up around her ears. He'd hurt her, and, for that, he was truly sorry. He would make damn sure he never did it again.

If she gave him the chance.

'I'll give you a baby, Millie.'

He knew, as soon as the words left his mouth, he'd said the wrong thing. She whirled around, waving the mug around. 'Thanks, but no thanks.'

He moved over to where she stood and gently removed the mug from her hand. This small apartment was too small for what he wanted to say—he needed more space for the big, important words he intended to say—so he took her hand and pulled her out of the kitchen and back into her much bigger lounge. Knowing he couldn't make her sit, he stood in front of her and looked down into her lovely, much-loved face.

'I'd like to give you a baby, Millie. But I'd like to love you more, share your life, be your lover and husband, be the father of your kids.'

She looked up at him and he saw the disbelief in her eyes.

'You told me that you couldn't, that you'd never allow yourself to become emotionally involved,' Millie said, pulling her hands out of his and walking over to the window. She sat on the narrow window ledge. When he looked up earlier and saw her standing in the window, his heart settled down from a galloping rush into a steady beat. She was what he needed. Having her in his life, whether that life was in Iceland or England, or anywhere else, was all that mattered.

He could only say the words and hope she believed them. He'd keep saying them, badly and over and over again, until he got them right. 'I love you, Millicent.'

Millie heard the three simple words, felt them settle on her skin and hauled in a deep breath. She fought the urge to fly to him, to wind her arms around his waist and bury her face in his neck. She couldn't allow him to walk back into her life after creating a tornado that had upended her psyche and torn through her heart. He had to work a little harder than that.

She tipped her head to the side. 'That's it? Is that all you've got?'

'No,' Ben told her as he slipped off his coat and threw it over the back of her couch. It looked, damn him, as though it belonged there. He looked as though he belonged in her flat, as though it was a space he'd always been part of. She'd felt the same when she was in his house in Reykjavik, completely at home, as though the house had been waiting for her arrival to make it complete.

Ben came to stand next to her, close enough for her to smell his heady cologne. But he didn't touch her and she was grateful. If he did, she might just shatter.

'I was stupid to run out of your life, to give up on what we had. I was scared. Love, being in love, is a scary business, Mils.'

Hearing him admit his fears made hers recede. Just a little. 'I'm scared, too, Ben. But not so scared that I'd prefer a life without you to one with you in it.'

The tip of his index finger ran down her cheek, along

her jaw. 'At the Harpa Concert Hall, I started to tell you that I wanted more than a December fling and I felt overcome with emotion. Then I tried to speak and my words wouldn't come. That petrified me.'

'You managed to keep arguing with me just fine,' Millie pointed out. She'd told him that the night they argued, but her words hadn't sunk in.

'I finally, with a little help, realised that,' he admitted, his hand cupping the back of her neck. 'Olivier helped me understand that my stuttering was a minor blip, not a complete meltdown.'

She narrowed her eyes at him, needing to make sure he heard her words and took them seriously. 'I said it a few nights ago and I'll say it again... I don't care if you stutter occasionally, I don't care if you stutter *all* the time. I'm in love with you and my love is *not* conditional.'

Ben rested his forehead on hers and closed his eyes. 'You don't know how much I needed to hear that, Mils.'

'But do you believe me?'

He opened his eyes, nodded, and Millie caught the sheen of emotion in his deep blue eyes. 'I— I really do.'

She swiped her lips across his, but pulled back before she got distracted. 'You have to talk to me, Ben, I need you to let me in. I can't be the only one talking all the time.'

He kissed her forehead, left his lips there before pulling back. When his eyes met hers, she saw capitulation in his. 'I know. I promise to work on that, but you've got to keep reminding me.'

She touched his jaw with her fingertips. 'Okay.'

Millie was happy to see his eyes were a lighter blue. He stroked her hair off her face before rubbing the back of his neck. 'If our kid has a stutter...you won't blame me?'

Our and *kid* in the same sentence… Millie thought her heart would burst with happiness. 'If *our* child stutters, we'll get him the best help possible, as early as possible. And we'll never let him think there's anything wrong with him,' she told him, sounding a little fierce. 'Because there is *absolutely* nothing wrong with you, there never has been.'

Ben's emotion-filled grin was a little crooked. 'We might have a girl, you know.'

She'd always been so certain she'd have a boy, but now she didn't care. 'I will take any gender you give me, Ben.'

He brushed his lips with hers in a kiss so tender it closed her throat, just a little. 'I love you so much, Millie. I can't contemplate a world without you in it,' he admitted.

All the tension of the past few days drained out of her. 'Good, because I've been miserable without you. Don't ever leave me again, Ben.'

'I promise I won't. And I hope you know that you can trust what I say, sweetheart.'

She did. He was the only man she'd ever trusted. She couldn't wait for the rest of their lives. She returned his kiss, winding her arms around his neck. Lovely minutes, or hours later, she pulled back and tipped her head back to send him a loving smile. 'Can I ask you a question?'

He brushed her hair back and swiped his thumb over her bottom lip. 'No,' he told her, a small grin touching his mouth.

She frowned, puzzled. 'Why can't I ask you a question?' she demanded.

His smile grew bigger. 'So far in our relationship, you've asked me to marry you and to give you a baby, and to sleep with you. I would like to be the one, just once, to ask a big question.'

'And what might that be?' she asked, her heart accelerating to warp speed.

'Well, I wanted to know if you'd marry me…' he softly said, love in his eyes. And at that moment, Millie saw her future in front of her, loving and being loved by this man. The money and the lavish lifestyle meant nothing—having Ben to support her, to love, and to do the same for him, was all she needed.

'We've been married a long time already, Ben,' she pointed out.

'In name only. I want to do everything we didn't do before, starting with the big engagement party, the church wedding, and the lavish reception.' His eyes held hers, as serious as a heart attack. 'I'll make a speech, Mils. I don't care what I sound like, as long as you hear how much I love you and how happy I am to make you mine.'

Although she was touched he was prepared to put himself in a highly charged, emotional situation for her, she knew she was his world and she didn't need him to prove it.

And she didn't need fancy, she just needed him. She shook her head. 'I don't need the big wedding and the fancy reception, Ben. I just need *you*.'

'What if we wrote our vows and said them under the Northern Lights?' he asked.

'Naked and in a hot pool?' she asked, laughing at him.

'It's an option, but I'd still like to see you in a wedding dress, with flowers in your hair. I want to put a ring on your finger in front of a few guests.'

So, not naked then. But, yes, that sounded completely perfect to her. 'I *love* that idea.'

'I'm so happy you are going to be my *wife*, sweetheart,' Ben murmured, pulling her into his body and burying his face in her hair. She felt his tremors and hugged him tight, knowing he needed to be loved as much as she did. They'd be fine, they had each other.

After a long, long hug, followed by an even longer kiss, Millie pulled back again. 'I was going to ask you to do something for me, Benedikt.'

'Anything.' He lifted his eyebrows and waited.

'Will you take me back to Iceland so that we can spend Christmas there? I feel that's where we need to be tonight, in the city where it all started.'

He nodded, smiling. Millie sighed, relieved. 'That was easy, I thought you'd insist on us going to bed first,' she said. To be honest, she was just the tiniest bit put out he hadn't.

His smile widened. 'There's a bedroom on the plane,' he told her, laughing. Then his eyes widened in mock horror. 'But no condoms, I'm afraid.'

She laughed, delighted at his willingness to embrace the future and give her the family they both wanted. 'I think I can deal,' she told him, love washing over her.

She didn't mind if it took ten weeks or ten years to have a baby, this man was the centre of her world. As long as she had him, she had her family.

'Let's go home, Ben.'

* * * * *

COMING SOON!

We really hope you enjoyed reading this book.
If you're looking for more romance
be sure to head to the shops when
new books are available on

Thursday 18th January

To see which titles are coming soon, please visit
millsandboon.co.uk/nextmonth

Introducing our newest series, Afterglow.

From showing up to glowing up, Afterglow characters are on the path to leading their best lives and finding romance along the way – with a dash of sizzling spice!

Follow characters from all walks of life as they chase their dreams and find that true love is only the beginning...

Two stories published every month. Launching January 2024

millsandboon.co.uk

MILLS & BOON®

Coming next month

THE BUMP IN THEIR FORBIDDEN REUNION
Amanda Cinelli

'Sir, you can't just–' The nurse visibly fawned as she tried to remain stern, her voice high with excitement and nerves as she continued.

'She knows me.' The man stepped into the room, his dark gaze instantly landing on her. 'Don't you, Isabel?'

Izzy froze at the sound of her name on Elite One racing legend Grayson Koh's perfectly chiselled lips. For the briefest moment she felt the ridiculous urge to run to him, but then she remembered that while they may technically know one another, they had never been friends.

It had been two years since Grayson had told her she should never have married his best friend, right before he'd offered her money to stay away from the Liang family entirely.

She instantly felt her blood pressure rise.

True to form, Grayson ignored everyone and remained singularly focused upon where she sat frozen on the edge of the exam table.

When he spoke, his voice was a dry rasp. 'Am I too late…have you already done it?'

Continue reading
THE BUMP IN THEIR FORBIDDEN REUNION
Amanda Cinelli

Available next month
millsandboon.co.uk